Seven Soldiers

Philip B. Storm

Eloquent Books
New York, New York

Eloquent Books
An imprint of AEG Publishing Group
845 Third Avenue, 6th Floor – 6016
New York, NY 10022
www.eloquentbooks.com

ISBN: 978-1-60693-875-1   1-606093-875-4

Printed in the United States of America

Cover Design: Peggy Ann Rupp, *www.netdbs.com*

Book Design: D. Johnson, Dedicated Business Solutions, Inc.

In loving memory of my wife, Maria.

⚮

She taught all who knew her
the meaning of love.

Chapter One

First Sergeant Virgil T. Turner stood tall on the troop review stand, glaring down on the arriving U.S. Army inductees. Bullhorn in hand, he bellowed, "Come on you sick, sorry pukes move your baggy asses off that bus and form up! Run! Run! Don't you dare walk in my army! Move your asses and move 'em now! You there, sissy-ass, what are you lookin' at? Don't you eyeball me, you wimpy-ass momma's boy! Move it!"

Like every new group of recruits before them, the men of Basic Training Company D began the army experience on post at Fort Dix, New Jersey, July 11, 1963. Falling-out in front of the reception center, they met the training cadre that would control their lives for the next eight weeks. One hundred eighty men began the process of becoming soldiers on that hot and sunny morning in the Pine Barrens of the Garden State. Few had any idea what lay ahead of them in the army, or in life.

Some of the men knew one another, having joined the army on the buddy system that guaranteed they could complete basic training with a friend. Many of them had just arrived at Newark Airport on the first airplane ride of their lives to be bused to Fort Dix. Others arrived directly by bus from New York, Philadelphia, and other East Coast cities.

They came from all the possible sources of basic trainees. About half had been drafted and therefore carried the designation "US" in front of their Army Serial Number, signifying a two year active duty obligation followed by four years of reserve status. Others had enlisted in the army reserve and were tagged "ER," or enlisted reserve, and would serve four to six months of active duty training and complete a six-year military obligation one weekend per month with an annual two week summer camp. "NG's," or National Guardsmen, had the same obligation as ER's, but were technically under the command of a state governor with limited exposure

1

to the regular army. The rest were "RA's," for regular army. RA's had voluntarily enlisted for at least three years, usually four, sometimes six. In 1963, the army expected RA's to be more committed to the art of soldiering than US's, ER's, and NG's.

The average age of the 180 men in Training Company D was nineteen years four months. Recruits averaged ten years of schooling. Sergeant Virgil T. Turner, whose eloquent greeting welcomed them to Fort Dix on that July morning, was the lead drill sergeant. First Sergeant Turner had a cadre of stripers attending him. Men with two stripes on their sleeves were corporals. There were several three-stripers, or buck sergeants. One of the men had three stripes up and one down signifying a staff sergeant.

First Sergeant Turner continued his welcoming speech. "Form up, form up! On the lines you fucking idiots! Are you blind as well as stupid? What in God's name is the army doing to me now? Sending me stupid-ass, sissy-mouthed motherfuckers that are blind? Goddamn this is gonna be a long eight weeks for the few of you that make it! You there Jody, what the fuck are you looking at? Keep your eyes down when I speak, son! You can look at officers; they don't get it! But don't you ever look a first sergeant in his eye! He just may kill you for it! Get it? Do you understand me, Jody? Sergeant Meeks, write this dumb fucker up! He just plain don't get it and he's too stupid to be in my army!"

Sergeant Turner's welcoming speech was having exactly the effect he wanted. The troopers were scared as hell, wondering what he would say or do next. All in all, a perfect beginning to basic training as the U.S. Army did it in the summer of 1963.

Chapter Two

Sergeant Turner's greeting got Private Mike Stott's full attention as he stood ramrod straight on the painted white line outside the reception center. Stott was both scared and impressed that one man could so quickly establish himself as the absolute authority figure in a group that contained some real tough customers. Or so Mike thought. Stott was seventeen-and-a-half years old on that July morning and had spent very little time away from his family other than Boy Scout campouts. He'd joined the army while still in high school with the commitment to report following graduation. His parents were furious with him for enlisting rather than starting college because he had received an academic scholarship to a local university. No one from either side of his family had ever attended college. Mike's father said he was a "damn fool" for blowing the opportunity.

Standing there, focused on Sergeant Turner, Stott was pretty sure that his dad had been right. That lost scholarship seemed particularly attractive to him twenty minutes later as the basic training troop labored to keep up with a series of commands for push-ups, squats, and jumping jacks fired at them with a speed that guaranteed noncompliance.

After an hour of exercise orientation, Company D formed up for the continuation of Sergeant Turner's welcoming. "All right troops, I've seen enough! You're the sorriest, poor-ass collection of sissies and faggots I personally have ever seen! I bet there's not one of you that's ever had a woman, or an idea. In fact, I bet none of you assholes has ever taken a good shit! You better get ready for my army! You got three, maybe four days of this reception center crap before you're all mine, so straighten up! Come Monday morning, you'll have your heads shaved; you'll be de-loused! You won't have those faggot duds on anymore! When you fall out Monday be ready to work your balls off! You sissies better give your souls to God 'cause your ass is mine for the next eight weeks! Sergeant Meeks, get these sick pukes out of my military sight!"

With that, Sergeant Turner executed a smart right face and strode past the soldiers at a brisk military pace. He wore a Smokey Bear-style drill instructor's hat and summer dress khakis. On his left shoulder was a Ranger patch and on his right a Screaming Eagle, indicating that he had served with the 101st Airborne Division. Above the extensive ribbon board on the left side of his chest was an oak wreath-enclustered long rifle badge worn by men who have served with an infantry unit in combat. A silver parachute was centered over the Combat Infantry Badge. Three stripes up and two down revealed Turner to be an E-7 first sergeant. Few if any of the new troopers understood what the patches and decorations meant at the time, but they all saw that First Sergeant Turner was a proud and powerful man.

Sergeant Meeks, the four-striper, took over. "You assholes are totally lucky! You caught Top in the best mood I've ever seen him in! Stand at attention you dickheads! We're gonna double-time to noon chow! Any man that can't walk the hand ladder don't eat, get it? Then you start cuts and shots, tomorrow you get army issue gear, and we burn that shit you're wearing! Tonight, get friendly with your new bunk mate and I'll personally Section Eight you, get it? Left face! Double-time, march!"

Private Stott had heard every word Turner and Meeks had screamed, but comprehended only parts of what they had said. Section Eight? Cuts and shots? Top? This was his first exposure to the language of the army and Stott wondered if the other guys understood more than he did. Mike thought back to the advice his brothers had given him, "Keep your mouth shut unless spoken to, never volunteer for anything, and always watch your back."

The youngest of seven children, Stott had grown up listening to his brothers boast about their time in the military. Those stories of adventure were a big part of why he had joined the army. All three brothers had been paratroopers.

Mike had visions of "going airborne" with all the glory and respect that would surely command from the girls back home. Joining the army seemed to be his best chance to escape an ordinary and boring life like the one his parents lived. But the first few hours at Fort Dix turned Mike's desire for excitement and adventure into a longing for home. Private Stott pondered what the next eight weeks—and four years—would bring.

As the troops double-timed to the mess hall, Stott looked around at his fellow recruits, wondering who among them could walk a hand ladder. More importantly, what exactly was a hand ladder? Arrival at the mess hall revealed it to be what was called overhead parallel bars in high school, but these were higher and longer. Sergeant Meeks explained the program. "Awright girls, here's the deal! Jump up and grab that first bar and hand-over-hand to the end. If you don't make it, you don't eat, get it? And don't fake it or I'll have your balls! Now go! Walk it or don't eat! If you can't walk it, you're too fuckin' fat to be in my army!"

Picture 180 men in line, hungry, nervous, waiting for the men ahead of them to hand walk 30 feet of overhead bars to enter the chow line. Stott was toward the back of the line and could barely see what was happening, but it was clear that not many of the men were completing the hand walk. When they failed, they had to return to the back of the line. This caused Meeks and the other sergeants great glee, as they chided the nonperformers. "You fuckin' sissy, you won't eat for weeks! By the time you make the walk, I'll be a first sergeant!"

But the recruits learned a valuable lesson in that first mess hall lineup. Those men who could not walk the bars after several tries were eventually allowed to get in the chow line. The food was edible—barely—and every soldier had to pick up after himself.

Sitting at that initial mess, Stott made his first acquaintance in the army, Private John J. Sharkey. John had stood a few places down from Mike in that first formation, but until noon chow none of the recruits had been allowed to speak. Sharkey was the shortest man in the formation.

"Where you from, please?" Sharkey asked Stott.

"Who wants to know?" Stott countered. His response drew the attention of the other ten men at the table.

"John J. Sharkey from New York." Sharkey spoke with polite confidence and looked directly across the table at Stott.

Before Stott could respond, Sergeant Meeks blew the loudest whistle the soldiers had ever heard and directed them as follows, "Awright, girls, out of the goodness of my military heart I let all you fat-asses eat, but that's the last time you chow down 'til you walk the ladder! Get it? Now, haul your limp dicks outside and fall in! Same order as before if you can remember it. And if you can't now, think how hard it's gonna be with all your fuckin' heads shaved, cause we're on our way to the cutshop!"

As the men formed up to double-time to the cutshop, Stott made his second army acquaintance. "Syl Mobliano, dickhead, and don't be fucking with my boy Sharkey! You punkass westerners don't play in our league!"

Stott turned to see the source of that friendly advice and got his first look at the "old man" in Company D. Sylvatore Mobliano was a short, powerfully built man who looked ten years older than the other trainees. He was completely bald, and this was before the cutshop. Syl's accent led Stott to believe he was another gracious New Yorker.

"What's your problem, pal? Yankees get their asses kicked last night?" It was the best smart-ass response Mike could come up with on the spur of the moment.

"I'll deal with you later!" Syl promised.

As Stott got his three-minute head shave—referred to by the army as a trainee trim—he observed Sharkey and Mobliano with their heads together glaring at him from the cut line.

"Hope they don't make you pay, Syl. That would be a real shame!" Private Stott couldn't resist a jab at Syl's hairless head. This brought the first ripple of laughter on day one of basic training from the troopers who caught his comment. Even Sergeant Meeks' hard-ass face broke momentarily.

Syl Mobliano was not amused. "Later." Syl's response sounded ominous.

There were 180 trainees, but only two barbers on duty averaging about three minutes per trim, so the barbershop formation consumed the better part of the afternoon. In the best army tradition, recruits not in the barbershop were standing at attention in the ninety-degree July sun. Sergeant Meeks remained in the shop, assuring all troops got their money's worth of haircut. Each man had to pay the barber two dollars for the privilege of receiving the worst haircut of his life, but they were learning the army way.

Keeping the troops in formation and in line was the remaining brain trust of Training Company D. Following Sergeant Meeks in descending order of authority was Sergeant Shitz. The good sergeant pronounced it "Sheeetz," but he was the only one who got it right.

As the trainees sweated at attention in the New Jersey sun, Sergeant Shitz offered his counsel, "You dickheads think this is hot? Wait 'til you get to Nam. You don't know what heat is! It gets so hot you have to cool down the momma-sans' tits 'fore you can suck 'em!"

Three words in that pronouncement got Private Mike Stott's attention. He knew what tits were, but could not imagine them too hot to suck. He assumed that momma-san referred to some form of female, but the term Nam baffled him. Though standing silently at attention, curiosity got the best of Stott. Instinct told him that speaking out was not in his best interest, so he raised his hand.

"What in hellfire do I see? Is some dumb-ass mother fucker raising his hand in my formation? Boy, you better be dying or have to talk to your momma or something really important or I will absolutely tear off your head and shit down your throat! Do you understand me, boy? Now, who's got a question?"

This brought a snicker from the troops who were supposed to be at silent attention. Stott knew he had messed up, but was pretty sure Sergeant Shitz had not really seen who had raised his hand, only that some fool had done so. Mike remained quiet with his hand down and hoped to God it was over.

"Oh, so that dumb-assed mother fucker that put his hand up lost his balls! That's worse and even dumber than raising your hand in my formation! Now, which one of you miserable assholes had his hand up?" Sergeant Shitz was glaring in Stott's direction.

Like a miracle, the guy next to Private Stott raised his hand! Sergeant Shitz ran down from his elevated review stand and got his nose one inch from the soldier's nose and screamed, "Are you the low-down sorry-ass mother fucker what raised his pissy little paw in my formation, trooper?"

"No, sir! It was him!" The recruit pointed to Stott.

Sergeant Shitz took a half step back from the soldier to Stott's right and threw a vicious, underhand punch to his midsection. The blow knocked the wind out of the trooper and sent him sprawling backward. Shitz then proceeded to kick the man in the ass all the way around the formation until he lined him back up in the slot beside Stott.

"What's your name, you sorry-ass, mother-fucking snitch?"

Though barely able to speak, the confused recruit managed the following response: "Smeall, sir."

The 170 recruits not in the barbershop were shocked and scared. Sergeant Shitz had kicked the crap out of one of them and, clearly, any recruit could be next. Sergeant Shitz strode back to the reviewing stand. "Now listen up troops, and listen up good! Two points. One, don't ever call me sir because I work for a living! Two. The army hates two things. The army hates a coward, and the army hates a snitch. Because a snitch is step one to being a coward, and we shoot cowards! Got it? Do you understand? If so, I better hear the loudest "Yes, Sergeant!" of your military lives!"

From 169 recruits came the loudest "Yes, Sergeant!" imaginable. Private Smeall was too hurt to speak. Next came another surprise from Sergeant Shitz.

"Now, listen up! Who had the hand up?" Again, he was glaring in Stott's direction.

"Sergeant Sheeetz, I did, Sergeant!" Private Stott screamed out.

"What's your name trooper?"

"Private Stott, Sergeant."

"What's the question?" Shitz asked.

"Sergeant, what is Nam, Sergeant?"

At exactly that moment, the final group of trainees exited the barbershop under the direction of Sergeant Meeks, who heard Stott's question to Shitz. Meeks ordered D Company to stand at ease and demonstrated the proper technique for doing so. He then mounted the review stand and delivered an explanation that the young soldiers would remember the rest of their lives.

A very serious, almost reverent Sergeant Meeks spoke, rather than yelled, "Listen up, troopers! You may have noticed that Sergeant Turner, Sergeant Shitz, and I wear Ranger patches. We served in the Tenth Rangers together since 1958. Nam is the short version of Vietnam. The Tenth has been there running recon since '56. You may have heard about Vietnam on the news or seen it in the papers, if you can read. There's damn sure a war brewing there, and some of us think it's gonna be a big one. Take this training serious, even if you're ER or NG, because you have a damn good chance of visiting Vietnam soon, courtesy of the U.S. Army! Sergeant Shitz, take these sissies to Barrack D and get 'em squared away. Late chow 1730. I'll see you girls at 0500!"

Double-timing to D Barrack, the reality of Stott's situation hit him. An "RA," Stott had a four-year enlistment ahead of him, and this was day one. He had alienated two bad asses from New York City that were now going to be in his barrack. He'd made no friends. Stott had raised the ire of Sergeants Shitz and Meeks and it wasn't even suppertime yet! Sergeant Meeks had just explained that there was a good chance he would have to go to war.

Although Mike had heard of Vietnam, he had no concept that it could in any way affect his personal plan for time in the army. Stott had it all figured out; he would get through training, go airborne and be assigned to a unit in Germany. He would then chase blonde-haired, blue-eyed, big-busted German girls around the countryside.

Now, on day one in the army, Stott had been told he might have to go to war! Mike began to focus on that other piece of advice his brothers had given him. "Watch your back!"

Chapter Three

At five-feet, two inches, John J. Sharkey, "JJ," was minimum height to be accepted into the army. This was the day Sharkey had been dreaming of for longer than he could remember. Even on that first day, John J. Sharkey knew he had found his home.

John Sharkey had no family whatsoever. His only memories were of St. Agnes Home for Orphans located in the unlikely community of Bedford, New York. The sisters of St. Agnes were disciplined and regimented. They operated on a meager, barely adequate budget that never provided enough of anything for the 600 or so orphans in their care.

Founded in 1902, St. Agnes occupied a sprawling and ramshackle estate that had been left to their order by the captain of a fleet of sailing ships, himself an orphan who had never married. Captain Estos Sharkey, however, had more orphaned children carrying forward his name than he could have imagined because the sisters encouraged those leaving their care to honor their patron by adopting his name. John J. had taken the name Sharkey gratefully, as he knew little of the world outside the orphanage.

When baby John had been left on the steps of a police station in the South Bronx in the fall of 1946, the odds were good that such a child would be adopted. But John had a dark complexion and was in poor health. During the post World War II baby boom, no family was found for him. John's world had been limited to St. Agnes and brief glimpses of the community around Bedford, New York, outside the orphanage walls.

The town of Bedford is one of the wealthiest bedroom communities within train-commuting distance of New York City. Comprised mostly of sprawling country homes on large estates, Bedford prides itself on having more Fortune 500 CEOs in residence per capita than any other town in America. The only people living in Bedford that weren't well-to-do were the staff and orphans of St. Agnes. On his occasional trips outside the orphanage, JJ had observed that everyone in America seemed to be rich, except the inhabitants of St. Agnes.

In June 1963, John J. Sharkey had completed twelve years of Catholic education at St. Agnes. John had no trouble finishing at the top of his class, but he believed the orphanage education was probably easier than regular high school. John had read every book he could get his hands on, particularly those about history and war.

The sisters of St. Agnes instilled respect for the Catholic Church and a deep sense of patriotism and love for America in all their children. For John Sharkey, the United States of America was everything. John enlisted in the army with Head Sister Mary Katherine signing his induction papers because John was not yet eighteen years of age. Although JJ had a few friends in the orphanage and had been well cared for by the Sisters, he had very limited emotional attachment to anyone. His life experiences had taught him to rely only on himself.

The sisters of St. Agnes knew that John was intelligent and obedient, but they never understood how a child could be so self-reliant. John's IQ had not been tested at St. Agnes. Had the orphanage the ability or resources to measure John's mental capability, they would have been astonished to learn that he was, in fact, a genius, with an intelligence quotient over 200 complemented by extraordinary intuition. Sharkey believed that the U.S. Army was his calling in life.

On that first afternoon at Fort Dix, John Sharkey was totally surprised when Private Stott took his inquiry about home as an offense. He was even more surprised when a fellow army inductee he had just met on the bus ride down from New York City had come to his aid and referred to him as "my boy."

John's seatmate, Syl Mobliano, had boarded the bus outside the Recruiting Center in Mamaroneck, New York, just a few moments before Sharkey, but had spent over an hour talking with the recruiters as they all waited for the last inductee to arrive. One of the recruiting sergeants, against army regulations and basic common sense, had revealed that the inductee they were waiting for was coming down from St. Agnes in Bedford. Syl knew about St. Agnes. The last man they were waiting for, John J. Sharkey, was an orphan.

Chapter Four

On that July morning in 1963, Sylvatore Anthony Mobliano was twenty-four years old and a recent graduate of Harvard Law School. A most unlikely army inductee, Syl had enlisted in the New York National Guard immediately after passing the New York State Bar Exam. Through a special program offered by the guard, Syl was headed for eight weeks of mandatory basic training at Fort Dix and then on to a guaranteed slot in Officer's Candidate School, OCS, at Fort Benning, Georgia.

Syl Mobliano was a gifted young man who had everything going for him. He had graduated magna cum laude from Brown University, Class of 1961. He then finished fourth in his class at Harvard Law, having missed honors by receiving two B's against his remaining A's. He completed his legal curriculum in two years.

As a starting middle linebacker at Brown, Syl had gained national recognition as a fast and aggressive player. Scouts from several pro football teams had tried to talk with him about a tryout, but Syl was not interested in professional football. The second oldest son in an Italian family of nine children, Syl had been programmed by his father for a much loftier goal.

Syl's father, Anthony Romero Mobliano, wanted all his children to reach for their highest achievable dream. Syl's older brother, Anthony Jr., was in his final year of residency at the Mayo Clinic in Rochester, Minnesota, on his way to becoming a neurosurgeon. Not blessed with Syl's athletic ability, Tony Jr. had focused on intellectual pursuits even as his younger brother had earned neighborhood and then statewide recognition as a scholar-athlete. Though four years older than Syl, Anthony understood and accepted that it was his younger brother whom his father and the entire Mobliano clan expected to become a U.S. senator, and then president.

14

Anthony Sr. and his two brothers had started a produce distribution business in Brooklyn in 1938 that now served the entire eastern seaboard. Mobliano Brothers' Produce, Inc. had made the family very wealthy. A guiding principal of the Mobliano brothers' success, however, had been not to flaunt their wealth. Anthony Sr.'s family still lived in the same Brooklyn brownstone he had purchased right after World War II. Though expanded to accommodate his nine children by acquiring the two brownstones on either side of his original house, Anthony Sr. still lived in the first home he had ever owned. His brothers, Romano and Gustavo, and their families lived on the same block. Family and tradition were extremely important to the Moblianos.

When he learned that the last inductee the group was waiting for was a boy without a family, Syl Mobliano took a special interest in John J. Sharkey. As John boarded the bus that morning to the jeers of his waiting fellow inductees, Syl was amazed to see how much John resembled his younger brother, Paulie. Though shorter and much thinner, John J. Sharkey could well have passed as a Mobliano. Syl resolved to watch out for the young man.

"How you doing? Syl Mobliano. Take a load off," he said to Sharkey as John hesitantly glanced at the empty seat next to him.

"Thank you. I am John J. Sharkey."

"Well, Sharkey, you don't look old enough to be joining the army, and I look too old! We make quite a pair! Good trip?" Syl asked.

"Excuse me, sir?" Sharkey replied.

"Sir? Do I look that old? I meant, was your trip down to catch the bus okay?" Syl asked.

"Yes, thank you." Sharkey was surprised by Syl's questions and friendliness.

"You know this trip?" Syl asked.

"No, sir. This will be my first trip to New Jersey." John sensed that Syl's friendliness was genuine, but he was uncomfortable talking so much to someone he had just met.

"Well, I grew up in Brooklyn, and this is my town! So I'll point out the sights along the way!" Across the George Washington Bridge, down the New Jersey Turnpike to pick up another group of inductees at Newark Airport, and all the way to the Wrightstown, New Jersey, exit, Syl bent Sharkey's ear, first about the scenery, then his life right up to the moment and about what he expected from the army.

"I'm a lucky guy, and I know it," Syl explained. "I've been fortunate to get a great education, and I'm going to put it to good use! I thought about going RA, but I decided I can serve my country better long term in the reserves. I'd like to run the Judge Advocates Office for the New York National Guard someday."

Throughout the trip, John J. Sharkey listened politely but said almost nothing. He had never met anyone quite like Syl Mobliano. He wondered if all the regular guys were like Syl. The kids at St. Agnes referred to the outside world as "the regular people," meaning those who had families. Syl had the largest extended family that John had ever heard of, and Syl seemed to be a nice person, but John preferred to listened rather than speak.

"You okay, kid?" Syl asked John several times during the trip. Syl worried that he had unintentionally caused John to be uncomfortable by talking too much about his own life and family. John had revealed absolutely nothing about himself during the ride, but Syl knew that John was an orphan. John's projected loneliness made Syl appreciate his own family and good fortune perhaps more than he ever had before.

As the inductees entered the main post gate at Fort Dix, there was a buzz of apprehension and excitement among the inductees. The most confident man on the bus was Syl Mobliano.

Chapter Five

Barry Milton Smeall was undoubtedly the most terrified basic trainee arriving at Fort Dix on that July morning. When Barry received his draft notice, the considerable wealth and power of the Pittsburgh, Pennsylvania, Smeall Family had been put to work to get Barry into an army reserve or Pennsylvania National Guard Unit, all to no avail. Despite their influence through contributions to senators, representatives and various other levels of local, state, and national government, no reserve slot opened up. Barry seemed destined to do what no Smeall before him had ever done: serve in the U.S. Army as a drafted private.

The very idea that her precious only son should have to waste his valuable time serving in the military was almost more than Bessy Smeall could bear. She wrote to her congressmen and called the governor of Pennsylvania with whom she had played golf, but it all happened too quickly. Her powerful and connected friends got involved, but alas, Barry Jr. received orders to report to the U.S. Army base at Fort Dix, New Jersey, on July 11, 1963, just four days after his twenty-second birthday.

Barry's father had avoided service in World War II because he was the co-owner of a business group that included a munitions plant in Nitro, West Virginia. As a critical supplies facility manager, Barry Sr. enjoyed the privilege of serving his country as a manufacturer rather than as a soldier. The thought of his son having to actually take orders from someone other than family made Barry Sr. physically ill.

His parents' anxiety about his having been drafted only added to Barry's own fear and dread of serving in the army. In his entire life, Barry Smeall had never been screamed at the way he had on that first day at Fort Dix. He was absolutely terrified.

When Barry saw Sergeant Shitz staring in his direction during the barbershop formation, fear drove him to raise his hand to explain. Sergeant Shitz's punch to his mid-section was the first time that Barry Smeall had been struck in anger or for a disciplinary reason. To have been called a "sorry-ass, mother-fucking snitch" completely befuddled the pampered son of Pittsburgh nobility. As Barry Smeall entered D Barrack, he was hurting from Sergeant Shitz's punch and very frightened about how his fellow trainees were reacting to him. Other soldiers were talking to each other and selecting bunks for the first night in the reception center, but no one spoke to Barry until Private Stott, the man he had pointed out in the barbershop formation, approached him.

"Learn anything from that ass-kicking you took, asshole?" Stott asked.

"I-I-I'm so sorry; I shouldn't have done that," Barry apologized. He noticed that Private Stott appeared to be much younger than him but seemed completely comfortable with the surroundings in the barrack.

"Can I take the bunk above you?" Barry managed to ask.

"You're kiddin,' right? You rat me out in formation and now you want to be buddies? What's the deal?" asked Stott.

"I didn't mean to do it! I-I-I was scared I guess. I would never do it again," Barry told Stott.

"How old are you, and where are you from? You never had your ass beat before? Are you ER or NG?" Stott wanted to know.

"My name is Barry Milton Smeall, and I am from Pittsburgh, Pennsylvania. I'm twenty-two years old, and I just graduated from the University of Pittsburgh. I was headed for law school before I got my draft notice. And no, I never had my ass kicked before. Is that so unusual?"

"Let me guess. You're a rich kid, and you never figured you'd wind up drafted, right? Your old man probably tried everything to keep you out, but here you are, a lowly private just like the rest of us! Get this: I'm RA, I'm going airborne, and I'm probably gonna be a lifer, so you and me are from different planets. You can take the bunk above me if you want, but get this: If you ever fuck with me again that ass-kickin' the sarge gave you will seem warm and comfy compared to what I'll do to you! Capish?" Stott minced no words.

"How old are you, Stott?" Barry managed to ask.

"Seven-fuckin'-teen, dickhead, but don't let that fool you! I won my weight in the Golden Gloves, and I don't take no shit from nobody!" Stott was convincing.

Barry observed that Stott was about his own height, five-eleven, but was much leaner. He appeared to have no body fat whatsoever and yet he seemed bigger than Barry, especially through the shoulders. Barry decided that a kid like Stott might be good to have as a friend and resolved to get on his good side.

Chapter Six

About the time Barry Milton Smeall and Mike Stott had made their acquaintance, Sergeant Shitz appeared in the barrack and blew his whistle for attention. "Awright assholes and faggots, here's the deal. I'm going to let you sorry fuckers double-time over to chow, but you'll have to walk the hand ladder if you want to eat. After chow you're on your own to get back to D Barrack, square away your bunks and tuck in. Corporal George will be on duty in D tonight and he will post a fire guard roster. Don't fuck up the fire guard! Corporal George will also post a KP list for 0400, and if your name is on either list, don't be late! If I check in D tonight and find the fire guard asleep, you'll run all night. Got it? Outside and fall in!"

As one of the first guys to walk the ladder, Stott was among the first to sit down and eat. To his surprise, the evening chow was damn good with strawberry shortcake and whipped cream for dessert. For the first time on day one at Fort Dix, there was no sergeant or corporal standing over the recruits shouting, so Mike had time to look around and reflect.

The guy sitting across from Stott hadn't said a word since he sat down, but started talking as Mike got up. "Hey, my name is Larry Allsmeir, and I'm RA, too. What military job are you going for?"

"How'd you know I'm RA?" Stott asked.

"Smeall told me and said you were a Golden Gloves champ, too!" Allsmeir seemed to know everything Smeall and Stott had discussed.

"You know Smeall?" Mike asked.

"Naw, just met him, but us Jews stick together! Seriously, Smeall wants to be your friend, and it's always good to have a multimillionaire as a friend," Allsmeir concluded.

"Private dickhead Smeall is a millionaire? Give me a break! Millionaires' kids don't get drafted! Allsmeir, I think you are completely full of shit! And how come a big shot like you is RA, smart guy?" Stott asked.

"Not all us Jews are rich, kid, but we're all smart! I joined before I got drafted so I could choose my MOS! I'm not getting stuck in the infantry with Vietnam about to explode!"

"What do you mean, about to explode? What do you know about Vietnam? What's wrong with the infantry?" Mike was amazed that Allsmeir seemed to be well aware of what Sergeant Meeks had told them about a country he had barely heard of.

Chapter Seven

Private Lawrence "Larry" Allsmeir graduated from Boston College in the spring of 1962 and received his draft notice a year later. After attempting to avoid military service by applying to graduate school, Allsmeir decided it was better to enlist and choose an MOS, Military Occupational Specialty, than chance winding up in an infantry unit. His three-year enlistment in the army guaranteed that he would be trained as a finance clerk. With a little luck, he'd be posted to a location where he could attend graduate school at night.

Allsmeir accepted serving in the army as a necessary evil. He hoped that basic training would be the hardest part of his military experience. Sitting beside Barry Smeall on the bus ride to Fort Dix, Larry had heard Smeall's life story. He began to angle for a way to take advantage of this very rich and scared young man who shared his religion. When Smeall had disgraced himself by squealing on a fellow recruit in the barbershop formation, Allsmeir figured befriending the obviously terrified Private Smeall might pay big dividends in the short and long term.

Although he shared Smeall's apprehension about the army, Larry resolved to make the best of it and bluff his way through the hard times. Allsmeir was a schemer and plotter who had an innate ability to get on the right side of a situation by sucking up to whomever he figured could help him.

Allsmeir had thoroughly researched his pending army service and was well aware of President Kennedy's commitment to support the Catholic leaders in South Vietnam. Had the potential for war in Vietnam not been so probable, he would have let himself be drafted instead of committing to a third year of active military service. Allsmeir saw no upside to fighting in an insignificant war 7,000 miles away, so clerking in a finance unit seemed to be the best way around a potentially tough situation. Meeting Smeall on the bus ride to Fort Dix seemed to be a good omen, and scheming to turn it into a big positive now preoccupied Allsmeir's thoughts.

Allsmeir overheard the exchange between Stott and Smeall in the barrack. He chose a mess hall seat across from Stott to begin cultivating a friendship with the cocky young boxer. Managing the Stott-Smeall relationship seemed like a natural to Allsmeir, and he began to manipulate both men. Allsmeir responded to Private Stott's three questions.

"Vietnam is going to explode because the power vacuum created when the French were defeated in 1954 must be filled. The Russians and Chinese see an opportunity to spread communism further down the peninsula and drag the U.S. into a guerrilla war with long supply lines. The various peoples of Vietnam hate each other almost as much as they hate outsiders. The poor bastards that serve there are going to be in a no-win situation. And if you are in an infantry unit you'll be fighting in some of the toughest terrain anywhere."

"How do you know all that?" Private Stott demanded.

"First, I was an oriental history major in college. Second, I've been reading everything I can get my hands on about the situation in Vietnam. President Kennedy thinks the North is going to invade the South and he sees it as a critical part of the world where the spread of communism must be stopped. We'll be sending more troops there, and soon." Allsmeir was adamant.

"So you believe what Sergeant Meeks said about running recon there since 1958?"

"First I heard about the U.S. being there that far back, but I'm not surprised. Apparently both the Russians and the Chinese have troops there doing the same thing," Allsmeir said.

"And you think we're going to fight the Russians and the Chinese in Vietnam?" Stott asked.

"I don't know who we'll be fighting, but I do think war on a large scale is a probability."

"There goes my plan for chasing big-titted German girls!" Stott seemed more concerned about that lost opportunity than going to war.

"If you're serious about going airborne, not chasing fräuleins may be the least of your worries! You're likely to be dodging bullets in the jungle in about six months. Maybe you should try for a different MOS," advised Allsmeir.

"Bullshit! I'm not afraid of being in a fight, and I'm sure as hell not afraid of carrying a rifle. I learned to shoot when I was four, and I've been hunting ever since. Where is Vietnam, anyway?"

Stott's attitude and bravado struck Allsmeir as particularly naive, but he was impressed nonetheless. "Well, good luck to you then, Stott, I plan to be fighting a desk while you're fighting the war! Meanwhile, help me take care of Smeall, and let's get him through basic, okay?"

"Smeall's gonna have to make it on his own, and ratting people out ain't the way to go about makin' it! Besides, I've already pissed off two guys from New York, so I'll be busy watching my back!" Stott actually seemed anxious for a confrontation.

"Those guys from New York that you're worried about just met on the bus ride down. They didn't even know each other twenty-four hours ago. Mobliano's just watching out for the orphan."

"Bullshit! He called Sharkey 'his boy' so they must be friends! And what's this orphan crap?" Stott demanded.

"Stott, you may be tough, but you've got a lot to learn! See you later," Allsmeir ended the discussion.

Chapter Eight

Leaving the mess hall that evening preoccupied with what Allsmeir had told him about Vietnam, Mike Stott met Fast Eddy Hale.

"Hey Stott! You seem to look for trouble wherever you can find it! I like that! I'm Eddy Hale, but my friends call me Fast Eddy, you know, like in the movies. Don't worry about Mobliano! He's just another rich guy from New York. And the midget orphan can't be any trouble either. You want to walk around and check out the post on the way back?" Fast Eddy fell in beside Stott.

"Hi Fast Eddy. So where you from and how you know Mobliano is rich?" Hale seemed to be the first more or less normal guy Stott had met in the army.

"I'm from Brooklyn, too, and I know Paulie Mobliano, Syl's little brother. I worked after school and summers in one of the Moblianos' produce markets. They made all their kids work there. The shoes Paulie wore to work cost more than I made in a month, but he was all right! And he worked really hard! Syl was a big-time athlete, so everybody knew about him. He got a full-ride scholarship to some Ivy League school to play football! Like he needed it! They should have given it to some smart kid who wasn't rich, like me!" said Eddy.

Stott was beginning to think that everybody in his training company knew everything about everyone else! He felt he knew absolutely nothing compared to these geniuses from the East Coast.

"So, Eddy, how did you wind up here at Dix? You get drafted?" Mike wanted to ask Eddy about his eyes, but thought he'd wait a while on that. Fast Eddy Hale had one brown eye and the most amazingly green right eye Stott had ever seen. It was disconcerting, like looking at two faces.

"Naw, I joined up. My brothers have all been in the service! I guess it's just what we Irish do when we're old enough.

Join the army and see the world! Or is that the navy? Hell, it beats hanging out in Brooklyn working in a produce shop! But this Vietnam thing kind of spooks me. What's up with that?" Fast Eddy admitted that he was concerned about Nam, just like Stott.

"I don't know about Vietnam, that's new to me, too. I kind of hoped I could get to Germany. You in for three or four years? What's your MOS?" Mike asked.

"Four years, RA all the way! I'm goin' airborne if I can, and I want to be a sniper!" Eddy said.

"You know how to shoot?" Stott asked.

"No, I've never fired a gun, but I'm good at everything I do! I know I'll be a great shot! You ever shoot a gun?" Eddy inquired.

"Yeah, I've done a little shooting. You may want to tone your expectations a bit. They say shooting is like golf; just because you're good at other sports doesn't mean you can hit a golf ball or shoot straight."

"Bullshit! You watch! I'll be the best shot in this training company, guaranteed!" Fast Eddy's confidence seemed genuine.

"Well, maybe, but that would mean you'll have to out-shoot me and that's not likely! I'll help you if you want," Mike said. Stott could relate to Hale, especially the family military tradition.

"Stott, I think you're full of shit, but I like you! We'll see who's the best shot! What's your MOS?"

"I'm slotted for AIT, Advanced Infantry Training, and then I was going to volunteer for airborne 'cause my brothers were all paratroopers. I've been listening to their bullshit about jumping since I was a kid. I guess I was hoping to see Europe by getting posted to the 173rd in Germany, but this Vietnam thing sounds serious." Vietnam was sticking in Stott's head.

"Shit, we're not there yet! Forget about it! Besides, I like chink girls!" Eddy looked on the bright side of every situation.

That was the first time Mike had heard anyone use the phrase "Forget about it!" the way Eddy did, but he soon learned it was a staple of New Yorkers' speech.

Eddy and Mike were taking a tour around the area between the mess hall and D Barrack when Stott realized they were lost.

"You know where we're at? I think we made a wrong turn. We should be walking toward the sun."

"Are you nuts? This is the right way. I never get lost!" Eddy's confidence prevailed.

After another five minutes walking in Eddy's selected direction, Mike knew they were on the wrong track. Just as he was about to discuss the route with Eddy, they came to a corner where the post hospital was located.

"Okay, genius, that's the six-story building we could see about a mile away out the second floor window in D, so you fucked up, Ed. We need to turn around," Mike said.

As Fast Eddy started to explain why his wrong direction was actually correct, a side door to the hospital immediately in front of the recruits was opened by a nurse in army greens. Her shapeliness got their attention, but not nearly as much as what happened next. The nurse placed a large wooden stop under each of the bifold doors to maximize the opening. Orderlies then began rolling out wheelchair-bound soldiers in various stages of impairment. Some were in casts, but some had missing extremities. The orderlies rolled the soldiers out onto a concrete patio and began lighting cigarettes for those who could not do it for themselves. Eddy and Mike were sixty feet from the patio stopped in their tracks.

One young soldier with a missing arm and leg looked up and saw Stott and Hale standing there staring at them. "Hey, guys, look at that! Got to be two dumb-ass new recruits that don't even have issue yet! What the fuck are you guys looking at? Get your sorry asses over here on the double!"

The authority in his voice caused Stott and Hale to quickly move to where the five injured soldiers were smoking. Each of the soldiers' wheelchairs was equipped with a stainless steel pole mounted on the right side of the chair back. The pole was designed to facilitate mobility for those patients who were on IV's, as were three of the five wounded men. Below the hooks that carried the IV's was a clipboard displaying the patient's condition and medication requirements. At the top of each clipboard was the patient's name and rank, along with any Purple Heart medals or decorations of valor they had received.

"Stand at attention in the presence of an officer!"

Stott and Hale snapped to attention.

"What are your names, privates?" Captain Albert demanded.

"Private Stott, sir!"

"Private Hale, sir!"

"At ease! Just arrive here at Dix?"

"Yes, sir!"

"Day one?"

"Yes, sir!"

"What's your MOS?"

"Infantry, sir!"

"Well, looky here guys! We are in the presence of two dumb-ass, brandy new 11-B's! Let me guess, you both want airborne, right? Both looking to be heroes, right?"

"Well, sir," Eddy began, but Captain Albert cut him off.

"Don't qualify a statement with 'well' in front of it! Yes or no! Airborne and heroes, yes or no?"

"Yes, sir!"

"You are truly two dumb fucks! Odds are only one of you will come back from Nam in one piece. You two sissies better change your MOS's! Now get your sorry asses out my sight! Now! Double-time out of my sight or I'll have you over here emptying bed pans! Move out!"

As Hale and Stott collided in their haste to depart, Captain Albert barked out another command. "Halt! You sorry fuckers did not salute me! Stand at attention! Salute! Dismissed!"

Hale surprised Stott by keeping pace with him as they triple-timed away from their first encounter with an army officer. Certain that they were well out of sight, Mike and Eddy looked at each and slowed down.

"Holy shit, Stott! What did you get us into?"

"Me? You're the dumb-ass that got us lost! Did you see those purple hearts? Seven between the five of them! Holy shit!" Mike said.

"And did you see those medals, Stott? What were they?" even Fast Eddy from Brooklyn was impressed.

"The only one I recognized was The Congressional Medal of Honor below Captain Albert's Purple Hearts. None of the other guys had one, but they all had Purple Hearts, so they were all wounded in combat."

"How'd you know that was a Congressional Medal of Honor? What do you mean about Purple Hearts?" Eddy was amazingly uninformed, but very interested.

"Well, Ed, I know about CMH's and Purple Hearts because there's one of each of them hanging over the dresser in my mom and dad's room. My oldest brother, who I don't even remember, was killed in Korea in 1951. He was a captain in the Tenth Rangers, the unit Sergeant Meeks said he served with. One of my earliest memories is of two army officers, all decked out in dress greens, arriving at our house one day to tell my folks that my brother had been killed in action. Mom was never quite the same again. My parents cried for days. Then they went to my brother's funeral in Arlington. My youngest sister and me stayed with our aunt, and that was the first time I'd been away from my parents overnight. People I'd never seen before came to the house crying, trying to console my mom and dad. A lot of them brought newspapers that had pictures of my brother in them, and that got mom stirred up all over again.

My folks went to Washington to receive my brother's Congressional Medal of Honor. When they got back, they had this glass-covered box, sort of like a picture frame, with my brother's military picture, captain's bars, Purple Heart and Congressional Medal of Honor mounted in it along with other medals and ribbons. They hung it on the wall in their bedroom and would stand there in front of it and cry. At first, they stood there most of every day, but after a while they stood there less."

Stott surprised himself, speaking out to Eddy Hale about his brother and family. Perhaps the encounter with the injured soldiers had brought it all back to him.

Fast Eddy Hale from Brooklyn remained silent as they made their way back to D Barrack. As they approached the formation area outside D, Hale gave Stott a sort of nod-salute and walked toward his squad bay one floor above.

Chapter Nine

Edward Robert Hale was seldom speechless, but Private Stott's story about his dead soldier brother had left him so. Eddy could not imagine life without his two older brothers, Sean and Patrick. He could not fathom how his father would have reacted if one of them had not returned from the service.

Though his family now lived in Brooklyn, Eddy had been born in Hell's Kitchen, that area on the west side of Manhattan that had, at one time or another, been home to every nationality of immigrants who had come to New York. Now predominantly Irish, Eddy still considered himself a "Mick from the Kitchen" because of his former residence at Thirty-third Street and Tenth Avenue. He had gone to high school at St. Xavier on the Brooklyn/Queens border. Eddy's mom died giving birth to his youngest sister, Mary Catherine, and his hard drinking, Irish cop father turned more to the bottle with each passing year. But Eddy's dad treasured his family and did the best he could for them. Sean Patrick Hale had been a New York City detective for over twenty years, with more than thirty-five total years on the force, counting his time as a patrolman. Stott's story made Eddy think about his own family, especially his dad.

His dad had always told him, "You gotta be tough!" Eddy worked hard to live up to his dad's expectations, but the past twenty minutes had truly moved him. Ed found himself fighting to hold back the tears as he walked into the barrack. In his distraction he bumped into the big black guy who had been standing next to him in formation.

"Watch out, man!" said George Washington Howard, the tallest recruit in Training Company D.

"Fuck off!" the encounter jarred Eddy back to the present.

"What'd you say, dice-eyes?"

This confrontation got the immediate attention of the dozen or so guys that were close enough to hear it, and a circle gathered around Hale and Howard.

31

"What'd you call me, nigger?" Eddy shot back at Howard.

The circle around the two boys got wider and deeper as the rhetoric heightened. Eddy sized up Howard and figured he was in for a bad time, the black guy being about half again his size. But he had used the word "nigger," and Eddy understood the consequences.

Private Stott heard two guys taunting each other as he climbed the stairs to the upper squad bays. When he heard the term "dice eyes" he instinctively new his new friend, Eddy Hale, was involved. By the time Stott got down to the circle of men anticipating a fight, Hale and Howard were squared off, about to start punching.

"Hold it! You, big guy, are about twice my friend's size and that ain't right! If you want trouble with Hale, you gotta take it through me, and you won't like that result!" Stott spoke in a loud, yet unexcited tone.

"What? Are you fuckin' nuts? You're no bigger than this white kid and this ain't your fight! Fuck off!" Howard was incredulous.

"Wrong on two counts, asshole. I am bigger than Hale, and it is my fight 'cause he's my friend. So how do you want to do this? Rules or no rules? Your choice." Stott's calmness surprised Howard.

"This dickhead called me a nigger, and I don't take that from nobody, mister!"

"Hale shouldn't have said that, but that's not gonna save you from getting your ass kicked if you want a fight. Rules or no rules?" Stott repeated.

"I'm gonna make it easy on you, whitey, and call rules! Just hands, no kicking. You won't last thirty seconds! When we gonna do it?"

"Right now, right here," Stott calmly said.

With that, the circle widened and Stott stepped forward. Hale didn't know what to do. If he let Stott fight for him he'd never live it down. But this big black guy looked real tough, and Eddy thought he stood little chance against him. Why was Stott so willing to stand up for him?

"Look, Mike, I can handle this. I'll fight him!" Hale exclaimed.

"I know you could, Eddy. But I haven't had a warm-up in a few days, so this will be fun. You'll owe me a beer."

Howard observed this exchange and just got madder. "Which one of you whiteys is it gonna be?"

"Me, now, put 'em up," said Stott.

Howard assumed what he thought was a boxing stance and faced Stott, figuring his first punch would deck this silly white kid. He started a long, right-handed haymaker punch toward Stott's head. That was the last thing Howard remembered until he saw Stott standing over him with a wet towel. The circle of recruits had gotten bigger, yet strangely quiet.

Dazed, Howard asked, "What happened?"

"Well, boy, you telegraph your moves, you're really slow, and you have a glass jaw. Other than that, you're a real tough guy," Stott was actually smiling at him and completely matter-of-fact.

Howard could not believe that this skinny white kid had just put him down. As he started to rise in protest, he realized his head felt disconnected from his body. He tried to prop himself up on one elbow, but fell backward slamming his head on the wooden floor. This brought a ripple of laughter from the thirty or so guys that had just witnessed Stott's one-two combination that had put Howard down and out for several minutes.

"We were about to call for help when you started coming around. You all right?" Stott asked.

"I-I-I guess so. What'd you hit me with?" Again, laughter from the surrounding circle.

"Just a soft left and a little harder right. I could see you didn't know what you were doing, so I took it easy on you," Stott's grin left Howard dumbfounded.

"Come on, sit up, put your head between your knees and keep this cool towel on your forehead. You'll be okay in a while. No hard feelings, right? I mean, after all, I don't want a big, tough guy like you mad at me!" Stott just didn't let up, but his grin made even Howard smile.

"Jesus-H-Christ, this is a bad start to a military career!" Howard exclaimed.

"You a lifer?" Hale moved in next to Howard. "Sorry about the name, but your crack about my eyes really got me."

"I'll forget it if you'll forget it, but your friend here really surprised me. You guys on the buddy system?" Howard asked.

"No, we just met. We walked back from the mess hall together and kind of hit it off. I guess I'm lucky he stepped in," Hale said.

"I guess I'm lucky Stott took it easy on me!"

"See you guys in the a.m. Try not to cause any more trouble tonight, Hale," Stott said as he departed.

Hale helped Howard to his feet. "You want some air?" Eddy asked Howard.

"Yeah, I need some. I'm still groggy."

After a time talking outside the barrack, Hale and Howard reentered the squad bay to find the only two remaining bunks were above one another.

"Well, Whitey Two, I guess we're gonna have to be bunk mates. Top or bottom?"

"Top, I don't want your big lard-ass falling in on me during the night! And what's the 'whitey' stuff?" Eddy had hoped the name calling was over.

"Well, as far as I'm concerned, Stott has earned the title of Whitey One, and that makes you Whitey Two. All you white guys look alike, so I'll have to assign you numbers!" Howard's grin made Hale smile.

"Okay. But I don't know how Stott will take being Whitey One. He's pretty edgy."

"If I can get over him kicking my ass in front of the whole company, he can learn to appreciate his nickname! I'm the one with the sore jaw!" Howard concluded.

Chapter Ten

Syl Mobliano and JJ Sharkey did not actually see the fight between Howard and Stott, but they heard about it right after it happened. One of the guys in their squad bay reported, "Goddamn! That Stott guy is something. The big spook didn't know what hit him, and he's twice Stott's size. And then Stott helps him up like nothing happened!"

"What's that, kid?" Syl asked the young recruit.

"You guys just missed the shortest fight of the century! Stott's buddy, Hale, got into it with that big black guy, Howard, and Stott steps in and decks Howard with two punches! The whole downstairs bay saw it, and Corporal George just watched the whole thing and didn't do nothin'!"

"Is that a fact?" Syl seemed more amused than impressed. "Well, JJ, I guess Stott is not just all talk. I still can't figure why he jumped on you at noon chow, maybe he's just a hothead."

"I thought most people liked to talk about their families and where they are from," said Sharkey.

"Well, JJ, you sure don't! We rode beside each other on the bus all the way down from the city, and you didn't tell me one thing about yourself! Still haven't." Syl thought maybe Sharkey would open up.

"I don't have much to tell, Syl. I'm really looking forward to getting our army issue clothing tomorrow! I'm going to hit the head before I turn in. I'll try not to disturb you when I climb up top. Good night."

"You won't disturb me, kid. I'll be awake for hours. I guess lights out is at 9:00 p.m."

"You mean 2100, right, Syl?" Sharkey actually grinned.

"Yeah, right, smart-ass!" Syl was glad to see JJ lighten up.

As Sharkey entered the latrine, there was Private Stott, brushing his teeth.

"Hey, Sharkey, what's up?" Stott seemed relaxed.

"Hello, Private Stott. Word is you're a great boxer. Congratulations on the knockout."

"Hey, the bigger they are, the harder they fall, but you probably know that. Ever do any boxing?"

"No, I haven't, but I would like to learn," Sharkey's interest seemed genuine.

"If we ever get any free time, I'll show you some moves. Did I hear the old guy call you JJ?"

"If you mean Syl Mobliano, yes, he calls me JJ."

"JJ cool with you? Call me Mike or Stott or whatever. You RA?" Stott inquired.

"Yes, I enlisted for six years," Sharkey told Stott.

"Six years! Holy shit! I thought I fucked up doing four! You a potential lifer?"

"Yes, that is my intention. I hope to be a good soldier."

"You know, JJ, I think you will be!" Stott stuck out his hand.

John J. Sharkey shook Stott's hand. "Sorry if I offended you at lunch."

"Forget about it! Just keep the old fart away from me so I don't have to hurt him!" Stott headed for his bunk.

Chapter Eleven

As the lights went out in D Barrack, George Washington Howard lay in his bunk and hoped Private Hale in the bunk above him didn't fart in his sleep. George's long legs caused his feet to hang over the end of the lower bunk, so they were jammed against the adjoining locker. George could not get comfortable, and he was too keyed up to sleep. Plus, his jaw hurt like hell.

What a day! He had just gotten into only the second fight of his life, and he had lost! To a skinny white kid, no less! At six-feet six-inches and 280 pounds, not many people had ever challenged George. When Private Hale had bumped into him, Howard had no idea that saying, "Watch out, man," would be taken as an offense. He was kidding more than angry, and the next thing he knew, someone called him a nigger! That hadn't happened very often to a guy his size, even where he grew up.

In the one fight he had been in previously, George had just reached out and slapped the other guy hard enough across the face to end the battle. No one had actually hit him before, ever. His head still hurt right between his eyes where Stott's "soft left" had tagged him. His jaw felt like it had been hammered with a stone! And then both of the white guys helped him get up and shake it off!

Howard had very limited exposure to white people. Having grown up in Benton County, Mississippi, with a thirteen to one black to white ratio, George had spoken with more white people in the past thirteen days than he had in his previous nineteen years.

When Howard went to Jackson to join the army, both of the recruiting sergeants were white. They assured him that the new army was fully integrated. "Hell, boy, you're gonna have an advantage! The army wants big, strong bucks like you, and we need black NCO's, so you're gonna have it made!"

"What's an NCO?" Howard asked.

"You know, son, noncommissioned officers—sergeants like me and Jim here. NCO's run the army; the officers just think they do! Just sign right here, and you're good to go!"

George Washington Howard had enlisted in the army for six years. He received orders to report to Fort Dix along with a one-way airplane ticket from the airport in Memphis, Tennessee, to Newark, New Jersey. George had been to Memphis twice before, but his trip to Jackson to join the army was the farthest he had ever traveled from home. He'd taken a Greyhound bus from Ashland to Jackson to sign up. George slept on a park bench across from the recruiting station that night and returned to Ashland on the bus the following morning.

George had four brothers and four sisters, all younger than him, and he hoped to be able to send money from his army pay back home to help his parents. George was the first man in his family to graduate from high school, and he considered himself very lucky to have done so. The high school Howard had gone to in Ashland, Mississippi, was segregated. Only five black students received high school diplomas in the Class of 1963. George was the only black male graduate.

Howard was quite surprised to see that about 10 percent of the trainees in Company D were black. He half expected to be the only black guy at Fort Dix. The few black recruits that had spoken to him so far shied away from him when they learned he was from Mississippi. George had trouble understanding them anyway. They spoke English, but it sounded very different from the way the folks in Benton County spoke. Amazingly, the only friendly contact he'd had so far in the army was from the two white guys he had gotten in the fight with!

George Washington Howard realized that he had been totally unprepared for the experiences of his first day in the army. He fell asleep calculating that he had 2,191 days left in his six-year enlistment.

Chapter Twelve

Days two, three, and four of Company D's army experience were consumed with standing in lines to get medical exams, a myriad of shots done mostly with airless needle guns, which hurt like hell, and waiting. On the morning of day three, they received their issue of GI clothing and began to look like soldiers. Corporal George and Sergeant Shitz were the only cadre the soldiers saw during this time, and they really didn't do much, except wait. Sunday afternoon, groups sat around outside D Barrack swapping lies and acting macho the way scared, nervous young men do.

The mess hall served chow between 1630 and 1800 hours on Sunday, and the men ate a reasonably good chicken dinner topped off with peach cobbler and vanilla ice cream. After chow, they were anticipating the first real day of basic training, which was scheduled to start at 0500 hours the following morning. Excitement filled the air.

Most of the guys had "buddied up," and circles of friends were developing. Mike Stott hung out mostly with Fast Eddy Hale and George Washington Howard, who Eddy had dubbed "Big Howie."

The three or four groups of black guys all avoided Howard. Big Howie seemed more comfortable around Hale and Stott than with any other group. They got a kick out of being Whitey One and Whitey Two. Big Howie had a good sense of humor, although his life experiences were so limited that Hale and Stott had to explain all kinds of regular stuff to him, like pussy.

Big Howie had never heard the term "pussy," but, after Stott and Hale explained it to him, it was all he wanted to talk about. Not that Howard didn't fixate on sex like every other red-blooded American boy, but pussy and eating pussy, as Eddy and Mike described it, really got Big Howie riled up. Never mind that Mike and Eddy had never done any of the things they described, they talked like pros.

As Hale and Stott lied about their many female conquests to Big Howie after chow that Sunday evening, Mobliano, Sharkey, Allsmeir, and Smeall ambled over and joined the conversation. Hale was in the middle of explaining to Big Howie why Irish girls were pure trouble when they joined in.

"So, Hale, how many women have you had?" Mobliano got right to the point.

"Lots!" was Hale's quick answer.

"Okay, how many is a lot to you? Ten? Twenty?" Syl kept digging.

"Between ten and twenty!" Hale exclaimed.

"What was the first one's name?" Mobliano demanded.

"I-I-I think it was Betty," Eddy murmured.

"Let me get this straight, Hale; you don't absolutely re-member the name of the first piece of ass you ever you got?"

"It was Betty or Sandy!" Fast Eddy screamed.

"So what color hair did she have?" Syl asked.

"Red!" Eddie screamed.

"So, did Betty have red hair or was it Sandy?" Mobliano's interrogation technique impressed the soldiers.

"Sandy!" Now Fast Eddy's face was flushed in anger.

"So, you think you remember that your first piece of ass's name was Sandy, and she was a redhead, right?"

"Yeah, Sandy was a redheaded Irish chick, and she had huge tits!" Hale said.

"Hale, you are absolutely full of shit! You know how I know you're lying? Because they don't call red-haired broads Sandy, and no Irish chick has big tits," Syl said.

"You calling me a liar, you bald-headed WOP?" Eddy had a pension for losing control and name calling.

"You trying to start a fight so your protector here, Stott, will jump in and save you?" Syl asked.

"Whoa, hold on, there Hale. Can't you tell when some-one's putting you on?" said John Sharkey, who had not spo-ken one word all day. "That mouth of yours doin' the name calling is a serious problem for you."

"Listen, dwarf, if I need any shit from you I'll squeeze your fuckin' head!" The men were all surprised at how quickly Hale had gotten angry and mean.

Then Sharkey really surprised them all. He dove directly at Eddy, headfirst, fists flying. It was probably dumb luck, but as Sharkey swung a wild right fist, Hale, in his surprise, leaned forward right into the punch. The soldiers heard a crack as Sharkey's fist connected with Hale's nose, shattering it in two places. Hale's eyes rolled back in his head, and he fell backward, out cold.

Stott, Howard, Mobliano, Allsmeir, and Smeall stared at Sharkey, hardly able to believe what they had witnessed. Sharkey was rubbing his fist, also in disbelief.

A moaning sound refocused the men on Hale as he came to and tried to sit up. Blood streamed down his face, and he was crying. His eyes were already turning black. Sharkey was as distraught as Eddy, although he wasn't crying.

First words out of Eddy's mouth, "You sucker punched me!"

The soldiers noticed that Hale no longer referred to Sharkey as a dwarf.

Big Howie spoke, "Jesus H. Christ, Hale, if I'd known you were that easy I could've saved myself a lot of crap with Stott, here!"

"Well, well, JJ, you're just full of surprises. Guess I don't have to worry about you after all!" Mobliano seemed pleased that Sharkey had a fighting spirit.

"Okay, guys, now here's the problem as I see it. We gotta get Hale fixed up, and we don't want to get anybody in trouble. Where can we get some ice for Hale's nose?" Allsmeir said, immediately figuring the angles.

"That nose is gonna need more than ice; it needs to be straightened and bandaged. If Hale misses morning formation, he'll have to recycle to another basic training company. You seven soldiers are turning into nothing but trouble," said Corporal George, the duty NCO, who had seen everything.

"Here's the deal. Mobliano and Stott, walk Hale over to the post hospital. Carry him if he passes out. I'll call a medic

I know and have him meet you there and fix him up, off the record. Allsmeir, you and the snitch here clean up the blood and police up this area. Slugger Sharkey, I'm puttin' you on first fire guard startin' now, and you don't get relieved 'til 2400. Private Howard, you and Hale seem to be in the middle of all the troubles around here, so you will clean every latrine in the barrack over and over until I inspect 'em and okay 'em. If any one of the seven of you so much as farts, I'm throwin' all you jerks in the stockade! Now move!"

"Can you walk, Hale, or do you want us to carry you?" Mobliano asked.

"I can walk, and I don't need you assholes to do nothin'!" whined Hale.

"Eddy, you couldn't find your way to the hospital or back! So we're walkin' you over like the corporal ordered, and if you give us any more shit you'll need carrying!" Mike said.

"Whose side you on, Stott? Why didn't you help me?" Hale demanded.

"Help you? You started your own trouble by bein' a hot-headed loudmouth! And what was I supposed to do? JJ's about a foot shorter than you and six classes lighter but still kicked your ass! You need to chill out." Stott was beginning to think Hale was more trouble than he was worth. Mobliano didn't say anything, but Mike noticed he observed everything.

Stott and Mobliano got Hale back to D just before lights out at 2100 hours and got him settled in his bunk above Big Howie. Corporal George's medic buddy gave Hale a small Red Cross cold pack so he could hold ice on his nose.

"If you take this pill, you'll sleep through the night, but somebody will have to get you to formation. Don't tell anybody where you got the downer!" were the last instructions from medic Smith.

The seven soldiers bedded down for the night awaiting the promised 0500 wake-up call and the first real day of basic training.

Chapter Thirteen

At the top and bottom of each stairwell leading to the individual squad bays in D Barrack was a thirty-five gallon galvanized steel garbage can painted army green. The men had each taken a turn emptying these cans under Corporal George's direction during reception. The cans were amazingly heavy, even when empty.

At 0415 hours on day one of basic training, Sergeants Turner, Meeks, Shitz and several other cadre each hoisted one of these cans high above their heads, and, on Turner's command, heaved them down the hardwood floors between the rows of bunks. Concurrent with the coordinated can toss, each of the sergeants blew their command whistles at maximum pitch. The effect was to literally shock-bounce the recruits out of their bunks as the sergeants began turning over lockers and bunks, dropping those troopers in the upper berths who were too slow to react some five feet to the floor below.

In the state of shock that this created and with the aid of an electronic bullhorn came First Sergeant Turner's real welcoming speech: "Awright, you worthless cocksuckers, on your feet! We start early in Company D, and you're already late! Ten minutes for the Three S's and then to formation! Fats, boots, and hats! All you motherfuckers on the lines by 0430 or you'll all run 'til you drop! Got it? Move your limped-dick fat asses! Now!"

The Three S's in ten minutes is impossible. For 180 recruits to get dressed and out on the line took until 0437. Big mistake for the boys in Company D. For those who hadn't managed to shit, shower and shave in ten minutes, personal comfort was a problem. At 0438 hours in the pitch dark of a rainy July morning, Sergeant Turner explained their predicament.

From an elevated review stand, bullhorn in hand, Turner began, "Did you worthless fucking faggots not hear me? Did

43

you think it was your mommy talking? Do you think I'm your fucking mother? I said 0430 hours! It's now 0440! All you scum-sucking motherfuckers now owe me and the army ten minutes! And the army and me have a rule! We collect our debts times ten! You all now owe me one hour and forty minutes! Got it? I'll decide when to collect! Sergeant Meeks, get 'em movin'!"

The first morning run lasted an hour. Half the guys puked within the first twenty minutes, but no one was allowed to stop. It was the first time that most of them had run in army boots. Many of the soldiers developed blisters on both feet, especially just above the heel where the army had cleverly specified a cross-stitched seam in the boot, guaranteed to irritate the skin.

At 0545, Sergeant Turner re-formed his company and marched them into their first basic training breakfast. After the hand ladder drill, they eventually got through the chow line, but few were capable of eating, given the stench from their puke-covered buddies. At 0630, the soldiers were back in formation and began an hour of calisthenics led by the first sergeant himself. Turner set a blistering pace for the exercises and barely broke a sweat.

Company D then practiced marching from 0730 hours until 0955 hours when they got a ten minute smoke break.

"Awright, girls, smoke 'em if you got 'em, pee if you have to! On me in ten!" Turner commanded.

The soldiers broke for noon chow at 1220 hours and were back to marching at 1300. As a break from the marching drill, they were treated to Sergeant Turner's exercise routine. Led by Turner himself, they started with jumping jacks, then hit the dirt for push-ups and sit-ups, back on their feet for deep knee bends, then more push-ups in a continuous cycle.

During one of the exercise breaks, Sergeant Turner noticed Hale's broken nose and black eyes.

"Well, Trooper Hale's setting a fashion tone with that mug! What happened, Hale, run into a door?"

"Yes, Sergeant!"

"Maybe you're not as dumb as you look, Hale," Turner said.

Company D drilled all afternoon right up to chow at 1730 hours. After chow, they were instructed in the fine art of spit-shining GI boots to a mirror finish and getting their gear squared away, army style.

"You sorry-ass troopers who can count will have observed that the army has issued you each two pair of high-quality black leather boots. You will alternate wearing each pair of boots on a daily basis. The pair that's not on your feet are to be resting on your foot locker in exactly this position and had better be shined to a mirror sheen! Good boots make good soldiers, so you sick pukes can at least look like soldiers by having perfect boots! That means every morning at formation the boots on your feet are parade-ready shined and your spare pair on your locker are just as good." Sergeant Turner seemed to have a thing about boots.

"Now, my twenty-two years in the army has taught me that some of you bright motherfuckers are going to try to trick me by keeping one pair of boots spit-shined on your locker so you only have to shine one pair each night! Trust me, assholes, the first trooper I catch not switching his boots everyday will abso-fucking-lutely wish that he was dead! Got it? Do you understand me, faggots? I'll see you girls at 0500!"

Sergeant Turner thus departed D Barrack at 1945 hours after the first day of basic training. He'd been with the recruits since 0415 hours that morning. Turner led the marching and exercises all day and had hardly stopped yelling at them the entire time. Yet, as he inspected each squad bay on his way out of D, he looked fresh as a daisy, like he just got up and performed the Three S's.

The troopers now had an hour to spit shine boots, two pair, prepare their gear for the next day, and make lights out at 2100 hours. Though exhausted, sleep came slowly as Stott and his buddies tried to comprehend what they had just been through on day one in Sergeant Turner's army.

"Stott, are you awake?" asked Private Barry Smeall.

"Yeah, Smeall, what's up?"

"You think tomorrow will be easier than today? We were on our feet for fifteen hours! I think I lost ten pounds, and I'm shaking all over! And did you see Sergeant Turner? He's some kind of superman! He didn't even sweat out there!" Smeall was all wound up.

"No, Smeall, tomorrow's gonna be harder and day three harder still. They're getting us in condition, breaking us down so they can build us up. You know, like in football camp!" Stott said.

"I don't know if I can make it if it's any harder!" Smeall's whined.

"Get some sleep, Smeall. You're gonna make it 'cause you have to! There's no slackin' off around Turner, so we'd better play his game!"

Day two in Sergeant Turner's army was, in fact, considerably harder than day one because it lasted longer. The men were rousted out of their bunks at 0430 hours and ran, exercised, and drilled right through to 1800 hours. Sergeant Turner proclaimed he was in a good mood because he had seen "a West Point Captain fall down a flight of stairs," so the recruits marched again after evening chow until 2030 hours.

Again, the troops spit shined their boots, squared away gear, and made lights out at 2130 hours. Even Smeall was too tired to talk. Stott's bunk bay had fire guard that night, so Mike was awakened by Private Shore at 0100 in the morning to walk the barrack floor until 0200, at which time he was to awaken Smeall for his turn at fire guard.

Stott shook Smeall, slapped him in the head, reached up under his bunk, and jabbed him in the back, but Barry just kept snoring. Mike was about to roll Smeall off to the floor below when he realized that he wouldn't be able to go back to sleep anyway. Stott let Smeall sleep, walked until 0300, and roused the next guy.

The collective snoring of the twenty or so guys closest to Stott kept him from falling asleep, so he lay there wondering how in the hell Sergeant Turner, who had to be in his forties, could set such a frantic pace and appear to be fresh at the end of the day. Just as Mike dozed off, the garbage cans crashed down the squad bay floor, indicating that it was 0430 hours, the start of a new day for the trainees in Company D.

The next twenty days of basic training were pretty much like the first two. Run, exercise, drill, and learn the army way. In fact, the first three weeks went by quickly for the men of D Company. They got Sundays off, but were restricted to the post and mostly laid around the barrack trying to recover from the grueling training schedule.

At the day's end formation on the third Saturday of basic training, Sergeant Turner informed the soldiers they were going to the field on Monday morning. "You troopers will 'eat, sleep and make love' to your assigned rifles for the next four weeks. We start range training at 0800 on Tuesday, and, providing none of you fucking idiots shoot one another, I will turn you into lean, mean, shootin' machines. And listen up, girls; we'll be marching out to the bivouac area on Monday, so you better rest up tomorrow!"

On Sundays, the mess hall served breakfast until 0930 hours. During the first three weeks of basic, Stott had lost fifteen pounds, and he wasn't heavy when he got to Fort Dix. The exercise regimen combined with no snacks, just good army food, was working well to get Mike and his friends into shape.

Chapter Fourteen

Through the first three weeks of basic training, the troopers in Company D had checked rifles in and out of the armory each day to use while marching and drilling. Now they were going to be assigned the rifle that would remain with them through basic training.

As Stott and his buddies hung out in D on the Sunday before going to the field, finally getting to fire a rifle was all they talked about. Fast Eddy Hale's nose was beginning to reduce back to a normal size with most of the black, red, and yellow bruising fading away. Along with his return to normal appearance, Eddy's chip-on-his-shoulder attitude was also coming back. The soldiers had all been marched to the barbershop for their second army headshave on the previous Friday, but this time the barbers left a little on top. Some of them had the beginnings of a flattop style that the army allowed. Eddy had purchased a product called Butch Wax at the PX and was leading the flattop styling contest in Company D.

"So, what do you think, Stott, my flattop styling cool or what?" Hale asked.

"Actually, Hale, you're just about the same degree of ugly as the first time I saw you, but now you're even skinnier!" Stott said.

Hale had resisted army food for a while at first and had lost even more weight than the rest of the recruits. "You'd better watch what you say to Sharkey now, 'cause I think he outweighs you!"

John J. Sharkey had taken to army food like a duck to water. He always cleaned his tray and, when allowed, went back for seconds and even thirds. Sharkey had actually gained weight through the first three weeks of basic training. He looked much stronger and healthier than the first day his buddies had met him in the reception center.

"That was a lucky punch Sharkey got in on me, Stott, and you know it! Next time, I'll kick his ass!" Fast Eddy's cockiness was definitely back.

"Well, if you want, I could arrange a rematch," said Private Mobliano, who had just entered Stott and Hale's squad bay.

"Yeah, that's a great idea!" said Private Allsmeir from behind Mobliano's shoulder. "We could set up an afternoon match, and I'll make book!"

"Allsmeir, I was kidding! You need to quit following me around!" said Mobliano. Mobliano was not all that fond of Allsmeir.

"So, what are you and your crew up to Mobliano? I thought you and Sharkey and the Jewish brain trust would be at church or something." Stott had started to get along pretty well with Mobliano and his guys.

"Yeah, right, Stott! Like Allsmeir and Smeall go to church on Sundays. Actually, JJ did go to church after he ate about three breakfasts!" Mobliano made all the troopers laugh at the thought of Sharkey going through the breakfast chow line three times.

"Yeah, JJ's at church, and then he said he was going to the library." Smeall seemed to keep track of everyone's movements.

"Where's your favorite punching bag, Big Howie?" Allsmeir inquired.

"Right here, dickhead!" Big Howie had walked up behind Mobliano, Smeall, and Allsmeir. He grabbed Allsmeir from the back and sat him up on an upper bunk with little effort.

"Now, what was that about me being a punching bag?" Howard asked Allsmeir.

Sitting on the upper bunk, Allsmeir was about eye level with Howard.

"I-I-I'm sorry, Big Howie. I was just kidding!" Allsmeir was truly panicked.

"You can call me Mr. Howard from now on, dickhead, get it? Only my friends, Stott and Hale, call me Big Howie!"

Mobliano, Hale, and Stott saw that Howard was messing with Allsmeir, but Allsmeir didn't know it.

"Yes, Mr. Howard!" Allsmeir was serious.

That was how Big Howie became Mr. Howard to the rest of the company. Like Sharkey, Howard had taken to army food and hadn't lost much weight. In fact, he looked even bigger and stronger than he did on day one.

"You know, Howard, you and Sharkey must be the only two guys in the company that have gained weight in basic! You really like this army food?" Mobliano asked

"Let me tell you, Mobs, this army food is great and all you want! I've had food here I never tasted before. Back home we lived on corn bread, beans, and polk salad. Couple of times a week we might have some salt pork or a little chicken, but there was eleven of us, so we didn't get fat!" said Howard.

"But you sure got big and strong! So it must've been enough," Mobliano seemed genuinely interested in what Howard said about his upbringing.

"I guess it was, but I was always hungry! I ain't been hungry since I got to Dix, so I'm beginning to think joining for six years wasn't so bad after all as long as little Stott, here, don't get mad at me again!"

The soldiers all laughed, except Allsmeir who was still perched on the bunk where Howard had placed him.

"Can I get down, now?" Allsmeir asked Howard.

"Didn't you mean, 'Can I get down, now, Mr. Howard?'" Big Howie was having fun.

"May I please get down, Mr. Howard?" Big Howie reached over and picked Allsmeir up, straight armed, and gently set him on the floor.

"You're learnin'," said Big Howie.

Stott, Smeall, and Mobliano were astonished by the display of strength they had just witnessed.

"You ever lift any weights, Howard?" Mobs asked.

"You mean like iron weights? No," said Howard.

"Well, tell you what. We got nothing to do until evening chow, so let's go over to the base gym this afternoon and see what you can do!"

"I can bench two hundred!" piped in Hale.

Mobs and Stott looked at each other, but Allsmeir beat them to the punch.

"I got twenty dollars that says you can't!" said Allsmeir.

As Big Howie, Mobliano, Allsmeir, Hale, Smeall, and Stott entered the gym, they were surprised to see Private John J. Sharkey working out on a light punching bag.

"Hey, JJ, what's this? I thought you went to the library?" Mobliano asked.

"Well, I know how to read, but I don't know how to box, so I'm trying to learn," JJ seemed embarrassed that his buddies had found him out.

"I told you I'd teach you!" Stott said.

"Yeah, but I wanted to get a head start!" Sharkey was serious.

Howard, Allsmeir, Hale, and Smeall were already by the weights, setting up a 200-pound bar for Fast Eddy. Sharkey, Mobliano, and Stott joined them just as Eddy was positioning himself under the 200-pound setup.

"Whoa, there, who's spotting for him?" Mobliano demanded.

"I don't need no spotter!" exclaimed Hale as he reached for the bar.

Mobliano and Stott each grabbed an end of the barbell and slowly lowered it to Hale's chest.

"You got it, Ed? Are you ready?"

"Let me have it!" Hale demanded.

They gradually let Hale have the full weight of the bar.

"Press," said Mobliano.

Although Eddy was able to hold the weight in the start position, to no one's surprise he could not push it up. After he strained and heaved for a minute or so, Mobliano spoke up, "That's enough, Hale; you'll rupture something!"

As Syl and Mike started to take the weight from Eddy, Big Howie grasped the bar in the middle with both hands and lifted the barbell and Eddy right up off the bench, because Hale would not let go. Howard actually got Hale and the barbell to full curl position as Hale continued to protest that he hadn't been given enough time.

Astounded at Howard's display of strength, Mobliano and Stott made Eddy let go and had Big Howie set the barbell back in its stand.

"Gimmie my twenty dollars, Hale, you didn't even come close!" Allsmeir demanded.

"Hold on, Allsmeir, settle that later. Put three hundred pounds on the bar." Mobliano was removing his shirt. Syl then did three reps with 320 pounds of weight, placing the barbell back in its stand by himself.

"I lifted weights for football conditioning since I was twelve to be able to do that," Syl said. "Howard, you want to give it a try?"

Howard positioned himself under the barbell and did ten repetitions when Mobliano stopped him.

"Holy shit, Howard! You really never lifted before? You think you could handle more weight?" Mobs asked.

With Howard still on the bench, his friends put another forty-five pound weight on each end of the barbell, raising the true dead weight to 410 pounds. To their amazement Howard bench- pressed the 410 pounds three times.

"Is that good?" Howard asked.

"Howard, if these weights are accurate, you're not far off the world's record!" Mobliano was dumbfounded, as were all his pals.

"Well, Mr. Howard, Hale's sure lucky I didn't know how strong you were in the reception center 'cause I would have let you kill him if I had known!" Stott said. All seven soldiers got a good laugh at Mike's confession.

"Didn't seem to matter, Whitey One! My jaw must not be strong!"

On that Sunday afternoon in the gym at Fort Dix, seven young soldiers from distinctly different backgrounds began friendships that none of them could have predicted.

Chapter Fifteen

On the fourth Monday of basic training, the cadre let the men of D Company sleep until 0500 hours. They didn't throw the garbage cans down the halls, either. Bugle reveille blasted through the barrack speakers at exactly 0500, and the soldiers all hit the ground running to make formation. To their amazement, Sergeant Turner led only a half hour of PT and then led them directly to the mess hall. No morning run! Something was up!

For the first time, the training sergeants, including Turner, spread themselves out through the mess hall and ate with the troops like regular human beings!

After an almost leisurely morning chow, Sergeant Turner called his troopers to formation and had them stand at ease.

"Listen up, troops! Today we force-march to our assigned bivouac area out past the rifle ranges. We got my favorite spot, which happens to be only about seventeen miles from where you're standing. First, we're double-timing over to the armory, where you'll be issued the rifle that will stay with you through basic. Then we're going back to D and pack up your gear—everything in your lockers—in packs and duffel bags. You may leave nothing behind! Get it? Everything gets packed! At 1000 hours we begin our march to the field! Remember, if you don't pack it, you'll never see it again! Get it? Sergeant Meeks, double-time to the armory and then to D and get 'em packin'!"

The armory was the most organized operation at Fort Dix. The men quickly got rifles assigned to them by their army serial number. A soldier's status in the army—ER, NG, RA, or US—in front of his social security number became his army identification code. The men were instructed to memorize the manufacturer's serial number on the rifle they were issued. Any trooper who did not return the same rifle he'd been issued would be court-martialed!

Rifles on shoulders, Sergeant Meeks marched them to the barrack to pack. The recruits had been issued three sets of fatigue shirts and pants, six sets of underwear, six pair of boot socks, two pair of high-quality leather boots, two base-ball-style hats, and a field jacket with liner. Each soldier also had a canteen, mess kit, and an entrenching tool, all with covers that allowed them to be attached to their web belts. A steel helmet or "pot" with liner, web belt, canteen, back pack, various pouches that attached to the web belt, and two pair of leather gloves with liners rounded out their field gear. The men had dress issue uniforms consisting of two sets of khakis, two sets of winter dress greens with two army dress shirts, two black ties, and an army winter overcoat complete with felt liner that alone weighed ten pounds. One pair of army dress shoes, two pair of dress socks, and a garrison cap rounded out their GI clothing.

Given that it was early August in New Jersey and the temperature made it into the low nineties most days, the winter dress greens, overcoat, gloves, and field jacket liner seemed unnecessary to the young soldiers, but not to the army!

As Stott and his buddies began to pack their gear for the march to the field, the training sergeants were circulating through the barrack barking orders and insults while offering helpful packing suggestions.

"You are un-fucking-doubtedly the dumbest group of recruits ever! Did you not hear Top say everything gets packed? That means every fucking thing, get it?" Sergeant Shitz seemed to be truly enjoying their packing dilemma.

"But, Sarge, its July and we won't wear our dress outfits or coats!" Private Hale just couldn't keep himself from whining.

"Hale, you are un-fucking-doubtedly the dumbest moth-erfucker in a company of severely dumb bastards! You take everything, get it? If you get to the field and you don't have it, you'll have to march back to D and get it! And if by some fucking chance stuff you left behind isn't here, you'll have to buy replacement gear, get it? Now pack that shit and get your fat ass—duffel bag overhead, wearable gear on your sorry-ass person—out to formation by 1000 hours or I will rip your head off and shit down your throat. Get it, Hale?"

Cramming all the aforementioned gear into a backpack and duffel bag was a formidable challenge. Most troopers had to pack, unpack, and repack several times to get it all in. Once this was accomplished, the duffel bag weighed seventy to eighty pounds.

At 0950 hours, the sergeants began shouting a warning, "All wearable gear on your bodies, get it? Pots and liners on heads! You think you march in your hats? You march with a weapon, you wear your helmet, get it?"

At 1000 hours on a steamy New Jersey morning, the 174 recruits remaining in Training Company D formed up, double deep, with wearable gear on, steel pots on heads, assigned rifles at the parade rest position, and duffel bags neatly positioned precisely in front of them.

No one knew what happened to the six men that were no longer part of Training Company D. One night they were there, next morning they weren't. During drill on that mysterious day, their lockers were cleaned out, and none of the remaining recruits ever heard from the missing six again. Stott and his buddies didn't really know any of the men who disappeared, but they sure wondered what happened to them.

Sergeant Turner was at the top of his game. "Awright, troopers, looks like those of you still with us are ready to march! Before we depart, however, our commanding officer wants to speak with you! We're waiting for him now!"

During the first few days of basic training, the recruits had been addressed by Captain Hargrove, Commanding Officer of D Company. Supporting Captain Hargrove were a couple of lieutenants, but the soldiers hadn't seen much of the officers since training began. Top Sergeant Turner and his cadre ran the show, referring to the officers only occasionally and then in not very complimentary terms. All the NCOs in Training Company D liked to scream out, "Don't call me sir, I work for a living! I don't play golf and I don't drink tea! Therefore, dickheads, don't fuck with me!"

Stott thought he must have heard that diatribe at least a hundred times since basic began. He observed that when the officers were within earshot, which was not very often, the sergeants did not subject the men to the usual profanity. When officers were present, the recruits were "troopers, girls or limp dicks." Sans officers, they were "motherfuckers, faggots, cocksuckers," and worse!

A Jeep roared up in front of the formation and out jumped Captain Hargrove and one of the lieutenants.

"Troopers! Ten-hut! Captain Hargrove up!" Sergeant Turner and his cadre were at smart attention.

"At ease, soldiers! Good to see you on this fine morning!" The captain was in dress khakis, so the soldiers knew he wasn't force-marching to the field with them. Stott noticed for the first time that Hargrove also wore a Ranger patch and had combat jump wings signaling that he was an airborne officer. Impressive!

"Sergeant Turner tells me you remaining troopers have been working real hard and that you're all making progress! That's great! I'm proud of all of you! Five weeks to go and you will have made it through basic training!" From Captain Hargrove's tone, one would have thought the men had all been awarded a metal for valor.

"Two things! I have a buddy from The Point that set a record here at Dix with Company B marching to their first bivouac! I hate to be second at anything! Then the same sob had 50 percent of that training company qualify as "sharpshooter" or "expert" at the end of range training! I want you boys to beat both those records! When my buddy's troopers set the marching record, they did it gear only, no duffel bags. But they got to bivouac in seven hours and twenty-three minutes in October! Today, you're gonna beat that time and in August! So here's the good news! I'm going to let you load your duffels on those deuce-and-a-half trucks over there, and then we're gonna haul ass out to bivouac Charley! Step and a half and double-time all the way! If you beat seven hours and twenty minutes and if more than half of you qualify as "sharpshooter" or "expert," I'm gonna give you all, every man-jack in the company, a three-day pass over Labor Day! Go to New York City, get laid, whatever! We'll pay you on Friday, and you won't have to be back on post 'til 0500 reveille the following Tuesday! How about it? Can you do it?"

Led by Sergeant Turner and the cadre, all screamed out, "Yes, sir, Captain Hargrove, sir!"

"Good men!" Captain Hargrove hopped back in his Jeep and disappeared.

For a couple of minutes, D Company remained at attention, absorbing what had just transpired. It was 1012 hours and at least ninety degrees. Sergeant Turner took command. "I fuckin' love a challenge! Sergeants, any of you fall out, I will personally kick the shit out of you! Troopers, you all will set this record! Shitz, you get the bags loaded! Meeks, you bring up the rear! Heitz, it's your lucky fucking day! Take my half-ton and run ice water to us all the way out, whatever you have to do to get ice water, I'll cover you! Troops! Hit the latrine now and back on me in five minutes! We will do this! Dismissed!"

Stott did the math in his head as he waited in line to pee. Seventeen miles in seven hours and twenty minutes! And in full gear! The trainees had to average one mile every twenty-five to twenty-six minutes! Certainly doable, but full gear shouldering an M-14 in the ninety-degree heat certainly made it challenging.

At precisely 1025 hours, D Company formed up, double-column, with Sergeant Turner on the front row right and Sergeant Meeks on the last row left. Sergeant Turner through his bullhorn boomed, "Awright, troopers, quick-time, march!" The pace was the equivalent of a very fast walk. Not quite double-time, but almost. The men had heard the various sergeants sing out marching tunes over the previous three weeks, and Sergeant Turner was, by far, the best march caller. He began:

> *I wanna be an Airborne Ranger,*
> *I wanna live my life in danger,*
> *I wanna go to Vietnam!*
> *I wanna make it to the hill at Bragg,*
> *I wanna kill me a slant-eyed fag,*
> *I wanna go to Vietnam!*
> *I wanna soak in the swamp at Benning,*
> *I wanna make it 'til the final penning,*
> *I wanna go to Vietnam!*

Sergeant Turner could call cadence like this for hours on end. Always to a marching beat, all directed to "going airborne," "making it as a Ranger," and, of course, serving in combat in Vietnam. There were other versions of Turner's tunes that involved everything from worthless officers to past wives and lovers, and they were all pretty catchy.

> *I know a girl that lives on a hill,*
> *She won't do it, but her mamma will!*
> *When that momma gets done with you,*
> *Won't be enough for a dog to chew!*
> *If ya don't give that bitch just what she need,*
> *She'll stroke it so hard she'll make it bleed!*
> *At's the lesson your momma done taught to me,*
> *Gotta pay her good, 'cause she ain't free!*
> *Private Hale knows what I'm sayin' is true,*
> *His momma gets two hunnert dollars a screw!*
> *Don't you pissy faggots be laughin' at Hale!*
> *She needs that money to pay his bail!*
> *Sound off, hut, two, three, four!*
> *Screw ol' Hale and beg for more!*

Sergeant Turner had a real talent for working the names of his current trainees into his cadence calling. He entertained the troopers nonstop for the first hour and a half of the march by working personal insults into his rhyme. They were making good time, and everybody was keeping up due to the proddings from Sergeant Meeks' swagger stick.

Turner's half-ton buzzed by, Sergeant Heitz at the wheel. As the column rounded a curve in the road that had turned to dirt, they could see Heitz and a couple of corporals setting up water bags and hoisting thirty-five gallon cans of ice into the top of the bags.

"Half-time, march! Company, halt! Are any of you girls thirsty? Awright! Fall out, take five, and I mean five! Get some water, pee if you have to, we form up in ten!"

It was 1200 hours, and Stott could see Turner and Meeks conferring over a map. "Company D, fall in! We're gonna go 'til 1400 hours, then take twenty to chow down on some C's, drink and change socks! Quick-time. March!"

At 1400 hours, the soldiers rounded another bend and, sure enough, there was Heitz with the truck full of ice water and C rations in the shade! It was the troopers' first experience with C-Rations, the mobile meals that U.S. servicemen had lived on during World War II and Korea, and they were so hungry the C's tasted great! As they ate and drank, Sergeant Turner tutored them. "Socks and boots, troopers, are what win wars! I told you all to pack socks in your back pack. Put fresh socks on now! We fall in five!"

The men changed socks, placing the sweat-soaked pair in one of their ammo pouches, and got back on the trail. It was amazing how much better their feet felt after the change of socks. Sergeant Turner was back calling cadence after Meeks, Shitz, and a couple of the other NCOs had taken a turn. The troop quick-marched another two hours, right up until 1620. Another fifteen-minute break, plenty of ice water, and back in step at 1635 hours. D Company was now well past the part of Fort Dix they had seen during the first three weeks of training.

The men marched past rifle ranges, M-60 machine gun ranges, artillery ranges, and various types of obstacle courses and campsites. Trucks and Jeeps passed in both directions. Once, a group of about twenty men double-timed past them, moving at a really fast pace. They were wearing camouflage fatigues and dark red berets and carried a variety of weapons that the men of D had not seen before. Their faces were blacked out as for night cover, and they looked very different from basic trainees. Just as the first of these guys passed Sergeant Turner, he sang out:

> *Red hat troopers don't have much fun!*
> *All they can do is run, run, run!*
> *Just two things that fall from the sky,*
> *Bird shit and fools, and that's no lie!*
> *Hooah! Hooah! Rangers!*
> *Hooah! Hooah! Rangers!*
> *Tonight them fools gonna sleep in the weeds,*
> *Diggin' out ticks and spittin' up seeds!*
> *If they were as tough as they think they are,*
> *They'd go down to Bragg an' run up the spar!*
> *Hooah! Hooah! Rangers!*
> *Hooah! Hooah! Rangers!*
> *One other thing them fools might could be*
> *Pisshead Pointers, just runnin' to pee!*
> *If they just wearin' wings and no Ranger patch,*
> *They can suck my Willie and kiss my ass!*
> *Hooah! Hooah! Rangers!*
> *Hooah! Hooah! Rangers!*

Just before the red hat men got out of sight, they gave D Company the universally recognized raised arm, one finger salute in perfect unison. The men in front said that "salute" actually made Sergeant Turner grin. Until that moment, none of the recruits thought he was capable of smiling.

Just after 1700 hours, six hours and twenty-five minutes into the march, Sergeant Turner looked at his watch one more time and screamed out the following, "Awright, troopers, we still got a shot at the record! Suck it up! Double-time, march!"

Somehow, the men all found the energy to fall in with Turner's very quick pace and ran hard for thirty minutes. Just when Stott thought they were all going to pass out, the troopers rounded yet another bend, and there was Captain Hargrove, his lieutenants and some other captain the men had never seen before standing in front of a cluster of twenty-man tents. The two lieutenants were actually holding a bright yellow "finish tape" that Sergeant Turner broke through at 1732 hours! Sergeant Meeks and the last two troopers passed through the check point at 1736 hours, meaning D Company had made the march in seven hours and eleven minutes. A new record!

When the last man crossed the line, the unknown captain took off his garrison cap, captain's bars and all, and slammed it on the ground. "Hargrove, you're the luckiest white man on the planet! You'd better share this with Sergeant Turner 'cause he made it happen!"

With that, an amount of money passed from the unnamed captain to Captain Hargrove, whose grin was indescribable.

"Thank you, Captain! It's been nice doing business with you!" Hargrove and his lieutenants then exchanged salutes with the mystery captain, who jumped in his own Jeep and roared away.

The troopers were pretty much washed out, still breathing hard and trying to recover from their toughest day yet.

Captain Hargrove spoke, "Troops, stay at ease! I couldn't be prouder of what you just accomplished! And Top, I owe you! Great job, particularly for a guy your age! Got a treat comin' for you all. Any minute now the deuce-and-a half's are gonna arrive with late chow. There's big steaks for all and seconds if you want 'em! Got ice cream for dessert! Tactical starts in the morning, tonight we're just gonna take it easy. Here comes chow! Enjoy!"

Mike Stott was standing close to Top Turner during the captain's speech and could see Turner flinch at the crack about his age. But the food was being set up and the trainees were being assigned bunks in the twenty-man tents. The trucks with the duffel bags had arrived ahead of the recruits. The recruits organized their gear and started going through the mess tent. No hand ladder to walk!

The captain and his lieutenants actually stayed and ate with the trainees, but they sat at a table with the cadre as the men spread out, picnic-style. The steaks were absolutely fantastic! Stott watched Sharkey and Big Howie eat three steaks each, and Big Howie had four servings of ice cream. As exhausted as he was, on that clear and relatively cool evening in the New Jersey pine forest at Fort Dix, Mike Stott's attitude toward the army was amazingly positive.

The sun was getting low in the sky, but the officers were still sitting talking with the cadre. The young soldiers were as relaxed as they had been since basic training started. Stott and his six new buddies were sitting in a loose circle when Sharkey spoke, "Guys, this was the greatest day of my life! We all made it! We broke a marching record! I just ate three steaks!"

His six buddies all laughed, but each was moved by Sharkey's statement. JJ seemed sincere about this being the best day of his life! Most of the troopers in Company D understood that Sharkey had been raised in an orphanage and had no family. To his credit, JJ never projected anything other than a great-to-be-alive-in-the-army attitude. He worked harder at everything and it showed.

"Sharkey, how much weight have you gained? You're really bulking up on this army chow!" Mobliano, now "Mobs" to his six buddies, inquired.

"Maybe ten pounds, but I feel great!" JJ seemed truly happy.

"I guess I musta gained some, too. That march damn near killed me!" Big Howie was still breathing hard.

"Sure didn't kill your appetite! The army would have a right to charge you extra for all you're eatin'! How many ice creams did you put away?" Hale, always the smart-ass, asked.

"One more than Sharkey, so probably five!" Allsmeir was keeping count.

Big Howie asked, "There any left? I could do one more!"

Mobliano said, "You know, guys, it's pretty amazing what we just did! Who'd have thought four weeks ago that this company of goofballs could have force-marched seventeen miles? And you gotta hand it to Sergeant Turner, he led all the way! I actually feel pretty good right now, like we really accomplished something!"

"Remember us when you're a big-time army lawyer, Mobs, some of us may need you to defend us!" Smeall seemed serious. "Hale will probably be in the stockade before basic is over!"

"Fuck you, Smeall! When I'm a sniper, I may just eliminate you for being a rich wiseass!" Fast Eddy said. Then he surprised the men, "You know, guys, I feel really proud to have made that march with you today, too. I wanted to just quit about mid-afternoon, but I didn't want to have to face you guys if I did."

Even Fast Eddy Hale seemed to be feeling more positive toward the army. Mike Stott was feeling proud, too, but remained silent.

"How about you, Stott? You're RA. Still going airborne?" Mobs asked.

Just as Mike was about to answer, the men were jolted out of their relaxation by Sergeant Turner's bullhorn. "Private Stott, listen up! Get your sorry ass up to Captain Hargrove's table on the double!"

Mike felt his heart pounding as all the Company D trainees turned their attention on him.

"What'd you do, now? You on Turner's shit list?" Hale asked Stott what they were all thinking.

As he hurried to obey Turner's order, all Mike could say was, "I have no fucking idea!"

Stott felt the eyes of the entire training company on him as he double-timed to the officer's table. When he reached their location, Mike realized he had forgotten his helmet!

"Private Stott reporting, Sergeant!"

Sergeant Turner spoke, "At ease, Stott! We're not going to court-martial you, YET!"

Oh shit!

"Where's your headgear, soldier?" Turner demanded.

"I forgot it, sir!" said Stott.

"Sir? Don't call me sir. I work for a living!" So Sergeant Turner wasn't afraid to use the line in front of the company commander! Captain Hargrove was seated just in back of Sergeant Turner, and Stott could see him grin at Turner's statement.

"Top, go ahead and ask Stott your question. We're relaxing tonight." Hargrove's easy attitude really had Mike worried now. But Sergeant Turner's next statement floored him!

"Awright, Stott! Take a chair!"

Mike could feel the eyes of every trooper in the company focusing on his back, and his predicament, as they strained to hear.

Sergeant Turner actually lowered his voice and spoke softly enough that only the officers, cadre, and Mike could hear him. "Stott, you're from Ohio, right?"

"Yes, Sergeant!"

"Lower your voice; we haven't started proceedings, yet!" Double holy shit!

"What was your dad's name?" asked Turner.

"Sergeant, my dad's name is Raymer Exton Stott."

The looks that were exchanged around the table sent a chill down Stott's back.

"Got any brothers, Stott?" Turner's tone was mystifying.

"Yes, Sergeant, two."

Again, looks were exchanged around the table.

"How old are they, and where do they live?"

Now, Stott was truly shaken. During the second week of basic training, a trooper had been summoned to the orderly room to be told that one of his brothers had been in a serious car accident. Mike feared the worst.

"I think thirty-four and thirty-five, but I'm not sure, Sergeant. Why?"

"I'll ask the questions, here, Stott! So your brothers are alive and well in Ohio?" The mood around the table seemed to ease.

"Well, yes, Sergeant, I guess so. What have I done?" Mike asked.

"I'll ask the questions, not you! Did you have an uncle named James William Stott?" Turner was staring intently into Mike's eyes.

"No, Sergeant, but that was my oldest brother's name. I don't really remember him; he was killed in Korea in 1951," Mike told them.

Every head at the table spun toward Stott. A silence lasted what seemed like forever. Sergeant Turner's eyes seemed to bore right through Mike.

"Jesus H. Christ! You're Captain Stottie's little brother? He musta been twenty years older than you! How is that possible?" Sergeant Turner face had drained of color.

Turner's statement put Stott in a state of shock, sitting there with the officers and cadre of Company D. Their focus had him totally on edge. What was this all about? Why was he there, talking about his dead brother? Captain Stottie?

"Sergeant, Turner, I don't understand! What's wrong? Am I in trouble?" Mike was scared and confused. Again, no one spoke for what seemed like a very long time.

"Relax, son. We didn't mean to be hard on you. It's just that we've heard Sergeant Turner talk about your brother many times! The Sarge was there, you know, the day it happened at Chozon. Sitting here, tonight, it hit us all that you have the same last name as a Congressional Medal of Honor winner that Turner has been telling stories about for years now. You don't even remember your brother?" The captain's tone was understanding, kind.

"Well, sir, no, not really. James was the oldest, and I am the youngest. My mom and dad never got over my brother's death. We didn't talk about James much since it made my mom so sad. He was twenty-two years older than me, so I know about him mostly from the stories my brothers and sisters told me. I'm sorry, I just can't really remember him." Mike felt like he had let them down, but it was all he could say. He fought to hold back the tears that would have disgraced him.

Sergeant Turner said, "It's okay, Private. I remember your mom and dad from the medal ceremony. You do your brother proud in the army, trooper, and maybe someday I'll tell you things about your brother that few people know. Go on back to your buddies."

As he made his way back to where Hale, Howard, Mobliano, Allsmeir, Smeall, and Sharkey were waiting, Mike could once again feel the company's eyes on him. He was fighting to get his emotions in check and wondering how much he should tell them.

"Christ, Stott, what's up? You don't look so good!" Hale expressed what they were all thinking. "What'd they get you for?"

"It wasn't like that, guys, they just had a couple of questions to ask me." Mike didn't know what, if anything, he should tell them. He regretted having talked to Eddy Hale about his brother on that first night in the reception center.

"Come on Stott, don't make us beat it out of you!" Big Howie was trying to lighten things up. "If these guys grab you, I might just set on you!"

Howie's words seemed to break the tension. "Look, guys, I gotta think about it. Maybe I can tell you later," Mike said.

Sergeant Turner jarred the recruits back to reality. "Listen up, troopers! Time to square away your gear and get prone! You won't get away with no morning run tomorrow, so rest up! Reveille at 0500 hours! Boots, fats, and hats for PT! Lights out at 2130 hours!"

Chapter Sixteen

Reverie at 0500 by piped in bugle with no crashing garbage cans was a treat! The troopers fell out for PT, did a two mile run, and were going through the chow line by 0630 hours. In the field, they ate from individual mess kits that they then had to wash in garbage cans filled with soapy, near-boiling water. Morning chow took a little longer in the field. They formed up again at 0730.

To the soldiers' surprise, there was Captain Hargrove and his lieutenants again, all the way out there in the weeds, as Sergeant Meeks called their bivouac location. Sergeant Turner called the men to attention. "Ten-hut! Captain Hargrove up! Listen up, troopers!"

"Good morning, champions! I wanted to come out and congratulate you all again on yesterday's march! Now you start the most important training you will receive in the army! Every soldier, every man-jack one of you, must be a rifleman first! No matter what your MOS, you must know how to use your weapons! Remember my deal with you! If more than half the company qualifies as "expert" or "sharpshooter" with the M-14, I guarantee the whole company a three-day pass over Labor Day weekend. In fact, troopers, I want to explain a few things to you this morning about your basic training regimen.

You've all heard that Vietnam is about to heat up! In anticipation of the buildup we all believe is coming, our training battalion here at Fort Dix has been granted unusual leeway to experiment with different ways of organizing basic training. In fact, you're the first training company to try out this new format! Those first three weeks of orientation, exercise, and army indoctrination will now be followed by four weeks in the field, right here in this bivouac area.

We're gonna attend classes, do PT, and shoot, shoot, and shoot some more! The last week we're even going to familiarize with the Colt 45 pistol and the M-60 machine gun!

We've been given unlimited ammo and unlimited range time, even at night! In addition to your training cadre, we've put together some of the finest training marksmen in the army to help make you be the best shooters you can be coming out of basic training! Any questions, troopers?"

One of the first things the recruits had supposedly learned in the army was to never, ever ask a question when questions were called for! It's just the rule! Officers always ask, "Any questions?" before they dismiss or turn over a formation to an NCO, but no enlisted man is supposed to ask them anything! The officer almost assuredly will not know the answer and will have to get one of their NCOs to bail them out. This embarrasses an officer, and then bad things can happen. Especially to the dumb-ass trooper that asked the unexpected question.

"Sir! Captain Hargrove, sir! Private Hale, here! A question please, sir!" Private dumb-ass Hale had his hand up!

Stott was looking right at Sergeant Turner and could see from the expression on his face that Hale had not acted in his own best interest.

"Yes, Private Hale, what's the question?" The look that passed between Captain Hargrove and Sergeant Turner did not bode well for Private Fast Eddy Hale's future.

"Sir! Thank you, sir! Two questions, please, sir! Do we get prizes if we shoot good? And why was Private Stott brought up on charges last night, please, sir?" Hale shouted.

Mike Stott decided that if Hale survived Hargrove and Turner after asking these two questions, he would kill Eddy himself, first chance he got.

"What? Prizes? Charges against Stott? Are you out of your fucking mind, trooper? What's your name, again, puke-breath?" Hargrove demanded.

"Sir, Private Hale, sir!"

"Sergeant Turner, is this kid for real? What the fuck is he talking about? Is he a potential Section Eight?"

Then, the worst possible thing that could have happened did! One of the troopers toward the back started laughing! Next thing you know, half the company was laughing.

But not Sergeant Turner and certainly not Captain Hargrove!

In a near-perfect repetition of the display the trainees had witnessed from the mystery captain the night before, when he had paid Hargrove, their captain ripped off his headgear, captain's bars and all, and slammed his hat to the ground.

"Of all the dumb-ass, cocksucking, motherfucking stupid things I've seen in the army, this is tops! Trooper Hale, I'm gonna spend all day thinking up something really special for you!"

To the soldiers' absolute disbelief Hale barked out, "Sir! Thank you, sir!"

This time the whole company burst out laughing including a couple of the training sergeants! Sergeant Turner's face was so flushed Stott thought he might just explode right there in front of the whole company.

"I don't fucking believe this! Sergeant Turner, get this brood of laughing swine out of my sight before I take out my .45 and start shootin'! Motherfucker!" It appeared the good captain was about to lose it.

Sergeant Turner screamed out a blood-curdling "Yes, sir! Company, right face! Double-time, march!" D Company fled the potential line of fire.

The area around the bivouac was divided into square mile grids or fire cuts; the recruits spent the next two hours double-timing around one of those loops. This on top of the seventeen-mile force-march the day before!

A little before 1000 hours, Sergeant Turner stopped the men in front of the tents and called a ten minute break. Turner grabbed Hale by his fatigue collar and dragged him out of site behind the compound.

At 1015 hours, Sergeant Meeks called the company back to formation and marched them to a staging area behind one of the M-14 ranges. Waiting there was a whole new group of NCO's. They began a lecture, tear-down demonstration of the internal working components of the M-14 7.62 caliber rifle.

As the recruits tried to focus on their first real M-14 lesson, most were wondering if they would ever see Fast Eddy Hale again.

At 1530 hours that afternoon, the range NCO's announced a fifteen-minute smoke break. When the trainees reassembled to continue M-14 training, Private Hale was standing at attention in front of the M-14 tear-down tables. He was dressed in white patent-leather army parade boots, a white MP's helmet, and pink lady's panties. Nothing else. He was holding a chrome M-1 parade rifle at present-arms. In bold, black lettering the words "PUSSY SNIPER" had been written across his chest.

After more than fifteen minutes, the laughter finally subsided enough so that the sergeant-in-charge of the range could resume his lecture. Private Hale remained in position until the end of the class at 1730 hours.

Chapter Seventeen

Serious M-14 training began the next afternoon as D Company prepared to fire the first rounds through their rifles. The training cadre now functioned as support staff to the range NCOs that organized and controlled the live fire. Interestingly, most of the M-14s that had been assigned to the men of Company D were brand new! The range NCOs could hardly believe the trainees had new rifles.

"We got guys carrying ten-year-old fourteens in Nam and you pussies get new weapons? That's fucked up!" was the first statement the privates heard from Master Sergeant Jenkins, the ranking NCO on the M-14 range. "But it does give you a real leg up in that the sights are good and black and zeroing your weapons should go fast! Anybody here think they know how to shoot?"

Fast Eddy just never learned. "Sergeant! Private Hale here, and I want to be first, Sergeant!"

"I didn't ask for volunteers, I asked if anybody can shoot. Well?"

The rest of the trainees had learned; never volunteer.

"Okay, then. You there, with the Coke-bottle glasses, get your ass up here!"

The range NCO had selected Private Barry Milton Smeall to be his guinea pig! His buddies could see the color drain from Smeall's face as he approached Sergeant Jenkins. The company was seated in what looked like high school football field bleachers. The seating faced an M-14 firing range that had placements for forty-eight troopers to space out and fire down range at soldier profile type targets spaced at twenty-five meter intervals extending out to 400 meters. Behind the farthest row of 400 meter targets was a forty-foot high sand bank designed to catch the projectiles after they passed through the profile targets. Each soldier profile target had a bull's-eye aiming zone centered in the heart position of the chest.

71

Private Smeall was instructed to hold his M-14 at present-arms position, essentially in front of his chest with the barrel pointing up at a forty-five degree angle from his left shoulder, down range. Sergeant Jenkins took Smeall's rifle, verified that it was not loaded and slammed it back in Smeall's hands.

"Private Smeall, I am about to hand you a loaded clip containing eight, standard-issue steel-jacketed 7.62 caliber rounds of ammunition. These are exactly the same as you will be issued in a combat situation! In the hands of a properly trained trooper with a properly sited M-14 on semiautomatic, that trooper should be able to kill eight VC at up to 400 meters away, no problem! The cadre here on Echo Range are among the best instructors in the army! Concentrate! Do not fuck up! Always keep your weapon pointed down range! Never, ever, let your weapon trail more than forty-five degrees from your assigned target down range! Do you understand, Private?"

"Yes, sir! I mean, yes, Sergeant!" Smeall screamed.

"Don't you ever call me 'sir,' I work for a living! And I am master sergeant, you miserable dickhead! Now, focus! I'll walk you to the firing line, you will load your clip, and, on my command only, chamber a round. Do you understand? Do all you dickheads in the bleachers understand? Are you watching? Focus! This is the most important day of your military career! Your lives and the lives of your buddies will depend on your ability to kill with the M-14-A2 Rifle! Do you understand?"

"YES, MASTER SERGEANT!"

"Sergeant Turner, on his left!"

Sergeants Jenkins and Turner then positioned Private Smeall on the firing line in the classic standing-fire stance. "Load the clip! Chamber a round! Do not touch the trigger! Site down range on the twenty-five meter target. Line the barrel end site up directly through the v-notch on the back site. Do not touch the trigger! Left hand two inches further forward on the stock! Make sure the weapon is firmly against your shoulder. Are you comfortable, Private?"

"Yes, I guess, Sergeant."

"Master Sergeant! Forget it again, and you will not see nightfall! Do you understand, Private? Are you or are you not comfortable?"

"Yes, Master Sergeant!" Smeall was learning!

"Close your left eye! Do you see the twenty-five meter target down the barrel sites?"

"Yes, Master Sergeant!"

"Steady, Private! Take a deep breath! Exhale! Still see the target?"

"Yes, Master Sergeant!"

"Slowly, gently wrap your right index finger around the trigger and focus on the target through the sites. Focus on the red center of the bull's-eye as you exhale. Ready? Gently squeeze."

BLAM!

To the complete amazement of every man on the range, they could see the twenty-five meter target slightly flinch as Smeall's first shot tore through what would have been the neck of the soldier target, about eight inches above the bull's-eye's center.

"Well, I'll be goddamned!" Sergeant Turner expressed the collective thought.

"Hold, Private! Finger off the trigger! Do you still see the target?"

An assured sounding voice from Private Smeall said, "Yes, I do Master Sergeant!"

"Slowly, gently wrap your right index finger around the trigger and focus on the target through the sites. Focus on the red center of the bull's-eye as you exhale. Ready? Gently squeeze."

BLAM!

Smeall's second shot hit the target half way between the first shot and the bull's-eye center, only an inch or so to the left.

"Well, I'll be a goddamned son of a bitch!" Turner said.

Smeall's third shot missed the target as did his sixth, but shots four, five, seven, and eight all were within the expanded bull's-eye area of the twenty-five meter target.

"Private Smeall, port arms! Check that your weapon is clear! Present!" Master Sergeant Jenkins seemed less surprised than the rest of Company D.

"How'd that feel, Private?" Jenkins asked.

"GREAT, Master Sergeant!" Smeall sounded and actually looked different than before he had successfully fired his M-14.

"Not too bad, Private, you sure you never shot a rifle before?"

"No, Master Sergeant, I swear!" Smeall was really fired up!

"Well, clearly, you got a well-sighted weapon. Let me see it!" Master Sergeant Jenkins took Smeall's M-14 and locked and loaded another eight shot clip.

"One hundred meter target, mark!" In very rapid succession Jenkins fired all eight rounds within one ring of the center of the hundred-meter target!

"Damn fine 14. Wanna try it, Sarge?" Jenkins asked Sergeant Turner.

The invitation put Sergeant Turner on the spot! He'd lose face if he said no, and clearly, Master Sergeant Jenkins had just put on quite an impressive demonstration of marksmanship. Turner took Smeall's M-14, locked and loaded a clip and called out, "125 meters, mark!"

A bit slower rate of fire than Jenkins, but Turner also fired all eight rounds to within three inches of bull's-eye center at 125 meters!

"Good shootin,' Sarge!" said Jenkins. "Okay, troops, you all see that the M-14 is a superior weapon. Even a new rifleman with proper instruction and good concentration can be successful! We'll see if Private Smeall can keep up the good example he set as distance and rate of fire increase. Smeall's weapon was delivered to him perfectly sighted as you all saw. Your individual 14s may or may not be set up as well. If they're a little out, we're gonna learn how to sight 'em in! And three weeks from Friday, I want you all to fire "expert." Now, let's get to work!"

Smeall's status within Training Company D had just gone from heel to hero. Stott wondered if Smeall's fire demonstration had somehow been orchestrated because most of the company had to work really hard to gain proficiency with the M-14-A2.

Mike Stott didn't remember much of significance over those next three-and-a-half weeks living in the field in twenty-man tents and learning to shoot, except that he thoroughly enjoyed it! He loved his M-14 and couldn't get enough of the firing range!

The only trooper in D Company who liked it more than Mike was John J. Sharkey. By that fourth Friday in the field, JJ and Mike had established themselves as the two best shots among the trainees. Even Sergeants Jenkins and Turner were impressed with their marksmanship. On M-14 qualification day on Echo Range, Sharkey and Stott both shot perfect hundreds on the fixed and rapid fire tests. No other troopers did that well, but nineteen trainees did manage to fire "expert" and seventy-one fired "sharpshooter," meaning that Company D had met Captain Hargrove's challenge!

Captain Hargrove showed up at Echo Range in time to watch Company D's final M-14 rifle qualifications on the seventh Friday of basic training. He jumped up and cheered when the results were announced. More importantly, Hargrove called for a fleet of deuce-and-a-half's to haul the trainees and their gear back to D Barrack! No forced march back as Sergeant Turner had been threatening! Captain Hargrove kept his word on the three-day passes too!

On Friday, August 30, 1963, Mike Stott, JJ Sharkey, and all their buddies got their first army pay, in cash, and a three-day pass with only one week remaining in basic training! Starting at 1730 hours, the trainees in Company D began signing out for their first leave off post at Fort Dix. They had money in their pockets, and New York City was a two-hour bus ride north!

Chapter Eighteen

"Awright, guys, here's the deal! The six of you assholes are hereby invited to the best Italian dinner available anywhere in the world! I know you're planning to see the city, but I want you to come to my family's house in Brooklyn Sunday afternoon for pasta and wine!" Mobliano's kind offer surprised his buddies.

"I'm giving each of you my address and phone number. Try to come together in a couple of cabs, around 4:00 p.m. Between now and then remember, there are a lot of hustlers in the city that want to take your money! And the pretty, friendly girls just want your money, too! Be careful! Have fun, but watch your ass! Especially you younger guys, Sharkey, Stott, and Hale. Don't let Hale's mouth get you all in trouble! I want to spend time with my girl and my family this weekend, not bailing you guys out! Got it?" Mobs' sincerity impressed his friends.

The seven basic trainees just made it to the 6:00 p.m. New York City bus out of Wright's Town by the Fort Dix Gate. They should have been exhausted from the first seven weeks of basic training, but they were young and excited about going to New York. Sharkey, Howard, and Stott had never been to the city and were really eager to see the sights! Mobs was headed straight for Brooklyn and his girl. Fast Eddy Hale surprised his buddies by saying he was going home too, to see his dad and brothers. Allsmeir was up for doing the town, but Smeall was strangely quiet.

"What's up, Smeall, you're awfully quiet for a guy who's headed for three days in N.Y.C.! You qualified 'sharpshooter,' you gotta be proud! Let's celebrate!" JJ was starting to come out of his shell, at least with his six buddies. He was still very guarded around the other troopers.

"Well, guys, I'm sort of embarrassed to tell you this, but my parents are waiting for me in the city. They want to take us all out to dinner, if you guys would be willing to go."

Barry Smeall seemed both anxious and nervous for his new friends to meet his folks. "Dad reserved a suite at the Plaza Hotel with three bedrooms you guys can share. I pretty much have to hang out with them."

The young soldiers were so surprised that no one said anything for several minutes. During the first weeks of basic training, the seven men had gotten to know each other to some degree. They understood that Smeall missed his folks most. While they were in the field those four weeks, the trainees were allowed to visit the PX on Sundays via the deuce-and-a-half shuttle, where phone booths were available outside the Post Exchange. Stott had called home once, but Smeall called every Sunday, collect, and stayed on the phone as long as the line of troopers waiting their turn for the phone would allow. Still, for Smeall's parents to have traveled to New York to be with their son on his first leave from basic training seemed odd to his six new friends.

Mobliano was the first to respond. "Well, Barry, that's a very kind offer, and normally I would gladly accept. But right now there's a girl named Maria waiting for me in Brooklyn, and I've gotta pass. But I tell you what, bring your family to our dinner on Sunday, and they can meet my family, and we'll all have a good time!"

"Let me get this straight, Smeall. You gotta chance to do the town, and you're stuck with your parents? Holy shit!" Fast Eddy said.

"You're making tracks to see your family, but Smeall's family visiting him is weird? Hale, as usual, you are completely full of crap!" Allsmeir always defended Smeall.

Sharkey, Howard, and Stott were amazed that Smeall's folks had the time and resources to come to New York and stay in a hotel. The idea that that they had reserved rooms for their son's army buddies was beyond their grasp.

"They really got rooms for us in a hotel?" Big Howie asked. "Man, I've never stayed in a hotel! Am I allowed, you know, like I'm a little darker than Sharkey!"

"Isn't the Plaza Hotel pretty famous? It must cost a lot of money!" Sharkey echoed what Stott was thinking. "And Howard, for the record, you're one hell of a lot darker than me! Don't make me kick your ass!"

"Look, guys, my family has a lot of money. I don't want that to make you think I'm different than you. My dad has always been generous, especially with our friends. This is no big deal to him. I'm sure the rooms are all charged to one of his companies." Smeall seemed anxious for his buddies not to be offended by his offer.

Sharkey, Hale, Howard, and Stott were simply incredulous, but Allsmeir and Mobliano seemed unfazed by Smeall's offer. "Look, guys, if Smeall's folks want to spend their money helping you enjoy your first army leave, what's wrong with that? I'm going to see my family, Hale's going to see his, and I bet if your families were closer you'd all be going home, too!"

Mobliano then realized how his statement might have affected Sharkey. "Sorry, JJ, sometimes I guess I say things that don't make it easy for you."

"It's okay, Mobs, really. I got a family. It's you guys and the United States Army!" Sharkey's statement brought another extended pause in the troopers' conversation as they considered the sincerity with which JJ had spoken.

Mike Stott thought that Sharkey just might be the gutsiest guy he had ever met. All during basic JJ had focused on becoming a good soldier. He never complained about anything. If he was lonely, he never showed it.

"Well, that puts it in perspective! JJ, you continue to amaze me! I can't wait to introduce you to my family!" Mobliano said.

"I look forward to it, too, Mobs! But between now and then, we're gonna have some fun!" The smile on JJ's face was contagious.

As the bus approached New York City, Sharkey, Howard, and Stott were awed by the sight of Manhattan. Seeing the lighted skyline of New York was magical. As the bus emerged from the Holland Tunnel, the sights and smells of the city on that hot August night made them forget they were still basic trainees on an unusually early weekend leave. White-side-wall haircuts and dress khakis, totally devoid of ribbons or decorations, identified them as recent recruits, but they were proud to be soldiers and thrilled to be in the greatest city in the world with their army buddies.

As the seven soldiers departed the bus at the Port Authority station in New York, Mobliano again counseled his buddies. "Hale and I are going to share a cab to Brooklyn. You guys can easily walk to the Plaza from the corner there across Forty-second Street to Sixth Avenue. Left on Sixth to Central Park South. Hang a right on Park South and you'll be lookin' at the Plaza at the end of that block. Probably take you twenty minutes. I better see you all in Brooklyn on Sunday!"

Mobliano and Hale jumped in a cab and were off. "I don't know about you guys, but I've done enough walkin' lately, and I'm starving! Let's grab a cab, I'm payin'!" Smeall now seemed in his element there in the city.

The five soldiers piled into a big, yellow Checker cab and headed up town. The white lights of Times Square dazzled Howard, Sharkey, and Stott as they stared in disbelief at the crowds.

"Come on, guys! Stop staring like a bunch of hicks! You can come back after dinner if you want and see the sights." Smeall was anxious to get to the Plaza.

"Won't it be closed?" Big Howie's question seemed natural enough.

Allsmeir and Smeall couldn't stop laughing. "Come on, Howard! Even a Mississippian ought to know better than that!"

"You been here before too, Allsmeir?" Howard asked.

"Yeah, sure, lots of times! Sharkey, you musta seen the city before! Bedford is only a one hour train ride away! You've never been in the city before either?" Allsmeir could be pretty insensitive.

"No, I haven't," Sharkey coolly answered Allsmeir.

"So it's only new to us 'experts'?" Howard was referring to the fact that Sharkey, Stott and he had qualified for the highest M-14 certification, "expert," while Allsmeir and Smeall had not.

"Yeah, it's just new to you kids!" said Allsmeir.

The cab driver saved them from a prolonged argument by asking, "You guys want to get laid?"

"How much?" Allsmeir was quickest to respond.

"Set you up with the best broads in town! Gimmie twenty dollars each and I'll bring 'em to the hotel!" the cabbie said as they pulled up in front of the Plaza.

Again, Sharkey surprised his friends. "Look, dickhead, if you think we're dumb enough to give a cocksucker like you money, I'm gonna kick your ass just on general principles when this cab stops! Get it?"

As the cabby turned to get back at Sharkey, Big Howie grabbed him by the shoulders and explained, "You start to turn on my boy Sharkey again, and I'll snap your fuckin' neck!"

The pressure Howard had on the cabby caused the blood to drain from his head.

"Just pay me and get the fuck out of my cab!" was all that the driver could manage.

Over his friends' laughter, Sharkey said, "So now I'm your boy too, huh, Howard? Too bad Mobs wasn't here for that exchange."

Stott noticed that JJ didn't mention Fast Eddy Hale. For some reason, Hale was always the seventh man in the group, and Sharkey, especially, kept his distance from Eddy.

"May I help you, gentlemen?" an elegantly dressed Plaza Hotel doorman inquired. Before the men could respond, a large and buxom woman with the reddest hair Stott had ever seen came bounding down the steps.

"Milteee, honeee!" The woman grabbed Smeall and began hugging and kissing him while continuing to shriek, "Oh, Milteee, babeee!" An elegantly dressed, silver-haired man joined in, wrapping his arms around both of them repeating, "Milteee, Milteee!"

This reunion was blocking the main entrance to the hotel and people exiting cabs were prevented from entering the Plaza. "Please, Mr. Smeall, sir, could you just move on in to the lobby and continue your homecoming," asked the doorman. His request functioned to bring the Smeall's back to earth.

"Oh, Milteee! These must be your friends! They're sooo cute! Why didn't you tell me how cute they were? Hi, boys! We're sooo happy to meet you! I'm Milteee's mom, Bessy, and this is my personal servant, Milteee senior!"

"Actually, I'm her king and ruler; she just hasn't figured it out yet! We are very happy you all are here. Call me Milt, please," Mr. Smeall then shook the boys' hands, looking them straight in the eye as he did so.

"I see why they call you Mr. Howard! How tall are you, son?" Mr. Smeall asked.

"About six-six, sir." Big Howie was clearly uncomfortable standing there in those elegant surroundings. Truth be told, Sharkey and Stott felt just as awkward as Howard. The three of them were in an environment that was very different from anything they had ever experienced.

"Milteee, have you and your friends had dinner? And we thought you were bringing six gentlemen; where are the other two? We want to treat you to the best steak dinner in New York!" Bessy Smeall was still holding both of her son's hands as though he had just returned from Mars.

"Mobliano and Hale wanted to go home to Brooklyn, but Mobs invited us all, you and dad, too, to dinner with his family on Sunday afternoon! But the five of us could use a good meal!" Smeall was starting to relax.

"We took the liberty of securing accommodations for your friends here at the Plaza. They have a suite just above ours with three bedrooms and a parlor. Hope they will be comfortable." Smeall senior was taking charge.

"Mr. Smeall, sir, I don't think we can afford a hotel like this." Stott doubted if they could afford to tip the bellman!

They had all just gotten two months army pay in cash that netted them about $150 each.

"Please call me Milt, and, son, don't you worry one bit about paying for anything! We are so pleased that Milteee's army buddies agreed to come to New York with him we insist on this being our treat. You may or may not know this, but we are fortunate enough to have accumulated a little money, and we believe in spending it! Please just enjoy our hospitality, and please don't feel uncomfortable. We are only too happy to have you with us!" Mr. Smeall seemed genuinely anxious to make his son's friends feel at ease.

"You listen to Milt, honey! Just enjoy and know that friend's of Milteees are like family to us! We love you all!" Bessy Smeall exuded warmth.

"Let's get you comfortable and then out to dinner! Here are the keys to your rooms, drop your things and come on down! We'll be in the bar!" said Mr. Smeall.

Each soldier had a dopkit with shaving gear, toothbrush, and changes of underwear. They had no civilian clothing. Barry Smeall led them to the elevators. Once inside and away from his parents, Barry said, "Don't mind my folks, they really mean what they say. They insisted on coming to see me this weekend, and when I told them I wanted to see the city with you guys, they decided to make it a party their way. Please just indulge them, and thanks for coming with me."

When Allsmeir, Sharkey, Howard, and Stott arrived at the eighteenth floor and walked into their suite, they were completely dumbfounded. The double doors opened into the most elegant living room any of them had ever seen. Stott said the room was bigger than his parents' entire house. There was a fully stocked wet bar on one wall with a silver ice chest full of Heineken. On one side of the parlor was a huge master bedroom with two king-size beds and the fanciest bathroom imaginable. Down a hallway on the other side of the living area were two more bedrooms, each with its own private bathroom. Two, queen-size beds in each of these bedrooms assured that Smeall's expected six buddies would be comfortable. The suite faced Central Park.

Sharkey, Howard and Stott were still speechless, but Allsmeir said what each of them was thinking. "Holy shit, Smeall! I didn't know places like this really existed! I thought they were only in the movies! This must cost a fortune!"

"Guys, please, just enjoy. Let me drop my stuff in mom and dad's suite and I'll meet you down in the bar," Barry said.

The four men just stood there, trying to comprehend the level of luxury that surrounded them. Big Howie's mouth was hanging open, and he kept looking around saying, "Golleee! Golleee!"

Allsmeir said, "Awright, guys, I'm blown away just like you, but I'm starving! I say we give Mr. Howard the master, and I'll flip you guys for who gets his own room!"

"You take it, Allsmeir! Me and Stott will bunk together," said Sharkey.

As they placed their dopkits in their room, JJ said to Mike, "Is this for real? Why are they doing this? Have you ever seen anything like this place?"

"JJ, I'm just as amazed as you, maybe more! No, I've never been to any place like this before. I guess we just gotta take them at their word and enjoy! They both seem really nice."

Sharkey kept shaking his head. Mike followed JJ back into the living room where Big Howie was still gawking around saying, "Golleee!"

"Awright, Howard, knock it off or I'll kick your ass! Just 'cause you're from Mississippi don't mean you have to act like a hick!" said Sharkey, stealing the line that Barry Smeall had used earlier.

Sharkey standing there threatening Howard, who was at least twice his size, made Stott and Allsmeir laugh out loud. "What, you don't think I can kick his ass? Just because he's twice my size? In case you haven't noticed, I grew more than an inch in basic, and I gained seventeen pounds. Another year and I'm gonna look Howard up and kick his ass just to prove it to Stott!"

"JJ, you can't even reach my jaw, so knock it off!" Stott noticed Big Howie had backed away a bit, just in case. Sharkey then feigned a move at Howard, who backed up so fast he knocked over a chair.

"Enough! We need a drink!" For once, Allsmeir was right.

As the boys entered The Oak Room, heads turned to look at them. The four young soldiers looked as out of place as whores in church.

"Your party is over there, gentlemen. Please follow me." A maitre'd led them to the Smeall's table. Barry was now wearing grey slacks, a pale blue mock-turtle pullover and a dark blue sport coat. He had on black Bass Weejuns and no socks! He looked like a civilian, except for the trainee-trim hairstyle.

"Sorry, guys, but I just had to get into civvies. Hope you don't mind," said Smeall, hoping to head off his buddies' harassment.

"You look swell," said Allsmeir, always the kiss-ass.

"Do you boys want a little drinkypoo before we eat?" Bessy Smeall asked.

"Are we allowed to drink, ma'am?" JJ asked.

"Don't you call me ma'am,' goddamn it! I'm not that old! Call me Bess! And yes, you're allowed to drink! How about a martini?"

"What's that?" Stott asked.

"Oh, boy! This is going to be fun!" Milt Smeall exclaimed. "Waiter, bring us seven double Smirnoff martinis, up, with olives!"

No mention of IDs, perhaps because the soldiers were with the Smealls.

As the waiter departed, Milt senior said, "You men like steak, right? We're going to Gallagher's at nine fifteen. Best steaks in town!"

Stott had never tasted vodka before and was pretty sure Sharkey and Howard hadn't, either. Allsmeir, being a big college man, probably had.

"To your time in the military, gentlemen! May it be brief and safe!" Mr. Smeall offered what he thought was a toast the men would all appreciate.

"Mr. Smeall, sir, I'm a lifer! I don't know about these guys, but I'm spending the rest of my life in the army!" With that unexpected announcement, JJ downed his martini in one long gulp.

"Well, son, that's a surprise! But all the best to you in your military career!"

As the boys took a sip of their martinis, Mike Stott had to work really hard not to throw up at the taste. Everyone else, including Big Howie, seemed to like it.

Bessy Smeall joined Sharkey by downing hers in one long gulp. "Whoee! That was good! We'll have another one!"

"Honey, the boys are starving and too many martinis on an empty stomach is not a good idea. We can start again at Gallagher's. Let's go eat!" Milt finished his drink. "Waiter, on my tab!"

Stott had managed only one sip of his drink. "You leavin' that, Stott? Whimp!" With that Sharkey downed the remainder of Mike's martini.

"Damn! These are good!" said JJ.

The Smealls and their guests piled into two cabs for the short ride to Gallagher's Steak House. The maitre'd greeted the Smealls and escorted them to an unusually large corner booth that could have accommodated a much larger party. Milt and Bessy sat beside each other in the back corner of the booth with Milteee on his mother's left where she could easily reach over and kiss him from time to time, as she often did. Larry Allsmeir was on Milt's right, but at a ninety-degree angle. Sharkey, Howard, and Stott essentially faced the Smeall family with Big Howie on the end so he would have room to stretch his legs.

"If you all like steak, I'd suggest the large New York cut, about twenty-two ounces, with Gallagher's twice-baked potato. Let's start with a twelve-count shrimp cocktail and then a Caesar salad. Save room for dessert! They have the best sweets in Manhattan! Okay with everybody? All you have to decide is the temperature of your meat." Milt had taken charge.

"First, bring us double Smirnoff martinis, up, with olives! Seven of them! I'd like you to bring us whatever is your best year Rothschild Beaujolais, hopefully '58, with dinner. We're going to be here talking for a while, so get it started! My boys are starving!"

"Madame, how may I prepare your steak?" the waiter asked.

"Medium, and don't you dare offer me a smaller cut! I can out-eat everyone at this table! And out-drink them, too!" Bessy Smeall was not to be outdone at anything. Sitting across from her, Stott couldn't help but notice how attractive she was. Not pretty, really, but she exuded a kind of sexy animalism and her boobs were incredible! She appeared to be much younger than her husband. Bessy acted like a twenty-year-old and, yet, she possessed a certain dignity that was unlike any woman Mike had ever seen.

"Gentlemen, how may I prepare your steaks?"

"Medium," the men said in unison.

The martinis arrived and once again Milt proposed a toast. "May your time in the army be everything that you want it to be! May you all lead long, happy, healthy lives!"

That was a toast even Sharkey could not take exception with, and everyone took a nice pull on their drinks. Mike noticed this one tasted better. Or was it the peer pressure?

Milt started the conversation. "Again, thank you for joining us tonight and this weekend. Bessy and I consider ourselves to be very blessed. We have each other, and we have our two children. Barry, here, is the apple of his mother's eye, and I kind of like him, too! Our daughter, Melanie, is a typical spoiled-rotten Jewish Princess, but we love her!

Let me be blunt. We are very, very rich. Bess and I were both born rich, and we've made ourselves richer. But money doesn't mean a thing unless you enjoy it! We know we're lucky to have a lot, and we've resolved to spread it around, especially with our children and their friends. Live it up this weekend, on us! Know that it is our great pleasure to see you enjoy yourselves! There's only one catch! You have to talk to us! Tonight at dinner, tell us about yourselves! If you're not comfortable talking tonight, maybe you will be later on. Just talk to us, and we'll be your friends for life!"

Sharkey, Howard, and Stott were staring into their martinis, shy about opening up to Smeall's folks. Allsmeir got the conversation going. "Well, I just want to thank you, Milt and Bessy, for inviting us to dinner and, especially, for providing us with those wonderful rooms at the Plaza. I've never stayed in such a beautiful and elegant hotel, and I'm pretty sure these other guys haven't either. Barry and I met on the bus ride down to fort Dix from Newark Airport, and we hit it off right away! We figured we just might be the only two Jews at Fort Dix, so we probably needed to stick together! As it turns out, we are the only two Jewish guys in Training Company D. We met our other five buddies right away during our time in the reception center as we were waiting for basic to start. Barry started off bunking above Stott, and I'm in the same bunk quadrant with Mobliano and Sharkey. Funny, all we have in common is being in the same basic training company, except of course for Barry and I being Jews, but us seven guys really hit it off!"

Allsmeir was laying it on heavy about how close the seven men were. Stott doubted that the other six men would have described the relationship as he did.

"So how many boys, I mean men, of course, are in the company? Do you all sleep in one big room?" Bessy wanted to know. Clearly, Smeall had not given his parents all that much detail about army life.

"We started with 180 men, but we're down to 171 now." Allsmeir had all the answers. "In the barrack, there are four squad bays designed for forty to fifty men each, but in the field we were all in a group of twenty-man tents."

"We're down to 171 guys? I thought we were 174." Sharkey questioned Allsmeir's numbers.

"No, JJ, Larry's right. Another three guys got recycled because they couldn't qualify with the M-14. Happened at the end of range time today. Was that really only eight hours ago?" Barry's comment made them all realize how their world had changed, at least temporarily, from Fort Dix to the Plaza in the past three and one half hours.

"Recycled?" Big Howie's first words.

"So you can talk! I was beginning to think we were going to have to tickle some sound out of you!" Bessy teased Big Howie.

"Yes, ma'am, I can talk, but I think Allsmeir's wrong about guys getting sent back."

"Yeah, recycled. Three poor bastards, Oops! Sorry, Mr. and Mrs. Smeall, three guys have to start basic all over again Monday morning. Plus, they all got weekend KP; no pass for those who didn't qualify because they're no longer part of Training Company D." Again, Allsmeir had the scoop.

"Milteee, how did you do shooting?" Milt asked.

Before Milteee could respond, old suck-up Allsmeir was right there. "He did great! Hit the target six out of eight shots the first time he ever fired a rifle! Then he qualified 'sharpshooter'!"

Stott could see the color drain from Barry's face as his father turned to stare at him. "Is that a fact?"

"Oh, that's great Milteee! I guess all that time shooting skeet with your dad paid off!" Bessy let the cat out of the bag about Barry's experience with firearms.

"Thought you never fired a rifle, Smeall!" Sharkey was incredulous. Stott wished JJ had been a bit more tactful.

"A shotgun's not a rifle!" Barry was defensive. Sharkey continued to stare intently at Smeall.

"Can I tell you the neatest thing I've seen in basic so far?" Howard filled an awkward silence with an incredibly detailed recounting of Master Sergeant Jenkins' selection of their son to be the first to shoot an M-14 on the firing range. "And then First Sergeant Turner said, 'I'll be a goddamned son of a bitch!'"

The Smealls seemed to truly enjoy hearing about their son's triumph on the range. "Do they use that kind of language often?" Bessy asked.

The five soldiers howled with laughter at her question. "What'd I say?" Bessy demanded. The men all started telling stories of how incredibly obscene the training cadre's language was, and that broke the ice for the evening. Everyone was talking at once, and the talking and laughing continued right through dinner. Sharkey, though involved in the conversation, talked the least. Maybe that was because the meal was so incredibly good. The steaks were fork tender and really tasty.

"You're not going to finish that steak, Stott?" JJ asked Mike.

"No, John, take it! I wouldn't want to jeopardize your feeding frenzy!" Mike said.

Mr. Smeall ate only about half his steak, and Big Howie finished it off. "How is it that John can eat as much as George? Where does he put it all?" Milt asked.

For a moment, Mike couldn't understand who George was, but then he remembered it was Big Howie's first name.

"We figure JJ and Howard owe the army money based on how much chow they've put away in the past seven weeks! Sharkey has been known to go through the breakfast chow line four times!" said Stott.

"Remember, Stott, I'm still growing, so you better watch it!" That was the first time JJ joined in light conversation. "I'm almost five-four now, and I weigh 135 pounds!"

Allsmeir said, "Sharkey and Howard actually gained weight in basic while the rest of us lost a lot of weight. Stott, you stayed about the same, right?"

"Yeah, I guess." Mike imagined the Smealls must have been really bored with this conversation, but, again, they surprised him.

"It sounds to me like, in spite of the pain, you all feel at least a little positive toward your army experience so far. We were afraid it would be awful for Milteee, but now it seems even our son has benefited from the experience so far," Mr. Smeall said. "Which of you likes the army the most at this point?"

"I do!" exclaimed Sharkey.

"Sharkey!" Allsmeir, Howard, and Smeall said in unison.

"Mike, I didn't hear your response. What's your opinion?" asked Bessy Smeall.

All his buddies turned to look directly at Stott. "Actually, so far I love it! Maybe not as much as JJ, but, after the initial shock of being constantly screamed and swore at by the sergeants, it's sort of like the Boy Scouts with guns."

"You were a Boy Scout?" asked Mrs. Smeall.

"Yeah, I was going for Eagle Scout when I discovered girls and kind of got distracted. I think I was about nine merit badges short of Eagle when I met Kathy Giuseppe." As soon as he said it, Mike regretted it. His buddies now had a name to use on him.

"So you been holding out on us, huh, Stott? You're all tied up with a nice little Italian girl!" Milteee seemed anxious to jump on the opportunity to tease Stott.

"Look! He's turning red, it must be serious!" Bessy Smeall said, digging in with her son.

Fortunately for Stott, two waiters then arrived with something called Baked Alaska, a dessert the Smeall's had decided the boys must experience. The lights over the table actually dimmed as it was served, showcasing the still-flaming treat. Bessy insisted that everyone have an Irish coffee with the Baked Alaska. So, on top of two martinis and a couple of glasses of wine, the young soldiers had a spiked coffee. Stott could really feel the alcohol, but it hadn't seemed to affect any of the other guys.

The Baked Alaska brought to the table could easily have served a dozen people, so JJ and Big Howie each had three helpings. Stott looked at his watch for the first time that evening and was astonished to see it was nearly 0100 hours, 1:00 a.m.! The soldiers at the table had been up twenty hours!

"Well, boys, Bessy and I really enjoyed this evening! If any of you would like, we could have a nightcap back at the Plaza, but what say we grab a cab and go on back?" Milt had noticed Mike's reaction to the time.

"Mr. and Mrs. Smeall, Milt and Bessy, I want to thank you for the best meal I have ever had. I will remember this night for the rest of my life. Thank you both, so much," Sharkey's sincerity truly moved his hosts.

"Son, it pleases us more than you know to have you all with us," said Milt. The Smealls had totally won over their son's friends with their gracious warmth and charm.

Though the cab ride back to the Plaza only took a few minutes, the combination of full bellies and a very full day began to affect the boys of Training Company D. As they entered the Plaza lobby, Milt asked, "Nightcap, anyone?"

"Sounds great!" Allsmeir said, not wanting to give up on the night or time with the Smealls.

"If you don't mind, I'm gonna turn in. I think the alcohol just hit me! Thanks again for a great dinner!" said Stott, slightly slurring his words.

"Me, too, but thank you again, so much!" Sharkey said.

"I'm gonna go with Stott and JJ if that's all right. Thank you, sir and ma'am." Big Howie was struggling with the informality the Smealls desired.

"You're so welcome and sleep well. Call us when you wake up, if you like, and we'll do some sightseeing!" Bessy had her arms around her son as though she'd never let go. "Good night!"

Howard, JJ, and Stott headed for the elevator as Allsmeir and the Smealls headed for the bar. Once inside the elevator, Sharkey said, "Let's give 'em a minute and head back down to Times Square!"

"JJ, not tonight. I'm a little light-headed and could really use a good night's sleep. Sorry, but I'm turning in," Stott said.

"Howie, you whimping out, too?" JJ demanded.

"Yeah, John. I'm seeing two of you guys right now, so I better hit it, too."

"Look, JJ, this will be the only time I'll ever let you down, but I just can't keep going tonight, Okay?" Mike said.

"Awright, Stott, since you put it that way. But I'm holding you to your statement. You just said you'd never let me down again, right?" Sharkey's intensity reenergized Stott.

"That's a deal, JJ," Mike slurred.

"You heard Stott, right, Howie? He made me a promise, and, in return, I swear to never let him down! You want in on this?" John seemed obsessed.

By this time, the boys were in the suite and JJ went to the bar. He opened two mini-bottles of Smirnoff and turned to Howard. "Me and Stott are about to drink to our pact. You in or out?"

"What do you mean 'pact'?" Big Howie asked.

"Well, Stott and me are making a pact to never let each other down, ever, no matter what. Our first allegiances are to each other, always. We've got a deal, me and Stott, and we're asking if you want in. Can't be more than three guys in a pact like this, two's enough. But I've been watching you all through basic and, if Stott agrees, I'd take you as our third man."

John Sharkey's statement sobered Mike Stott right up. He could see how deadly serious JJ was about his pact proposal. They hadn't talked about this; JJ had made up his mind.

"I can see you and Stott, JJ, 'cause you're so much alike. But why me? I'm a Negro, and you know I'm not as good as you guys at soldiering. And I've never really had a friend, not like your talkin' about," Howard, now extremely serious too, confessed.

"Howard, don't you ever underestimate yourself again! I can see that you're smart and, more importantly, you are loyal. If you join our pact, I know you'll keep up your side of the deal. In or out? You get only one chance with us. In or not?" Sharkey was staring intently at Howard.

"Mike, you want me in, too?" Howie asked.

Talk about on the spot! Mike wasn't that surprised at Sharkey wanting a commitment of friendship from him, but JJ's feelings toward George Washington Howard was a surprise.

"We got off to a pretty bad start, Howie, but the way you've handled yourself has impressed me, too. What John's proposing is forever. No matter what, right, John? If you want in, yeah, it'll be the three of us."

Howard just stood there looking back and forth between Sharkey and Stott. Tears were streaming down his cheeks.

"I'm in," said Big Howie.

JJ opened a third mini-bottle of Smirnoff. The men took the vodka in their left hands and clasped right hands together.

"Loyalty, from this moment forward," Sharkey said.

"Loyalty," Howard and Stott repeated.

Mike Stott thought at the time he knew how much that pact meant to John Sharkey and believed Howard took it seriously, too. He liked both these guys, especially Sharkey, but he doubted that he would ever have initiated such a pact.

They downed the little bottles of vodka, but Sharkey held on to their hands. "Understand, brothers, there is nothing I would not do for you two."

Mike felt that Sharkey meant it when he said it, but Stott could not have comprehended what that pledge meant to John J. Sharkey.

Chapter Nineteen

That last two ounces of Smirnoff, on top of the other drinks, combined with the emotion of their pact had Mike Stott's head spinning. He managed to take a shower and brush his teeth, but when he lay down on that luxurious bed, he was out. JJ was still talking, but it didn't matter. Mike vaguely remembered that it was after 0200 hours, 2:00 a.m.

At 10:30 a.m. the next morning, Sharkey shook Stott awake. Mike recognized JJ but couldn't get a grip on where he was. "Is it reveille?" Mike asked.

"Get your ass up and moving, Stott! We've got a city to see! I've already had breakfast and we're meeting the Smealls at 1100 hours for brunch! Howie's in the shower, so haul ass! I sure hope you can learn to handle a little booze!" JJ looked fresh as a daisy, and he had on blue jeans, a black T-shirt and Converse All Star gym shoes!

"Where the hell did you get those civvies?" Stott asked.

"Right off the street! Me and Allsmeir been up since 0700 hours! We went downtown someplace that Larry knew about on the subway. Look! I got the same stuff for you and Howard!"

Sure enough, Sharkey had laid out jeans, shoes, and a shirt for Mike. "You found clothes that will fit Big Howie? How in the hell did you do that?"

"Yep! Size fourteen All Stars and all! I've wanted a pair of Converse All Stars my whole life and now we got 'em! Move your ass!" Sharkey was positively jubilant.

Stott completed the Three S's in record time and, sure enough, there was Big Howie in civvies like JJ had. "I've never had overhauls without bibs before! And gym shoes! These are my first!"

Mike realized he'd had a pampered childhood compared to these two guys. "What do you mean 'bibs,' Howard?"

"You know, bibs and 'spenders! You don't have to wear nothing else! We worked the fields in overhauls with no shoes. I feel like the king of the Negro world in these duds!"

"Don't get uppity on us, Mr. Howard! We could take the All Stars back!" This, from Allsmeir, who had just emerged from his shower.

"You just try it, Allsmeir, and I'll flatten you like a johnny-cake!" Howard said.

"Like a what?" JJ demanded.

"You know, johnnycakes! Them things you put molasses on for breakfast!"

"Never heard of them! Come on guys; let's not keep the Smealls waiting!" Larry said.

Allsmeir had also bought some civvies, but he had dress slacks and loafers.

"How much we owe you for these clothes, JJ?" Mike asked.

"About thirty-five dollars, but don't worry about it! You guys have to keep me in food and drinks the rest of the week-end!" Sharkey had it all figured out.

"I'd rather pay you! I've seen you drink! Where'd you learn to put away booze like that, John?" Stott asked through his hangover.

"Other than communion wine, that's the first alcohol I ever had! Didn't seem to affect me at all! That's just one more thing I'm better at than you, Stott!" JJ was in rare form.

"Name another thing!" Pact or no pact, Mike wasn't letting JJ get away with a statement like that.

"Shooting and brains!" said JJ.

The elevator opened, and there were the Smealls, all three, looking like they owned the world. Hell, maybe they did!

"Good morning, dears! I'm starving, and I need coffee! Let's go eat!" Bessy had on skintight stretch slacks tucked into white ankle boots and an even tighter long-sleeved T-shirt. She looked gorgeous! Milt and Milteee looked like they just left a gentlemen's fashion shoot in their Saturday casuals.

"Where'd you guys get the regular clothes?" Milt asked.

Allsmeir related the early morning trip that he and Shar-key had taken to Orchard Street.

"They were open on the Sabbath?" Bessy asked.

"Some were, but we got this stuff off the carts! I taught JJ about bargaining and you should've heard him! When he asked about extra large sizes, the venders started laughing, and I thought we were gonna get in a fight! But we got all this stuff and it even fits the guys." Allsmeir liked to tell everyone's stories.

"Amazing! But let's find some food!" Bessy took charge.

They walked a few blocks to a place called The Stage Delicatessen. Piles of eggs and pancakes served with bacon, sausage, and something called lox. Fresh-squeezed orange juice and the best coffee Stott had ever tasted, with cheesecake for dessert.

The soldiers spent the entire day with Barry and his folks, seeing all the touristy sights of New York. The Statue of Liberty was Stott's favorite, but Sharkey and Howard would have stayed on the observation tower of the Empire State Building forever. The day was very hot, but clear. It felt like they could see forever.

Toward the end of the afternoon, the Smealls decided the group should take a carriage ride through Central Park. They split up to fit into two carriages, with JJ and Mike in a rig with Bessy. She sat across from them, and all the boys could think about was the way her boobs jiggled as they bounced over the roughly paved streets.

"Well, John, we know Mikey has his Kathy, have you got a girlfriend?" Bessy asked.

"Uh, no, ma'am. Not yet," was JJ's mysterious answer.

"What do you mean, 'not yet'? What are you waiting for?" pressured Mrs. Smeall.

"First, I have to establish myself. Then I'll find a woman," Sharkey stated.

"Find a woman? What's that mean? Why not a girlfriend?" Bessy asked.

"Mrs. Smeall, you know exactly what I mean. I don't mean to be rude or disrespectful, but I believe the relationship between a man and a woman is 90 percent sexual." Sharkey's words made Mike want to crawl under the carriage seat.

"John, you may be right, but how on earth did you reach that conclusion at your age?" Bessy inquired.

"It's just what I feel." Sharkey tried to end the conversation.

But Bessy Smeall would not give it up. "Don't you want to be loved, have a family?"

"I want to be the best soldier in the United States Army. After that, I'll see what's next," JJ stated.

"Mikey, is John for real?" Bessy Smeall asked.

Stott didn't know what to say or think.

"Stott feels the same as I do! He's just less vocal about it than me." JJ was staring straight at his buddy.

They rode another ten minutes or so in complete silence. Sharkey and Mrs. Smeall seemed less bothered by the silence than Mike. It was nearly 1900 hours, 7:00 p.m., when they arrived back at the Plaza after the ride through Central Park. The soldiers' heads were spinning from all that they had seen and experienced during the past twenty-four hours, thanks to the hospitality of Barry Smeall's parents.

"Last night, you folks treated me to the best meal I'd ever had. Today, you've showed us sights that I will never forget. From the bottom of my heart, I thank you." Sharkey's words were moving.

"The day is not over, John! Let's freshen up and head down to Chinatown for dinner! We were going to do Italian, but since we're all invited to Mobliano's tomorrow, let's do something fun tonight! Back here in the lobby at 7:30?" Milt seemed to be having as much fun as the soldiers. Bessy, too.

Howard, JJ and Stott took a separate elevator; it was Mike's first chance to question Sharkey. "What was that talk about women and sex with Mrs. Smeall? I was so embarrassed I wanted to jump out of the carriage!"

"What's that?" Big Howie was all ears.

"John got in this big philosophical discussion with Bessy Smeall that scared the shit out of me!" Stott could feel his face turning red at the memory of it.

"Stott, stay cool. She understood it, didn't she? When you get older, you will, too!" Sharkey said.

"Older, my ass! We're the same age, dickhead, and I've got a girlfriend!" Now Mike was getting mad.

But Sharkey just smiled, "You got a girlfriend, but have you ever gotten laid? Plus, I'm two months older than you and much wiser! And don't call me dickhead again until you outrank me, which will be never!"

That got Big Howie laughing pretty hard and he said, "You know, Stott, I think JJ's been holding out on us! I think he's been around more than he lets on! When is your birthday, anyway?"

"Been around, my ass! December 20, 1946, if it's any of your business! And Sharkey, I'll make sergeant before you, for sure!" Stott did not appreciate their comments.

Now JJ and Howard were both laughing and enjoying the discussion. "Remember when I called you 'kid' that first day? Guess I was right again! And there's no fucking way you'll make sergeant before me! I got a month's pay that says I'm an E-5 before you!"

"Bullshit! You're on, and let's put a steak dinner on top of the month's pay! I can't wait to make sergeant so I can put your sorry ass on KP!" Stott shouted.

But Mike's speech only made Sharkey and Howard laugh harder! "Got to him, didn't we?" they said in unison. This intellectual exchange had taken place as the boys freshened up, yelling back and forth between the bathrooms. Allsmeir had stayed out of the discussion.

As the four of them got in the elevator to go meet the Smealls, Howard asked Allsmeir, "I didn't hear you piping in with your usual wiseass remarks. You sick or something?"

"If I've learned one thing in basic, it's not to get between the three of you!" Allsmeir spoke in total seriousness.

"Good decision," Sharkey said.

The elevator door opened and there were all three Smealls dressed in blue jeans and wearing black nylon zip-up jackets with "NYPD" printed on the back in big, gold letters.

"Aren't these the greatest? We got one for each of you! I hope Mr. Howard's fits!" Bessy was positively beaming. She had on skintight jeans and black-strap high heels, making her about four inches taller. Her flaming red hair was piled up on the top of her head, and she had on more makeup than before. All this in about twenty minutes.

"We saw these jackets around the corner, and I just had to have one! Then I decided we all had to have one! I put on my sophisticated hooker look, so tonight people will think you guys are cops that just arrested me! What do you think?" Bessy struck a pose with her chest pushed out and her chin in the air. Clearly, she was having fun, and she looked absolutely fantastic! It was hard for the boys to remember that she was Barry's mother.

"You look terrific, Bessy!" JJ was the only soldier to speak.

"She's wound up tonight, gentlemen, so I hope we don't all get arrested! I'm starving! Let's head down to Chinatown and get some chow!" Milt Smeall seemed used to having his wife cut up. "Oh, I decided we ought to stick together tonight, so I got us a limo."

Sitting at the curb outside the Plaza was the first stretch limousine Stott had ever seen. It was a 1962 Cadillac, black with black leather interior. The car had room for eight people in the back area that was sealed off from the driver by a glass partition. Milt Smeall talked to the driver through a microphone!

"Chinatown, please, driver! Put us right in the middle of the restaurant section off Canal Street."

The limousine had a bar in the back and, sure enough, there was a large bottle of Smirnoff vodka on ice! Stott was the last to enter the car, and Bessy was already mixing martinis for everyone.

The driver went down Fifth Avenue for a long way. By the time they arrived in Chinatown, all were on their second drink. Milt had the driver drop them at a restaurant called The Peking Palace/New Peking. Exiting the limo, Stott, Howard, and JJ felt like they had arrived in another country. The lighted signs were in Chinese characters, and Chinese dialects were more common than English. They entered the restaurant to the sounds of some strange stringed instrument playing a mournful, sing-song melody. The Smeall group appeared to be the only non-oriental customers dining in The Peking Palace that evening. The maitre'd recognized the Smealls and gave them a warm welcome.

"Have you joined the New York City Police Department, Mr. Smeall?" the owner, Mr. Lee, teased Milt.

"No, Mr. Lee, we just bailed Bessy out of jail, and they were so glad to get rid of her they gave us these jackets!" Milt said.

"Oh, Mr. Smeall, I know not true! No one want get rid of Miss Bessy!" said Mr. Lee the politician.

"Drop the small talk and serve up some booze, honey!" Bessy instructed Mr. Lee, who was now surrounded by several assistants.

"Yes, Miss Bessy! Smirnoff martini straight up with olives, yes?" Clearly, the Smealls were not strangers at The Peking Palace.

"Right! And my six attending slaves will also have one!" Stott wondered if Bessy considered how the word "slave" might affect Big Howie, but she was on a roll. "Chop-chop! I'm thirsty, and I get mean when I get thirsty!"

Milt Smeall just rolled his eyes and said, "Well, boys, you can see Bessy's ready to party! What's your favorite Chinese food?"

"Mr. Smeall, er, Milt, I've never had Chinese food before, and I don't think JJ or Howie have either, so maybe you could choose for us, if you don't mind," Mike said.

"None of you three have had Chinese food before?" Bessy Smeall was incredulous. "You're teasing us, aren't you Mikey?"

"No, ma'am, I wouldn't do that. I've never been in a restaurant like this before, and I've never tasted oriental food," Stott confirmed.

"Mr. Howard, JJ? Have neither of you had Chinese food, really?" Milt was also totally surprised. The Smealls weren't being rude, but their guests' total lack of sophistication became clear to Milt and Bessy, sitting there in The Peking Palace.

"Actually, I have had Chinese food, but not in a fancy restaurant," JJ confessed.

Bessy was the first to recover. "Well, then, this will really be fun! I'll order all my favorite dishes, and we can all share! How does that sound?"

"Great!" said Howard and Stott together.

Sharkey remained silent.

"If it's okay, I really like the spicier dishes," said Allsmeir. "I was an Oriental history major at Boston College, and I love all things Oriental!"

"How'd a nice Jewish boy like you wind up going to B.C.?" asked Milt.

"Best languages department, and B.C. was looking to integrate!" Allsmeir's comment brought laughter from the three Smealls. Howard and Stott missed the humor, but both noticed Sharkey perk up at the mention of B.C.'s languages department.

"You never mentioned an interest in languages before, Allsmeir. What languages do you speak?" Sharkey's question got all their attention.

"Well, getting cursed at by pros like our sergeants hardly encouraged any intellectual-type language discussion, JJ! But, for your information, I speak three Chinese dialects and, of course, Yiddish."

"Which dialects?" Sharkey demanded.

"What's Yiddish?" Big Howie asked.

"Cantonese, Mandarin, and Mongol. Yiddish is our Jewish language, Mr. Howard, based mostly on German."

"Say something in Mandarin!" JJ was intensely interested in Allsmeir's professed language skills.

"Well, I'll tell you what! Mrs. Smeall, if you don't mind, point at the dishes you would like to order, and I'll tell them to Mr. Lee in the dialect of his choice. Would that satisfy you, JJ?" Larry was a little put off at Sharkey's obvious skepticism about his language skills.

"Gotta see it!" was Sharkey's reply.

The dinner party was a little surprised at this exchange between Allsmeir and JJ, but Bessy wasn't going to let anything interfere with a good time. "Oh, that'll be fun! My menu is only in English, so this will be a great test!"

By this time Milt had ordered a second round of drinks, but Sharkey, Howard, and Stott had respectfully asked to switch to beer. That had actually pleased Milt who joined them in the switch and instructed Mr. Lee to bring Shenzdou beer, which none of the soldiers had ever heard of. The Shenzdou came in big, green bottles, ice cold, and tasted great! Way better than Smirnoff. Stott hoped he had some chance of remembering his first Chinese dinner if he could lay off the vodka.

"Are we ready to order, please?" asked Mr. Lee.

What happened next was astonishing. Larry Allsmeir began speaking Chinese, and Stott thought Mr. Lee was going to pass out! Mr. Lee called all of his staff over, and, frankly, everyone in the restaurant focused on the Smealls' table. Apparently, Mr. Lee asked Larry to start over with the order, and there began an exchange of such exuberance the whole restaurant cheered when Allsmeir and Mr. Lee finished.

But what occurred next would provide lifelong memories for Mike Stott and all at the table.

John Sharkey had been intently focused on the ordering exchange, looking over Bessy's shoulder as she pointed to her selections and had Larry articulate them in Mandarin. After Allsmeir's language ability was cheered by the staff and customers of The Peking Palace, JJ spoke. "You forgot the pork and onions in the peanut sauce."

John Sharkey then proceeded to speak to Mr. Lee in what sounded like the same language Allsmeir had used, but faster. The Smeall dinner party soon learned that JJ had repeated the entire nine-dish order that Bessy had selected, finishing with the pork in peanut sauce that Larry Allsmeir had missed.

Total silence befell The Peking Palace. Larry Allsmeir was absolutely chalk white, and Mr. Lee's mouth was hanging wide open. The wait staff was standing wide-eyed as well, staring in disbelief at Sharkey.

JJ then said something else in their language that made all the Chinese in the room howl with laughter. Mr. Lee, his staff, and most of the customers in the restaurant began shaking Sharkey's hand and bowing to him! The chatter back and forth between Sharkey and the Chinese was amazing! Mike could see that Allsmeir understood some, but not all, of what was being said. Allsmeir just kept staring at Sharkey in disbelief.

The Smealls, Howard, and Stott were speechless. All had their mouths hanging open too, because JJ turned to Stott and said, in English, "Shut your mouth, Stott. Stop acting like a hick!"

That made the entire restaurant laugh uncontrollably, except for Stott, who still couldn't believe what he had just witnessed. JJ gave Mike that "gotcha!" look that Stott came to know so well over the years, and, with his finger, made a little check mark in the air, completing his triumph.

Mr. Lee announced to the entire restaurant, "In honor of having not one, but two young Americans in one party speak our language here tonight, I am sending champagne to every table! We will drink a toast to them, but especially to Mr. Sharkey whose excellent pronunciation makes me think he must have Chinese girlfriend!"

The entire restaurant stood and cheered, and when the champagne arrived they stood and cheered again.

"To Mr. Sharkey and Mr. Allsmeir! You honor us by speaking our language. You will always be most welcome in my restaurant and my home!" Mr. Lee's toast brought tears to Bessy Smeall's eyes.

"Who could have predicted such a night? Thank you, thank you JJ and Larry! What a surprise and what a wonderful gift of communication you both have. I haven't had this much fun since Milt fell off our boat and had to be pulled out of the Allegheny River by the Coast Guard!" Bessy Smeall said.

Bessy then proceeded to tell her guests the story of Milt's plunge into the river. But Mike barely heard what she was saying. John J. Sharkey spoke Chinese! How in the hell did he learn it? Why hadn't he told his buddies before? Why did he let Allsmeir spout off about his own language skills and say nothing? And what had he said to Mr. Lee and the other Chinese that had made them laugh so hard?

When Bessy finished her story, Stott asked, "JJ, what the hell? Where did you learn to speak Chinese? What did you say that made them all laugh so hard? Damn!"

All eyes turned to Sharkey. "I told them that perfect Mandarin only comes out of perfectly sized people. Captain Estes Sharkey owned whaling ships that sailed the China Sea! He requested that at least some of the sisters in the orphanage he founded maintain Chinese language capability. Not many of the kids were interested in the language, but Sister Mary Katherine told me that to learn another language is to live another life." That inspired me. Just before I joined the army I helped her translate papers for an orphanage in Taiwan."

Allsmeir said, "So you can read and write Chinese, too? Holy shit!"

"Well, yeah. The sisters started with the characters first and then taught us the sounds."

"How many kids learned Chinese?" Bessy asked.

Sharkey blushed, "Really, just me. It wasn't hard. Fun, actually, like a puzzle."

The food arrived and the Smealls and their guests ate and ate and ate. Especially Howard, Sharkey, and Bessy. They kept eating after the rest had finished. Mike Stott sat sipping his beer, still trying to comprehend Sharkey's language skills.

As JJ finished the last of what had to be his fifth or sixth plate of Chinese chow, Stott asked him, "JJ, you know any other languages?"

"Uh, yeah."

"So do I have to beat 'em out of you or are you going to tell us?" Stott demanded.

"Don't threaten me. Latin, of course, and a little Italian," JJ seemed reluctant to fess up.

Bessy spoke up. "I knew you were intelligent! I just knew it! Didn't I tell you Sharkey was the smart one, Milt?" She realized how that sounded and added, "Not that the rest of you aren't smart, but John's intellect just shines through."

Now Sharkey's face was flushed, and he was truly embarrassed.

"Mrs. Smeall, Bessy, could you please tone it down a little? Me and Howard gotta live with this guy, and he's plenty proud already!" Stott said.

"Why just you and Howie? Aren't all you boys in basic together?" Bessy asked.

It was a fair question that Bessy asked, and Stott knew she wanted an answer. As Mike was trying to come up with a response, Sharkey said, "Yes, ma'am, we're all together now, but Howard, Stott, and me are lifers. We're going on to Advanced Infantry Training while the other guys will take a different track. Mobs will be an officer and then an army lawyer. College guys like Larry and Barry, here, will probably get desk jobs, and Hale will probably get court-martialed. But Stott and me and Howie want to be real soldiers, in the thick of it! Me and Stott are going airborne! We'll probably be in Vietnam while they're all coasting through. No disrespect intended; that's just how it is."

"Is there a lot of talk about Vietnam in the army, son?" Milt asked JJ.

"Yes, dad! All the time. Ready guys?" Barry Smeall started calling Sergeant Turner's favorite cadence and his buddies all joined in:

I wanna be an Airborne Ranger,
I wanna live my life in danger,
I wanna go to Vietnam!
I wanna make it to the hill at Bragg,
I wanna kill me a slant-eyed fag,
I wanna go to Vietnam!
I wanna soak in the swamp at Benning,
I wanna make it 'til the final penning,
I wanna go to Vietnam!

The soldiers realized they had once again gained the attention of the entire restaurant when they were applauded at the end of their performance.

"Oh, Milteee! I don't want you going to Vietnam, no way!" moaned Bessy Smeall.

"No, we sure don't, son," said Mr. Smeall. "But we don't want any of you to have to go. Kennedy should never have put our boys there in the first place!"

"That's for sure! I would have let myself be drafted instead of enlisting if it weren't for Vietnam!" Allsmeir said. "Could've been in for two instead of three years!"

"What do you boys think? Will you fight in a place nobody has ever heard of?" Bessy asked.

"To tell you the truth, I've been trying not to think about it. I joined the army for adventure, but I really didn't think about having to go to war!" Mike confessed.

"What about you, Mr. Howard?" Milt inquired.

"Sir, I never even heard of Vietnam 'til I got to Fort Dix! I want an army career, so I guess I'll have to go if they send me," said Big Howie.

"That leaves you to give us your opinion, John," said Bessy.

"I don't understand how these guys didn't know about Vietnam! President Kennedy says it's where we must stop the spread of communism! Of course, I want to go to Vietnam or any other place my country needs me!" It was the first time his friends had heard Sharkey offer his opinion on Vietnam or war. "Besides, wars have existed since the beginning of civilization, so nations need armies, and armies need good soldiers. I intend to be the best soldier in the United States Army!"

"But, John, with your language skills and intelligence, you could be anything you want! Why not an interpreter at the United Nations or something more grand than being a soldier?" Bessy asked.

Sharkey stared intently at Bessy Smeall after she asked those questions. JJ paused before he responded and then said, "All due respect ma'am, but that's insulting to me. I'd rather die in this chair than work for the commies in the United Nations! There is no more honorable profession than serving one's country in the army."

At that moment, Mike Stott began to understand how special his new friend was. Mike reflected back to the pact that he had made with JJ and Howard the night before. Stott looked across the table at George Howard and found him staring back, both wondering if they would be able to live up to Sharkey's expectations.

Sharkey's speech had taken some of the gaiety out of the evening, but, fortunately, Mr. Lee returned to the table with a bottle of plum wine and a beaming smile on his face.

"We celebrate big night! Have two young Americans that speak our language! We are so happy to have you here! This is very special wine bottle. It survived great earthquake in San Francisco! We drink tonight to everyone's luck and health!"

When the Smeall party finally left The Peking Palace, it was after midnight. Everyone was a little tipsy, especially Stott. The limo was right there at the curb, waiting for them. "Driver, show us around the theater district on the way back to the Plaza. And start by going through the village before you head up town; my boys are still enjoying the sights!"

So Bessy mixed her guests another short martini, and they rode around with the windows open, experiencing midnight Manhattan. Over by Times Square, the working girls made offers the boys might have fallen for under other circumstances, despite Mobliano's warnings.

By the time they returned to the Plaza it was nearly 2:00 a.m., and the young soldiers were pretty wasted. They again thanked the Smealls profusely, but Milt Smeall summed up the night. "I can honestly say this was one of the most interesting evenings of my life! Even Bess was speechless at John and Larry's language skills! Hell, we'll be celebrities at The Peking Palace from now on! Good night! You're on your own until the limo leaves for Brooklyn at three thirty tomorrow, I mean, today!"

When the boys got to the suite, JJ wanted one more drink! Mike was fighting to stay upright, but Sharkey opened four mini-Smirnoffs and insisted on putting one in his hand. Then Allsmeir said, "JJ, I'll never forget tonight! You absolutely humbled me! I'm serious! I've studied Chinese for six years, including immersion courses, but your ear and your enunciation blew me away! Here's to you, man! Do you have a Chinese girl?"

"Well, thanks, Larry. You did just as good as me, but thanks!" JJ seemed pleased to receive Allsmeir's praise.

"What I want to know, asshole, is what else you're holding out on us?" Stott knew he was slurring his words, but it was a serious question.

"Nothing of importance! You'd better lie down before you fall down!" JJ said.

But it was too late! Mike Stott passed out right in front of his three buddies. They had to pick him up and put him on his bed.

Mike dreamt of Sharkey speaking Chinese, and Bessy Smeall's boobs.

Chapter Twenty

Mike awoke at 1300 hours, 1:00 p.m., Sunday afternoon. Sharkey was shaking him awake, but JJ didn't look as if he'd been up and about for long, either. John had opened both of the blackout curtains, revealing a cloudless first day of September 1963.

"Allsmeir's gone already, but Howie's still asleep. Here's something I think you'll like. It's called café latté from that snooty restaurant downstairs. I've had two, and they're pretty good. We need to go get some breakfast! Get your ass moving!" Sharkey had on his jeans and another civilian shirt.

"Another new shirt?" Mike asked.

"Oh, yeah, I bought them downstairs. Got you and Howard one, too, but different colors. I figure we needed some more civilian duds for Mobliano's house this afternoon."

Stott took a sip of the fancy coffee, and it was damn good. He sat all the way up and looked out the window at the incredible view of Central Park.

"Thanks for the coffee, JJ, it helps my head. Don't you have at least a little bit of a hangover?"

"I'll admit to a small disturbance in the back of my head. You know, Mike, I still can't believe what the Smealls have done for us! They must have spent a thousand dollars! Are you okay with letting them do that?" JJ, like Stott, couldn't really grasp why the Smealls were treating them so well.

"JJ, it's all strange to me, too! I've never experienced living like we have the past two days. Never ridden in a limo before and sure never stayed in a place like this! I've eaten the most fabulous food of my life, and I've got to admit I've had a great time with Milt and Bessy." As Mike spoke he realized this was the first really personal conversation he'd had with Sharkey.

"So, your life was a little different from Barry's, huh?" JJ asked in complete seriousness.

Mike stared at Sharkey and realized his question was sincere. "John, are you fuckin' kidding? My family's not poor, but we're sure as hell not rich! I worked in a Kroger's grocery store for spending money! I had to pay my mom and dad room and board as soon as I started making any money. My dad is a union guy in a GM plant. Mom works at a department store. They're great people and I hope you meet them soon, but they are nothing like the Smealls! My folks simply won't be able to understand how you and me have spent a weekend in New York living like millionaires! In fact, I'm not sure I'm going to tell them because it is a little weird!"

"Mike, you know I grew up in an orphanage. I know this weekend is real because I'm here with you and Big Howie, but I doubt if you can ever imagine how this feels to me. I got to tell you, though, the best part of the weekend for me, by far, is the pact we made. Have you thought more about it?" JJ turned serious.

"Yeah, John, I have. I'm totally flattered that you wanted to form a pact. But after your display of language ability last night and hearing some of the conversations you've had with the Smealls, I hope I can carry my weight," Stott admitted.

"That's strange! I was afraid you and Howie wouldn't want to team up with me, and you're worried because I know a couple of languages?" JJ seemed surprised. "You know when I decided I wanted you to be my best friend? When you shook my hand in the latrine that night after you had the fight with Howard. You looked me right in the eye, and I knew we had put that first meeting behind us. You were the first regular guy that ever offered to help me."

"What do you mean, 'regular guy,' John? And what did I offer you?" Mike asked.

"At St. Agnes, we called the people with families 'regular people.' You offered to teach me to box, and then you coached me on my M-14. You showed me how to aim by instinct, not Master Sergeant Jenkins! Only you and me hit every target! That was the proudest day of my life! We're gonna do great things in the army, Mike. I promise."

"So, you're pretty sure you're a lifer, JJ? I mean, the first seven weeks haven't exactly been a picnic! And I doubt we'll ever have a weekend like this again in our lives! By the way, you said last night that you were well aware of the situation in Vietnam. You actually want to be in a war? I mean, hell, I'll go if they send me, but that's different than wanting to go!"

"Serving in combat is how you make it in the army. Once you've earned a Combat Infantry Badge, the army treats you better. I want to get one right away!" JJ said.

"You can also get killed in combat, JJ!" Just for an instant Mike considered telling Sharkey about his brother, but something stopped him.

"I know that, Mike, but you and me are not going to die in combat." JJ said it matter-of-factly.

"And how do you know that, John?"

"I just know it. You know, President Kennedy authorized a new part of the army called the Special Forces. I think that's the place for you and me!" JJ announced.

"What the hell is that? I never heard of it. How do you know so much?"

"Because I read, dickhead! You should learn how! It would be a good offset to your propensity for physical action," JJ said.

"You know, Sharkey, when I make sergeant ahead of you, you're gonna wish you hadn't called me a dickhead so often!" Mike said.

"That's one thing I won't have to worry about because there's no fucking way you'll make E-5 before me!" JJ shouted.

"Are you guys still worrying about whose gonna make sergeant first?" Big Howie walked in their room wearing the grin he had been wearing ever since he arrived in New York. "Hell, I'm just afraid this is all a dream, and I'm gonna be woke up for fire guard or KP! For a Mississippi boy like me, this just doesn't happen! Are we really here, in the Plaza Hotel? Do I really have a pair of Converse All Stars? Damn!"

"Get away from the window! You're blockin' the light, Howard! Who do you think will make sergeant first, me or Stott?" JJ asked.

"Probably Stott," Big Howie told Sharkey.

"What! Why would you say that?" JJ was shocked.

"Because you're gonna get put in the stockade for sexual misconduct! I seen the way you been starin' at Mrs. Smeall's tits, and I figure it's just a matter of time 'til you reach out an' grab one! Mr. Smeall will use his influence, and next thing you know, you'll be lookin' at five to twenty in the stockade!" Big Howie explained.

Howard and Stott roared with laughter. Not Sharkey. JJ's face was crimson red, and he knew they had him!

"I was not!" JJ screamed. He actually lunged at Big Howie, but Mike saw it coming and grabbed him from behind, pinning his arms at his sides. JJ used both feet to push off from one of the nightstands, sending both boys sprawling backward out through the bedroom door and into the hall. But Stott didn't let go of his arms, and that got Sharkey really pissed!

"Let go of me! I'm gonna kill you both! Let go, goddamn it!" said Sharkey.

Big Howie was standing over them, laughing uncontrollably. "You know, I take it back! I'll make sergeant before either of you because you'll both be competin' with each other so hard I'll just slide on past you!"

Allsmeir entered the suite with the Smealls while Mike was still hog-tying JJ on the floor.

"What's this? Children at play? Will you guys grow up? We came to see if anybody was hungry!" Allsmeir said, trying to restore order.

At the mention of food, Sharkey said, "Time out! Before I get really mad and hurt you, let's go eat!"

Mike and JJ got up, brushed themselves off, and went to brunch with the Smealls.

Milt had made a reservation for the seven of them to have brunch right in the hotel lobby. Actually, brunch was a new term to Howard and Stott, but Sharkey explained that it meant a combination breakfast-lunch menu served mostly in upscale restaurants in Manhattan. When the group arrived at the lobby restaurant entrance, the maitre'd eyed their blue jeans and seemed on the verge of discussing proper attire with them. Milt shook his hand, leaving behind a folded twenty dollar bill. They were seated immediately.

"Well, Mr. Sharkey and Mr. Stott, what was that scuffle about upstairs?" Bessy asked.

When neither Mike nor JJ answered, Big Howie said, "These two guys are always arguing about who's gonna make sergeant first!" He then went on to explain what had just happened upstairs.

"So, you two were fighting?" Bessy asked.

"No, it wasn't a fight. JJ was about to go after Howard, and I was holding him back," Mike said.

"John was about to go after Howard?" Milt Smeall said, now disbelieving.

"Goddamn it! Why is that so unbelievable? If Stott can whip him, so can I!" Sharkey just wouldn't let it go.

Big Howie then told the Smealls how he and Stott met because of Hale's mouth. "I never been hit like that before!" Big Howie concluded.

"And now the three of you are best of friends?" Bessy asked, still not understanding.

"Mr. and Mrs. Smeall, it was no big deal, really. But I just realized that JJ here has quite a temper, too. Kind of like Hale," Stott thought that would get Sharkey really riled up again.

But Sharkey wouldn't take the bait. Bessy said, "Come on, John, we've got to hear your side of this! I can't believe you are a hothead!"

JJ coolly said, "If Stott says it, it's right. I know he didn't mean that comment about me being like Hale. Mike thought that would get to me, but it didn't. I can keep my cool when I have to, and that's just one more reason I'll make sergeant before him."

Everyone laughed except Stott.

"So, John, let me ask you to explain again how it is you know Chinese and, what, two other languages?" Milt asked, referring to what had happened the previous night.

"Well, Milt, there wasn't that much to do for fun where I grew up, so we had to kind of entertain ourselves. One of my earliest memories is of Mother Gina telling us that languages were one of the keys to life. I didn't really understand what she meant until she said, 'Imagine you are adopted by a family from Italy! They take you home to Bologna to live with them, but they only know a little English! Wouldn't you want to show your gratitude by learning their language?' That sure put it in perspective for me! The sisters knew a variety of languages among them, and they were thrilled if us kids showed any interest in learning one of them. My favorite sister, Mary K, knew Italian and three Chinese dialects because she had lived in China before World War II. We studied Latin as part of our Catholic education, and Italian came pretty easy on top of the Latin."

Bessy interrupted JJ. "But I've heard oriental languages are particularly difficult for Americans to learn. Wasn't it terribly hard?"

"No, not really. I started learning the characters when I was four, and they seem as natural to me as the English alphabet. Sister Mary K and I started speaking to each other only in Mandarin or Cantonese when I was about eight. I loved it because none of the other kids could do it! And, truth be told, it got me a lot of attention. I was always the smallest boy in my age group, so I focused on the languages to earn respect. There was one Chinese carryout in Bedford and, when I was sixteen, I was allowed to work there from 4:00 p.m. to 8:00 p.m. on Thursday and Friday and noon until seven on Saturday. That really helped my ear and, if I may say so, I think I may just kind of have a natural ability in languages."

Everyone listened intently to Sharkey. Stott was reminded once again that his life had been much easier than JJ's.

"So you had eaten Chinese food before!" Big Howie voiced what Mike was thinking.

"Did you take the SAT's, Sharkey?" Allsmeir asked.

"Uh, no. I knew all I wanted to do was join the army," JJ said.

"Why the army instead of the air force or the navy?" Milt asked.

"When I was twelve, an army recruiter came to St. Agnes to talk to the older guys that were finishing school. I sneaked in to listen, and he saw me hiding in back. He never said anything until he was finished with the older guys. Then he ran to the back of the room and cut off my escape path. Scared the hell out of me! But then he asked my name and if I remembered my parents. When I explained that I had no memory of them, he sat and talked to me for two hours! That was the first time I had talked very much to a regular guy, you know, not a priest, and he was really nice to me. He told me that he was an orphan, too, and that he joined the army as soon as he was old enough. His name is Sergeant Bill Patterson and he still writes to me every Christmas. Right now, he's in Germany. He got married three years ago, and he and his wife are going to have a kid. If I ever get to Germany, I'll look him up, or maybe I can see him somewhere else. Two years ago, Sergeant Patterson got into something called the Army Special Forces. President Kennedy personally gave him his beret at Fort Bragg!"

As Sharkey was talking, the food came. When JJ finished speaking, everyone just sat and ate in silence. Even Bessy didn't have anything to say. JJ, of course, concentrated on the excellent eggs Benedict. Stott had been hungry, but Sharkey's story had him thinking.

"You gonna eat those eggs, Stott?" Sharkey asked.

That brought Mike back to reality. Stott knew he would have to act fast or his chow would be in JJ's stomach. But Milt Smeall was way ahead of them. Just as JJ inquired as to whether his buddy was going to finish, a waiter showed up with seconds for both Sharkey and Howard.

"I didn't want you guys to start fighting over brunch!" Milt's comment lightened the mood and they all began talking about the trip to Brooklyn and dinner at Mobliano's.

"Milt, I'd like to take some wine," Bessy said.

"Oh, no, mom! Mobs explained to me that if we brought anything other than ourselves, he'd kick my ass! So nothing!" Barry Smeall had obviously been talking to Syl.

As he finished his second serving, JJ asked, "You talked to Mobs since Friday?"

"Yeah, he called to ask if you were in jail, Sharkey. When I told him we'd been mostly with my folks, he seemed relieved. I think he said something like, 'I knew if Hale was with you guys you'd all get in trouble, but I was also worried about Sharkey,'" Barry said.

"Mobs really said that?" JJ couldn't believe it.

This provided Stott with an opportunity. "Yeah, John, Mobs made me promise to personally keep you out of trouble."

"Now I know that's bullshit, Stott! Mobs would never trust you ahead of me! Would he?" Sharkey wasn't so sure.

"I'm telling you, JJ, Mobs called the other morning while you and Allsmeir were out buyin' clothes just to make sure you weren't in big trouble!" Mike said.

Sharkey was staring intently into Mike's eyes. Stott was trying really hard not to let on that he was teasing him when JJ said, "You're full of it, Stott! You were out like a light and would never have heard a phone! I can see I'm gonna have to watch it with you, pact or no pact!"

"What pact?" Allsmeir and Smeall asked in unison.

Sharkey knew he had talked out of turn. "Uh, nothing, guys, nothing."

"Come on, JJ, what are you and Stott up to now?" Barry Smeall persisted. "Stott, you gonna tell us?"

Mike looked Sharkey and then Howard straight in the eye. "No idea," was all he said.

Sensing an awkward moment, Milt Smeall said, "Okay, guys, we better get moving! It's after three o'clock and the limo is waiting! Let's make tracks for Brooklyn. If we get there early, we'll sightsee!"

As they left the Plaza lobby to head for Mobliano's home, Sharkey and Stott lagged behind the group. "Did Mobs really call you?" JJ demanded.

"No, John, he didn't! We were just teasing you. Teasing can't violate our pact! Howard knew I was kidding you! So did Smeall. You gotta lighten up!"

"All right, but I'll still make sergeant first!" Sharkey stated.

As the limo crossed from Manhattan on the Brooklyn Bridge, Milt pointed out the landmarks along the way. "Brooklyn, by itself, would be the ninth largest city in the states. It's really very different from the other boroughs. The part we're going to is almost exclusively Italian, but there are sections of Brooklyn that are all Jewish and others that are all black. Very ethnic, but very cosmopolitan," Milt concluded.

"What do you mean, 'boroughs,' Mr. Smeall?" Big Howie asked. Sharkey, Allsmeir, and Stott had gotten comfortable calling the Smealls by their first names, but Howard just couldn't do it.

"New York City is comprised of five sections called 'boroughs.' The one people think of when they hear New York is the island borough of Manhattan. Then there's Brooklyn, the Bronx, Queens and, finally, Staten Island," Milt explained.

"Do Negroes live in all five boroughs?" Howard asked.

"Yes, Mr. Howard, I believe they do. Does that surprise you?"

"Well, back in Mississippi, we don't live, you know, mixed in with the white folks. I've even seen Negro men walking on the street with white women here in New York. Back home, they'd be hung if they did that." Big Howie's words shocked them all.

"Are you serious?" Bessy Smeall asked what they were all thinking.

"Yes, ma'am, Mrs. Smeall! Least in Benton County where I'm from. In the mornings, when we line up on the county square for day work, we're on the southeast corner of the courthouse and the white men are on the northwest side. Wouldn't dare go to their side."

"Are you serious, Howard?" Mike asked again.

"Yeah, Mike, I'm dead serious. It's why I've been so surprised at you guys I've met here in the army. You treat me just as bad, no worse, than you treat everybody else! Seriously, I never expected to make friends with a group of white guys. And I will never be able to explain to my folks what I've done this weekend! They just wouldn't believe me. They couldn't. They know I don't lie, but they just wouldn't be able to understand."

"You know, Howard, you're the first black guy I've ever known," Sharkey said. "I guess I never really thought about you being different than any of us. We didn't have any Negro orphans at St. Agnes. Are you serious about your folks not being able to believe we're friends?"

"Yeah, JJ. Totally serious," said Big Howie.

Stott could see that they had finally hit on a subject that the Smealls were uncomfortable discussing. To his great surprise, Barry Smeall spoke up. "First time I ever spoke to a black person was when I went to college. We were pretty segregated in Pittsburgh, too. I've got to say, you are my first black friend. I just think of you as one of the three musketeers! The biggest, I might add!"

"You referring to Howard, Stott, and me?" Sharkey asked Smeall.

"Actually, no. Howard, Stott, and Hale. I guess I think of you as more buddied up with Mobliano," Barry said.

Stott could see that Smeall's opinion did not please JJ, but he said nothing further. At least they had somehow gotten off the subject of the pact.

"Well, we're just about there!" Milt announced. "Just around that corner, right, driver?"

"Yes, sir, Mr. Smeall," the driver answered. But when they got to the corner to make the turn the entire street was blocked off! An NYPD squad car sat crossways between two parked cars, denying access to all vehicles.

"Street's closed for a party at the Moblianos', Mac!" one of New York's finest said to the driver. "Find another route to get where you're going!"

"But, officer, I'm taking these folks to the Moblianos'!"

"Why didn't you say that, Mac? What do you think I am? Psychic? Are you waiting on your party? If so, I'll let you park it right at the curb there!" the officer said.

As the Smealls and the soldiers got out of the limo, they could see that the whole block, both sides of the street, had been turned into a carnival. There were colored lights and streamers running across the street between the houses. Lines with alternating American and Italian flags canopied the entire block. In the center of the street were dozens of tables covered with red-checkered tablecloths, and four bars had been set up, one on each corner of the table arrangement. At the center of the tables, a shiny hardwood dance floor had been assembled. Off to one side of this floor, an eight-piece band was playing Italian songs.

Already, hundreds of people were in the street, laughing and talking and singing with the band. At the far end of the block Stott could see another NYPD squad car. In addition to the people in the street, folks were hanging out of windows, talking, and joking with those in the street. The street had an appealing aroma of grilling sausages, wine and beer, and cigar smoke. Toward the far end of the block, a mini-Ferris wheel, perhaps thirty-feet high, had been erected and children were lined up to take a ride. Standing next to the Ferris wheel, helping the kids get in the seats, was Syl Mobliano in a clown suit!

"Holy shit!" Sharkey and Stott said at the same time when they saw Syl.

"My, my, what a party!" said Bessy.

"Are we in the right place?" asked Milt Smeall.

At that moment, Syl Mobliano came rushing out of the crowd to greet his guests. "Sharkey! Stott! Howard! You're here! You must be the beautiful Mrs. Smeall with her servant! Welcome! Welcome! Come meet everybody!"

Stott was perplexed. He looked back down the block, and, sure enough, there was another Syl in the clown suit! "Syl, hold on! I thought that was you down there in the clown suit, but you're here! Do you have a twin brother?" Mike asked.

Syl and the people around him roared with laughter. "That's my pop, you idiot! He'd never let anyone else wear his clown suit!" Syl exclaimed.

Next began a whirlwind of introductions by which the Smealls and Syl's army buddies met three hundred to four hundred people, many of whom were named Mobliano. As these introductions took place, they were working their way down the block, winding through the tables and past the band. Someone had taken a drink order, and all had wine or beer or some other drink in hand. Everyone was speaking English to the newcomers, but Italian to the "family" as they slapped their backs, shook their hands and, very often, kissed them. It was absolutely fantastic! Syl was more or less dragging Sharkey through the crowd to meet everyone. It seemed to Stott that Syl had a definite mission in mind. When they got to a very pretty older woman with snow white hair Syl cried out, "Momma, momma, turn around! Wait 'til you see my buddy, JJ!"

As Mrs. Mobliano turned in response to her son's request, she came face-to-face, maybe three feet apart, from John Sharkey and Mike Stott. At first, she looked directly at Mike and gave him the most radiant smile he'd ever seen. "Welcome, welcome!" she said. Then, she looked directly at JJ. The color drained from her face and for an instant Stott thought she might pass out.

"My God! My God!" Maria Mobliano exclaimed. She grabbed Sharkey and hugged him and kissed him. "Syl, Syl! He looks exactly like Paulie! My God! Get Paulie over here! Somebody find my Paulie!" At Mrs. Mobliano's demand, half the people on the block began calling, "Paulie! Paulie Mobliano! Get over here! Come here!"

Mike could see that Sharkey was embarrassed to death at all this attention, but he was trapped by the crowd. All the commotion searching for Paulie Mobliano caused Mr. Mobliano, Syl's father and exact look-alike, to come running over to investigate. The crowd parted for the senior Mobliano.

"Pop, this is John J. Sharkey and one of my other buddies, Mike Stott," Syl said.

Anthony Mobliano smiled at Mike, but, when he saw JJ, his reaction was as extreme as his wife's, but different. For an instant, Stott thought he saw fear in Mr. Mobliano's eyes, but he quickly recovered his composure. Still looking Sharkey directly in the eyes, the senior Mobliano said, "Son, your resemblance to Syl's little brother, Paulie, is absolutely remarkable! Welcome to the party! You too, Stott! Where's the rest of your party? Somebody find Paulie!"

At Mr. Mobliano's command, everyone started searching for the elusive Paulie. As Mike and JJ had wound their way through the crowd and introductions, they had become separated from the Smealls, Allsmeir, and Big Howie. As the newcomers were reunited, Syl introduced all to his parents. Bessy Smeall and Maria Mobliano seemed to hit it off at once. They joined arms and began talking. Milt Smeall was explaining to Anthony Mobliano about all the fun he had had with "his boys" in the city. Milt then said, "Thank you so much for inviting us to this incredible party! We are honored to be here!"

"You are most welcome! We're going to have some fun!" Anthony was cut short by the appearance of the much sought after Paulie Mobliano.

"Come here, you!" Maria Mobliano commanded. "Meet your twin! Stand right next to him! Right there! Paulie, this is Syl's friend, John Sharkey. John, this is my son, Paulie."

As JJ and Paulie shook hands their uncanny resemblance became clear to all. Paulie was two years younger than JJ, but about the same height. John outweighed Paulie by a few pounds, but their faces were remarkably alike.

"Let's give Paulie a GI haircut, and they'll be twins!" Syl barked out and grabbed his little brother as if to hold him for the cut. As everyone but Paulie laughed at Syl's remark, Stott couldn't help but notice the way Mr. Mobliano continued to stare at Sharkey. He also could not help but notice how much Syl and his father looked alike as they stood there, side by side. Anthony was obviously older, but he and his son were the same height and had the same muscular build. Both Syl and his father were completely bald. Paulie, on the other hand, had incredibly thick, black hair as Sharkey's had been before his trainee trim.

Mike shifted his gaze to Maria Mobliano, who was still engaged in intimate conversation with Bessy Smeall. She was very beautiful with her prematurely white hair and wonderful smile. Stott remembered that she had had nine children. For the first time since entering the army, Mike was homesick.

Then Stott was jolted back to the moment. Through the crowd that was now engulfing his group, through all the laughter and noise, walked two of the most beautiful creatures he had ever seen. Mike felt his knees start to buckle as these two young goddesses ran up and threw their arms around Syl.

"JJ, Mike! Meet my little sisters, Briggetta and Briegeita! Are they cute or what?" Syl had an arm around each one. One of the girls whispered something to her brother in Italian that made the other goddess blush and laugh.

"Well, are you guys going to say 'hi' or just stand there like a couple of hicks?" Syl said, laughing at Mike and JJ.

Stott was speechless, but his buddy, John J. "Show-off" Sharkey, said in what Mike later learned was perfect Italian, "Please forgive my unsophisticated, Midwestern friend for his inability to speak. I am sure that he is completely overcome by your beauty, as am I. I am pleased that you think that I am cute, but was it Briggetta or Briegeita that so thinks?"

When Sharkey spoke in Italian, all of the people around them stopped to listen, especially Syl, his parents and his sisters. Syl recovered first.

"JJ! You speak Italian? And you didn't tell me? My God! And such perfect Italian! Where did you learn? How did you learn?" Syl asked.

Sharkey, probably as much to irritate Stott as to impress Briggetta and Briegeita, answered, in Italian. Everyone in the crowd began speaking Italian to JJ and he was the instant star of the party. Frankly, it pissed Mike off! He could have cared less except that Briggetta and Briegeita were now each holding one of Sharkey's hands, showing him off to their friends and neighbors. As he was being absorbed into the crowd around the Mobliano's, JJ looked back at Stott and gave that check-in-the-air sign that infuriated his buddy.

From behind Mike, Big Howie said, "Don't know which of you'll make sergeant first, but I sure know who's making time first!" Howard, Allsmeir, and all three Smealls were choking with laughter at Howie's observation. It didn't seem funny to Stott.

The six new guests were shown to a table and sat down for another round of drinks. Almost immediately, people came and sat with them, engaging them in conversation. Next thing Stott knew, Bessy Smeall was out on the dance floor stealing the show with an awesome jitterbug that got the whole crowd cheering. Mike sat drinking beer, wondering if Sharkey was changing his mind about being a lifer! In the distance, he could see JJ still hand in hand with the Mobliano girls, laughing and talking with Syl and a large group of people.

The crowd seemed to have doubled since they arrived, and Mike realized it was after six o'clock. They had already been at the party for more than two hours! Anthony and Maria Mobliano came and sat down with them, and the party seemed to center around their expanded table. There were so many people around them it was hard to get another beer, but Big Howie kept working through the crowd, returning with pitcher after pitcher.

Big Howie was the only black person at the party, and he was treated like a celebrity. Things were going along really well except, of course, that Sharkey was still with the two prettiest girls Stott had ever seen. Big Howie leaned toward Mike and said, "You know what, Stott? Hale's not here."

Frankly, Mike hadn't thought a moment about Fast Eddy Hale, especially after he saw Briggetta and Briegeita. But Howie's observation made him stop and think. Had Hale decided not to come to Mobliano's party or was he in jail? Hale's dad was a cop, so he must have just decided to do something else. Mike stood up and looked in the direction where he had last seen Sharkey, Syl and the goddesses. To his absolute horror, there was Eddy Hale talking to the four of them!

Then things really took a bad turn! JJ let go of one of the girls' hands and Fast Eddy took it! As Stott watched in envy, the five of them began walking toward him. Paulie Mobliano re-emerged from the crowd and started talking with Hale. That made Mike remember that Eddy had said he knew the Mobliano family through Paulie. Stott surmised that Eddy must have, for once, been telling the truth.

The closer the group got, the more Stott could see how truly beautiful Briggetta and Briegeita were. They had gorgeous olive skin and coal-black hair. One had her hair rolled up on top of her head while the other's hair fell radiantly over her bare shoulders.

Both girls were wearing bright-colored sun dresses cinched at the waists, showing off their slim middles and robust chests. Mike felt himself getting aroused and wondered how to hide his rapidly rising third member. He quickly sat down to hide his interest. But not soon enough!

As Mike sat back in his chair, Bessy Smeall leaned across the table, took his hand in hers and laughingly said, "Mikey! I think you like the Mobliano girls! Naughty, naughty!"

Stott was absolutely mortified! Howie asked, "What's wrong, Stott? You don't look so good!"

Bessy answered for Mike. "Oh, he's perfectly fine, Georgie! Just a little overwhelmed by the party!" The grin on her face scared the hell out of Stott.

As the Moblianos, Sharkey, and Hale approached the table, Syl began introducing Eddy Hale to everyone. "Hey, it's Mr. Howard and Whitey One! What's up, guys?" Hale yelled out.

"What did he call you, Mikey?" Bessy Smeall asked.

"Uh, Whitey One. Big Howie, here, started calling me that early in basic, and the name kind of stuck with the guys," Stott said. Big Howie then told the story of their first meeting all over again for the gathered crowd.

To Mike's complete exasperation, at the end of Howard's tale, one of the goddesses said to him, "So, you're a fighter, not a lover, huh, Mr. Stott?"

Before he could respond, Mike's former pal, John J. Sharkey, made matters worse. "Oh, Mike's a lover all right! But his girlfriend, Kathy Giuseppe, is back in Ohio, waiting for him!"

"So you like Italian girls, huh, Mikey?" one of the goddesses teased.

Clearly, everyone in the crowd was enjoying this exchange except Stott, who still hadn't recovered enough to say anything. Bessy Smeall spoke up. "Oh, that's for sure! Want to know how I know Mikey likes Italian girls?"

Mike wanted to evaporate! Was Bessy about to describe his aroused condition to everyone at the party? Mike was too embarrassed to protest.

Bessy continued to the delight of the gathered masses, especially Mike's former friend, Sharkey. "I know because just before you folks joined us Mikey was telling me how beautiful Syl's sisters were! In fact, he was just saying the goddess with her hair piled on her head was the most beautiful creature he had ever seen!"

The crowd laughed and cheered. Mike Stott prayed to just disappear.

"Well, forget about Briggetta, Stott, because I'm in love with her! Maybe Briegeita will talk to you!" JJ said.

"I certainly don't talk to boys that are spoken for," Briegeita with the long hair teased. As Mike was struggling for anything intelligent to say the band started playing their version of "Rock Around the Clock" and lots of folks started dancing. Unfortunately, Sharkey and Briggetta and Eddy and Briegeita were among them. Parting the crowd as she came through, yet another gorgeous, olive-skinned beauty emerged from the crowd. She also threw her arms around Syl, but this one gave him a kiss that indicated she wasn't his sister!

"Mike, George, Milt, Bessy! Meet my fiancée, Maria Marinelli!" Syl exclaimed through the biggest grin in Brooklyn. Maria also had an outrageously beautiful smile, and she kissed each of them on the cheek as she and Syl headed for the dance floor.

Mike was really surprised to see how well JJ and Hale were doing jitterbugging with the goddesses! They looked like professional dancers! The band stayed with rock and roll and next played "Whole Lot A Shakin' Goin' On" to the delight of the crowd.

Bessy Smeall grabbed Mike's hand and literally pulled him up out of his chair to the dance floor. "No chance to say you can't! You're dancing with me, right now!"

Mike wasn't much of a dancer, but anybody would've looked good with Bessy. The way she moved was incredible, erotic. Stott could feel lots of eyes on them, her! And she smelled absolutely delicious! Next came the Elvis Presley hit from the late fifties, "Love me Tender," a beautiful, slow love song. Bessy—Mrs. Smeall—wrapped herself around Stott and led him through the dance! The way she moved got Mike all aroused again, and he was embarrassed beyond description. When the song ended, Bessy gave him a devilish grin and said, "Honey, we better sit this one out!"

As they exited the dance floor, Milt got up to dance with Bessy, and Mike was off the hook! Big Howie leaned over and said softly to his pal, "You better watch out, boy! That lady got trouble written all over her! And I thought it was Sharkey she liked!"

Mike thought about another fight with Howard right then and there, but remembered his weight lifting exhibition.

"Lay off, dickhead!" he said to Howard. That, of course, played right into his hands!

"Well, well! Whitey One got big trouble!" Howie said. He had his hands on Mike's shoulders, insuring he couldn't move. Stott felt what the cab driver must have felt that first night in the city when Howard restrained him.

"Get off me, goddamn it!" But Big Howie kept Mike in his seat and kept muttering, "Big, big trouble!" through his laughter.

After a while, the band went back to Italian music, and many of the dancers left the floor. As Milt and Bessy returned to the table, she gave Mike an absolutely wicked wink seen, unfortunately, by Howard. Still standing behind Mike with those huge hands on his shoulders, Howie gave Stott a pressure squeeze to let him know he hadn't missed the wink.

"Bessy says you got to dance with her after dinner, Mike, so get ready!" Milt Smeall instructed Mike.

Syl's look-alike father, Anthony Mobliano, took the band's microphone and addressed the crowd. "Welcome everyone! What a great night! What a great party! You all know us Moblianos like to party and what better reason than when Syl brings home his army pals!" Mr. Mobliano then introduced each of the young soldiers and made them stand for applause. He continued, "And a special welcome to Barry Smeall's parents, Milt and Bessy Smeall! Bessy's the beautiful lady lighting up our dance floor, and we're thrilled you're both here! Among the other beauties on the floor tonight are my lovely daughters, Briggetta and Briegeita, and, of course, my wife Maria. And the gorgeous lady standing next to Syl is his fiancée, Maria Marinelli. We hope they'll set a wedding date soon! Now, on a serious note. You all know that us Moblianos are the rarest of minorities in Brooklyn. We are Republicans! And proud of it!"

At this point, the crowd gave Mr. Mobliano a combination of applause and Bronx cheers. But the detractors still reflected good spirits and respect for their host, even as they dissented with his political persuasion.

Anthony Mobliano continued: "Though we are Republicans, we wholly support our president, John F. Kennedy, as he strives to defeat communism in southeast Asia. We don't agree with the president's domestic agenda, but all Americans must support their president when it comes to foreign policy. Many of the young soldiers I just introduced to you here tonight will very likely be called on to serve in combat in Vietnam. Join Father John Omidus in our prayer for them here tonight. Father John!"

Mr. Mobliano's final few sentences brought a hush to the crowd. Stott thought to himself that if Vietnam was serious enough to be praying about, maybe he should take it more seriously.

Father John began: "Heavenly Father, hear our prayer. Bless all gathered here this glorious Sunday evening, but especially bless the young soldiers here with us tonight. Bless President Kennedy as he backs the government of South Vietnam in its struggle against communism and to preserve a Catholic stronghold in Asia. Bless our young people as they choose life partners and begin to form their own families." Father John prayed for several more minutes and concluded with the following words: "Heavenly Father, we again ask for your guidance and blessing for the soldiers with us. Some of them may kill others in battles to preserve our Christian way and create a democracy in Vietnam. Forgive them their transgressions as they fulfill their duty to God and country. Keep them safe and bring them home to their families, or accept them into Heaven should they be killed in the line of this glorious duty. Amen."

Father John's words temporarily stole all the gaiety from the evening. The crowd was silent as Anthony Mobliano again took the microphone to speak. "Thank you, Father, for your wonderful prayer and sobering words. God bless our soldiers! God bless Brooklyn! God bless America and the great Republican Party! God bless the human spirit that goes forward in the face of adversity to do the right thing! But now, tonight, let us celebrate being alive and together in the greatest city in the greatest country in the world! Let's have some fun!"

During the time that Father John and Anthony Mobliano spoke, John Sharkey had moved back to the table where Howard and Mike were sitting. As Mr. Mobliano encouraged his guests to return to partying, there was JJ, next to Big Howie. John put his hand out to Mike and took Howard's hand and placed it over theirs. "To our pact, to the U.S. Army and to America." There was a tear in each eye as Sharkey finished, "I love you guys," he said.

Mike looked across the table and saw Milt and Bessy Smeall staring at the three of them. They had heard JJ's words, and both had tears in their eyes.

The band struck up again with a happy Italian song that most guests sang along with. Lines began forming to go through two buffet lines offering the best food Howard, Sharkey and Stott had ever tasted. Beer, booze, and homemade red wine flowed freely. A happy and gay atmosphere retuned to Chester Street.

Everyone ate and drank and danced and sang until well after midnight, but Father John's prayer, Anthony Mobliano's words, and Sharkey's pronouncement had moved Mike Stott like nothing before in his life. He would remember that night as a turning point in their lives as three seventeen-year-olds began the transition from boys to men.

Chapter Twenty-One

The party was still going strong at 2:00 a.m. when Mike, JJ, Big Howie, Allsmeir, and the Smealls expressed their thanks to the Moblianos and departed to the applause of the remaining partiers! Just as they got in the limo, Briegeita took Mike's hand and said, "Maybe I'll see you again sometime." Stott nearly passed out from delight!

As the limo pulled away, yet another New York City cop bid them a good evening and wished them a safe journey. It occurred to Mike despite his semi-drunken state that Anthony Mobliano was a powerful man. This mattered to Stott only because he was in love with Anthony Mobliano's daughter.

To Mike's astonishment, Bessy mixed all of them a Smirnoff for the ride back to Manhattan. It was nearly 3:00 a.m. on Labor Day, September 2, 1963, when Howard, Sharkey, and Allsmeir helped Stott into the elevator and to his bed at the Plaza. His friends kept drinking vodka as Stott fell into a deep, alcohol-induced sleep filled with visions of both Briegeita and Bessy Smeall!

At noon, JJ shook Mike awake. Sharkey looked fresh and alert even as Stott struggled to get to the head.

"Gotta get you to hold booze, dickhead! Move your ass; we've got to check out! Barry says the limo is taking us back to Fort Dix with a stop in Trenton, New Jersey, for chow before we go back in." JJ had packed for both Mike and Howie. With Allsmeir's help, he got his buddies down to the lobby. There were the Smealls all dressed up and looking fabulous.

"It was a fabulous weekend, men! What a party last night! The limo will drop Bessy and me at Teterboro and then take you guys back to the base. I've never had more fun! Thanks for letting us share your first leave!" Milt said.

All piled into the limo, and the driver loaded about a dozen of Bessy Smeall's suitcases into the trunk. They left

Manhattan across the George Washington Bridge on a beautiful Labor Day afternoon looking back down the island of Manhattan from the car windows.

Sharkey spoke. "Mr. and Mrs. Smeall, Milt and Bessy, I will remember this weekend for the rest of my life. No matter where we go or what we do, Stott, Howie, and I will be forever in your debt. I thank you from the bottom of my heart."

At the airport, Milt said, "We love you like sons. Never hesitate to call on us for anything, and we expect to see you again, soon." Stott and his friends said good-bye to Milt and Bessy and watched them walk to their waiting plane.

With tears in her eyes, Bessy turned to them and said, "I'll see you all soon."

"Is that their plane?" Big Howie asked Barry Smeall.

"Uh, yeah, it is," Barry Smeall said.

"All theirs, just for them to use?" asked Howard, trying to grasp that the plane belonged to the Smealls.

"Yes, it is registered to one of my dad's companies, but just the family uses it," Barry confirmed.

"Damn!" Big Howie expressed what JJ and Mike were thinking.

The driver got on the New Jersey Turnpike, headed south. "Mr. Smeall, sir, your father directed me to take you gentlemen to the Black Horse Inn in Trenton for dinner and then return you to Fort Dix. Is that okay with you?"

"Sure," was Barry's simple response.

The soldiers rode in silence for quite a while, each consumed in his own thoughts. Finally, Sharkey said to Barry, "Smeall, thank you. I'm still sort of struggling with the reality of the last three days, but thanks. Is this just how your family lives? I mean, you know, spending that much money, eating in fancy restaurants and being driven around in a limo?"

It took Barry Smeall a few moments to collect his thoughts, and then he said, "Guys, the simple answer is 'yes.' I'm a few years older than you are, but in a strange way

I've learned more from you guys and my army experience over the past two months than everything I did for the past twenty-two years. I guess I took the way my family lives for granted. We've always had everything. I've been humbled by how hard your lives have been compared to mine. Especially you, JJ. And, of course, I'm still very ashamed of what I did in that first barbershop formation, Mike. But I'll never forget the way you guys cheered for me when I got lucky and hit the target on that first range day. First time I ever felt like part of any team. Hell, we may never see each other again after next Friday, but I'll always consider you guys among my best friends."

Smeall meant what he said. But the level of luxury that Sharkey, Howard, and Stott had experienced over the past seventy-two hours made them understand that Barry Smeall lived in a world to which they simply could not relate.

"Barry, I got to ask you! Is your mom a lot younger than your dad?" Stott asked.

Barry laughed loudly at the question. "No, just a couple of years. My mom's a real live wire! Always has been! She's very kind and tenderhearted but projects that 'in-your-face' attitude and flirts with everyone. I think she wanted to have more than two kids, so she reaches out to young people. Unfortunately, she and my sister don't really get along that well because my sister's a totally spoiled brat! But my parents truly had one of the best weekends of their lives! They told me so! Thanks!"

Once again, Smeall was thanking Stott, JJ, Howie, and Allsmeir for letting his family spend a small fortune on them.

Howard hadn't said a word except "thank you" since leaving the airport. "Barry, guys, I believe there is hope for the world! You all have made me believe we can live together, after all."

"What are you talkin' about, Howie?" JJ asked.

"JJ, you ask me that again in about six months if you don't understand by then," Big Howie said.

The trainees stopped at the Black Horse Inn outside Trenton, New Jersey, and had yet another great meal, just the five of them. When they were finished, Sharkey asked for the check.

"It has been previously arranged," said the waiter.

The limo dropped the soldiers back in front of D Barrack at 1920 hours on Labor Day, September 2, 1963. There at the desk in the Orderly Room was Corporal George waiting for the troopers from Training Company D to return from their three-day passes. "What's this? You sissies got civvies? Are you out of your fuckin' minds? Top will kick your asses, dickheads!"

"But only if you tell him, Corporal, and that is not in your best interest." Sharkey's statement surprised Corporal George. As he got up to scream at them, Big Howie put his hands on the corporal's shoulders and gently but firmly helped him sit back down.

"You're just an E-4, mister. Think about it," was all Howard said.

The men went back to their respective squad bays and began squaring away their gear for the last week of basic training. Over the course of the evening, the rest of the troopers from Company D returned from whatever they had done on their first army leave and prepared for four more days with First Sergeant Turner.

At 0500 hours on Tuesday, September 3, 1963, the bugle played reveille on the barrack speakers, and Stott and his buddies were back at it—PT, the morning run, and then the mess hall for morning chow. Over the next four days, the company was trucked to different ranges where they received initial instruction and fired the M-60 light machine gun and the Colt .45 pistol. On the last Friday, they once again practiced with the M-14s that they had qualified with, but it was anticlimactic.

At the end of the eighth Friday of basic training, D Company assembled for words of wisdom from Captain Hargrove. "Great job, men! All of you standing here have made it! Tomorrow morning we'll hold a final formation where you'll get your training completion ribbon and the appropriate M-14 qualification badge. Also, we assign each man his next duty station for training in your Military Occupational Specialty. Most of you will leave immediately for that post, so this is your last night together. Pack up your personal gear, turn in your steel pots and other field equipment following this formation. Be ready to leave for your next post tomorrow! I'll be traveling to the West Point-Purdue football game later tonight, so good-bye and good luck! First Sergeant Turner, take over!"

D Company came to attention and saluted their first commanding officer, remaining in formation after the captain and his attending lieutenants departed.

First Sergeant Turner offered his summation. "Well, girls, this was different! I've done dozens of basic trainings, and you guys got off easier than any group yet! I must be getting soft in my old age! And this new format is bullshit! Way too easy! But you made it, and it's official! Dress shoes and khakis with garrison caps tomorrow, ready to travel! Be ready to roll to your next training base when you fall out for morning formation, which, by the way, will be at 0900 hours!"

That brought a cheer from the boys in Training Company D as they realized they'd done their last morning run with First Sergeant Turner.

"Given that we have a dick-headed private named Hale in this company, I hesitate to say this, but, any questions?"

Even Hale knew by then to keep his mouth shut.

"Awright, ladies! 0900 hours! Eat before if you wanna! Dismissed!" Turner executed that smart right face that he was famous for and strode away.

"Geez! It's over! How about that?" Syl Mobliano said.

By tradition, the recruits were allowed to go to the NCO club for beer that night, but most got packed up in anticipation of changing bases the next day. Allsmeir, Hale, Howard, Mobliano, Sharkey, Smeall, and Stott ate supper in the mess hall, and then got Cokes from the PX and sat outside talking.

"Has it really been eight weeks? Went by so fast!" Eddy Hale exclaimed.

"Eight weeks with you asking dumb-ass questions was like eight months!" Sharkey said.

The friends all laughed.

"Think we'll keep in touch?" Barry Smeall asked.

"Probably not, but let's at least say we'll try," Mobs commented.

"Does everybody know for sure what MOS they got?" Hale asked.

That surprised his friends because the sergeants had told everyone what MOS they were slated for. Mobliano knew where he was going because he had been pre-assigned to Fort Benning, Georgia, for Officer's Candidate School.

"You don't know, Hale?" Smeall asked.

"No, do you?"

"Yeah, Finance Clerk School at Fort Harrison near Indianapolis," responded Smeall.

"Military Police School at Fort McClellan," said Howard.

"Stott and me are 11-B's, Advanced Infantry Training, but we don't know where yet," Sharkey said. "We're hoping it'll be to the same place. How about you, Allsmeir?"

"I got totally fucked! I've been assigned to Artillery Training at Fort Sill, Oklahoma! Some goddamn deal I made, volunteering!" Larry Allsmeir had kept this to himself until then.

"Maybe they're sending me directly to Sniper School!" Fast Eddy Hale speculated.

That made all his friends except Allsmeir laugh. "Fat chance, Hale! You only qualified 'marksman'!" said JJ. 'Marksman' was the lowest of the three M-14 qualifying categories.

"I thought you signed up for infantry," Stott said to Eddy.

"I did. All the guys like you and Sharkey have been told they're going to AIT, but the sarge says there's no word on me, yet."

"Probably have to repeat basic for being a smart-ass, Hale," Smeall observed.

"Actually, Ed, I'll always remember you standing there in your pink panties and chrome liner during that first M-14 class," Mike said. All but Hale got a good laugh at the reminder, even the still pissed-off Allsmeir.

Attempting to change the focus, Fast Eddy said, "Remember how we all met because of Stott's fight with Howard!"

"Come on, Hale! Don't bring that up! Besides, it was your fault, anyway, for callin' me a nigger! You started it! Come to think of it, all the trouble D Company trainees had was because of you!" Big Howie said.

"Stott, you never told us what the captain and Sergeant Turner talked to you about that night after the march to bivouac. What was it?" Smeall wanted to know.

All six of his buddies focused on Stott. "It was personal, guys. And I want to keep it that way."

"Come on, Stott! Tell us!" insisted Hale.

"Shut up, Hale! He said it was personal!" Sharkey's tone indicated he might want to take another swing at Fast Ed.

"Come on, you two! Let's not end basic the way it started with you two going at it," Mobliano said. "I want you guys to think about me tomorrow night because as you're all heading for your new training posts, I'll be with my Maria! I got ten days before OCS starts, so I got a ten-day leave! How about that?"

"Officers get all the breaks!" complained Hale.

"You going to Brooklyn right after formation tomorrow, Mobs?" JJ asked.

"Yeah, I'm going to try to catch the 1300, I mean 1:00 p.m. bus!" Mobs said.

Mike knew exactly what Sharkey was thinking! If they had any time off, he wanted to head for Brooklyn, too! Both had the goddesses on their minds.

"Well, gee, JJ! You wouldn't be thinking about bothering my little sister, would you, kid?" Mobs teased.

"Oh, so now I'm a kid, huh, Mobs! I'm starting to think you officers are all a pain in the ass!" They all laughed at Sharkey, especially Mobs.

"What are you laughing at, Stott? I hear you made arrangements to see my other little sister! I'm gonna have to keep an eye on both of you!" Mobs continued.

"Briegeita told you that?" Mike asked.

"Yes, she did, and I've told all my brothers to watch out for both of you! Seriously, you both know you are always welcome at the Moblianos'," Syl stated.

"So what do y'all remember most about basic?" Big Howie asked.

They all thought about Howie's question for a while, but for Mike Stott the answer was obvious. "The most memorable part of basic training didn't happen at Fort Dix. It was the weekend we spent in New York with Barry's folks! I saw and did things I couldn't have dreamed of before that weekend! First hotel I ever stayed in was the Plaza! Incredible! But the one thing I will never, ever forget is that night in Chinatown when JJ started speaking Chinese! Allsmeir's talent surprised me, but he's a big college man! When Sharkey started talking, it was magical! And the affect on everyone in the restaurant! Especially Milt and Bessy! And then the asshole also speaks Italian so he could talk to Briggetta and Briegeita! I have to admit that JJ's language exhibition was the most memorable part of my basic training experience!"

"I didn't get to see JJ perform at the restaurant, but I gotta agree with Stott! JJ worked ten times harder than the rest of us these past eight weeks, and I know he's smarter than me! And I'm a genius! Seriously, for a seventeen-year-old guy to speak seven languages having never left Westchester County is absolutely amazing! Plus, he gained weight in basic! Now, if I can just keep him away from my little sister, I'll always remember him as a great friend!" said Syl.

"What's the seventh language?" Stott demanded. "I know about his Latin, Italian, three Chinese dialects and English, but what's the seventh? Damn!"

"Sharkey, you holding out on your best friend?" Mobs asked JJ.

"Yeah, Sharkey, what's the seventh? I'm starting to get an inferiority complex!" Allsmeir admitted.

Sharkey remained silent, pissing Stott off once again.

"Goddamn it, Sharkey! Tell me! What's the other language? I thought we had a deal!" Mike was truly mad.

"Tell you what, Stott! Tell us what Captain Hargrove and Sergeant Turner talked to you about, and I'll tell you about my other languages! And we do have a deal!" JJ was becoming a real pain in the ass!

"Yeah, Stott! I had to stand there in panties because of you, so you owe me an answer!" Hale put in his two-cent's worth.

"It's the one big mystery of basic, Mike. Are you ashamed of something?" Syl Mobliano knew exactly the right words to get to Stott. "If you fess up, maybe I'll put in a good word for you with my sister!"

All eyes focused on Mike. What is there about other people's business that makes humans so curious? Stott would have held out on this group of busybodies until JJ said, "Please, Mike. Don't hold out on me. I speak Spanish and French. Don't be impressed. Languages seem to be the one thing that comes easy for me."

"Spanish and French! Damn!" Allsmeir voiced what all were thinking.

"Wait a minute!" screamed Hale. "I know what it is!"

Before Fast Eddy could say anything, Sharkey grabbed him in a headlock and capped his other hand over Hale's mouth.

"Nobody asked you," was all Sharkey said.

"All right, all right! JJ, let him go! Let's not ruin this last night. And Hale probably does know the answer, so I might as well tell you all. As he was going over the company roster that night, Sergeant Turner realized that he had known someone with my same last name. They called me to their table to ask me if I had a brother named James William Stott. I did. That was my oldest brother, who was killed in Korea. He was a captain in the Tenth Rangers. I guess Sergeant Turner served under my brother. My brother was posthumously awarded the Congressional Medal of Honor. Sergeant Turner said maybe someday he would talk to me about him," Stott said.

It seemed that the silence lasted a very long time. Syl spoke first, "Geez, Mike! That's incredible! That's the most distinguished honor a soldier can earn. You must be extremely proud."

Sharkey said, "You have some standard to live up to, Mike."

As the soldiers headed into D for the last time, JJ softly said to Stott, "I want to hear all that you know about your brother. Now."

John Sharkey and Mike Stott stayed up for a long time talking about Captain James William Stott, Congressional Medal of Honor winner, and their future in the army.

Morning formation held yet a few more surprises, the biggest of which was Private Fast Eddy Hale's MOS assignment. Sergeant Turner was reading off the names and next duty stations, but he had skipped over Hale. Sharkey and Stott were both assigned to the same Advanced Infantry Training Company right there at Fort Dix. Close to the goddesses!

After every man except Hale had received his orders, all troopers were waiting to hear Hale's fate. Sergeant Turner spoke. "Not very often that the army surprises me, but this takes the fucking cake! Of all the cocksucking travesties of justice I ever heard of, this is the worst! Private Eddy Fucking Loudmouthed Hale is hereby assigned to Army Intelligence Training at Fort Monmouth, New Jersey! What's that big word the captain used? Oxymoron? Jesus Fucking Christ! Hale in Intelligence is like an officer working! Just don't make any sense! Any questions?" Sergeant Turner glared directly at Hale.

Silence, thank God!

"Dismissed! Get the fuck out of my military sight! Except for Privates Stott and Sharkey! I'll see you dickheads in the orderly room, now!" said Turner.

Holy shit! Now what?

The troopers had said their goodbyes and most made tracks for the bus stations and airports. Big Howie had a flight to Birmingham, Alabama, the following day, so he was hanging around waiting for Sharkey and Stott. Everyone else left.

Mike and JJ, duffel bags in tow, reported as instructed to the orderly room in D Barrack. First Sergeant Virgil T. Turner was sitting behind the desk with his highly polished jump boots carefully balanced on one corner of the desk so as not to mess up their shine. It was the most relaxed they had seen Turner. Sharkey and Stott naturally came to attention as they entered the room.

"At ease, assholes! Do I look like a fuckin' officer? Pull up those two folding chairs and sit down. Sharkey, how fuckin' tall are you? How'd you get in my army anyway? Did you somehow fake your height?" Sergeant Turner could be cruel.

The thought that someone could fake his height made Stott laugh. Big mistake!

"What the fuck are you laughin' at, dickhead? Did I say something funny? You think I'm funny, Stott?"

"No, First Sergeant! I just don't see how anyone could fake his height, Sergeant," Mike said.

"Maybe not! But if anyone could, it would be some dickhead like one of you! I ask again, how tall are you, Private Sharkey? I want a fuckin' answer!"

"First Sergeant, I'm now five-feet, four and a-half inches! I grew two and a-half inches in the last eight weeks, Sergeant!" JJ screamed out.

"Bullshit! Nobody grows that much in eight weeks! Are you fuckin' with me, boy? 'Cause if you're fuckin' with me, I'll take you outside and kick your ass right fuckin' now!"

"No, First Sergeant! I grew more than two inches and gained seventeen pounds!"

"Bullshit! Did this little dickhead really grow that much, Stott?" Turner asked Stott.

"Yes, First Sergeant, I believe he did!" Mike said.

"Goddamn it! I didn't order you assholes here to talk about how fuckin' tall Sharkey is! Sit fuckin' down! Now! Listen up, privates! You two dickheads did something we hardly ever see! You both fired perfect qualifying rounds with your M-14s in basic fuckin' training! Wouldn't have believed it if I hadn't seen it myself! I guess, Stott, I can understand you doin' it, but how this little dickhead managed it, I'll never fuckin' know!"

"First Sergeant Turner! Stott taught me, Sergeant! And I could do it again, anytime, Sergeant!" JJ shouted.

"Shut up, goddamn it, Sharkey! You're startin' to irritate me! Keep your fuckin' mouths shut and listen, get it? As I was saying before you started running your mouths, the fact is you both managed perfect scores on Echo Range. Captain Hargrove pulled some strings and got you both assigned to Advanced Infantry Training School here at Dix. You start 11-B training Monday morning in the same AIT Company, but right now I've got a question for you both. How serious are you about the army? You first, Stott."

"I'm serious, First Sergeant! But, to be honest, I'm also a little scared about Vietnam!" Stott said.

It got very quiet in the orderly room. Sergeant Turner just kept his eyes locked on Mike's. Finally, he spoke. "Stott, your brother was the bravest man I've ever known. Absolutely fuckin' fearless! If you ever admit to being scared again, I'll shoot you myself! What about you, hot shot? Are you both serious and scared, too?"

"No, First Sergeant! I'm serious, but I'm not scared! And neither is Stott, really!" Sharkey said.

First Sergeant Turner sat there staring back at Sharkey and Stott for a very long time. Finally, Turner spoke. "You'd be stupid not to be scared about Vietnam, boys, but you can never admit to being scared if you're going to make it in this man's army. I've been in the army for almost twenty-three years. Went in as soon as I could after World War II started. I was seventeen, just like you dickheads. Saw my first combat in Africa with Third Army and then went in with the first wave at Omaha wearing Ranger Patches and three stripes. What a cluster fuck! More guys in my unit died on the beach than made it up the hill! I have no fucking idea why I'm still alive after that day, but somehow I'm still here.

I stayed in when II was over 'cause I just didn't have anywhere else to go. Was about to get out when Korea heated up, and I figured I'd get extended anyway, so I signed on for six more years. Two years of combat in Korea, and I've already been to Nam twice. Probably go again soon. Fact is, I wouldn't be talking to you dickheads now if Stott's brother hadn't done what he did, so I'm talking to you boys more than I should! Still can't believe Stottie had a brother as young as you, but here you are, in my fuckin' training company! What are the odds?

So listen the fuck up! Some of the shit-brained officers in the Pentagon are trying to reorganize the army for what they call the new dynamics of war! Recon in Nam, if nothin' else, has taught us that conventional infantry tactics don't work very well in that hellhole of a country. And the indigenous people just could be the key to shuttin' down the bad guys' supply lines, so the generals' brain trust in Washington is willing to try some different approaches."

"You mean like the Special Forces?" Sharkey interrupted First Sergeant Turner.

"What the fuck do know about that?" Turner demanded.

Sharkey told Turner about his buddy, Sergeant Bill Patterson.

"So you're an orphan?" Turner asked Sharkey when he finished his story.

"Yes, First Sergeant," JJ said.

Again, Sergeant Turner sat and stared at Sharkey for what seemed like a long time. "No family at all?" he asked John.

"No, Sergeant, but Stott here, is my best friend. We're going to be lifers together, just like you. And what did you mean about the 'indigenous people'?" JJ asked.

Mike and JJ endured another lengthy silence as the first sergeant seemed to reflect on what he had just heard.

"Back to why I called you in here, dickheads! Captain Hargrove and me noticed you both volunteered for jump school after AIT, so here's the deal. Captain pulled some strings and got you pre-assigned to jump school at Benning starting Monday, November 4. So, if you don't fuck up or shoot somebody in AIT, you're going straight to bird shit school from here. No time off, dickin' around waiting for a unit. If, and it's a big if with you two dickheads, you keep your noses clean through jump training you might have a chance to volunteer for an experimental program that the army is trying to kick off at the first of the year, get it?" Turner asked.

"What program, First Sergeant?" JJ beat Mike to the question.

"Can't tell you yet, and you've got to prove yourselves between now and then. But this is no bullshit. You two fit a certain profile that the army's looking for, and your marksmanship didn't hurt you none! Hargrove got his major's slot back in the Tenth Rangers startin' November 1. Let's just say that the captain, er, major might be involved in this new deal, okay? So keep working hard, don't fuck up, and maybe you'll make me proud! You both got to report to Company A, AIT I, right down the street there, by 1700 hours tomorrow. If you go see First Sergeant Macleod over there right now you can sign in, square away your gear, put on those faggot civvies I hear you own, and fuck off until reveille at 0500 Monday! Get out of my military sight before I decide to kick both your asses on general principles!"

"First Sergeant, how'd you know about our civvies? And you didn't tell us about the indigenous people." Mike thought JJ knew better, but he asked the question anyway.

"I know fuckin' everything, dickhead! Now move it or I'll re-fuckin'-cycle you both, 'experts' or fuckin' not!"

The two buddies beat it out the door.

"JJ, are you fuckin' nuts? Why'd you ask him about the civvies?" Mike asked.

"Because I wanted to see his reaction! Corporal George must have told him about our civvies, but he didn't rat Big

Howie out for sittin' him back in his chair! That's interesting!" Sharkey analyzed everything.

As Mike and JJ rounded the corner there was Big Howie, waiting for them. "What's up guys? Get your asses chewed out? Why you grinning like that, JJ?" he asked.

"Cause Sergeant Turner told me to look you up and kick your ass, and now I've found you!" With that Sharkey feigned going after Howard, but Big Howie was way ahead of him. Howard pitched his fully-loaded duffel bag right at JJ who had no choice but grab it in self-defense. As JJ grabbed the eighty pound bag, Big Howie grabbed JJ and the duffel in a big bear hug and exclaimed, "What now, tough guy?"

The sight of Howie holding JJ and the duffel about three feet off the ground as Sharkey flailed about helplessly was hilarious! Mike's laughter, of course, made Howard laugh and Sharkey madder.

"Goddamn it, Howie, that was a cheap trick! But now you're in trouble because you can't hold me up here forever, and when you put me down I'll kick your ass back to Mississippi!" Sharkey screamed.

First Sergeant Turner rounded the corner and saw Sharkey's predicament and Stott howling with laughter.

"Two minutes after I tell you to keep out of trouble and you're out here fighting, Sharkey? Jesus fuckin' Christ! Stott, I am hereby promoting you to E-2! Right now, on the spot! Your first order is to get these two dumb-ass privates under control or you all go to the stockade! Goddamn!" Turner walked away shaking his head.

"You two heard the first sergeant! Attention!" Mike screamed.

It worked! Howie dropped JJ and they both stood at attention! But just until Turner got out of sight. "Okay, JJ, you owe me a month's pay and a steak dinner 'cause I got promoted first! Howie, you're my witness! JJ owes me, right?" Mike said.

Even Sharkey had to laugh! "Come on, guys! Let's dump our gear at AIT and head for NYC!"

"Man, I fly out of Newark at 1535 hours tomorrow, and I can't miss that flight! I'll have to take all my gear!" Big Howie said.

"I got it!" JJ yelled. "We'll catch the bus to Newark Airport, you can check your duffel with the airline and then you just have to get yourself back to catch your flight! That's an easy ride back to Newark on a bus or even a cab! From Newark we go right to Brooklyn, er, I mean the city."

But when JJ called Briggetta from Newark Airport he learned the girls were out in the Hamptons with their cousins.

JJ, Big Howie, and Mike spent that night walking the streets of Manhattan. They chipped in and got one cheap hotel room, but they should have saved their money! The three friends had a big steak dinner and drank a lot of beer. They went back to that area just off Times Square where they had seen the working girls with the Smealls, but the ladies weren't interested in three young soldiers on foot instead of in a limo! Finally, around 5:00 a.m., as they were staggering back trying to find their room, the boys ran into a hooker who worked the hotel. Sharkey talked her into doing all three for one low price! Or did she talk them into it? Mike, JJ, and Big Howie lost their virginity to the same New York City working girl early on Sunday morning, September 7, 1963. She finally left their room at about 9:00 a.m. after she talked Big Howie into bringing coffee and Danish for all of them!

Seeing her in the morning light sobered all three boys right up! After she left, they flipped a coin to see who got to shower first! Exiting his shower, Big Howie started the conversation. "So let me get this straight. All that crap you guys and Hale were telling me about all the girls you had was bullshit? That was the first piece of ass you ever had? Both of you? And your first turns out to be a thirty-dollar-a-night New York City whore that we shared?"

Sharkey and Stott looked at each other and started to laugh. "Yes to all four questions, dickhead! So what!" JJ said.

"So all that talk about eating pussy was lies?" Howie wouldn't stop.

"Absolutely!" JJ and Mike were now laughing hysterically. "But you believed it!"

Just for a minute, Mike feared Big Howie might come after them. But then he started laughing, too. "So the first time any of us got laid just happened! With a whore in NYC! You white guys are truly full of shit!"

"Tell you what, Howard! We keep this between the three of us and me and Stott won't remind you that you went third! Change the subject. How did you get assigned to Military Police Training? I thought you were going to AIT with us," JJ said to Howie.

"Beats me! I was as surprised as anybody. Maybe because of my size?" Howie speculated.

"Good thing the army doesn't know about your glass jaw!" JJ teased Howie.

"But they do, JJ! One night toward the end of bivouac Sergeant Turner called me to the orderly tent and asked me about my fight with Mike in the reception center. He knew all about it, he just wanted to hear about it from my side. After I told him, he asked me how come we became friends. I told him it was because Mike made sure it ended right after the fight. I mean, you know, Mike worked hard to put it behind us. Then he asked me about you two guys, you know, being best friends but kind of rivals. The sarge seemed to be aware of everything happening in the company."

"So, when you're an MP, will you look up Hale and arrest him for being a wiseass all through basic?" JJ asked.

"He'll probably be a general by then!" Howie exclaimed.

JJ, Mike, and Howie checked out of the scene of the crime and said good-bye at the bus station. Howard headed for the airport, and, after a couple more hours walking around the theater district, JJ and Mike took the Wright's Town Bus back to Fort Dix to begin Advanced Infantry Training.

Chapter Twenty-Two

Mike and JJ started AIT at 0500 hours on Monday, September 9, 1963. First Sergeant Mike Macleod ran a very different training environment than Sergeant Turner had. Maybe it just seemed easier after basic, but AIT was pure fun! They did PT and a morning run every day and had to jump when any NCO spoke, but mostly AIT trainees focused on infantry weapons and tactics.

For the entire eight weeks of Advanced Infantry Training, the soldiers stayed in A Barrack, which was newer and nicer than D Barrack in basic. They never went to the field! The trainees posted fire guard every night, but never got KP! Sharkey and Stott were assigned to different squads but talked every night and were in all the same classes. AIT took on a much more serious tone as the officers and NCOs talked constantly about Vietnam, encouraging the men to take the training to heart because their lives would depend on being good infantrymen.

During Advanced Infantry School, RA's, men that had volunteered for three or more years, were treated very differently than US's, ER's, and NG's, especially during weapons training. The instructors made sure that RA's were proficient with the M-60 light machine gun and Colt .45 pistol. Trainees also received 105 mortar training and learned to throw grenades.

Mike and JJ crawled on their bellies under low-strung, barbed wire during nighttime, live-fire exercises as the range NCO's fired M-60s and AK-47s overhead. Every sixth round was a tracer shell so they could see the stream of the bullets streak by only a few yards above their heads.

"If you panic and stand up, you're dead!" the sergeants screamed out over their bullhorns.

There was a vertical obstacle course that required troopers to climb up progressively wider-spaced rungs until, at the top, one literally had to stand up and reach for the top rung while fifty to sixty feet in the air. At first, there was a safety net to catch those who fell, as many did. By the middle of the sixth week, the safety net was removed. Topping the course was truly difficult for troopers who were scared of height. One man in their unit fell from about forty feet up and broke his leg as well as arm. As the medics were taking him away, First Sergeant Macleod explained, "That trooper lost his concentration. Lose it in combat and you die."

The soldiers never saw that trooper again. Training took on a more serious tone.

AIT was scheduled to be an eight-week course, six days a week. The men had Sundays off and were not restricted to post, but most were exhausted by Saturday night and spent Sundays recovering and resting up.

At the end of week one, Sharkey came to Mike with a plan. "Look, Mike, I owe you for teaching me to instinct-shoot the M-14 in basic. There's something I'd like to do for you now that we have a little time at nights before lights out and all day Sunday. Here's my offer: I'm going to teach you ten Chinese words every day. Just ten! But we'll review the previous day's words every night and build on what you remember. If you are as smart as I think you are, you'll know maybe five hundred Chinese words by the end if AIT! Then you can say you speak Chinese! If you can use five hundred words, you can basically communicate with people, sort of. What do you think? Will you try it?"

"Are you nuts? I can't learn Chinese! You started when you were four, and it took you, what, five or six years?" Stott thought JJ had lost it.

"Look, Mike. Just ten words a day. Just sound association. I know some tricks! You can do it! It would mean more than I can explain if you would do it. Please!" Sharkey pleaded.

It was the first time JJ had asked Mike for anything since they had met. Sharkey was standing right in front of Stott with his arms folded across his chest, staring into Mike's eyes.

"Please, Mike," Sharkey said again.

"All right, I'll try, but don't get your hopes up! I took French for two years in high school, and all I remember are cuss words!" Stott said.

"Great! Here we go!" Sharkey coached Stott right up until lights out. Mike was truly surprised at JJ's patience. At 2200 hours, lights out, on night one, Mike had eighteen words memorized. He went to sleep going over the sounds in his mind and hoped to God he would remember any of them by reveille!

At the end of week six, Saturday, October 19, Sergeant Macleod decided to give his AIT Company the afternoon off. "I'm tired of looking at you assholes," the First Sergeant explained at 1100 hours that morning. "Tell you what, we're done until 0500 Monday morning. Go to town if you want, but don't fuck up and get back late! I notice some of you dickheads have civvies tucked away where you think I don't see 'em. Wear 'em if you want, but you'll have a harder time getting back on post late Sunday or early Monday in civvies! Get out of my military sight!"

Sharkey and Stott met in the front of Mike's squad bay. "Brooklyn, right?" Sharkey said.

"Okay, but I haven't talked to Briegeita since that night of Mobs' party. She probably doesn't even remember me!"

"Probably not, but Briggetta remembers me! We're gonna meet 'em at a malt shop about a half mile from their house! I got the address, now move your ass! We can still make the noon bus!" said Sharkey.

Mike and JJ just made the bus to the Port Authority bus station in Manhattan. As they rode up the New Jersey Turnpike toward New York City, the trees were close to peak color on a beautiful, cool autumn afternoon.

"Okay, before we really start to relax, let's review your Chinese!" JJ proclaimed. He wouldn't let up! After about forty-five minutes and several hundred words, Sharkey said, "I'll be damned! You're doing pretty good for a hick from Ohio!"

"That's it! I'm done for the day! You're giving me a head-ache, and then you call me names! You're starting to remind me of Fast Eddy Hale!" said Stott.

The two friends rode in silence for a long time. "You're pretty quiet for a guy going to see his girlfriend." Mike tried to get Sharkey stirred up.

"You know, Mike, we'll be through AIT in two weeks. Then we head for jump school at Fort Benning. This may be the last time we get to New York for a long time, maybe forever. I have mixed emotions about seeing Briggetta again. She's real cute, but we don't have a future, and I know it. Christ, she's in college! Maybe we should just, you know, find a working girl like we did before and skip going to Brooklyn," Sharkey said.

JJ's words surprised Mike. Sharkey didn't seem disap-pointed about Briggetta, though he had really liked her. "Come on JJ, what's up? I thought you were really anxious to see her again. What's wrong?" asked Stott.

"I guess the reality of our situation, yours and mine, hit me looking out the bus window just now. After jump school, we could get assigned to an airborne unit and be in Vietnam by Christmas! And here we are going to have malts with a couple of college freshmen! We'll be living in a very differ-ent world from them! Seems silly to go see them. What do you think?"

"Well, JJ, you sure took the fun out of our weekend pass! But I know what you mean. I got to tell you, though, our ex-perience with that whore didn't set so well with me. I spent the next three weeks hoping my dick wouldn't fall off from some God-awful disease! Let's go see the girls and just talk to them and have some fun! It's not like you're gonna ask Briggetta to marry you, right?" Stott teased.

That brought a smile to JJ's face. "That's for sure! Okay, you're right! Sorry to be a party pooper!"

It was the first time Sharkey had revealed his melancholy side to Mike, and it reminded Stott once again how differ-ent their backgrounds were. Mike had not gotten homesick in the army, mostly because he had been kept so busy. And then that incredible weekend with the Smealls filled his only off time. But Sharkey had no home to miss! That realization really jolted Mike.

"JJ, what do you think about that special program Sergeant Turner told us about? You think it's for real? Or was he just working us to stay in line?" Mike asked.

"I think there's something to it, Mike. You know, we'll be E-3s after jump school. If we get assigned to an airborne unit we'll just be airborne grunts for a long time. I want to try for anything that gets us ahead in the army, so I'm hoping it's for real," said Sharkey.

"If Hargrove's a major back in the Tenth Rangers, does that mean the special program would be run by the Rangers? I hear that's really tough training!" Stott told his friend.

"But your brother did it, so you can too!" Sharkey brought up Mike's brother every chance he got.

"Yeah, I guess, but is that what you want, JJ?" Mike asked.

"Sergeant Turner's marching songs got to me! I keep hearing 'I want to be an Airborne Ranger' playing in my head! Yeah, I'd go for that if I got the chance," Sharkey said.

Stott sensed that he had lightened JJ's spirits talking about their military opportunities. As they arrived at the Port Authority, Mike just couldn't resist messing with JJ a little bit more.

As they exited the bus, Mike said, "I don't know, JJ, there may be a minimum height requirement for Ranger training!"

"That's it, goddamn it! I'm gonna kick your ass right here, right now!" Sharkey screamed, drawing the attention of one of New York City's finest, who was watching people depart from the buses.

"Quiet, JJ! There's a cop right behind you!" Stott pointed out.

"I don't give a damn! I'm kickin' your ass right here!" JJ was fired up.

"Pipe down, son. There'll be no fighting on my watch!" the big cop said to JJ.

Sharkey turned to look at the source of that comment and had to look up considerably at the policeman.

"It's nothing, officer. He was just kidding me!" Mike said.

"Move on, troopers and don't land in one of my jails! The chow's worse than army food!" The cop sized them up immediately.

As they moved away, JJ said, "Goddamn it, Stott! You almost got us in trouble! I'm still gonna kick your ass, but later!"

"Better grow about another foot, dickhead!"

Sharkey spun around, but there was the cop, right behind them!

"Later!" Sharkey reminded Mike of that first day in the army when JJ and Syl had been mad at him.

Sharkey decided to splurge and take a cab to Brooklyn. As they hopped in the taxi, JJ cooled down. "You really like to mess with me, don't you Stott? But you only do it when we're alone. Why?"

"I don't want to embarrass you, but somebody has to keep you humble. That's my job! It's part of our pact!" said Stott.

"Goddamn it!" was all Sharkey said all the way to Brooklyn until he gave the driver the street address.

"That's not a bar or a whorehouse, son, that's a malt shop!" the driver said.

"Why'd you say that?" JJ asked.

"Well, it's obvious you're young soldiers, so I figured you were going to drink or get laid," returned the driver matter-of-factly.

The cab ride cost ten dollars; Stott lost the coin flip to see who paid.

JJ called Briggetta from the phone booth outside the malt shop at 1445 hours, 2:45 p.m. "They're on the way," JJ told Mike. "They said they have a surprise for us and to wait outside!" Sharkey was back in good spirits. Stott, on the other hand, was apprehensive about seeing Briegeita. That apprehension melted away immediately, however, about two minutes later.

Briggetta and Briegeita pulled up in front of the malt shop in a brand new, shiny red Chevrolet Impala SS convertible with the top down and rock and roll music blaring from the radio! Both girls had their hair wrapped up in bandannas and the boys couldn't tell one from the other. But the passenger jumped out and gave JJ a big kiss, so Mike assumed that was Briggetta!

"Look what we got for out eighteenth birthday! Isn't it cool? And we both just got our licenses! Stop standing there with that dumb look on your faces! Come on, get in!" Briggetta exclaimed.

JJ and Mike exchanged glances, trying to comprehend the girls and their new car. JJ got in the back seat with Briggetta, and Mike sat shotgun. Briegeita leaned over and kissed him on the cheek and said, "Welcome back to Brooklyn, honey!"

Mike Stott was too happy to speak!

"Where do you want to go? We have to be home by eleven thirty, but we're all yours until then!" Briegeita said.

Mike finally managed, "Is this really your car?"

"Sure, silly," she said. "You think because we're from Brooklyn we stole it or something? Our folks said to say hello and Syl called from Fort Benning just a while ago. He said we better watch out for you, Mr. Stott, because JJ's a gentleman, but he's not so sure about you! I told him I hope he's right!"

Mike was completely ecstatic. Then he blew it! "What motor does this have in it?"

From the backseat, Briggetta yelled, "Here you are with two beautiful Italian girls in their convertible and you want to know about a motor? Are you retarded or something, Stott?"

JJ, laughing heartily, said, "You know, I'm beginning to think he is! He was worried that Briegeita wouldn't remember him! And now he asks about your car's motor? You gotta wonder about these guys from Ohio!"

They were still setting at the curb in front of the malt shop. "I ask again, where do you guys want to go? We know our way around!" said Briegeita.

"I bet you do!" said JJ. "I've never been in a convertible before, so I'll enjoy anywhere just looking up at the sky!"

Stott was still intrigued with the car. It had red vinyl interior with bucket seats in front separated by a console. As Briegeita pulled away, she gassed it pretty good and made the tires squeal!

"Must be a 327," Mike said.

"One more comment about the car and I'm putting you out at the next corner! Tell me you're glad to see me and that I look cute!" Briegeita demanded.

"You look beautiful, and I am glad to see you. How's Syl doing in OCS?" Mike asked.

"Syl's always fine! Do you guys have any money or do we have to take you to dinner?" she teased.

From the back, Briggetta said, "I know! Let's take a ride to Westchester! We can find one of those country inns and eat and talk. We can barely hear you back here with the wind rushing by!"

"Great idea!" Briegeita changed directions and said, "Get out money for tolls! Mikey, do you want to drive?"

"Huh, me drive? I have no idea where I'm going!" said Stott.

"You know how to drive?" Sharkey yelled from the back.

"Well, yeah, but I never drove in a city like this!" Mike really didn't want to take the wheel.

"Okay, I'll drive; I love driving!" said Briegeita. By this time, they were crossing a bridge over both water and a lot of railroad tracks.

"Bye-bye Brooklyn, hello Bronx! Next stop, Westchester!" Briegeita shouted.

She really was a pretty good driver and not at all afraid to push the gas pedal. "How long have you been driving?" Mike asked.

"About two weeks!" she said, after turning onto a divided highway that seemed to take them quickly out of the city.

"You know where to go?" Mike asked.

"Sort of," she said. "Isn't this fun?"

It was. Sharkey and Briggetta had their heads together, talking in the back. Mike and Briegeita couldn't hear them at all because of the wind noise.

"Syl tells us you are both lifers in the army. Is that right Mike?" Briegeita asked.

"Well, yeah, I guess right now we're both thinking that way. JJ is more sure about it than me. All he talks about is being the best soldier in the army."

As the foursome drove past a series of reservoirs on Route 22, Stott saw a sign that read "Bedford, 8 Miles."

"Hey JJ! Isn't Bedford the town you grew up in?" Mike yelled.

"Yeah, why?" responded Sharkey.

"Cause we're almost there!" Briegeita and Mike said at the same time.

"What?" screamed JJ.

"Well, that last sign read 'Bedford, 8 Miles,' and that was about two miles back as fast as she's going!" Stott said. He turned to look at Sharkey and saw a completely bewildered look on his buddy's face.

"Oh, John! Let's stop and see your orphanage!" Briggetta exclaimed.

Mike realized they had been set up; it was no coincidence that they had found their way to Bedford! But he didn't think Sharkey had caught on. JJ was speechless and looked befuddled.

JJ said, "We could if you really want to."

The town of Bedford was little more than a crossroads with quaint little shops and restaurants. There was one gas station.

"Which way do I turn, John?" Briegeita asked.

"Just stay on twenty-two, and you'll see St. Agnes about a mile up on the right."

The sun was fading fast and it was getting a little cold with the top down. They had rolled up the windows a ways back and that made it easier to hear back and forth between the front and rear seats. Briegeita drove into St. Agnes through a stone archway that looked ancient. There were rusted black wrought iron gates that hadn't been moved for a very long time. A series of buildings surrounded what appeared to be a main house made of block granite. Strangely, there was no one in sight; neither children nor nuns.

"Geez, JJ, it looks deserted," Mike said.

"No, it's Saturday, so everyone's at four o'clock mass. They'll be coming out soon."

As if on cue, the doors to the chapel swung open, and children began streaming out. There were sisters coming out with them, but Stott was struck by how somber everyone was. Many of the younger children were holding hands with each other and with the sisters. Everyone was moving toward what appeared to be the dining hall. Mike turned to speak to JJ and saw there were tears in his eyes. Briggetta was holding his hand. Stott could see the sad little boy in his army buddy. Mike fought to hold back his own tears.

Both girls looked ready to cry, the sight of all those orphans was so incredibly sad. "Maybe this wasn't such a good idea," Briegeita said, confirming Mike's suspicion that Bedford had been a predetermined destination.

But Sharkey didn't pick up on the comment. "Let's go see Sister Mary K," JJ said.

They went around to the side of the large stone house that faced the driveway. A light shone through the thick, antique panes. JJ knocked on the door. A considerable time passed before the door slowly swung partially open. "Who's there, please?" an almost timid female voice asked.

"Sister K, it's me, JJ."

The door swung full open and a diminutive little woman in an all-black habit viewed the four teenagers with an incredulous stare.

"Oh, John! It is you!" She opened her arms creating a mini-cavern with her full habit, and John stepped in and hugged her. They held each other for some time. Sister Mary K, on her tiptoes, reached up and softly kissed Sharkey's cheek.

It was the most touching scene Stott had ever witnessed.

"John, you're taller! And you've put on weight! You look wonderful! Are you going to introduce me to your friends?" Sister Mary K asked.

"Sister K, this is my best friend, Mike Stott from Ohio. Please meet Briggetta and Briegeita Mobliano. They're the sisters of another one of our army buddies, Syl Mobliano. They surprised us when we met them in Brooklyn with their new car, so we took a ride, and here we are!"

"Hello, children!" Sister Mary K exclaimed. "I am delighted to meet you! And you are JJ's best friend? I am thrilled that he has made a best friend! Are you Catholic, son?"

"Uh, no, Sister, I'm not. It's nice to meet you, too." The look that passed between Sister Mary K and the Mobliano girls convinced Mike they had met before.

"Please come in. Would you like to stay for dinner?" the Sister asked.

Briggetta answered, "Thank you, Sister, but no. We don't want to be a burden. We're going to find a country inn and have dinner and talk. Would you like to join us?"

Stott was speechless. The girls were inviting Sister Mary K to go to dinner with them? He was absolutely convinced that these three women had met before.

"No, but let me make you tea! John and I used to have tea often after dinner, didn't we, JJ? And I would like a private word with John if you don't mind."

They sat in Sister K's office, a small, but cozy room with an oversized fieldstone fireplace covering one wall. A wood fire was softly burning and there was a hint of apple aroma in the room. JJ brought in two more chairs from somewhere as Sister K reappeared with a silver tray and tea service for five. The girls commented that the china was beautiful and the tiny nun beamed with delight.

"It was Captain Sharkey's tea service! We still have china and silver for eleven people. We used to have china for twelve, didn't we John?"

Her comment made JJ blush. "Sounds like a story there," Mike said.

"Yes, there is. You probably don't know this, but John and I share a love of languages. I remember that he started learning Chinese characters when he was only four years old, right along with the English alphabet! One of the other nuns and I were so amazed at his interest that we made a project of challenging him with several languages at the same time! To our surprise, the more we challenged John the more he seemed to absorb different dialects. By age ten, JJ could switch back and forth between Mandarin, English, and Italian words in the same sentence! It became our game! We nuns loved to hear him alternate words. By age twelve, his language skills far exceeded ours, and we studied with him to advance our skills!"

John Sharkey's face showed both embarrassment and pride as Sister Mary K told his friends about his language proficiency. He said nothing. Stott noticed that Briggetta was still holding his hand.

Sister K continued. "Then JJ played a trick on us! Once a month, we tried to take the children to the library in Bedford to give them some exposure to the outside world. When John was thirteen, during one of the library visits, he 'borrowed' a self-study French language course. Frankly, he stole it! Along with a little handheld recording device that was the property of the head librarian! She called us and asked if one of our children could possibly have taken her recorder 'by accident.' No one fessed up. Three months later, however, I was walking by the chapel late one night and thought I heard children whispering! I quietly crept to the back of the altar, and there was JJ, by himself, practicing speaking French with the recorder! Right under the statue of the Virgin Mother! I stood and listened for sometime before I confronted him. When I touched him on the shoulder in an effort not to startle him, he jumped straight up, knocking over and breaking a certain teacup and saucer. JJ had been borrowing a cup of tea in the evenings as he practiced his French! He was mortified! He started to try to explain, and he was speaking French! And I didn't know the language! I finally got him to switch to English! 'John,' I said, 'where did you get that little recorder? And is that the French language lesson that the Bedford library reported missing?'"

Now JJ was crimson red, but Mike was truly enjoying the story! "What did he say?" Stott couldn't wait!

"JJ said, 'Yes, Sister. I intended to return both on the next trip to the library. I have learned French and no longer need the recorder or the tapes.' It was at this point that I pointed to the broken cup and saucer lying at John's feet. He hadn't seen it until then. He was speechless with grief! In all John's seventeen years with us here at St. Agnes, it was the only time anyone ever saw him cry!

I was so moved by his tears that I volunteered to join in his sin! 'John,' I said, 'let's make a pact. You and I will return the recorder and tapes to the library, but we'll leave them in the librarian's office. The library will have its things back, and you won't be in trouble. What do you say?' As he wiped the tears from his eyes, John looked at me and said, "No, I can't let you be involved in this. I'll take the things back and confess next visit."

Sure enough, the next Wednesday a group of our children went to the Bedford Library and John went and confessed to the librarian. You tell them what happened next, John."

They all turned their attention to JJ, but he looked only at Mike. Finally, John spoke. "The librarian made me tell her, word for word, what Sister Mary K and I had discussed. And then she asked, in French, why I didn't take Sister K's offer to form a pact of secrecy. I answered her, in French, that I would reserve my pact participation to honorable endeavors. She then said that she considered my borrowing the tapes and recorder as worthwhile because I had learned French, but I had to make a pact with her not to steal or lie again, ever. That was the first pact I made."

"What about the broken cup and saucer?" Briggetta asked.

"I am obligated to replace it first chance I get," came Sharkey's answer as he turned to face Sister K.

"John, have you made any more pacts?" Sister Mary K softly inquired.

"Just one more," John said.

"And you clearly are not prepared to share information about it, are you?" Sister Mary K knew John Sharkey very well.

"No," answered JJ.

Briggetta and Briegeita exchanged knowing looks again and Mike figured he'd never understand girls. "Won't you go to dinner with us and tell us more JJ stories?" Briggetta pleaded.

"No, children, I won't. But you run along and enjoy yourselves. Let me have just a minute alone with John, please."

Stott walked to the car with the girls in silence. "Think we should put the top up?" Mike asked.

"No, not until after dinner. We're just going down by Armonk for dinner. We'll put the top up after we eat," Briegeita said.

Mike knew at that moment that the trip to Bedford had definitely been pre-planned. "Why did we do this? You had this all planned, didn't you? What's up?" Stott was both curious and a little agitated.

"It was for John," was all the girls would say.

A few minutes later, JJ walked back down the driveway and got in the car. To the girls he said simply, "Thanks."

Briegeita drove a few miles back the way they had come and turned in a gated driveway toward what looked like a Victorian mansion. The small bronze sign read, "Val Hallow Inn."

"Are we dressed for this place?" JJ asked.

As the four approached the maitre'd, he spoke directly to the girls, "Welcome back, Misses Mobliano. You have the balcony table by the fireplace per your request."

The two couples enjoyed a wonderful dinner of steak and potatoes, salad and bread. They drank Cokes and had cheesecake and coffee for dessert. The girls talked about college, the Moblianos' extended family and their futures. Briegeita was even prettier than Mike recalled. After he stared at her and her twin sister through dinner, Stott thought he could tell them apart.

Sharkey was fairly subdued during the meal, though he listened closely when the girls talked about college. He asked for the check.

"But, sir, this is their restaurant!" said the maitre'd.

"What?" JJ and Mike said at the same time.

"We are full of surprises!" exclaimed Briggetta. "My dad and uncle bought this place about ten years ago! Isn't it great?"

Sharkey voiced what Stott was thinking. "It's really nice. Thanks, but it makes Mike and me feel, well, strange. Over Labor Day, Barry Smeall's folks treated us to that incredible weekend in the city and now you girls take us and buy us dinner. Why?" JJ asked.

"Why not? You're soldiers, we're patriots! When we told our parents you were coming to see us, Dad suggested we come up here. So we thought we'd surprise you! Wasn't it okay?" Briegeita retorted.

"Yeah, sure. Thanks."

The evening had turned cool, and Briegeita put the top up for the drive to Brooklyn. When they arrived at the Moblianos' home on Chester Street, she pulled around to an alley in back where there were garages behind the family complex. As if by magic, Paulie Mobliano appeared and opened the bifold doors.

"Hi guys! Did you have steaks? That's what I always have! Hey, Sharkey, you're taller!" Paulie was exuberant. "Dad says you gotta come in and say hello."

Mike and JJ said "Hi" and "Thanks" to Mr. and Mrs. Mobliano, and the girls walked them out the front door. "Are you going back to Fort Dix tonight or tomorrow?" Briegeita asked.

Sharkey may have made a pact not to lie, but Mike hadn't. "Actually, we're gonna stay at the USO on Forty-ninth Street," he said.

JJ gave Mike a "what the hell?" look, but for some reason Stott needed to get away from these girls, who had planned the evening so carefully and mysteriously.

"Thanks! Drive that car carefully," Mike said.

"Call us anytime," Briggetta said. She gave JJ a hug; no kiss. Briegeita just said, "See ya."

As Sharkey and Stott walked down Chester Street toward the boulevard where they'd seen a row of bars, JJ said, "Thanks. I wanted to get away from them, too. We just don't play in their league, do we Mike?"

"No, it's not only that. Being taken care of just doesn't feel right! Let's go back to Manhattan and look up that whore!" said Stott.

"Good idea," said Sharkey. "But this time let's get one each!"

They did. Mike and JJ arrived back at Fort Dix early Sunday evening, way ahead of when they had to be back. They'd spent all their money, but it was their choice! Besides, payday was only eleven days away!

During the last two weeks of AIT, Mike and JJ qualified with the M-60 machine gun and re-qualified with the M-14-A2 rifle. Sharkey and Stott achieved "expert," the highest qualification one could achieve, on both weapons. In AIT, they fired their M-14s on full automatic, which was a hoot! The recruits also qualified with the Colt .45 pistol, which First Sergeant Macleod explained was unusual for enlisted men.

"The .45 is basically an officer and senior NCO weapon, but the army has decided all 11-B's must qualify with it! The .45 is only reliable up to about twenty-five yards, but if you get a good one, they're accurate to a longer distance. Watch this!" Macleod then took out his personal .45, which had been fitted to him by an army gunsmith. He put three magazines, twenty-four shots total, into the extended bull's-eye of a fifty-meter target, utilizing the classic left-palm-supported standing firing position.

"Any of you dickheads wanna try that?" he challenged.

Mike Stott's father had taught him to shoot his own "worked" Colt .45 from the time Mike was ten years old. Though he knew it was crazy to volunteer for anything in the army, it was the last week of AIT, and Stott was feeling pretty cocky.

"First Sergeant Macleod, I'd like to try it, Sergeant!" Mike screamed out.

"Is that you volunteering, Private Dickhead Stott?" Macleod responded.

The rest of the troopers gave him a combination of Bronx cheers and catcalls as Mike responded to the First Sergeant's command to double-time up to the firing line.

"You won't even hit the twenty-five meter target, Private!" Macleod barked.

"First Sergeant, is your weapon trick-sighted?" Stott asked.

"No, Private! It's accurate as hell if you can fire it right!"

"Can I try fifty meters, First Sergeant?" Stott asked.

"What? You better try twenty-five meters, trooper!"

"Fifty meters, mark!" Stott said, imitating what he had heard the sergeants say.

"Bullshit!" said First Sergeant Macleod.

Mike managed to put all eight rounds in the kill zone of the fifty-meter target. That brought a cheer from the troopers and an "I'll be damned" from the sergeant. Stott clear-checked the .45 and handed it, grip first, back to Macleod.

"Any other hot shots in the troop?" he asked.

No one else was stupid enough to volunteer.

"Meet me in the armory after chow, Private Stott!" ordered Macleod.

That evening, Mike was rewarded for his good shooting with Macleod's .45 by having to clean every pistol in the armory. There were 168 of them; he got back to A Barrack at 0100 hours. Lesson learned.

On the morning of Friday, November 1, 1963, AIT Training Company A put its troopers through a final, qualifying obstacle course and declared them army riflemen, Military Occupational Specialty # 11-Bravo, or 11-B's as the army preferred. At the graduation ceremony, each trooper was awarded his weapons' qualification medals and a light blue, braided shoulder rope signifying his status as an infantryman.

The lieutenant colonel that commanded all Advanced Infantry Training at Fort Dix addressed the final formation. "Congratulations, men! You are now part of the backbone of the United States Army! It is the infantryman that carries the burden of combat on his back! Remember the Infantry Creed: 'Lead, follow, or get the hell out of the way!' Be a leader! Serve your country proudly! Many of you will be assigned to units that will see combat in the country of Vietnam soon. Remember your weapons training and give 'em hell! I am proud to see that some of you have volunteered for jump school. Those of you headed straight for Fort Benning will experience one of the great thrills of your life in the next few weeks when you take that first jump! But always remember, whether you arrive at the battle on foot, by helicopter, or parachute, you are an infantryman! Dismissed!"

The soldiers had all received their forwarding orders prior to the last formation, and, as promised by Sergeant Turner and Major Hargrove, Sharkey and Stott were headed for jump school at Fort Benning in Columbus, Georgia, on a Delta Airlines flight out of Philadelphia at 1030 hours Sunday morning, November 3, 1963. Mike and JJ stayed in A Barrack that Friday night and took the 9:00 a.m. bus from Wrightstown to Philadelphia Saturday morning to see the sights in the City of Brotherly Love. After seeing the

Liberty Bell and Betsy Ross's house, Mike and JJ decided to see a bar.

They managed to make the flight to Columbus and arrived at Fort Benning Airborne Training Center via military bus from the airport late Sunday afternoon. Real army began the next morning.

Chapter Twenty-Three

Basic training had been a shock because the army way was all new to Mike and JJ. AIT had actually been more relaxed than basic and had lulled them into thinking the hard part of training was behind them.

When Sharkey and Stott fell out for 0445 reveille on November 4 in Training Company B, Airborne Training Center, Fort Benning, Georgia, they were greeted by a whole new army. It was intense! The purpose of jump school was to get troopers in shape to handle hitting the ground at twelve to fifteen miles per hour via parachute, laden with up to 110 pounds of combat gear. It was all about conditioning, discipline, and toeing the line!

The night before, in the barrack, Sharkey and Stott were quite surprised to learn that most of the men in their training company had been in the army much longer than they had. Most had been assigned to an airborne unit and then sent to jump school. There were sergeants, corporals, and PFCs—privates first class—starting jump school right alongside "green grunts" as JJ and Mike were called!

At that first formation, Mike and JJ met Master Sergeant Bill Boulter. His greeting was memorable. "I am Master Sergeant and Jump Master Bill Boulter. If you're religious, think of me as God. If you are not religious, consider me to be your king and supreme ruler for the next three weeks, or you will wish you were dead. I don't care what your rank is, how long you been in the army, or if you are in some fuckin' special unit! You are whale shit at the bottom of the ocean to me! Don't forget it! I am God, until you earn your jump wings! Got it, girls?"

"Yes, Master Sergeant Boulter!" the troopers shouted so loud it hurt their ears!

"I can't hear you pussies!"

"YES, MASTER SERGEANT BOULTER!" they said even louder this time.

"We never walk in jump school, we run. Everywhere! To the john, to chow! We fuckin' run! Got it?"

"YES, MASTER SERGEANT BOULTER!"

Thus began a level of intensity Mike Stott had never experienced nor could have imagined. The soldiers were on their feet, running, for nineteen days straight. The morning run seemed to last forever. Several men dropped out that first morning and were dismissed from jump school on the spot! Gone! Back to their units or whatever, in disgrace.

Master Sergeant Boulter and his training cadre were incredible physical specimens! They drove the men through a continuous exercise regimen that paused only when they were attending classes in jump instruction, parachute rigging, and jump survival indoctrination.

The chow was way better than in basic or AIT, if one had time to eat it! Soldiers were ordered not to be overly communicative with jump school mates.

"You're not here to make friends or fall in love, dickheads! That comes later at the unit level! Especially for you 'Special' guys! You're here for one reason only! To earn your jump wings and join the army's elite, or leave in disgrace! Those are the options! My fuckin' way! If you talk back to any of us in any way, we'll break your fuckin' legs! Or nose! And if you think 'cause you're an officer you're immune, just fuckin' try me!"

Stott came to think of Boulter as pure evil.

There was time allotted for church on Sundays, but other than that the troopers worked, running everywhere. They first learned to jump off progressively higher fixed towers as they prepared for the first real jump from a C-119 "Flying Boxcar" airplane.

By the time Mike was loading into that first C-119 for jump number one, he had lost twelve pounds and could do 300 push-ups, nonstop. The training and conditioning were so intense, and the trainees were so scared of Master Sergeant Boulter and his cadre that the nineteen days went by in a flash.

The weather turned cold and rainy the last week of jump school, and weather was the only thing that Master Sergeant Boulter could not control. B Company was scheduled to do its first real jump on that third Wednesday of jump school, but zero visibility kept the 119s on the ground. Thursday was worse, but Friday was supposed to be clear.

Bad weather had made Master Sergeant Boulter's mood even meaner than usual, so men ran and exercised, packed and re-packed chutes eighteen hours a day on that Wednesday and Thursday. Boulter explained their dilemma. "If you don't get your three good jumps in, you don't get your wings! That means you do this all over again, and I hate repeaters! If the birds can fly tomorrow we've been cleared to get in your three qualifying jumps all in one day! Formation at 0530 hours in the a.m.! We'll do calisthenics, but no run!"

That brought a cheer from the troopers.

"Shut the fuck up and listen! Chow hall will be open, but if you eat and throw up in my plane, I'll personally throw you out chuteless, get it? We'll load in the first 119s at 0645 hours and get in three waves of jumps by 1300 hours! We're down to seventy-eight troopers, so it should be no problem! That means you earn your wings and get the fuck out of my military sight by late chow! Dismissed!" said Boulter.

Sharkey walked up to Stott's bunk bay and said, "Mike, this is it! We earn our silver chutes tomorrow! We'll be jump qualified and get to wear bloused jump boots! And we're supposed to get PFC stripes! What a day! You gonna eat in the morning?"

"Hell no! You're not even a little nervous, JJ?" Mike asked.

"Come on, pussy! Hell no! We're ready!" JJ said.

"You know, John, despite all the chow you been eatin', even you lost weight these last three weeks! But I think you grew an inch! What do you weigh?" asked Stott.

"I'm five-six, and I weigh 140 pounds! Which means I can probably kick your ass, so watch it! See you at 0500!" Sharkey was beaming with pride.

As he left, Stott yelled, "I think you gotta be five-eight for Ranger school!" but he got no response. Instead, an older trooper about two bunks over who had not spoken one word to Mike all through jump school walked over and peered down at him as he lay in his bunk.

"You think you got a shot at Ranger training, kid?" he asked. His tone was less than friendly.

"Don't know. Maybe. Why?" the guy really pissed Stott off.

"How long you been in the army?" the guy asked.

"Since July," Mike countered.

"This past July, '63?"

"Yeah."

"You're full of shit! You gotta prove yourself before you get to Ranger school, asshole," Mike's new buddy said.

Then to Mike's great surprise, another older soldier who hadn't spoken to either of them walked up and said, "Go back to your bunk, mister!" The guy did.

He then said to Stott, "You gonna make a career of the army, son? If so, you go for Ranger school! Don't pay attention to that retread. How old are you?"

"Seventeen," Mike said.

"Go for it! You and Sharkey too!" With that, the mystery soldier departed.

As Mike lay there contemplating that strange exchange with two guys he had never talked to before, Master Sergeant Boulter appeared from nowhere and stood staring down at him. Boulter didn't say a word. He just stared at Stott for a long while and walked away.

As tired as he was, Mike had trouble falling asleep, probably because the next day he was going to jump out of a perfectly good airplane. Stott thought about his brothers who had been there at Benning before him, especially James.

Mike fell asleep wondering why in the hell he hadn't taken that scholarship.

Chapter Twenty-Four

Company B troopers formed up that Friday to a cold but clear morning. Stott had a half cup of coffee and was amazed to watch Sharkey eat his normal, huge breakfast. "Damn, John! Remember what Master Boulter said! You don't want to lose it in the plane!"

"No problem for me, sonny! Let's jump!" Since Sharkey had learned he was two months older than his friend he had taken to calling Mike "sonny" every chance he got.

Men began rigging jump gear and parachutes just off the flight line at 0645 hours. There were four C-119s warming up, their flight crews walking around checking out the planes and drinking coffee. Mike was nervous and excited as Master Sergeant Boulter personally checked out each first-time jumper.

"Remember to bend those knees before impact! Any one of you breaks a leg, I'll kill you!" said Master Sergeant Boulter, full of compassion.

The troops boarded the planes, nineteen or twenty first-time jumpers in each of the four Flying Boxcars. A jump school sergeant coordinated with an air force sergeant as jump masters in each plane. Stott wound up in a different plane than JJ, with Master Sergeant Boulter as his jump master.

Mike was the eleventh man out of the 119. When the green "good to go" jump light came on, Master Sergeant Boulter checked the clipped static lines and pointed each man out into the slipstream at very close intervals.

It was incredible! The static line popped the chute immediately and Stott felt that false sense of being jerked upward as the chute deployed. There wasn't a lot of hang time on that first jump, but Mike would always remember looking around thinking, as he descended, *this beats the hell out of college!* The ground was coming up fast, and he focused on bending his knees and preparing to forward roll into the landing.

Thump! Stott touched down, knees properly bent, and rolled forward on his right side. His chute billowed out behind him, caught up in a slight cross wind. Mike broke the air from the chute and gathered it in as he had been taught to do. He checked himself out and all was well! Nothing broken or even bruised! He'd done it! First jump!

Other troopers had landed close by, and Mike looked around for Sharkey. Sure enough, there he was about 200 yards downwind from Stott, giving him a thumbs-up sign. Glancing around, it appeared all the troopers had landed successfully. Then Stott noticed one guy was still on the ground several hundred yards past where he had spotted JJ. The trooper had collapsed his chute, but was still on the ground. As Mike watched, one of the jumpmasters reached the trooper and bent over to speak with him. The sergeant signaled for the medics' jeep that came and put the trooper in back. Only one broken ankle among the seventy-eight jumpers.

Mike and JJ never learned whether or not Master Sergeant Boulter later shot the guy who broke his ankle, but the remaining seventy-seven troopers loaded up and completed two more qualification jumps before noon, 1200 hours!

Completing the third qualifying jump meant that the army now had seventy-seven more airborne troopers, and two of them were John J. Sharkey and Mike B. Stott. JJ had just turned eighteen, and Mike was a month shy of his eighteenth birthday. The newly qualified jumpers were ordered to clean up, don their dress greens, and report to the mess hall for late midday chow and to receive their jumpers' credentials, those coveted silver-winged parachutes. They were once again treated to steaks and ice cream.

More than half of the jump school troopers were going back to the airborne units to which they had previously been assigned. The rest of the men were to receive orders for their next posting.

At 1400 hours, Master Sergeant Boulter called the paratroopers back to the final formation of Training Company B,

Airborne Training Command. "Airborne troopers! Ten-hut! Colonel John Rushing, executive officer, 101st Airborne Division!"

"At ease, men!" directed Colonel Rushing. "You will all remember this day as one of the proudest days of your life! You've earned the right to blouse your jump boots and hold your heads up high! You are paratroopers! Congratulations! I hope all of you can serve with the 101st, but wherever you hang silk, be proud to be airborne!"

That brought a spontaneous cheer from all. Mike could actually hear Sharkey's "hooah" above all the other voices.

Colonel Rushing continued. "Some of you will return to your airborne units, others are going to new assignments. I understand seven of you have volunteered for Ranger training! Hooah! There's a big one starting in southeast Asia, and you'll get to be a part of it!"

At this point in Colonel Rushing's speech, a captain ran up onto the reviewing platform from which the colonel was speaking and saluted him. He then approached Rushing and spoke directly in his ear, handing him a parchment-colored paper as he did so. The captain backed off, saluted again, and ran from the platform back in the direction from which he had come. Very strange!

The colonel stood looking at the paper he had received for several minutes. "Troopers, ten-hut! Listen up! I've just been informed that President John F. Kennedy has been shot in Texas! His condition is unknown! All active-duty military personnel are on full alert effective immediately! You are to report to your units at once! Those unassigned troopers will remain with the training company until further notice. Master Sergeant Boulter, return these troopers to A Barrack. Men, no further information is available at this time. Pray for our president! God bless America! Master Sergeant Boulter, take charge!"

Colonel Rushing left the reviewing platform with all of his attending officers. Master Sergeant Boulter mounted the platform and stood looking out at the men in silence. All were in a state of shock.

Boulter visibly gathered himself and said, "At ease, men. This situation has no precedent that I know of. All leaves are canceled. I'll do my best to keep you informed about what's going on, but we probably won't get much reliable information anytime soon. I'm going to move that TV we have in the orderly room out to the lower squad bay in A so you all can at least see the news. Dismissed!"

Sharkey and Stott walked back to A Barrack in silence. Not one of their fellow paratroopers said a word. It seemed the only thing they could do was sit in the barrack and collect themselves. Most soldiers had packed their clothes in anticipation of leaving for new assignments. Some men started unpacking. Finally, Mike heard one of the older guys speak. "Is this for fuckin' real? Can it be? Who could have done it?"

After a long, silent interval a soldier down the hall stood up on a footlocker and shouted, "Listen up! Until we know something further, we can stay in shape and be ready to go! Who'll join me in a run?"

Stott stepped from his bunk bay and saw the trooper who had come to his aid the previous evening standing on that footlocker. He still had his dress-green jacket on from the formation. Mike was astonished to see that he had three stripes up and three rockers down with a star in the middle! The guy was a sergeant major!

Sharkey was standing beside Mike with tears in his eyes. "Where'd the sergeant major come from?" JJ asked.

"He was in our jump class! I met him last night! He wore unmarked fatigues all through jump training. Can you read his name tag from here?" Stott asked.

"Looks like C-A-R-T-W-R-I-G-H-T. Cartwright. Put your fatigues on! Let's go run with him!" JJ was off to change.

Nearly all of the troopers that weren't headed back to their assigned units came out to join Sergeant Major Cartwright.

"Let me introduce myself, men. I'm Sergeant Major Colin
Cartwright, and I went through jump school with you after
twenty-one years in the army! No, I haven't lost my mind!
I'm joining a new unit, and I need to be jump qualified.
Proud to have jumped with you! You young guys try to keep
up, okay? Fall in by fours! I'll call! Let's go!"

Sharkey and Mike fell in behind Sergeant Major Cartwright two rows back. His cadence calling lacked First Sergeant Turner's color, but was very forceful and kept the paratroopers in step:

> *Here we go! Up the hill!*
> *Down the hill! Airborne!*
> *Here we go! Up the hill!*
> *Down the hill! Ranger bound!*

The men jogged around the Airborne Training Center at Fort
Benning for a very long time, all thoughts focused on President Kennedy and what might happen next. Sergeant Major
Cartwright kept a slow, sustainable double-time that worked
well to relieve their tension. Mike and JJ's group passed many
other columns as well as many lone officers, all, apparently,
coping with the terrible news by doing all they could do;
stay in shape and be ready. After more than two hours, Master Sergeant Boulter pulled alongside in a Jeep and shouted
to Cartwright, "Come on back, Sarge. There's news."

When Cartwright's men arrived back at A Barrack, Master Sergeant Boulter, the remainder of the jump school cadre
and probably another hundred troopers, presumably from
other training companies, gathered in the open space between A and B Barracks. Some were in sweaty fatigues, but
most of those gathered were in dress greens.

"Men, gather round," said Boulter. No formation!

Boulter spoke clearly and distinctly, but in a tone very different from his command voice. "Fellow soldiers, we've just
been officially notified that President John F. Kennedy died
from gunshot wounds suffered earlier today in Dallas, Texas.

President Lynden Baines Johnson has already been sworn in. There's no other official information, but apparently one or more gunman fired several rounds into President Kennedy's motorcade and there are other casualties. First Lady Jackie Kennedy was sitting next to her husband when he was shot, but she wasn't hit. Governor Connolly of Texas was among the wounded. Assigned troopers are cleared to return to their units. Troopers awaiting assignment are to remain here on post until we get further orders. The mess hall's staying open awhile if anybody wants chow. The NCO club is open to all enlisted men, but don't drink too much. We don't know what's next. I'll be in the orderly room in A, probably all night. See me if you need to. Pray for our country."

Sharkey and Mike walked back into A Barrack in silence. No paratrooper said a word. The guys that had been in Stott's bunk bay had departed for their units, so JJ went and got his gear and took the bunk across from him. Sergeant Major Cartwright appeared in the walkway and said, "We'd better get some chow before mess closes. Let's go."

Mike, JJ, and several other troopers joined Cartwright in a somber walk to the mess hall and were the last group to go through the chow line before it shut down. They received large helpings of chow. Seven men sat and ate in silence until Cartwright spoke. "If the Cubans or Russians are behind this, it'll mean a war. Kennedy was a great man. Our nation will miss him."

"Sergeant Major Cartwright, do you think it has anything to do with Vietnam?" John Sharkey asked.

After reflecting for some time, Cartwright said, "Probably not. But President Kennedy understood the importance of Vietnam as a roadblock to the spread of communism. I doubt that Johnson will have the same vision. I need a beer, let's move to the NCO club."

Two beers later, Sharkey asked the sergeant major, "Sergeant Major Cartwright, why'd you go to jump school now? You're wearing Big Red 1 patches, are you going to a different unit?"

"I've been selected to serve in the Fifth Special Forces Group, Private. Jump qualification is a prerequisite."

"Do you know Sergeant Bill Patterson, Sergeant Major?" JJ asked.

Cartwright turned to look squarely at Sharkey. "I did. Sergeant Patterson was killed in Vietnam in May. Why do you ask?"

The color drained from Sharkey's face as he struggled to hold back the tears. "He was my friend," said JJ.

Mike put his hand on John's shoulder, but said nothing.

"How did you know Sergeant Patterson, son?" inquired Cartwright.

JJ swallowed hard, straightened his shoulders and lifted his head. He retold the story of how he had met Sergeant Patterson at St. Agnes.

"I'm very sorry, son. Patterson was a fine soldier. He brought honor to his beret. I'm proud to have known him. Honor his memory." With that, Sergeant Major Cartwright bid Mike and JJ farewell.

Sharkey and Stott walked around the Airborne Training Center grounds until well after midnight when an officer of the guard commanded them to return to the barrack.

There was no reveille on Saturday morning, November 23, but most troopers woke early anyway. Those remaining in A Barrack were temporarily unassigned, so soldiers like Sharkey and Mike felt essentially lost. No sergeants were screaming at them to "move their asses."

Stott woke hoping it had all been a bad dream and that President Kennedy was still in office. He rolled over on his side to see if JJ was awake and found him staring back, his eyes filled with tears.

"How can it be? Why would anyone want to kill our president? What does it mean?" JJ questioned.

"I just don't know, John. Let's go get some coffee. I don't think I can eat, but maybe there'll be some news in the mess hall."

Mike and JJ shaved and showered and dressed in fatigues to go to the mess hall. A few of their jump school mates were up and about too, but the barrack was eerily quiet. Guys nodded without speaking and just shuffled about.

It was almost 0800 hours when JJ and Mike entered the nearly empty mess hall. The cooks had the breakfast line open, but it looked like almost no one had eaten. The two friends took eggs, bacon, and toast with black coffee and sat at a table by themselves.

"I'll be right back, I've gotta call Sister Mary K. I know how bad she's hurting," JJ said and left for the phone booths outside the hall.

Mike sat staring into his coffee, picking at his food. He felt depressed and decided to call his parents. Stott realized he hadn't talked to them since the first day he'd arrived at Fort Benning to begin jump school.

"Private First Class Stott, ten-hut!" a booming yet familiar voice sounded from behind Mike. He instinctively snapped to attention. It was Syl Mobliano with Sharkey, and he was wearing first sergeant stripes! To Stott's surprise, Syl hugged him.

"Good to see you, Mike! One hell of a time, huh?" Syl looked as serious as he sounded.

"Where'd you come from?" Mike asked, still shaken by Syl's unexpected appearance. "And what's with the first stripes?"

"Well, I came looking for you guys from OCS over on the other side of the post. I've got two weeks to go and then I'll be a '90-day wonder,' otherwise known as a second lieutenant! I wear these stripes because I'm an OCS squad leader. Big deal! How you doing?" Syl asked.

"I guess okay. I mean, we got through jump school and were riding high until the news about President Kennedy. I think JJ's taking it worse than me, but it's really awful. John, did you talk to Sister K?" Mike asked.

"Just for a minute. She's totally broken up. I was standing out there trying not to cry when Syl found me. Mobs, it's really good to see you. You'll be an officer in two weeks?"

"Yeah, I should get my gold bar on Saturday, December 7, Pearl Harbor Day! If you guys are still here, come to the graduation so I can order you around after I'm a lieutenant!" said Syl.

"That sounds pretty miserable! Are your sisters coming to the graduation?" JJ countered.

"Think I'd tell you if they were? Actually, they might. Dad and mom are coming for sure. You got the day off? Are you restricted to base?" Syl asked.

"Yeah, we're restricted. But we don't know what's up. I guess we should hang around the barrack. Heard any news about who shot President Kennedy?" Mike asked Syl.

"No, I haven't heard anything. If you hang around the barrack you're likely to get a detail. I think the NCO club is going to open early. Let's go over there and have a drink," Syl suggested.

The friends were surprised at how many guys were already at the club, drinking. JJ, Syl, and Mike sat at a big round table with a bunch of guys they didn't know and discussed the awful events.

"Heard from the Jewish brain trust or Howard?" JJ asked Mobs.

"No, but Eddy Hale stopped by the house last weekend to say 'Hi.' He told my dad he's in a sixteen-week intelligence training school and hopes to finish just before Christmas. Claims he'll be a corporal at the end of his school," Syl explained. "You guys haven't heard from Big Howie?"

"Not yet," said JJ. "The thought that Hale might outrank us by Christmas is more than I can stand to think about. Let's have a beer!"

"I've got barrack duty this evening, and I've got some studying to do, but I'm off all day Sunday. If you're still just hanging around, walk over to the other NCO club by the infantry museum tomorrow and we can have lunch. That club does good cheeseburgers! I figure JJ can get by on four or five of them! See you then!" Syl Mobliano's visit had brightened the boys' spirits.

Sharkey and Stott kept checking back at A Barrack, but there was no news and no orders. They decided to do a run, just to take their minds off Kennedy's assassination.

"You realize we don't have to run, but we are? This airborne thing has worked on our heads," Mike told JJ.

"Shut up and keep up," was all JJ said.

When they returned late Saturday afternoon, Master Sergeant Boulter was looking for them. "Sharkey, Stott, orderly room," a corporal directed them.

"At ease, men! Is one of your dads a big shot or something? A senator or congressman? Who do you know?" Boulter demanded.

"No, Master Sergeant Boulter!" Mike and JJ screamed.

"Bullshit! One of you dickheads knows somebody or you're the two luckiest PFC's in the fuckin' army! You both got orders for Ranger training! Un-fucking-believable! Starting 6 January, 1964! Until then, you're both temporarily assigned to the Airborne Training Center right fucking here! You'll be acting corporals in jump schools here 25 November through 5 January, 1964. Son-of-a-fucking-bitch! Move your shit to Cadre Barrack B and report to Master Sergeant Dupree by 0900 hours Monday morning. Get out of my military sight!"

"Master Sergeant Boulter, thank you!" Sharkey shouted.

"Get out of my fuckin' sight! Now!"

Sharkey was absolutely ecstatic, but Stott wasn't so sure.

"We did it! We made it! Can you believe it?" JJ cried when he and Mike were clear of the orderly room and Master Sergeant Boulter.

"John, I'm not so sure this is a good thing! Most of the guys we're gonna be with in Ranger school have been in the army a long time and are older. How in the hell did we get assigned now? Christ, we've only been in the army for five months!" Stott sounded scared.

"Goddamn it, Stott! Don't rain on my fuckin' parade! We're gonna make it! We got a month here to get in shape and get ready! We'll do what we're told and keep our mouths shut! You know the drill by now! Christ, you're tougher than I am, and I'm gonna do it! So are you! Let's celebrate!" The news of their orders had temporarily made them forget about the national tragedy.

It came crashing back down on them as they entered their squad bay. A trooper who had been in the NCO club with them said, "Did you hear? The guy that shot Kennedy is an ex-marine that trained in Russia! He's got a Russian wife! He's in custody! Did the Russians program him to shoot our president? Christ, what a mess! By the way, did that big nigger find you guys? Said he was a friend of yours! He was going to the NCO club to look for you."

Sharkey and Mike found Big Howie sitting outside the NCO club with his head in his hands, staring at the ground. He had on dress greens with PFC stripes and a military police unit patch on one shoulder and a "screaming eagle" on the other. When he saw his friends he cried out, "Lord, Lord, boys! What is this world coming to? How could it happen?" There were tears in Howard's eyes as he stood to shake their hands.

"Good to see you, Howie, but what are you doing here at Fort Benning? You didn't go AWOL on us, did you?" Stott asked.

"Hell no, Stott! I done finished MP school, but they sent me here to go to jump school! I been assigned to the 101st Airborne Division Military Police, so I got to go to jump school!" Howard looked desperate.

Despite the situation and circumstance, Sharkey and Stott started laughing.

"What's so damn funny?" Big Howie demanded.

"When do you start?" JJ asked.

"Monday morning! Got to report right here to Training Company B, Airborne Training Center."

Now his buddies roared with laughter.

"That's where we just got our wings! And we may be in your cadre! I'm gonna ride your ass to the moon!" JJ was doubled over with laughter.

From the look on Big Howie's face, Mike was pretty sure he didn't believe Sharkey. "Is he kiddin' me, Mikey?" Howard asked.

Mike was laughing, too, but not as hard as Sharkey. "No, Howie, he's not! We're both laughin' at the thought of you hanging under a parachute! You might be over the weight carry limit! Plus, we know how much you hate to run, and that's all you're gonna do for the next three weeks!"

"Was gettin' out of the plane hard the first time?" Howard wanted to know.

"No, because if you don't go out on your own, the jump master will throw you out!" JJ said.

"Damn! And you have to run everywhere? Even in the barrack?" asked Howie.

Together Sharkey and Stott said, "Abso-fucking-lutely!"

"Damn! So where are you guys going next? Got any idea?" Howie asked.

"Well, yeah! Just before we heard you were here look-ing for us, we both got orders for Ranger training starting in January! We're temporarily assigned to the Airborne Train-ing Center right here until we start. JJ wasn't kidding! We may be part of your training cadre. We're acting corporals reporting to a Master Sergeant Dupree. I guess we're lucky because we will be running with you trainees so we can work on getting in shape for Ranger school. JJ's excited. I'm a little scared," Mike admitted to Howie.

"I heard you had to be in the army a while before you can volunteer for Ranger training. How'd you guys get in so fast?" Big Howie asked the question that had been on Mike's mind.

"Well, we did volunteer, but I bet it's because of Mike's brother. You know, being a Congressional Medal of Honor recipient's little brother can't hurt in the army!" Sharkey speculated.

"Maybe, but if Vietnam is really about to get hot, the army will need more Rangers. Maybe you'll get assigned after jump school, Howie! You seem to be following us around!" Stott couldn't resist messing with him.

"First, I gots to make it through jump school, and I don't have a buddy to do it with like you guys had!" Howard was worried.

"Quit worrying! You'll make it or I'll personally kick your ass, got it?" Sharkey was already acting like a sergeant.

"The last time you said that we all got in trouble, JJ! Knock it off! Let's go in and have a beer! Howie, we saw Mobs this morning! He's finishing up OCS, and we're gonna see him tomorrow," Mike said.

The three of them got a little wasted as they drank nickel draft beers and listened to the news on the NCO club TV. Big Howie bunked in the cadre barrack that night so he couldn't be identified for a detail. They were learning the army way!

On Sunday, November 24, 1963, Big Howie, Sharkey, and Stott met soon-to-be-Second-Lieutenant Syl Mobliano at the other NCO club at Fort Benning. Together, they watched the national tragedy get even stranger as Jack Ruby assassinated Lee Harvey Oswald live on CBS News.

None of them had duty on the day of the funeral or Thanksgiving Day, so they met at the NCO club and tried to cheer each other up.

Despite President Kennedy's funeral and the national time of mourning, the army's training regimen got back on track the first week in December. Later in the month, Mobs got his gold bar, Big Howie made it through jump school, and JJ and Mike got a taste of command as they ran new troopers through jump school classes.

Sharkey and Stott decided they should stop drinking beer and concentrate on preparing for Ranger training. They kept hearing stories of how incredibly difficult Ranger school would be, so Mike and JJ passed on a longer leave and requested a six-day leave over Christmas 1963.

Chapter Twenty-Five

On December 24, 1963, John Sharkey and Mike Stott began their first six-day leave from the army. The month of December had felt like light duty in some ways because Master Sergeant Billy Dupree took care of his cadre. Mike and JJ had gone from lower-than-whale-shit trainees to order-givers over that last weekend in November. The change in the way they were regarded by the army could not have been more extreme. But the boys knew they'd revert back to lower-than-whale-shit trainees in Ranger school come the first Monday in January.

Mike's parents insisted that he bring Sharkey home with him for Christmas, so Mike and JJ purchased Delta Airlines military personnel airfares from Columbus, Georgia, to Cincinnati, Ohio. They arrived at the Boone County Airport serving Cincinnati at 3:00 p.m. on Christmas Eve, 1963.

Sharkey and Stott splurged and had their dress greens tailored to fit them like officers' uniforms. With their bloused trousers tucked into mirror-shined jump boots and their dark red airborne berets, Mike and JJ couldn't have been prouder of their uniforms as they walked down the airplane steps and across the tarmac to the terminal doors.

To Mike's surprise, Kathy Giuseppe was waiting with his folks in the terminal. She was standing there holding his mother's hand and came running toward him, throwing herself in his arms. Mike's mom started crying, but his dad remained his normal reserved self as Mike introduced JJ to them.

"I love you. Welcome home," his mom whispered.

"You look different, son," Stott's father said. "Welcome to Cincinnati, John. We're happy you came with Mike. Got any luggage?"

The boys were each carrying a medium-sized army gym bag in which they had packed only army-issue clothing. They were carrying their winter great coats and finally needed those winter gloves that had been issued to them way back in basic training. As they piled into Mike's dad's old DeSoto, Kathy and Mike's mother were both talking at once, telling John and Mike about all their plans for the holiday.

John was very quiet, but he listened patiently to all the news about two families he had never met. During one of the unusual lapses in the women's chatter, Mike's dad said, "Looks like you lost some weight, son. What do the scales say?"

"Well, I am lighter than when I went in, but not by much. JJ and I have been trying to get ready for Ranger school, so we've been running constantly and lifting weights along with the calisthenics the army recommends," Mike told his father.

"Ranger training?" his folks asked in unison.

"Uh, yeah. John and I start at Camp Darby on January 6," Mike said.

His mother started crying and his father just shook his head.

"What's Ranger school?" Kathy wanted to know.

"Why the hell did you volunteer for that?" his father asked.

"Dad, it just sort of happened. We met a sergeant that knew James, and he sort of encouraged us," Mike told him.

When Mike mentioned James, his mom began crying harder.

"James who?" Kathy inquired.

"My brother James, Kathy. I never told you about him."

They were crossing the Ohio River on the suspension bridge at this point, and Mike looked up to see the Christmas lights on the Carew Tower, the tallest building in Cincinnati. He realized how insensitive he had been to let the conversation take this course. Mike knew he should have waited to tell his parents about Ranger training.

"Why are you so upset, Mrs. Stott?" Kathy asked.

When no one responded to Kathy's question, JJ spoke softly to her, "Ranger training is the toughest training in the army. James Stott was Mike's oldest brother and he was a Ranger captain who was killed in Korea. He won the Congressional Medal of Honor."

Kathy just stared at Mike. "You never told me any of this," was all she could say.

"Why, son? Why do you want to go through all that? Hasn't our family given enough already? Don't do it!" Mike's mother was truly distraught.

"I'm sorry, Mom. I should have explained it to you later and in a different way. It just seemed like something I had to do. Now I've got to do it!" Mike said.

They rode in silence the rest of the way home. Mike's brothers and sisters and their families were waiting for them at his parents' home. They weren't home more than ten minutes when Mike's father announced, "Well, you might as well all know. Mike starts Ranger training when he goes back. He and his buddy both. I guess he didn't listen to you guys telling him not to volunteer for anything."

Both Mike's brothers' jaws dropped open. All his family just stared at him. "Are you crazy, Mikey? And how the hell did you guys both get assigned to the Rangers now? You just got though jump school!" Raymond, Mike's older brother, was incredulous.

"It just happened, Ray. Our first sergeant in basic served with James in the tenth. When he found out I was his brother, I think he might have helped us," Stott said.

Mike's mother started crying again, and his sisters joined with her. Not exactly the way a family gathering on Christmas Eve was supposed to go. Fortunately, Mike's young nieces and nephews didn't understand the adults' grief. Their excitement about Santa Claus relieved the gloom to some degree, and the family focused on them. Mike's two young nephews, Chris and Davey, were very interested in their uniforms, and Sharkey seemed to enjoy explaining the meaning of the marksman badges and winged parachute to them.

Mike's brothers began scolding him for volunteering for the Rangers. "Damn, Mikey! Why'd you do it? It guarantees that you'll be in the shit! And with Vietnam building up, you'll be there next year! Damn!" Raymond exclaimed.

"I still don't know how you got assigned after only six months! Most guys go to Ranger school after a second enlistment," Bill said.

Stott's dad found Mike and his brothers talking in the basement. "Who was the sergeant that knew James?" he asked Mike.

"Sergeant Virgil Turner, Dad. He said he met you and mom at the medal ceremony. James was his commanding officer. He was there with James, you know, in Korea."

Mike's father's eyes glazed over as he reflected back to one of his most painful memories. "I remember him. He was a World War II vet. I'm surprised he's still in the army, he must be pushing fifty. Still gung-ho army?"

"Oh, yeah!" By this time Sharkey had found them and he told Mike's dad and brothers about Turner leading the forced march to bivouac. JJ explained that Mike had helped him learn to shoot and that they both fired perfect scores on the two parts of M-14 qualification.

"No shit? You both shot one hundreds? That doesn't happen very often. I worked a basic training M-14 range my last four months on active duty, and I never saw a trainee shoot perfect scores. I guess we started you pretty early, huh, Mikey?" Bill said.

"You had never fired a weapon before basic and still scored one hundred, JJ? Now, that is impressive!" Raymond told Sharkey.

"Thanks. Really, it was Mike's talking me through it! And I've gotta tell you about his knocking out the biggest guy in our basic training company in the reception center!" JJ went on to relate Mike's run-in with Big Howie because of Fast Eddy Hale.

"You've gotta stop being a hothead, son. Are you keeping up with your boxing?" Mike's dad asked.

"No time, dad! I haven't hit a bag in months."

"Well, your training equipment in still over there in the corner. You guys can work out while you're home. Sounds like you'd better be in shape when you get back if you're going to make it through Ranger training. I wish you hadn't volunteered, but now that you have, finish it. You too, Sharkey! Don't let me down! Now, no more army talk! It's Christmas, you're home!" Mike's father went back upstairs to join the family.

"Wow! I see where you get your toughness!" JJ said.

"Actually, JJ, you don't. Mom's the tough one," Raymond said. "You guys stay together and make it as Rangers, and you'll be golden in the army!"

"We're not stopping with becoming Rangers! We're gonna go for Special Forces!" JJ pronounced.

"What the hell is that?" Mike's brothers asked.

"We don't even know yet! Drop it JJ! Let's just get through Ranger school! That's enough!" Mike said.

"Nope! We're earning berets! I promise!" JJ was dead serious.

"You guys are both nuts! Let's go have a drink and celebrate Christmas! No more army bullshit tonight!" Raymond put his arm around Sharkey and said, "Take care of my little brother, little brother! You're part of our family now!"

JJ had to stay in the basement a while to dry his eyes. Raymond's words had moved him deeply.

Sharkey received lots of Christmas presents from Mike's family, and he was overwhelmed. Mrs. Stott baked them spice cakes and chocolate chip cookies virtually every day, and Mike and JJ worried about getting back in shape for the Rangers. JJ and Mike spent a lot of time talking with his dad and brothers about everything imaginable, including girls.

JJ also made Mike work on his Chinese. One day they were in the basement practicing Mandarin when Mike's mother came down to do a load of wash. "Are you boys drunk? Sounds like you're both speaking in tongues," his Mom said.

"Uh, no mom. JJ's teaching me Chinese. I think I'm up to about six hundred words," Mike said.

"You wouldn't take your French serious in high school and now you're learning Chinese? And how do you know that language?" she asked JJ.

JJ started explaining about learning Chinese from Sister Mary K. Mike's mother sat down on a bench by her washing machine and listened to John for several minutes. When JJ finished, she got up and put her arms around him and just stood there, hugging him. JJ put his head on Mike's mother's shoulder.

On the day before JJ and he were to return to Fort Benning, Kathy asked Mike, "Are we kind of, you know, over? You are so different now. You haven't even tried to feel my boobs! Mikey, what happened?"

"Kathy, I'm gonna be gone for a long time. You want a family and kids, and I'm still just a kid who happens to be a soldier. Don't wait around for me," Mike said.

The last night before Mike and JJ were to leave for Fort Benning, Mrs. Stott fixed another big family dinner. Everyone came over again, almost like another Christmas. JJ and Mike had a few beers, maybe more than a few, and started talking about their Labor Day weekend in New York City. Next thing they knew, the whole family was focused on their story. The boys didn't leave anything out. They even fessed up about the working girl, although they did omit the detail.

At the end of what turned out to be an hour-long tale, the family sat in total silence for several moments.

"Did it really all happen, just like you told us?" Mike's sister Ann asked.

"I know it's hard to believe, but yeah, it did. Just like we said. I didn't know anybody in the world had the kind of money to live like the Smealls, but I guess they do. I'll never forget it," Mike said.

"But I wouldn't trade ten weekends like that for the time I've spent with you guys," JJ said. "Thank you. I love you all."

The next day, before Stott's dad took them back to the airport, he and Mrs. Stott took JJ and Mike into their bedroom. "JJ, you've mentioned our son James several times while you've been with us. We thought you might want to see his Congressional Medal of Honor. You are the only person outside our family we ever let see it. You are part of our family now, so there it is. Remember that our pride is surpassed only by our grief. Be Rangers if you must, but come back to us when your army time is over. Just come back in one piece. You don't need to be heroes! Just please come back."

Stott's mother hugged and kissed both boys. "You're always welcome here, John. Come back. Mike, don't you be a hero. Just come back," she said.

JJ, Mike, and his dad rode the twenty miles back to Boone County Airport in silence. Mike watched the city he had grown up in go by the window in framed slow motion. It was the last time that Mike Stott ever felt like a little boy.

Chapter Twenty-Six

Sharkey and Stott decided to get a head start on Ranger training by giving up alcohol. They didn't even drink on New Year's Eve, 1963! Mike and JJ were still assigned to the Airborne Training Center as acting corporals, but there were no jump schools during the holidays and Master Sergeant Dupree was really good to them. He knew they were reporting to Camp Darby on January 6, so he assigned them no duties.

"Run, exercise, and rest, boys. Don't drink alcohol, and don't drink coffee. If you're gonna make it through the next eight weeks you've gotta have the right mental attitude, and you've got to be able to take the physical pain. Remember this: The cadre will act like they want to wash you out. But really, they don't. It is extremely unusual for young recruits like you two to get assigned to Ranger school. I know you both can make it; the question is 'how bad do you want it?' Don't break! You, Stott, just might be the youngest man to ever get Ranger patches if you make it! That would be something! Go do it!" said Dupree.

PFCs Sharkey and Stott reported to Camp Darby at 1700 hours on Sunday, January 5, 1964. Hell started immediately.

Ranger school is divided into three parts: Crawl, Walk and Run. The sessions take place at three different locations, Camp Darby for Crawl, Camp Merrill for Walk and Camp Rudder for Run. At Camp Darby, Stott and Sharkey were pushed to their physical and psychological breaking points through twenty to twenty-two hour days during which they never stopped moving. Mike and JJ crawled on their bellies for miles, ran everywhere when they weren't crawling and rested by standing chin deep in swamp water. The Ranger training company that Sharkey and Stott were assigned to started with eighty men in the first formation at 0001 hours on January 6. Twenty days later, transitioning from Crawl to Walk, there were fifty-six men left.

On day twenty-one, as Mike and JJ began the Walk phase, they were introduced to Ranger Captain Gonzalez Gonzalez. "Think Crawl was hard, boys? Think you're pretty tough now? Think you're on the downhill? Fuck you all! You're mine, now, and only half of you will make it to Run!"

The remaining fifty-six men were standing in formation in an icy, cold rain on a foggy swamp bottom somewhere within the confines of Camp Merrill. They were in alphabetical order. JJ was standing on Mike's right. It was 0300 hours and pitch black.

Captain Gonzalez held the men at attention and strode through the rank with a flashlight that he aimed in each man's face for a minute or so as he personally sized up each trooper. Approaching from the left, he first peered into Stott's face before moving on to Sharkey. Mike was surprised to see that Captain Gonzalez was exactly JJ's height.

Gonzalez's eyes were yellow. Not yellow-brown, not sort of yellow, but pure yellow, like the eyes of a cat.

Troopers had learned to hold their eyes absolutely locked forward, unmoving when a Ranger officer or NCO faced them. If one's eyes flinched, that man was assured of a serious ass kicking. Captain Gonzalez challenged Stott's gaze for a very long time before moving on to Sharkey.

"How fucking tall are you, you little shit?" Captain Gonzalez screamed at JJ.

"Captain Gonzalez, sir! Five-six sir!" Sharkey screamed back.

Captain Gonzalez knocked JJ out cold with a vicious shot to the side of his head.

Stott knew it was a test for both him and Sharkey; he didn't flinch. Minutes passed before Sharkey regained consciousness.

"Stand up or quit, you miserable little undersized prick!" Captain Gonzalez yelled.

Somehow, through pure mental will, JJ resumed his position in the formation next to Mike. This incident took at least five minutes, maybe longer, because Sharkey was out cold for some time.

For the first time in Stott's life, he felt true desire to kill. Ways of murdering Gonzalez raced through Mike's head as he struggled to maintain his composure.

If complete silence can become quieter, it did at Camp Merrill that morning. Stott could feel Sharkey struggling to stay upright as Captain Gonzalez once again stood nose-to-nose with JJ staring into his eyes.

"Fucking dwarf!" said Gonzalez and moved on to the trooper to Sharkey's right.

So began the Walk portion of Ranger qualification.

Trainees were under strict speak-only-when-spoken-to discipline. Not a word could they utter unless prompted to do so by cadre. For the next twenty days, the entire Walk segment, Captain Gonzalez tortured John Sharkey by using him for every hand-to-hand combat demonstration and assigning him to even more shit details than the rest of the men. That JJ was able to endure this treatment amazed every trooper in the company.

Sharkey never once complained. Not even to Stott, during Walk, or later.

Once, when they had the chance to speak to each other alone Mike asked JJ, "You okay"

"Yes, shut up!" was his only response.

The Run phase of Ranger school moved on to Camp Rudder, closer to the Florida-Georgia border. The training company was down to forty-three men. "If you can make it to Run you should make it as a Ranger," they were told by Major Hargrove as they began the final nineteen days of Ranger qualification. "Show me that you can lead or follow in a team and that you never, ever lose your composure. Don't blow it now. You are each nineteen days away from personal accomplishment that will change the remainder of your life. Get there!"

Sharkey and Stott had been surprised to see Hargrove again, but they understood that their previous exposure to this officer was irrelevant. JJ and Mike were assigned to different teams and were totally separated for the first time since their military experience began. As they waded away into yet another cold, miserable swamp, JJ gave Mike a brief "air check." Stott resolved not to fail over the next eighteen days.

At the midpoint of "Run," the Ranger trainees got a four hour midday break in one of the few clearings at Camp Rudder on a sunny, but cool afternoon. There really was no explanation for the downtime. Perhaps it was to see if the men were all still mentally competent. They hadn't had a hot meal for days, maybe weeks; it seemed like longer. The army trucked out chow to the trainees in marmite containers full of steaks, potatoes, and salad. It tasted fantastic. Men were allowed seconds and everyone dug in. There was even coffee! First they'd had in quite a while.

Tactical training conditions had been called off for the break. After chowing down, the trainees were sprawled out on the side of an embankment, letting their first hot meal in seven weeks settle in their stomachs. They were as relaxed as they could be given they were still Ranger trainees.

Captain Gonzalez came walking up out of the woods just as the soldiers finished their meal. The mere sight of Gonzalez set them on edge, but he called out to them in a previously unheard "soft" voice, "Listen up, troops! Stay relaxed! You're on your one break in Ranger training, so just stay cool."

As Gonzalez got closer to the men, they could see that the captain was carrying a small black snake, perhaps two feet long, in his left hand. Not unusual to see the snake, they were everywhere. Normally, one didn't pick them up. Captain Gonzalez continued. "Just stay relaxed troops! While you're on your break, I just wanted to demonstrate to y'all how a Ranger captain kills a snake."

With that introduction he had their full attention. Captain Gonzalez then transferred the snake to his right hand, holding it firmly with just the snake's head and perhaps one inch of its body protruding from the thumb side of his right fist. The snake's body was wiggling, trying to escape Gonzalez's grasp. As the soldiers watched to learn a Ranger captain's snake-killing technique, Captain Gonzalez stuck the snake's head into his mouth and bit off the snake's head. Blood spurted and dripped from the captain's mouth as he chewed on the snake. Gonzalez dropped the snake's headless body to the ground and then spit out the head.

"Not bad," he said.

Every single Ranger trainee in the company lost it! They threw up all that they had just consumed, plus some! On themselves and on each other! It was the sickest and most repulsive thing the trainees had ever seen. The combined stench of the trooper's puke was overwhelming. As Captain Gonzalez stood there watching their agony, troopers saw him smile. It was the first and last time that Gonzalez ever showed an emotion other than anger.

Stott heard later that Captain Gonzalez always pulled that trick on Ranger trainees at their one and only break. Rangers said they had seen him bite off the heads of rabbits and other rodents if a snake wasn't available. For years, every snake Mike saw, and he saw plenty, reminded him of Captain Gonzalez.

Just four days before Run was to conclude, an unusual warm front swept over the Georgia-Florida border region. It was February 24, 1964, and the company was running a night ambush exercise deep in a cottonwood patch. Stott's team had been issued some early-generation, night-vision assistance goggles, and they helped at least a little to see into the moonless night. An aggressor team was creeping toward Mike's unit from several directions. The plan was to let the aggressors crawl past his position and then infiltrate their flank, cutting their force in two.

Previous night exercises had found the trainees struggling not to shiver from the cold, but this night was actually hot. By that point in Run there were few portions of any trooper's exposed skin not completely covered by insect bites. Resisting scratching these infestations took real willpower. Mike lay motionless, fighting the urge to scratch, watching one of the aggressors crawl by his position less than twenty feet away. Stott wondered why the aggressor couldn't smell him. It had been seven days since his last shower.

Suddenly the aggressor that Mike was watching screamed out in pain and raised himself up on to one knee. He then fell over on his back, his body writhing in convulsions. His scream caused another soldier to move into a trip wire and the entire area was immediately illuminated by flares. The glare from the flares made Stott's goggles feel like he was looking directly into a sunrise. By this fifty-fifth day of Ranger school, Mike was disciplined enough to remain motionless and concealed, calculating that this was probably yet another test of troopers' concentration. Then Stott saw the snake, probably a cottonmouth and the biggest one he had ever seen.

Human instinct overrode Mike's Ranger discipline. "Man down! Medic! Snake bite!" he screamed out. More flares went off, and Stott saw that there were several troopers much closer to his position than he had realized. Mike rose to a crouch and moved toward the fallen trooper, careful to avoid the snake's path of departure. Still fearing this was all some trap within the exercise, Stott put his hand on the still writhing trooper and could see that his eyes were rolled back in his head.

From somewhere, a lieutenant colonel appeared dressed completely in black, but with "OBSERVER" where his name badge should have been. "What the fuck?" were the first words out of his mouth.

"Sir! Pretty sure it was a cottonmouth, sir," Stott said.

The colonel raised a flare pistol and fired a yellow distress flare into the air. "Tactical off! Grid A-5 red, trooper down! Cottonmouth bite! Get me a chopper, now!" he screamed into his radio. "Name, son!" the colonel said to Stott.

"Stott, sir! Mike B. Ranger training . . . "

"Shut the fuck up! I know who you are and the team you're with! Do you know his name or where he's bit?"

"No, sir!"

"Start cutting his clothes off, now! Got to find the bite!"

A medic showed up from somewhere and several other troopers from both Mike's team and the aggressors had now converged on the site. Another trooper helped Stott cut the bitten trooper's clothes off. They saw two very small, but rapidly swelling holes in his right thigh just above the knee.

"Shit! Bad place," the medic said as he cut X's over both fang marks. The medic then began squeezing the area around the bite, trying to force the venom back through the X cuts. Another medic arrived and stuck three syringes in the downed trooper.

"Pulse racing! We gotta get him stabilized!" said the second medic. Stott backed away as the medics took over.

Major Hargrove emerged from the semi-darkness as more flares went up to mark the position. "Who called off my exercise?" were the first words out of his mouth. Then he saw the observer/colonel and saluted him. "Didn't see you, sir. What happened?"

"Ask Trooper Stott, major. He made the first noise."

"That right, Stott?"

"Sir, no sir! The guy who got bitten screamed out, and I froze, thinking it might be part of the exercise. Then I saw a big snake right by the guy and figured it got him, sir," Mike said.

Major Hargrove glared at Stott. Mike heard a chopper's blades beating the tepid air. The colonel set off two more bright flares and a green smoke canister indicating to the helicopter pilots that they had clearance for a landing zone. The medics got the bitten trooper in the helicopter, and it lifted off immediately.

"Goddamn it! This fucks up my tactical. Cadre, call in the teams! Now!" said Hargrove.

It took about twenty minutes, but finally all personnel involved in the exercise had gathered at the scene of the incident. There in black aggressor garb was Sharkey with the rest of his team.

Including the colonel that he had originally encountered and three other observers, Stott counted sixty men; forty-two trainees and the rest cadre. It was now just past 0600 hours and the faintest of morning light lit the eastern horizon.

"On me, men. Squat in front, stand in the back." Major Hargrove reset the exercise. The men stayed with it for another thirty hours. The trainees later learned that the trooper bitten by the cottonmouth died in the chopper.

The last two days of Run consisted of a series of tests of physical endurance and mental discipline. Somehow, both Sharkey and Stott made it through the final hurdles of Ranger school. They had earned their patches and were to receive promotions to E-4, corporal, as well.

On Saturday, March 1, 1964, a ceremony was held at the main parade ground at Fort Benning to award 142 men Ranger qualification patches. The men were told that this was an unusual location because troopers from three other training companies would also receive their patches in a combined ceremony attended by several generals and a plethora of army brass. The army public relations guys were going to film the ceremony for use both with the public and as a recruiting film for new inductees.

The forty-two troopers in the graduating group spent Friday afternoon, evening, and Saturday morning spit-shining their boots and polishing brass. The dress greens that JJ and Mike had tailored after jump school now fit loosely around their waists but were tight in the shoulders. Mike and JJ were in truly remarkable physical condition.

The new Rangers formed up by training company and marched into the main parade ground to an army band playing "Stars and Stripes Forever." The parade ground was partially surrounded by bleachers that were full of troopers' families as well as hundreds of officers and their families, all anxious to hobnob with the generals at a reception following the ceremony.

The generals and their staffs, as well as a huge complement of other officers were seated on a large reviewing stand at the front the assembly area. The band was off to the right side. In typical military fashion, the reviewing stand was positioned so that the officers could look down on the troops. Conversely, the troopers had to look up at the officers. The army way!

The men marched into the parade ground to the applause of literally hundreds of people, maybe thousands. The four companies were called to attention and then parade rest. Then began a series of speeches by the generals and colonels about how great the accomplishment was to become Rangers. Pretty heady stuff. Sharkey and Stott were side by side; Mike could feel the pride emanating from his person.

After the field grade officers made their speeches, the cadre from each Ranger training company made the presentations of badges and patches to their trainees. To Mike's great surprise, Captain Gonzalez assisted Major Hargrove in the awards to his group. As the senior captain in the Ranger training regiment, Gonzalez was given the honor of closing the ceremony.

Holding with military tradition, just prior to dismissing the new Rangers at the end of the ceremony, Captain Gonzalez said, "Congratulations, Rangers! Any questions? Dis—"

Before Captain Gonzalez could complete pronunciation of his last word, "dismissed," Corporal John Sharkey screamed out at the top of his lungs, "Captain Gonzalez, sir! Corporal John J. Sharkey, sir! Question, please, sir!"

An indescribable hush fell over the parade grounds. People and officers that were starting to get up from their seats sat back down. The band that was ready to sound off sat back down! It was unheard of! A newly made Ranger had a question?

Captain Gonzalez stared at Sharkey from the reviewing stand. After several long minutes of dead silence Gonzalez spoke, "What's your question, Corporal Sharkey?"

"Captain Gonzalez, sir! Where will you be ten years from today, sir?" Sharkey screamed.

You could have heard a pin drop. Every new Ranger, all the training cadres, and all of the people attending the graduation waited for Captain Gonzalez's response. "Why, Corporal Sharkey, do you want to know where I'll be in ten years?"

"Captain Gonzalez, sir! In ten years I estimate that you will be approximately fifty years old, sir! I will be thirty. I figure by then I'll be able to kick your ass, and I want to be able to find you, sir!" JJ screamed at the top of his lungs.

For an instant, the crowd remained silent. Then one of the generals laughed out loud. That started it! The entire crowd roared with laughter. When the cheering and laughter finally subsided, Captain Gonzalez responded, "Corporal Sharkey, I make you this promise! I'll find you ten years from today! Dismissed!"

There is another military tradition whereby soldiers sling their headgear into the air following a graduation. The night before the ceremony, two of the more senior guys that had made it through Ranger school circulated in the four barracks and got all of the men to agree not to pitch their garrison hats. Instead, the 142 newly pinned Rangers screamed out the loudest "HOOAH!" ever recorded! The generals led another round of applause for them! It was the proudest day of Mike Stott's life.

Chapter Twenty-Seven

On that memorable day that Corporals John J. Sharkey and Mike B. Stott became two of the youngest Rangers in the army, Second Lieutenant Sylvatore Anthony Mobliano was attending his monthly drill weekend at a National Guard armory just south of Albany, New York. He had been assigned to the New York National Guard Judge Advocates' Office and rotated to various facilities around the state, gaining exposure to his duties. Syl reported to a major that had twenty-five years in the guard and was coasting toward his military retirement. Frankly, Lieutenant Mobliano was bored. This was the third monthly drill weekend he had experienced since receiving his commission. He sincerely hoped future drills would be more fulfilling.

As he sat at lunch with the major at a country club close to the armory, Syl asked, "Sir, is there anything more I could be doing to help you, sir? I've finished reviewing the two cases you gave me this morning and the clerks should have my analyses typed for signature when we return. Will you have time to review them with me, sir?"

"Relax, lieutenant. Didn't you learn never to volunteer for anything in basic training? Frankly, I don't have much to do for the rest of the weekend, either. Unless one of our guardsmen commits a crime while in uniform during a drill, this is pretty good duty. Relax, son. You could be commanding an active duty rifle company, working your balls off, instead of enjoying this government-sponsored lunch! Let's have another drink," suggested the major.

Syl was perplexed. Martini lunches and wine with dinner on drill weekends was certainly not what he had expected from the New York National Guard. "Sir, begging your pardon, sir, but I guess I'm feeling a little guilty about my contribution, sir. Two young guys I went to basic with are getting their Ranger patches at Fort Benning today. They've been through real tough training, and now they'll probably go to

Vietnam. What a pair they were, sir! A boxer and an orphan, both just now eighteen and gung-ho beyond belief."

"You say they were in basic with you and now they're through Ranger school? Didn't know that was possible, lieutenant. They already got through jump school, too?" asked the skeptical major.

"Yes, sir, they did! The one kid speaks Chinese and a couple of other languages. And all he wants to do is be a good soldier, sir." Syl still marveled at JJ's dedication.

"Good for him. Order me another vodka martini, lieutenant. I have to take a piss."

As Syl watched his commanding officer walk toward the men's room he prayed to God to never become as jaded as the major. His thoughts turned to the firm he had joined. Syl was thankful that his civilian career was challenging. Whittlesea and Polk, PC was one of the most prestigious law firms in Manhattan. Syl was proud to have been accepted into its junior staff. Whittlesea and Polk boasted two retired U.S. senators as partners, and Syl had already met with of them!

The major returned. "Here's to your young Rangers! Better them than us, lieutenant! Dessert?"

"No thank you, sir," was all Syl could manage.

As Second Lieutenant Mobliano sipped his coffee, Corporal Eddy Hale was staring at a stack of reports that he had to type before day's end. He had made the mistake of bragging about his typing skills. Now he was a clerk/secretary to Captain James Downs in an analysis section in the Pentagon. Eddy lit a cigarette and reflected on his luck in the army. The one skill that Eddy possessed was the ability to type very rapidly and almost never miss a stroke. Given that some army documentation required as many as seven carbon copies, Fast Eddy's typing skills earned him selective treatment and great duty, assuming one's ambition was to be a typist.

But Eddy Hale still dreamed of being a sniper! How could he possibly admit to his father and brothers that all he did was type documents, smoke cigarettes, and drink coffee in the army? The last time he spoke with the Mobliano girls

they had told him that John Sharkey and Mike Stott expected
to receive their Ranger patches today! And they had already
been to jump school! His big accomplishment was to get
through seven long documents before making his first error
of the day on his IBM typewriter! Goddamn! Those guys
had all the luck!

Private First Class George Washington Howard was in
a bar outside Ramstadt, Germany, on that first Saturday of
March 1964. But he wasn't drinking and having fun! In fact,
he was just about to have to step in and break up a fight between two young airborne troopers that had been taunting
each other over a fräulein. He was backing a 101st Airborne
military police sergeant named Jimmy Lee from Carthage,
Tennessee, and he knew how much the sergeant liked to use
his billy club.

"You ready, Private Howard? The little guy's buddies over
there are drunk, too, so they'll probably jump in to help their
boy. I'll get the two Romeos! You watch my back! Any one of
these dickheads move, you smack 'em, got it? Don't hesitate!
You got to show tough with these punks! They think because
they been to jump school they can whip the world! Here we
go! Let's kick ass!" Sergeant Lee swung into action.

As Howard positioned to cover his sergeant, he reflected
back to the fight he had with Mike Stott. Hopefully, none of
these young troopers could box! He remembered that today
was the day his buddies, Sharkey and Stott, were to get their
Ranger patches if they made it through the course. Since arriving in Germany, Howard had been so lonely it hurt. He
wished he'd tried to get through Ranger school with Mike
and JJ. As the only black MP in the 101st, making new friends
had been just about impossible. He missed his buddies. He
thought of their pact. Would he ever even see them again?

A bar chair came flying through the air in his general direction. George knew it was time to focus on the present!
Good luck, boys, he thought.

PFC Larry Allsmeir sat looking out through the front flap
of the twenty-man tent he called home. An icy rain was fall-

ing, turning to snow as he watched. He felt totally trapped out here on the west side of Fort Sill, Oklahoma, loading artillery shells into the 155 Howitzers belonging to the 1st Infantry Division, the "Big Red 1." How the hell could this have happened? Allsmeir carried a copy of his enlistment papers with him at all times, still hoping some NCO or officer would help him out of this miserable situation. Could he endure two and a quarter more years of this shit?

After completing his eight-week MOS training in artillery at Fort Sill, Allsmeir had been assigned to the Big Red 1, but held at Sill with a brigade that was practicing close-in infantry fire support tactics just across the post from where he had trained. As a junior PFC in his unit, he had been denied any holiday leave and was beginning his seventh month in the prairie land hell called Oklahoma. Larry was the only enlisted college graduate in his unit. Most of the guys seemed to hold his education against him. There was no opportunity to attend graduate school classes and very little to do in his off time other than read.

"Allsmeir, Buckley, Mitchell, Rinehart, and Weil! Front and center, now!" Allsmeir's platoon sergeant screamed out.

Oh shit! Now what? It was Saturday, for shit's sake, his Sabbath!

"Listen up, troopers! You five dickheads have been assigned to a new training school, right here in beautiful Oklahoma! Pack up your shit; you're goin' back across post to learn firebase construction techniques! You'll move tomorrow, start class 0730 Monday morning! Dismissed!"

Now what? Firebase construction? Fuck!

Allsmeir's buddy, Milt Smeall, was fairing considerably better. Specialist Smeall was waxing his Stingray convertible inside a maintenance facility at Fort Harrison on that first Saturday in March 1964. As a finance clerk specialist, Smeall worked an eight to five duty day, Monday through Friday. He nearly always got the weekends off. When he made specialist, E-4, he was allowed to live off post if he could afford it, and, clearly, he could.

When he had gone home for the holidays the past December on a fourteen-day leave, Barry found a new Corvette in his space in the family compound. It was silver blue with black leather interior and a white convertible top. The car had a 375 horsepower fuel-injected motor and a four-speed transmission. "We figured you needed a toy out there in Indianapolis," his dad had said. "Hell, you can drive home most weekends if you want to, or I can send the plane. You've only got seventeen months to go and I've got a feeling they're going to keep you right there at Fort Harrison. Need more money, son? Is there anything to spend it on?"

In fact, Miltee had found something to spend his money on. Her name was Beverly Sue Parsons. She was twenty years old and worked as a cashier at Harmon's Men's Store in downtown Indianapolis. When Milt went into Harmon's to buy some civvies to keep in his new apartment, Bev had helped him select ties. The first thing he noticed were her tits. Had to be 40D's, and they sat north of a wonderfully small waist. Beverly had green eyes and auburn hair and a fantastic smile.

"Where you going to wear all these ties? I thought you said you were a soldier," Beverly asked. "Are you planning on asking me out to dinner or something? If so, and if I say yes, we don't have to go to a fancy place. I know soldiers don't make much money, so we could just go for Chinese. Are you going to buy that blue blazer?"

"Huh? Yeah, I'm going to buy the blazer. Do you want to go out with me? Really?" Smeall was mesmerized.

"Well, honey, you've got to ask. Maybe I'll say yes and maybe I'll say no. But you won't know unless you ask. Wow! All this stuff you're buying comes to over $400!"

"Okay. Would you like to go to dinner sometime?" Milt timidly asked.

"Well, it just so happens I'm free tonight! Or at least reasonable!" Bev teased. "Do you have a car? Where are you going to put all these clothes in the barracks?"

"Uh, yeah. I've got a car. You really want to go out to-night? It's 1620 hours; I mean 4:20 p.m. When do you get off? Where do you live?"

"Not so fast, cutie! First of all, what's your name? You're not married, are you? I would never go out with a married guy!" Bev coyly stated.

"No! Of course I'm not married! My name is Barry, Barry Smeall. Look, if you're serious, I'll pick you up after work and take you to the best restaurant in Indianapolis for dinner! What do you say?"

"Really? You mean like St. Elmo Steak House?" Beverly was surprised.

"Sure. Tell me when and I'll go drop these clothes off and freshen up. Then I'll come get you unless you want to meet me at this place, what is it, St. Elmos?"

"I get off at six! But sometimes it takes a while to clear the register. Will you really pick me up and take me to St. Elmos? For dinner, really?" Bev questioned. "You must be an officer!"

"No, I'm not an officer! Look, let's have dinner and talk. If we don't get along, I'll just drop you at your car, okay?"

"Okay! Pick me up at 6:15! Promise you're not just fooling with me? You'll really be here?" Beverly asked.

"Of course I'll be here! See you at 6:15!"

Milt Smeall had a tugging in his gut that he had never felt before. What was he in for? Beverly was absolutely gorgeous, and she liked him before she found out he was rich! She called him cutie! God, please let her be Jewish, Milt prayed.

When he returned to pick Beverly up, the town was emptying out. Barry found a space right in front of Harmon's. It was 5:50 p.m.. Milt put a nickel in the meter and walked around looking in store windows until just before 6:00 p.m. At 5:59, he entered Harmon's just as the manager was locking the door.

"I'm sorry, young man, we're just closing," said the manager.

"Uh, I'm here to meet Miss Parsons," said Barry.

"Is that so? Beverly! There's a young man here says he's to meet you! That so?"

"Yes, Mr. Smith! I'll be out in five minutes!"

Barry stood pretending to inspect more ties, but his eyes kept darting back in the direction Bev's voice had come from. When she came into sight Barry felt his knees start to buckle. Miss Beverly Parsons had piled her auburn hair up on her head and put on evening makeup. Somehow, she had found a light green sweater dress to change into, and it clung seductively to her body. Bev now had on high heels and the combined effect was to make her look a bit older, and even more beautiful.

"Hi, cutie! How do I look?" Bev asked.

Barry Milton Smeall was tongue-tied! He simply couldn't speak! Mr. Smith, waiting to lock the door behind them said, "Young man, are you all right?"

Finally Barry managed, "You're beautiful! I mean, I'm sorry, but you look like a movie star! You're taller!"

"Well, honey, high heels will do that! You cleaned up pretty good yourself! Let's go! Have a good Sunday, Mr. Smith. Good night!"

At the sidewalk Bev asked, "Where did you park? We could walk to St. Elmos, it's not very far."

"Uh, I'm right here," Barry said as he opened the door to his Corvette.

"Oh, my God! You're kidding me, right? You have a Stingray? Oh, my God!" Now Bev was stuttering.

Barry was happy. Bev recognized a Stingray! "Yep! And it's a Fuelie! What do you think?"

Bev was running her hands over the vet's dashboard and caressing the shifter. "Is it really yours?" she asked.

"Yeah. It is. Where is this St Elmos?"

"Two blocks over and two down. But take me for a ride! We can eat later! I've never been in a Corvette! Is it new?"

"I got it last Christmas," Barry said and then realized how that might sound. "I mean, I got it back in Pittsburgh when I went home for the holidays."

"So it's brand new! You're from Pittsburgh? I've never been that far east. Fact is, I've never been anywhere! Have you?" Bev asked. She reached over and put her hand on Barry's thigh, causing him to release the clutch too quickly. The vet's tires broke loose just a little, giving a healthy squeal as Barry pulled out from the curb.

"Neat!" Bev screamed. "Do it again!"

Barry popped second gear and got another squeal from the vet's posi-traction rear axle. The car lurched a little to the side, but Barry straightened it up and slowed down. They were on the main drag in downtown Indianapolis.

"I love this car!" Bev yelled. "To heck with dinner! Let's go for a ride!"

"You sure? I'm kinda hungry. A big steak sounds good."

"Just drive, silly! We can eat later. I know, let's go the Pole! We can order burgers and malts and eat in the car!"

"What's the Pole?" Barry asked.

"It's the neatest drive-in in town! It's out towards the race track. Turn here!"

Several times during the short drive to the Pole, Barry barked the vet's tires and each time Beverly squealed with delight. They sat in the car and ate cheeseburgers and drank huge, extra-thick chocolate malts. When she finished her burger, Bev let out a man-sized burp. "Oh, excuse me!" she said. "I guess I'm so excited I gobbled down my food. You're still eating!"

Barry was still eating because he had been focused on Bev's breasts way more than on his burger. "Guess I'm a slow eater," Barry offered.

"That's because you've been staring at my chest!" Bev explained. "It's okay; I know my boobs are too big! Don't you think so?"

Barry Smeall struggled hard not to choke on a french fry. "No I haven't! I mean, I haven't been staring at your boobs, and they're not too big for me! I mean, if I had noticed them, I wouldn't think they're too big!"

"You'd think they were if you saw me with my bra off! I just don't know what to do with them," Bev cried.

Barry Smeall was absolutely smitten. The most beautiful girl he had ever been close to was explaining to him that she thought her tits were too big! She wasn't embarrassed talking about them. She just sat there, normal as could be, discussing her size 40D bazooms. Barry tried to recover. "Want to go to a movie?" he asked. Might be too cold for a drive-in, but I think I saw a theater just back a ways."

"Got any other ideas?" Bev asked in return.

"Well, yeah, I do, but I just met you three hours ago! I mean, I don't know what you like, so you choose," Barry said.

"I still live with my folks pretty far out of town. But I told them I was staying with Jeanie tonight. She's my best friend. So I've got the whole night! Now do you have any ideas?" Bev teased.

Barry felt the sweat popping out on his forehead. Was this gorgeous creature suggesting what he hoped she was? Hell, might as well go for it!

"Well, Beverly, I have my own apartment off post, and I've got a swell new RCA color TV. Want to go watch some TV?" Barry ventured.

"You're not an officer, and you have your own apartment? How old are you, honey?" Bev asked.

"I'll be twenty-three in June," Barry answered. "How old are you?"

"You should never ask a lady her age!" Bev retorted. "But I'll tell you 'cause I like you! I'll be twenty-one in May."

Barry missed three shifts on the ride to his apartment. Bev didn't say anything. She just kept her hand on his right shoulder. Barry had chosen a second floor apartment in a new complex on the northeast side of town to be close to Fort Harrison. The building was so new that he had no neighbors below or next to him yet.

As they walked through his front door Bev exclaimed, "Wow! This furniture looks brand new! And look at that TV! It's the biggest one I ever saw! Are you rich or something?"

It was a question that Barry was prepared for. "I'm just careful with my money," he said. "Want a beer?"

"I don't drink alcohol. But I'd love a Coke! I have to use the little girls' room, okay?" She kicked off her shoes and headed down the hallway. When she emerged with her hair let down, she had removed the sleeved sweater, revealing bare shoulders. The effect was stunning.

"Wow!" Barry said. "You really are beautiful."

The first program that came on was the *Lawrence Welk Show*. Bobby Grayson was doing a version of the Elvis Presley million seller, "Love Me Tender." They listened to several other songs until Beverly said, "Barry, don't get the wrong impression of me, but when you walked into Harmon's today, my heart fluttered. If you don't really like me, please don't hurt me."

Barry slowly, cautiously moved to Beverly and softly kissed her lips. Her response was to melt into his arms and very gently return his kiss. Barry was so aroused he began to shake. "Not here, let's do this right," Beverly whispered. "I'm a virgin, Barry. Is that okay?"

As they entered the bedroom hand-in-hand, Beverly whispered, "Let's take our time. I want to remember everything." She sat Barry back on the pillows and unbuttoned the front of her sweater dress. The dress fell to her waist and she put both hands behind her back to loosen the five hooks on her bra. Her breasts seemed to rise rather than fall as Bev removed the brassiere. She let her dress fall to the floor and stood there in her panties facing Barry.

"I don't have any, you know, hair down there, okay?" She sat on the side of the bed and slowly removed her panties. Then she stood again and stared down at Barry, revealing a body like he thought only existed on the air-brushed pages of *Playboy*.

All Barry could manage was, "Oh, my God!" By Sunday noon, Barry Smeall had decided to ask Beverly Sue Parsons to marry him.

Chapter Twenty-Eight

The Saturday night following their certification as Rangers, Sharkey and Stott drank free all night in the NCO club at Fort Benning. They couldn't buy a drink! Sharkey's challenge to Captain Gonzalez had spread across Benning like wildfire, and all the enlisted Rangers wanted to buy the "Shortest Ranger" a drink. Mike drank free too, as his buddy. Stott told the story about how Gonzalez cold-cocked JJ during the first hours of "Walk" a hundred times. Fortunately, several other guys in their training company who had also witnessed the incident were there to back him up. It was an incredible tale!

"I had that sadistic motherfucker in 'Walk' also," recounted an older Ranger. "Meanest guy I've ever been around! Watch your ass, Corporal Sharkey! Gonzalez will be gunning for you! I mean that literally!" As Mike and JJ got drunker and met more Rangers they heard the warning about Captain Gonzalez "gunning" for JJ several times. Stott began to worry that it could be for real. But drink they did!

Sunday, March 2, 1964, Sharkey and Stott were to report to the Sixth Ranger Training Brigade right there at Benning. When they arrived at the Sixth's orderly room, they met Master Sergeant Pete Ryan and their commanding officer, Colonel William Duckworth.

"You both look like shit! Did a little celebrating last night, did you, troopers?" Master Sergeant Pete Ryan inquired. "Corporal Sharkey, it says here you are fluent in three Chinese dialects. Is that true?"

"Yes, Master Sergeant!" JJ barked out.

"Pipe down, you're not a trainee anymore, you're a Ranger now! Save the yelling for your girlfriend! How'd you manage to learn Chinese?" Ryan asked.

Sharkey recounted the story of learning the language to honor St. Agnes's benefactor, Captain Estes Sharkey. Colonel Duckworth spoke for the first time, "You two met in basic training?"

"Sir, yes sir!" Mike and JJ said.

"And you've been together ever since? Seems odd. Any explanation?"

"Sir, no sir!" both of them said again.

"Corporal Sharkey, you're the guy that caused the uproar at your graduation ceremony, right?" the Colonel asked.

"Sir, yes sir!" said JJ by himself this time.

"Did you think Corporal Sharkey was amusing yesterday, Corporal Stott?"

"Sir, no sir!" Mike said.

"Why not, Corporal?" the officer wanted to know.

"Sir, I knew he was dead serious, sir!" Stott responded.

Master Sergeant Pete Ryan and Colonel Duckworth exchanged a very serious look.

"Your records indicate that you both know how to shoot. Who's the better shot?" Sergeant Ryan asked.

"Master Sergeant Ryan, Stott is! He taught me how to instinct fire, Master Sergeant!" JJ said again, a little too loudly.

"That so? What do you mean by 'instinct fire?' That's a new one to me," Ryan said.

"It refers to keeping both eyes open unless you're more than about a hundred yards out, right Corporal?" Colonel Duckworth explained.

"Sir, yes sir!" Mike said.

"And I'm bettin' your dad is a pretty good shot, right Corporal?"

"Sir, yes sir! The best you've ever seen with a pistol, sir!" Now Stott was being too loud.

"Um-hum. Well, there's something funny going on in my army, and I don't like it!" Duckworth fired off.

Holy shit! Now what?

"You two corporals are hereby assigned to the army's Languages School in Monterey, California, close to Fort Ord. I guess I get it with Sharkey, but how you got assigned there, too, Stott, baffles me. You got connections? If so, you better tell me now! I don't need any connected troopers in my command, get it? Got anything to tell, Corporal?"

"Sir, no sir!" Mike said, trying to keep cool.

"Sir, may I speak, sir?" Sharkey asked.

"Why not? I'm not getting anywhere with your buddy, here. Go ahead, speak freely Corporal Sharkey," directed Duckworth.

It took all the willpower Mike could manage not to smack JJ right then and there because he knew what JJ was going to say! It was Sharkey's one weakness; Mike's brother's CMH.

"Sir, Stott's brother won the Congressional Medal of Honor in Korea, sir! I think that's why we got to Ranger school so fast, sir!" JJ said.

Colonel Duckworth and Master Sergeant Ryan stared at Mike for some time. "Is that correct, Corporal Stott?" Duckworth asked.

"Sir, yes sir!" Stott said.

"You have a lot to live up to, soldier," Colonel Duckworth softly said. "But that wouldn't have anything to do with your posting in the army and certainly nothing to do with you, Corporal Sharkey! Fact is, I have your orders right here. They actually arrived ahead of your graduation yesterday. Very strange. You start 10 March; need to be there 9 March. Transport via train! Damn! Your unit's going to Bragg Monday; makes no sense to take you guys there and then start you back west. Master Ryan, cut transport orders and put 'em on a train! I want you boys speaking Hmong to me when you get back! Dismissed!"

As Mike and JJ waited for their papers, Master Sergeant Ryan continued to question them as his clerk typed their documents. "Think you can shoot bad guys as well as you can hit targets, troopers?" he asked.

"Yes, Sergeant!" they said.

"Good answer! Looks like you get a train right out of Columbus on 4 March and take four days to get to Ord. Don't let the infantry guys goad you into any fights unless you're sure there's no MPs around! Then kick their march-lovin' asses. I expect you to run with us in the a.m. and then you're good to go! Get out of my military sight!"

"Yes, Master Sergeant!"

When they got outside, Mike blasted JJ, "Goddamn it, Sharkey! Stop telling people about my brother's CMH! You know it pisses me off, but you keep talking about it every chance you get! Knock it off!"

"Mike, if I had a brother that won a Congressional Medal of Honor I'd be so proud I'd tell everyone. You should, too," John said.

"Do me a favor and drop it! Okay?"

"Only if you buy me a steak at that joint in town! We're not restricted to post, so let's go!"

When Sharkey and Stott finally hitched their way into Columbus, everything was closed! Nothing was open on Sunday, not even the gas stations! They wound up walking all the way back to the barrack after they stopped in the NCO club. It served beer seven days a week, even on Sundays!

Sharkey and Stott made 0500 hours formation with the Sixth Rangers on Monday, March 3, and were introduced to yet another physical training technique. They ran backward! For about a mile around a cinder track, they actually ran in reverse. Then they did Ranger calisthenics for one hour and ran two miles the normal way.

Mike and JJ sat down in the mess hall at 0700 hours and made many new acquaintances among the troopers in the Sixth. They were friendly, but reserved. The boys knew they'd have to earn respect from these guys when they returned from languages school.

An older guy wearing E-8 stripes described their challenge. "We heard about you, Corporal Sharkey, sounding off at graduation. Don't do that again. Look around you. The troopers in our teams have years in the army. You and the other new guys have months. That pisses us off. You'll have to earn your way in the Sixth. Don't get outta shape out there in the land of

fruits and nuts! You'll need to be tough when you return. I'm
gonna need shooters! Lay off the caffeine! Pack up and shove
off. By the way, I'm Master Sergeant Snook."

Master Sergeant Snook stood up and left. Nearly all the
Rangers that were still in the mess hall followed him out.
Across the hall, Mike and JJ spotted four Rangers who
looked about as green as they did. Stott recognized a couple
of them from the graduation ceremony. One very tall and
young-looking corporal walked over to where JJ and Mike
were sitting.

"I'm Pete Netting," he said. "Got my patches with you
guys. Remember you 'cause of Sharkey's blowout with Gonzalez. Mind if I sit down?"

They shook hands as Netting sat down. "Come on over,
guys." He motioned for the other new guys to join them.
Mike and JJ shook hands with the other three men, and then
Netting said, "Heard you two are going to languages school.
We're all leaving for sniper school tomorrow. We've got a
question for you guys."

Netting's tone was odd. "Shoot," JJ said.

"How long have you guys been the army?" Netting
asked.

"Why?" Stott countered.

Netting stared at him. Mike had the feeling he and Netting
were not going to be friends, but then Pete lightened up.

"Look, the four of us are RA's, in for four to six years
each. We all volunteered for jump school, but then got
pushed into Ranger training. I'm not telling you who, but a
couple of us feel that better guys than us got washed out of
Ranger school even though they performed better than we
did. Two of us are twenty years old, but John and Bill, here,
are still nineteen. And now, like you guys, we find ourselves
in the 6th Rangers. None of us have been in the army longer
than a year. So, I ask you again, how long you guys been the
army?" Netting asked.

JJ and Mike looked at each other and decided Netting
might be okay after all. "Stott and I met in basic training at

Fort Dix this past July. We've been in the army about eight months. Tell you the truth, we've both wondered how, exactly, we got to be sitting here as Rangers, too," JJ told their new group of buddies.

"You've been in the army for less time than us!" the guy named Bill exclaimed. "How old are you guys?"

"We're both eighteen," Mike said.

"Holy shit!" all four responded.

Netting seemed to be the spokesman for the four of them. "We're not trying to get into your shit, here, so hear me out. Why do you think you guys got fast-tracked? You think it was just the luck of the draw?"

Mike gave JJ the "I'll answer that" nod. "We don't know. We both shot perfect hundreds on M-14 qualification in basic. We've both kept our noses clean, at least until JJ sounded off to Captain Gonzalez!"

That brought a chuckle from their new friends. Stott continued. "Our captain in AIT got promoted to major in the Tenth Rangers and our Top told us he pulled strings to get us directly into jump school. Then, the officer, Major Hargrove, showed up as cadre in Ranger school. But we don't really know if Hargrove helped us or not. Sounds like you guys have developed some ideas about what you're asking us about. So why don't you share them with us?"

Netting gave his three buddies a "should-we-share-it-with-these-guys look." He made a decision to open up. "Let me ask you guys this. Are you orphans?"

The question astonished Stott, but not Sharkey. JJ said, "Yeah, I am. And I'd bet you, John, and maybe Bill are, too. Am I right?"

"We all are, Sharkey," Corporal Netting confirmed.

The six new Rangers sat there in absolute silence for several minutes. The mess sergeant broke the spell by telling them to vacate his mess hall or get put on KP. It was 0850 hours. The men walked outside, still without speaking.

Netting finally spoke, "Okay. So you're a regular guy, Stott? You have a family?"

"I do," Mike said. "JJ, how did you know these guys were orphans? I just don't get it." Stott really did not understand anything at that moment. To learn that five out of six brand new army Rangers sitting at one mess table together at Fort Benning were orphans seemed extremely unusual.

"Mike, I can't explain it, but my guess is these guys were pretty sure at least one of us was an orphan when they approached us. Correct?" JJ stated.

"Yes," they said in unison.

Netting continued. "Okay, so now we're all communicating. We've noticed that you two are pretty tight, so here's something to think about as you're out there learning to speak to the natives. Of the 142 men that earned Ranger patches last Saturday, we know for a fact that eleven guys, all with less than one year in the army, are orphans. There may be more, but Sharkey makes the eleventh that we've confirmed. Six of those eleven are going on to sniper school right now. We just think it's odd. Nice to meet you both. See you when you get back. Hooah!"

"Hooah!" Mike and JJ shouted.

The two friends headed back to the barrack to prepare for their cross-country train ride. "What do you make of all that, JJ?" Stott asked.

"Assuming Netting's right, it's a little strange. Let me clear something up. You asked how I identified those guys as having come from orphanages. It's just a sixth sense you develop when you grow up in an orphanage. I can't explain it more than that. And I bet it's not unusual to have 10 percent of any group of young servicemen be orphans. What else are they going to do when they turn eighteen?" Sharkey, as always, brought a certain clarity to the situation.

Mike needed to get back to something he could understand. "You looking forward to the train ride?" he asked.

"You bet!" JJ said. "So far I've made it to four states since I joined the army. I figure we're gonna go through ten or twelve more on the way to California, and then we'll see the

Pacific Ocean! I'm going to teach you at least another 500 Chinese words on the trip, so it's gonna be great!"

Holy shit! Ninety hours on a train with Sharkey pitching Chinese every waking hour! Holy shit!

Actually, the train ride was great! It wasn't crowded and the conductors and porters were really nice to the young soldiers. Ranger patches and airborne berets made a difference! Mike and JJ arrived in Monterey at 1500 hours Friday afternoon, March 7.

They didn't have to report until 1700 hours March 9, so they chipped in and got a cheap hotel room about three blocks from the beach in a town called Seaside. There were lots of soldiers from Fort Ord in the area, but they were all infantry pukes, so Mike and JJ hung out in a surfer bar called the High Tide. After about ten beers Friday night, Stott finally got up the courage to ask a local beauty to dance. The next thing he knew, he and JJ were making it in the sand with two really groovy California girls. One of them had an old Chevy pickup truck with the roof chopped off it. They hauled beer and firewood to a secluded spot behind some big rocks and built a huge campfire right on the beach. The girls kept Mike and JJ company all night. Sharkey and Stott decided they would retire to California someday.

When they reported to the Army languages school on Sunday, March 9, Mike and JJ learned that classes ran 0800 to 0500 hours, five days a week, and that the instructors were civilians! They were assigned a room in what looked more like a college dorm than an army barrack. No duty other than to show up for classes!

"Don't think this will be easy, gentlemen," a civilian administrator told them. "You'll have lots of homework every night and on the weekends, too. On the sixth Friday, April 18, we will administer a four-hour oral test to evaluate your skills. The army expects you to be able to handle basic communication utilizing at least 800 sounds. Do either of you have any exposure to Oriental languages?"

The question seemed odd. You would have thought the languages school would have had military files describing Sharkey's proclaimed language skills. JJ was quick to pick up on the advantage they had. He spoke directly to Mike in Mandarin, basically saying, "These folks are uninformed. We can play with them, no problem."

Mike understood him well enough, but before he could attempt to respond in Mandarin the administrator stated in perfect Mandarin dialect, "Silly man, we are not fools! Watch your tongue!"

Sharkey and Stott realized they were in the big leagues!

"Let me get this straight," Stott said in English, of course, "you civilians run this school? We're not under some NCO or officer's direction?"

"There will be army observers in with the class and, of course, all eight students are either army or marine personnel. Military evaluators will monitor the final test. Understand, you are participating in the first Hmong class to be taught here in Monterey. We will be adjusting the curriculum as we go based on the students' ability to absorb and retain."

"Like going to college for six weeks," JJ observed.

"Maybe, but remember, we've gotta be in shape when we get back! If classes start that late every day, we can train in the a.m.," Mike said.

"Right." Sharkey seemed lost in thought. "Can we see a list of who else is in the class?"

"I don't see why not. You'll meet them in the morning, anyway. Here."

The administrator handed them a copy of the class roster along with a six-week schedule ending with the final exam on April 18 between 0900 and 1300 hours.

"Goddamn! The other six students are officers! And two of 'em sound like women's names!" JJ exclaimed.

The list set forth name, rank and branch; nothing else. It read:

Lieutenant Colonel Ronald Warner, U.S. Marines
Major Marjorie Stoggsdale, U.S. Marines

Major Michael Holland, U.S. Army
Captain Olivia Stroth, U.S. Army
Captain William Vespos, U.S. Army
Captain Christopher Mays, U.S. Army
Sergeant John J. Sharkey, U.S. Army
Sergeant Mike B. Stott, U.S. Army

Sergeants Sharkey and Stott! What the fuck! JJ and Mike shot each other looks of wonder, but said nothing.

"Thanks for the info. Will we see you in the morning, sir?" JJ asked.

"Yes. I'll be there to help launch the class, but you will have two full-time instructors: Mr. Anderson and Miss Kim. Until the morning then."

Sharkey and Stott walked outside and turned to face each other. "What's going on?" they asked in unison.

The boys found their rooms and squared away their gear. They had been told back at Fort Benning that the uniform for languages school would be dress khakis. Both men had spent considerable time during the train ride to Monterey sewing Ranger patches and corporal stripes on their kakis. Their papers declared them to be "just made" corporals. Mike and JJ were, in a word, bewildered.

"Christ, JJ. We're going to show up at class with corporal's stripes on, and we're supposed to be sergeants! I just don't get it!" Stott lamented.

"Me either, Mike. Let's just play it by ear! Come on! Let's go run on the beach, and then we can polish our jump boots! We gotta look sharp and be sharp!" Sharkey's bounding enthusiasm was contagious. They ran until they were winded and then prepared for the morning.

There was a dining hall in the dorm and instructions said breakfast would be served there six days a week from 0645 to 0745. JJ and Mike awoke at five, ran three miles, did calisthenics, performed the Three S's, and made it to the chow line at 0700. To their great surprise, there were thirty or so people having breakfast and no one had on a uniform! Everyone turned to look at them as they entered, all decked out in their fresh-pressed khakis. No one said a word.

JJ softly said to Mike, "Do you get this? Are these people civilians? And what's with the broads?"

"Keep it down! Let's just eat and go to the classroom," Stott said.

The chow was really good! Students could order omelets or just about any breakfast item one could think of! Then, waitresses brought it to where they were sitting! "Man, I haven't had an omelet since New York!" JJ said. "I think I'm gonna like this place!"

Mike and JJ chowed down, drank lots of fresh-squeezed orange juice and went to class. Surprises continued. At 0750 hours they were the first to arrive and saw that the classroom was very different than any either of them had seen before. There was room for twenty students, each having his or her own cube with glass partitions four feet high. These stations each had a microphone and a headset connected to what looked like an oversized shortwave radio. In the front of the room there were four more of these stations, but these sat on an elevated platform perhaps two feet above the main floor. The elevated stations faced the other twenty cubicles. There was a pull-down movie screen in back of the platformed stations.

Personalized nameplates for each of the eight students were arranged alphabetically, not by rank! At exactly 0800 hours, the door opened and in filed persons who had been at breakfast plus an extremely tall, older man who could not possibly have been in the military. He was accompanied by a diminutive woman no more than four and a half feet tall. All in civilian clothes!

"Well, I'll be damned! You two must be Sergeants Sharkey and Stott! We saw you in the mess, er, dining room, and we thought you could not possibly be our classmates because you're so young! Damn! I'm Major Mike Holland." The major then introduced Sharkey and Stott to the other officers, all of whom were friendly except for Colonel Ronald Warner, the ranking officer in the room, and a marine.

Colonel Warner said, "How old are you two? How long have you been in the army? What's with the corporal's stripes? Are you, or are you not, sergeants? You first, Stott!"

Colonel Warner's tone brought Mike back to reality. "Sir, eighteen. Eight months, sir. And sir, we're not sure, sir!"

Stott's performance caused the other five officers to laugh out loud. Not Colonel Warner. "What the fu—er—heck do you mean you're not sure! The schedule says you're both sergeants! You're wearing corporal's stripes! And you both look like you ought to be in grade school! Get straight, now!"

"Hold on, sir. Give him a chance to talk," said Major Marjorie Stoggsdale. "Now, soldier, the colonel has a point. Slowly, clearly explain yourself."

"Sir, er, ma'am," Stott started, but Major Stoggsdale interrupted.

"Just relax, son. You're in no trouble, but you must understand that we all are a bit surprised to meet two obviously young, very junior enlisted soldiers here at this school. Now, just give us a little history."

Mike recounted their path in the army from basic training to AIT to jump school and then Ranger qualification in only eight months. He continued. "Then we got sent here right after making Ranger. We got our promotions to corporal just two Saturdays ago, on March 1 when we got our Ranger patches. We were totally surprised that we were listed as sergeants! We can't explain it. Sorry, sir and ma'am."

The officers just stood there staring at them. "Is that just how it happened Sergeant, er, Corporal Sharkey? Just like Stott described?" Major Stoggsdale demanded.

"Ma'am, yes ma'am! Just like he said, ma'am!" Sharkey snapped.

Mr. Anderson intervened. "We verified their military IDs when they checked in yesterday. Their orders are straight. Miss Kim and I are here to teach you Hmong. I, frankly, am interested only in your collective abilities to concentrate and learn this very challenging language. May we get started?"

At 0825 hours on March 10, 1964, John Sharkey and Mike Stott began a sound association immersion program to learn the language of the hill tribes of central Vietnam with six military officers. After that shaky beginning, John and Mike resolved to best the officers by the widest margin possible just to show 'em!

At the end of class on that first day, Mr. Anderson brightened Mike and JJ's perspective. "Well, ladies and gentlemen, you questioned Stott and Sharkey's right to be here this morning, but, if I were you, I'd be worrying about keeping up with them! Clearly, Mr. Sharkey has a gift for languages! Good work boys! Civvies tomorrow, okay? Good night, and do your homework!"

The dorm dining room only served breakfast and lunch. The boys had been given a daily dinner allowance of $6.75 each. There were several restaurants within walking distance of the school and a pizza carryout less than a block away. "Pizza and then back to study?" JJ suggested.

"Let's call those two surfer girls we met! They said call anytime!" Mike had been really impressed with the one named Muffin.

"Maybe this weekend. I gotta keep you on the straight and narrow 'cause we're going to stick it to that arrogant bunch of dickheaded officers!" JJ was fired up. "But, Mike, how did we get here, to languages school with all officers after eight months in the army?"

"You're doing it again, JJ! You're searching for army logic! There isn't any! We're here, we can do this course, and then we can go back to soldiering. Pepperoni and mushrooms?" Mike asked.

They ate pizza at a picnic table right in front of the carryout window. By 1900 hours, JJ and Mike were back working with the recording devices they had been issued, practicing the words and sounds together. Stott was amazed at how quickly and perfectly JJ got all the homework words for the night down pat. Sharkey was able to mimic the sounds exactly, and he seemed to forget nothing!

"Is it really just that easy for you?" Mike asked.

"Yeah, Mike, it is. Don't get discouraged! This is the one thing that just seems to come natural to me. That and being a lady's man, of course! Look at this!"

JJ produced a letter from Briggetta that had been waiting for him at the school. "How the hell did she get the address before we even got here?" Stott asked.

"Actually, it was forwarded from Benning. It came air-mail, and we came on the train, get it? You know, like planes are faster than trains? Do I have to explain it to you again?" JJ could be a real smart-ass!

"Let me read it!" Mike said.

It was a long letter, nearly four pages. Briggetta had excellent penmanship. Mostly, it was about the girls' college crap and a Mobliano family update. The last paragraph read:

John,

> *I can't stop thinking about you. I'm not sure what it means, but I'd like to see you when you get a leave. Try to come to Brooklyn. And Briegeita says to bring that retarded friend of yours with you.*

Love,
Briggetta

Holy shit! Love! And Briegeita said she would like to see Stott?

"Okay, JJ, you've been holding out on me! What's this 'love' stuff?" Mike asked.

"Beats me. I did call her once just before we started Ranger school. She's pretty sharp, remembering that you are retarded and all!" said Sharkey.

"Very funny! We don't stand much of a chance to get to New York anytime soon, though. Maybe they could come visit us!" Mike hoped.

"I don't want them to, Mike. We've got to be the best in this class! No time for fooling with them. Besides, they're not likely to give up their virginity to us! So let's just make it with the California girls! We met two that put out. Count your blessings!" JJ said.

For the next six weeks Sharkey and Stott settled into a serious work routine. They got up at 0500 every morning and did their Ranger workout, running at least three miles and usually four or five. They were the first in the classroom every day and studied five nights a week, at least four hours. Sharkey pushed Mike every minute.

But the two friends did have fun on the weekends! The surfer girls picked them up late each Friday night after they had completed their homework and brought them back very late Sunday night, sometimes Monday morning. The girls even taught them to get up on a surfboard. Muffin's sun-tanned, muscular body, and her 38C's stayed in Stott's memory for years.

The officers kept to themselves in and out of class and never stopped being officers. An intense competition developed between JJ and Major Stoggsdale to be best in class. Mike and JJ learned the major was thirty-seven years old, a registered nurse, and had two other college degrees. She was a real loner. Even her fellow officers kept their distance from her, especially Captain Olivia Stroth.

On the final exam on April 18, JJ finished with the highest skill level ever recorded for Hmong as assessed by the testing board. Mike just edged out Major Stoggsdale for second. The test results were announced to the assembled class at about 1600 hours. Sharkey and Stott let out a Ranger "Hooah!" and were very surprised at what happened next.

"Troopers Sharkey and Stott, I want to say something to both of you, in front of your fellow students," said Marine Lieutenant Colonel Ronald Warner. "I'm proud to have been in this class with you! I don't impress easily, but your work ethic has impressed me. Maybe you were just determined to beat us officers! That's great! Go get 'em, troopers! Officers, I want us to give these young Rangers a big Hooah!"

"Hooah! Hooah! Hooah!" the officers screamed out.

"Can we buy you a beer?" Captain Olivia Stroth asked.

JJ and Mike suggested the High Tide Bar, and the six officers as well as both instructors drank many beers with them right up until their surfer girls showed up at 2200 hours. Sharkey and Stott said goodbye to their language school classmates and made the best of their last few days in California.

Chapter Twenty-Nine

Sharkey and Stott had received orders to return to the Sixth Rangers from Fort Ord via a Military Airlift Command flight through Wright Patterson Air Force Base in Dayton, Ohio, to Pope AFB in Fayetteville, North Carolina. Why they had traveled by train to languages school remained a mystery. Perhaps it was because the military was in the process of dropping civilian train transport for its troops in favor of utilizing a combination of public air transport services and MAC flights.

While Mike and JJ had been studying Hmong, components of the Sixth Rangers had been redeployed to Fort Bragg, North Carolina. They reported to Master Sergeant Frank Snook "on the hill" at Bragg at 1630 hours on Wednesday, April 22, 1964.

"Looks like you boys put on weight livin' the good life out there in Monterey! We'll run it off you starting in the morning! Colonel Duckworth wants to see you guys. Wait here."

Mike and JJ understood that when a colonel wants to see a couple of lowly corporals in his command, it's not good news.

Stott spoke softly to JJ, "Christ, now what? We just got back! Did you do something I don't know about?"

To Mike's horror, Sharkey answered, "Maybe!"

"Goddamn it, Sharkey! Haven't you learned to keep your mouth shut, yet? You've already got a crazy captain gunning for you! Isn't that enough?" asked Stott.

Stott and Sharkey waited in the makeshift orderly room for more than an hour, but Master Sergeant Snook never returned. A familiar face they remembered well appeared at 1750 hours. Sergeant Major Colin Cartwright boomed through the tent flap, grinning from ear to ear.

"Hello boys; welcome home!" he said.

Mike and JJ had automatically snapped to attention when the tent flap moved in anticipation of an officer. Their surprise at seeing Sergeant Major Cartwright must have been evident to him.

"Stand easy, boys. I wanted to talk to you before we see Colonel Duckworth. What made you write this letter to me, troopers? Make no mistake, I was proud to receive it! But what made you do it? Whose idea was it?" asked Cartwright.

"It was my idea, Sergeant Major Cartwright! You're the only guy we know in the Special Forces, and we remembered how you kept the troops motivated on November 23, Sergeant Major! I, er, we heard that the Fifth Special Forces Group was setting up shop in the central highlands of Vietnam, and now we speak Hmong! Plus, we made it through Ranger training! So we wanted to volunteer for Five Group!" Sharkey said.

Mike Stott was dumbfounded. What fucking letter? Then it got stranger.

"So which one of you wrote the letter that you both signed?" the sergeant major asked.

Mike was smart enough to have figured out that JJ had written a letter to Sergeant Major Cartwright concerning his command, and then he that realized the little shithead had even forged his name!

"I wrote it Sergeant Major! We want to join the Fifth! What do we have to do?" Sharkey just kept pushing.

"You haven't said a word, Corporal Stott! What do you say? You as anxious as Corporal Sharkey to sign your life away to the army?" asked Cartwright.

Stott was trapped! Sharkey knew it! If Mike said "no" he was cooked! If Mike said "yes" he was in for something he didn't even know about!

"Yes, Sergeant Major!" It was all Stott could say, given the circumstances.

"If you both are truly serious, there just might be an opportunity to try out for Special Forces, but you need to be sure of what you're signing up for. First of all, there's no guarantee that you would wind up in the Fifth, despite your languages skills. And the first thing you have to get through is a psychological profiling that eliminates most applicants. But even before that, you have to have the support of your current commanding officer, and Colonel Duckworth doesn't even know you. That's why I'm here. When I got your letter I called Top Turner, and he said you were both total dickheads, but to give you a shot! But then Major Hargrove called me back and said he'd back you! Pretty goddamn unusual! So, boys, you ready to sit down with Colonel Duckworth and tell him you want to leave his command?"

"Yes, Sergeant Major!" JJ said.

"Stott?"

"Yes, Sergeant Major!"

"Wait here."

As the sergeant major exited, presumably to check access to Colonel Duckworth, Stott said to Sharkey, "I will absolutely kick your ass for this! When did you send this letter, goddamn it?"

"The Sunday after we got our Ranger patches! Even before we went to languages school! Pretty cool, huh?"

"What part of "you are a total fucking dickhead" do you not understand, Sharkey? You could have at least talked to me about it!" Stott was truly upset.

"I didn't want you distracted at languages school. And you weren't! You beat all the officers! And now, thanks to my initiative, we might have a shot at Special Forces! You should be kissing my ass instead of being pissed off!" JJ's cool was making Mike even madder!

Stott said, "Goddamn it! I'll get you for . . . " but before he could finish, Sergeant Major Cartwright reappeared.

"Okay, boys! Colonel Duckworth will see us now!"

As they entered Duckworth's office, they snapped to attention. "At ease, goddamn it! This is my executive officer, who you two dickheads already know, Major Hargrove. Just came over from the Tenth. Major Hargrove, meet Sergeant Major Colin Cartwright."

Sergeant Major Cartwright saluted and then shook hands with Major Hargrove. Then Colonel Duckworth illustrated why he was a colonel by firing off a series of questions.

"Now, what's this bullshit about two green-ass young Rangers brash enough to want an SF tryout when they just made Ranger less than two months ago? I thought there was a time-in-grade and time-in-unit limitation before you green hats would even consider troopers. And why, exactly, are you involved in this, Sergeant Major? And Major Hargrove, you remember these two dickheads from all the soldiers you commanded through basic training? It's my cocktail hour, and I better get some goddamn sensible answers right fucking now! You first, Major!"

"Sir, I do remember these two for several of reasons! First of all, they both shot perfect hundreds on each M-14 qualifier section, and I was there to see it. Just doesn't happen that often! Second, they showed exceptional dedication and leadership qualities all through basic training. Third, Corporal Stott, here, is the young brother of a Congressional Medal of Honor winner from the Tenth in Korea, Captain James Stott. He never brought it up. My Top, First Sergeant Turner, was there when his brother distinguished himself, and I heard about Captain Stott a hundred times from Top Turner. Then his younger brother shows up in our basic training company! When I came back to the Rangers, these two were in training, and they made it through despite a 50 percent washout rate in that class. Also, Corporal Sharkey is the trooper that sounded off to Captain Gonzalez at his graduation ceremony, and I believe, sir, you remember that!"

Colonel Duckworth shook his head, recalling JJ's challenge. "How could I forget that? Christ, what moxey! Okay, Sergeant Major, your turn!"

"Sir, I was a ground-pounder my entire career until I got the opportunity to join the Fifth. I had to get jump qualified, and these two were in my jump class. We finished on November 23. You all remember that day. I organized a run with the holdover troopers, and these two were first to run with me. If I may say so, sir, I believe I can pick out the good ones after twenty-two years in the army. I liked these two youngsters then, and I like 'em more now given that they made it through Ranger training in one of Captain Gonzalez's Walk/Runs! They wrote me this letter, sir."

Sergeant Major Colin Cartwright handed over "their letter," which Stott still hadn't seen. To Mike's surprise he saw that the letter was three pages long and ended with two signatures. Colonel Duckworth read it, twice, and handed it to Major Hargrove.

"Thank you, sir, I've read it. Sir, begging your pardon, sir, but I had a chance to talk with Sergeant Major Cartwright when he came looking for you last week. You were still on leave, and I haven't had a chance to brief you, sir. It seems the SF guys have a couple of 'experimental' recruitment programs that they are trying out right now. Not secret, are they Sergeant Major? Can we talk about them in front of our boys, here?"

Our boys?

"No sir, major, they're not secret, and I'm happy to discuss them openly. Fact is, we need good men. Many of the older soldiers we test simply can't, or won't, make the sacrifices necessary to make it in our units. Vietnam is about to get super hot! You, sir, are well aware of that! Five Group needs to double in strength and then double again over the next two years to accomplish the missions we know of, not to mention the missions yet to come. Command has decided, out of necessity, to rethink prequalification criteria. Clearly, if your two troopers here had another year in the army and had accomplished the training they've already finished, we'd be after them! SF command has identified several hundred young RA's, all with above average intelligence, to help 'fast track' through training. It was no accident that Sharkey and Stott have been on the schedule they've been on. You need good, young Rangers too, but these two guys wrote that letter, essentially begging to be considered for a Special Forces opportunity. We'd like to put them through the psych-ops screening to see how they stack up. If they don't wash out with the headshrinkers, we'd give them a shot. With your permission and support, of course, sir," said Sergeant Major Cartwright.

Holy shit!

"You two know what you're in for?" asked Colonel Duckworth.

"Sir, we can do it, sir!" Sharkey shouted.

"How about you, Corporal Stott? Does Sharkey always speak for both of you?"

"Sir, no sir! I speak for myself, sir! But if this little dickhead can make it, I can sure as hell do it, sir!" Stott said.

"So, it's like that, is it?" Colonel Duckworth said. Mike could see that Major Hargrove and Sergeant Major Cartwright were suppressing grins.

"Sir, question please, sir!" JJ barked out.

"Yes, Corporal Sharkey?" the Colonel responded.

"It's for the Sergeant Major, sir! Are a lot of the identified potential Special Forces candidates orphans, Sergeant Major?" Sharkey asked.

Both officers turned to look directly at Cartwright. "Yes, Corporal Sharkey, nearly 50 percent of our target group are orphans. Most of the rest are special cases like your buddy, here, that have an extraordinary connection to the army. And, of course, we're searching for potential lifers." Then, to the officers he said, "Many candidates have the physical skills required. It's what's between their ears that causes our washout rate to be so high. I spoke to a jarhead Colonel named Warner that was in languages school with these men. Seems they finished first and second against six, highly educated officers. Colonel Warner said he'd take 'em in recon anytime."

"God damn jarheads! Next thing you know the fucking marines will be trying to steal my young Rangers! Major, what do you say?" Colonel Duckworth did not look happy.

"Sir, that's quite a letter! I think we give these two Boy Scouts a psychological evaluation right away. If either of them qualifies, let them go for it. Hell, they'd probably be the two youngest soldiers in all Special Forces! Right, Sergeant Major?" Hargrove asked.

"Sir, yes sir! If they started with the next training group and made it, they would be the youngest by a wide margin. Major, sir, did you know that our recruitment code name for this program is 'Boy Scouts?'" asked Cartwright.

"No, I didn't, but for once you guys came up with something logical! Sir, do we let them go?" Hargrove directed his question to Colonel Duckworth.

"Test 'em! If either of them makes it, let 'em go!"

Sharkey barked out a "Sir, thank you, sir!"

Colonel Duckworth said, "See if you still want to thank me in about five weeks, Corporal Sharkey! All of you get the hell out of here! I'm thirsty!"

Outside Duckworth's office, Sergeant Major Cartwright said, "On the supposition that the colonel would do the right thing, we prescheduled you both with our shrinks beginning tomorrow at 0900 hours. Do yourselves a favor. Make formation with the Sixth in the morning, eat a light breakfast and show up in dress khakis here." He handed both men a three-by-five card with an address and appointment schedule on it.

"Don't drink alcohol tonight. Get a good night's sleep. And Stott, wait to kick Sharkey's ass until after the testing! I don't want you guys showing up all bruised and battered!" Cartwright commanded. He continued, "Don't think I don't know that Sharkey signed both signatures on the letter! Clearly, you have had some surprises here in the last hour, Corporal Stott! But you kept your cool and supported your buddy, just like Sharkey said you would in the letter. Get through it over the next three days! We've got you slotted to start an SF prep course Monday morning! Do it!"

"Good luck, troopers!" said Major Hargrove, giving them a wink! Mike and JJ snapped to attention and saluted him.

As Cartwright and Hargrove departed, Mike turned to confront JJ. But the little dickhead got the jump on his buddy.

"Don't you ever call me a little dickhead again! I don't mind 'dickhead,' but nix the 'little'! I probably outweigh you now, so watch it!" JJ's gall made Stott laugh.

"So you sign my name to a secret letter you wrote to volunteer us for a unit I don't know anything about, and you have the balls to be mad at me for calling you a 'little dickhead?' You are something else! What was in the goddamn letter, anyway?" Stott asked.

"I'm not gonna tell you! It got us where we want to be! That's all that matters! If YOU can fool the shrinks over the next few days we're going to be the two youngest soldiers in the Special Forces! Can you imagine what that means?" Sharkey was puffed up in anticipation.

"Yeah, it means we're going to keep working our balls off, nonstop, to try to earn the privilege of spending the rest of our short lives in Vietnam! And what do you mean, 'if I can fool the shrinks?' You re the one that's nuts! Completely goofy! I mean it! I'm gonna kick your ass at the first opportunity!" said Stott.

Sharkey just stood there, grinning. "Come on, buddy, I'm starving! Let's get to the mess hall before it closes!"

Over the next two and a half days, Mike and JJ were tested and interviewed by teams of doctors, psychologists, officers, and senior NCO's. Pete Netting and Bill Murphy, two of the guys they had spoken with in the mess hall just before they went to languages school, went through testing at the same time.

To Mike's surprise, even the completely insane John J. Sharkey was cleared to start the Special Forces preparation course along with the other three of them on the following Monday morning "back in the woods" at Fort Bragg. Stott called his folks on Saturday night, April 25, 1964, and told them he'd been accepted to try out for Army Special Forces. His mother began crying hysterically, but his dad said, "If you start it, finish it." Mike's brother Raymond promised to kick his ass as well as Sharkey's for being so damn stupid as to "go Green."

Stott spent Sunday trying to get mentally prepared for the "prep course" and considering ways to get even with Sharkey for getting him into the mess. He refused to go to morning chow with JJ, so Sharkey knew his buddy was really upset. They'd been told to pack up their gear and move to a restricted area at Fort Bragg even further out in the boonies. As Mike was finishing packing, Sharkey returned with Netting and Murphy. Stott could see that JJ was once again up to something.

"Looks like you're ready to go, huh, Mike?" JJ started.

"What the fuck is it to you? And what are you up to now? Don't say nothing, 'cause I can see by the look on your face you're about to make me even madder!" said Stott.

Sharkey then switched to the Hmong dialect that they had practiced all those weeks in Monterey. In Hmong, he said, "These two unworthy bastards don't believe we know Hmong. Speak only in Hmong until I give you the signal. And if I raise my right hand, switch to the Mandarin I taught you. Now, which of these two idiots is uglier, Netting or Murphy?"

Instinctively, Mike responded in Hmong, "Two very ugly bastards! But not as ugly as you, you little rat!" Stott wanted to use the term "dickhead," but he didn't know the Hmong sound for it.

But Mike couldn't deter his friend! JJ went on to describe the weather and the smallness of Netting's brain, all in Hmong. Despite Stott's previous mood, JJ's perfectly cadenced Hmong insults to their clueless buddies made him smile.

Netting and Murphy were standing there with their mouths hanging open. Netting said, "My God, that's incredible! How many words do you know? Can you talk about everything in that language?"

"Of course we can! We beat six officers in our class, and we'll be teaching this to guys like you before long! Now pay me!" Sharkey demanded.

Netting and Murphy each handed JJ a ten dollar bill. He handed one on to Mike and pocketed the other. "So here's the deal! We'll teach you both five words a day until you get the hang of the rhythm of the language. You'll have to pay us a dollar a word! If you guys can keep up with us in Special Forces training, we'll have you speaking a couple of hundred words in Hmong when we get our berets! Deal?"

"Deal!" Netting and Murphy yelled out.

How could Stott stay mad at the conniving little bastard? As Netting and Murphy left to finish their packing, JJ said to Mike, "Stick with me, sonny, and I'll make you rich! Get moving! There's a deuce-and-a-half that'll take us to the field at 1400 hours."

"Sharkey, I reserve the right to kick your ass at some point in the future!"

"Sure thing," was all JJ said.

The men loaded up in the deuce with ten other SF candidates and rode for quite a while in a north-by-northwest direction. Mike had the sensation that they drove over the same terrain several times, but out there in the middle of nowhere everything looked the same. They finally arrived in a small clearing in which three tents unlike any they'd seen before had been erected. As the men climbed down from the truck, they were met by a soldier wearing camouflage fatigues with his face blackened. There were no markings on his fatigues, and he said not a word! He gave them the universal forefinger over the mouth "hush" signal and motioned to follow him. They entered a tent that was about half the size of a twenty-man tent used in AIT.

When the tent flap closed, Stott heard the deuce-and-a-half drive away and his group was left in total darkness. It was quite close within the tent. Eyes were adjusting very slowly to the darkness because they had entered the tent from a late but still bright afternoon sun. The tent flap opened just a crack and a fragmentation grenade rolled in among the men. It went off as they were diving away from the direction the

grenade had entered. In the close quarters the sound was defining, but to their relief the grenade did not fragment. The
ten trainees were sprawled out across and over one another,
trying to comprehend what was happening when the tent
flap opened again and the brightest light they'd ever seen illuminated the interior.

"Jesus fucking Christ! We got us a group of faggots, here!
Will you look at these sissies, Clive! Three of 'em done
pissed themselves, two have tears in their eyes, and, from
the smell of things in here, a couple of these dickheads must
have shit their pants! Are you two faggots holding hands? I
swear to God you won't leave this tent alive if you're fuckin'
holding hands! On your feet! Outside!"

The afternoon sun still blinded the men as they departed
the tent filled with the smell of cordite, urine and, yes, human excrement.

"Two lines of five! Now! I see four of you faggots wearing ranger patches! Drop and give me a hundred, right now!
The rest of you sissies give me fifty! I fuckin' hate Rangers! They get double glory for nothin,' so I work 'em double
hard just to get even! I know it's hard for you Rangers, but
straighten your fuckin' backs when you do push-ups! What
do you think you are? Fuckin' worthless-ass recon marines
or something?" The speaker was wearing master sergeant
stripes on standard issue fatigues and double lightning strike
patches. He had a double-A—Army Airborne—patch on his
other shoulder, but no Ranger patch!

"I'm Master Sergeant Smith! That's all you need to know!
Since you fuckers were all dumb enough to follow a trooper
you didn't know into an environment you didn't understand,
I doubt that any of you will make it to assessment and selection anyway, but we're gonna see what you're made of over
the next thirty days! Or whatever part of thirty days you make
it through! If you have no basic instinct for directions you
might as well just quit right now and go back to your dumb-
ass airborne units if they'll take you back! Those fuckers are
lost all the time anyway, and you can stay lost with them!

But for the one or two of you that have an IQ over one hundred and can piss standing up, we're gonna teach you to use a compass and then the stars! You'll be able to navigate with a sexton, and you'll know how to spot yourself anywhere in the world! Over there is a stack of shelter halves. Take two. You'll live out of a pup tent for the next thirty days. I said, 'out of,' not 'in.' Dig in over there in the woods. No closer than fifty meters a man! You fuckin' Rangers go the furthest! I don't want to have to smell you! Now move! Triple-time, Goddamn it!"

So began thirty very challenging days of near constant movement during which the Special Forces candidates averaged only a couple of hours rest per twenty-four hour period. The men spotted and recovered, learning to find their way over very difficult terrain in total darkness. They ate a combination of C rations and K rations and other unusual food. They drank only water. No coffee, no milk, and no beer!

"Get tougher, boys! For the few of you that make it to phase two, you'll look back on this as living in the Ritz! And then you face the qualification course! Now move your sorry asses!" said Master Sergeant Smith.

At the end of thirty days, the training group had decreased from forty to nineteen men, who advanced to survival training, twenty-four more days of living off the land, accomplishing individual and team missions. Far more mentally challenging than physically difficult, the survival indoctrination can best be described as hide-and-seek with life-or-death consequences.

Sharkey and Stott had been assigned to different training teams. They didn't talk for fifty-four days. At his low points during the exercises, when failure seemed imminent, Mike focused on the ass-kicking he owed Sharkey. Stott lived to get even with the little bastard! And then there was that fucking pact that they had made! Once, Mike got a glimpse of JJ getting the shit kicked out of him for missing a checkpoint, but Sharkey bounced up like a rubber ball and got right back on track! Damn, how JJ's undying dedication motivated Stott!

Somehow, Stott made it to the training formation on day fifty-six, and there was Sharkey, back next to him in the lineup, giving Mike that air-check, thumbs-up sign. The fifteen remaining Special Forces candidates in the group waited to hear their fates. How many of them would be selected to continue on to the qualification course?

One of the evaluation team officers that controlled their destiny, a major named Hammond, spoke, "Interesting group. About normal to this point. Just over half of the soldiers you started with have been disqualified or quit. If I don't call your name, you will return to your previously assigned unit. Goodbye and good luck. The following men will report back to their units to await a slot for continuing their Special Forces Training: Sergeant Mike Aswann; Sergeant Richard Barnett; Sergeant Bill Cushing; First Sergeant Howard Jones; Staff Sergeant Michael Mulaney; Staff Sergeant Barry Norris; Sergeant Kyle Ryan; Staff Sergeant Jim Stein; Sergeant Bruce Wolynski. Troop, dismissed!"

Stott felt his knees buckle. The blood drained from his face. Could it be? He hadn't made the cut? Sharkey hadn't made the cut? It was the most devastating moment of Mike's life. He turned to face Sharkey. The tears were trickling from JJ's eyes.

"Hey, troopers, heads up! I almost forgot! The following 'Boy Scouts' are to report directly to individual skills training on Smoke Bomb Hill: Corporal Bill Bickes; Corporal Mike Ceiake; Corporal Bill Murphy; Corporal Pete Netting; Corporal John Sharkey; Corporal Mike Stott. Dismissed!"

The goddamn major had been fucking with them! As Mike shook Sharkey's hand in congratulations, JJ said, "That son-of-a-bitch major got us, didn't he! I just couldn't believe we hadn't made it!"

The six "Boy Scouts" reported to Master Sergeant Gills the next morning as directed. "Listen up, scouts! I'm gonna read off your name and new, primary MOS specialty training assignments: Corporal Bill Bickes—18B-weapons sergeant; Corporal Mike Ceiake—18D-medical sergeant; Corporal

Bill Murphy—18C-engineering sergeant; Corporal Pete Netting—18C-engineering Sergeant; Corporal John Sharkey—18E-communications sergeant; Corporal Mike Stott—18B-weapons sergeant. Corporal Ceiake, you're gonna be gone awhile; your MOS is a forty-four week school! Rest of you boys will be doing twelve to fourteen weeks training in your specialty! One thousand percent is all we want! Two of you are on four-year enlistments: Bickes and Stott. See me before you do anything! Here's your envelope with orders; get it done! Hey, I almost forgot! Any of you idiots have any skeletons in the closet? We start 'top secret' clearances for all of you if you make it to Five Phase!"

Bickes and Stott went straight to Master Sergeant Gills as the other guys departed for their training classes. Sharkey and Mike gave each other a nod. They didn't see each other for fifteen weeks.

"Bickes and Stott, you got a choice to make. We're not spending any more training dollars on you unless you extend your enlistments by four more years right now! Sign here or go back to your units!" Gills laid the paperwork in front of them.

Stott barely knew Bill Bickes. They'd had little contact. Bickes was a tall kid with movie star good looks and a quick smile. "No, Master Sergeant. I won't do that," Bickes said.

"Sergeant Hines, get this limp-dick mother fucker outta my sight! Back to the Sixth! Now! What about you, Corporal Stott? Balls or no balls? Yes or no?"

Mike Stott extended his enlistment by four years.

For the next twelve weeks, Stott was immersed in the study of virtually all of the medium and light duty weapons used by the armies of the world. He learned how to disassemble and reassemble the weapons and learned their most effective uses. Stott and his training mates fired and cleaned these weapons, all the while being indoctrinated with the culture and traditions of the Special Forces. The training was so interesting and intense that Mike never thought of anything other than living the life of a Green Beret. He learned to appreciate the AK-47 automatic rifle used by most of America's enemies. It was indestructible and would keep firing even covered in mud. Most interestingly, although still very much in the position of having to prove his worthiness, Stott was increasingly treated like he was already on the team. A couple of times during this training, Mike participated in a "beer break" with other trainees as well as Special Forces cadre.

The Saturday night before 18-B training was to conclude, the officers and cadre who had served both as their instructors and evaluators sat down with the candidates over beer and pizza and just "shot the shit" with them from 1800 hours until way after midnight. It was the Saturday of Labor Day weekend, 1964. Just for an instant, Mike thought of that incredible Labor Day weekend the year before when he and Sharkey had experienced New York City with their five basic training buddies as guests of the Smealls. Could a whole year really have passed? A year ago in Manhattan, Mike still felt like a civilian. Now he felt like he had been in the army his whole life.

A couple of the senior Special Forces NCO's had spent years in southeast Asia, including Vietnam, dating way back to coordination maneuvers with French troops in the mid-1950s. Mike's favorite 18-B instructor was Master Sergeant Morgan Wright. He'd served with a Ranger reconnaissance team in World War II and was one of the first men to earn the right to wear the Green Beret. Master Sergeant Wright was as tough as the rest of the cadre, but reminded Mike of his father in many ways. Stott felt sincere admiration for him.

The teaching cadre all deferred to Master Sergeant Wright as one of the world's foremost weapons experts. They were allowed to call him Master 'Pop' Wright and sometimes "Top Pop." Stott hoped to earn the right to speak to him on that level someday. Master Sergeant Wright had earned six Purple Hearts, two Silver Stars for valor and three Bronze Stars. Toward the end of that evening, he was finally convinced to open up and tell the group some early Vietnam stories.

Master Sergeant Wright told many memorable stories that evening, but one stuck with Mike the rest of his life, especially when he was about to eat breakfast. A Special Forces doctor, Major Jim Harkin, said to Master Wright, "Master Pop, I've heard it many times before, but would you please share your 'Russian' story with us again?"

"Okay, if you insist, Doc. Back in 1958, shortly after the Russians successfully launched their 'Sputnik,' my boys and me, along with about a dozen Montagnards, were monitoring one of the supply trails way over on the Laotian side of the border. For several weeks, we had regularly seen a very Russian-looking chap traveling with the bad guys as we observed them through our binoculars. We nicknamed him, of course, Ivan. He seemed to be giving orders that were more or less followed by a band of Laotian smugglers that were trading arms for opium. He wasn't the first Spetznaz trooper I'd seen, but he was the first to operate openly, even in the daylight. We were under strict orders not to kill any Russians because 1958 was a rough point in the cold war, and Ike didn't want to ruffle any feathers. Pissed me off! Here was a Rusky obviously directing the bad guys, and I couldn't just take him out! What bullshit!

"Although military supplies and ammo were always in short supply, it was amazing what was available even way out there in the jungle. One of our Montagnard villages had, of all things, several canisters of helium left by the French. God knows what the hell the Frenchies were doing with helium out in the middle of nowhere, but there they were, gathering rust. The Yards—for you youngsters that's what we call our Montagnard allies—had held on to them because they thought they might have use as weapons, but, of course, they didn't. Then fate dealt us a hand! We used to get supplies dropped from a C-119 or 130 every few weeks, and, on the next drop, instead of the bazooka ammo we'd asked for, we got dropped two skids of Navy weather balloons! Go figure! My guess is some group of dumb-ass Seabee's got my bazooka rounds and probably died trying to open them, thinking they were edible! You guys know, all the navy does is eat!

"Then it hit me! I was under orders not to kill any Russians, but I wasn't under orders not to give 'em a lift. Me and the boys humped four helium canisters and two of the Navy's balloons about twelve clicks over to where we'd regularly seen Ivan and the smugglers. Two nights later, just before first light, we saw Ivan and three Laos humpin' down the trail, probably headed back to wherever their hooch was. We hustled up and got ahead of them, set up a pretty decent ambush, and caught 'em flatfooted! We bound and gagged all four of them and made them trek back with us to where we'd stashed the helium and balloons. We rigged Ivan to the balloons with an old chute harness. At first good light, when we knew all the Lao villagers would be up and about, we opened the helium canister valves and inflated the balloons. It took about six Yards to hold down our 'package' until we got a favorable breeze. I ripped the gag off Ivan as we released our hold-downs, and up he went, screaming his head off! Ivan was drifting up in a northwesterly direction, raising about ten feet per second. When he got about two clicks high, maybe 200 feet, he was exactly over an unfriendly Lao tribal clearing, and we could hear them screaming about a 'god in the air!' I let my best shooter take his silenced 7.62 sniper rifle and shoot both balloons. Near as we could tell, Ivan fell right into the middle of their village! We heard later they ate him for breakfast. No one ever saw those three smugglers again, either."

During the week following Master Sergeant Wright's fantastic story, Mike Stott successfully completed the 18-B weapons sergeant training course. He was told to report to the SF training battalion orderly room back "on the hill" closer to the main post at Fort Bragg. To Mike's surprise, John J. Sharkey was waiting in the same orderly room.

First words out of his mouth were, "I outweigh you now, I'm sure! You look skinny as hell, so you better rethink kickin' my ass! Did you pass 18-B?"

"Would I be here if I hadn't? Guess you must have made it through 18-E. They say it's the easiest SF MOS!" Stott said.

Master Sergeant Frank Snook came out to greet them. "Humf! Didn't think I'd see you two dickheads again! They must have really loosened up the standards if you clowns got through your MOS courses!"

Then Master Sergeant Snook really surprised Mike and JJ! He began speaking in perfect Hmong dialect!

"Your new names are Rat I and Rat II. Stott, you're I 'cause you're bigger. Heard of Panama, the country? No matter, you're headed there for your team and unit training. Wonderful place, Fort Sherman! The army's jungle warfare school is tailor-made for you two sports! You're gonna love it! MAC flight out of Pope, 20 September, total of six A trainer teams plus cadre. Really got nothing for you 'til then. Want to take some leave?"

"How much leave could we take, Master Sergeant?" JJ asked.

"You can leave now, if you want. Got to be back here 19 September, 1400 hours, so a seven-day leave would work. By the way, you've both completed languages school, so if you don't fuck up in 'team' you just might make it yet!"

It was the first time any NCO had sounded that positive about their prospects. That made Sharkey and Stott very nervous.

"You can store your gear in B Barrack. I'll cut your leave papers. Come back at 1200 hours, and you'll be good to go. Stott, I'm counting on you to keep Sharkey out of trouble!" said Master Snook.

"Thank you, Master Sergeant!" JJ and Mike said together.

Chapter Thirty

"Where do you want to go?" JJ asked. "I haven't spent any money in months, so I'm rich! Want to go to Brooklyn?"

"No, let's stay closer. Even if Briggetta and Briegeita would see us, we wouldn't get laid. Let's go to the closest beach and just relax and look for broads," Mike suggested.

"Okay, but how we gonna get anywhere? Greyhound bus? I'm up for anything as long as there are no swamps and no snakes," JJ said.

"How much cash you got?" Stott asked.

"I've got more than $1,200!" JJ said. "Plus, I opened a savings account!"

"Well, I've got about that much. Let's go buy a car! Just something cheap!"

"You sure you can drive?" Sharkey asked. "I've never driven a car."

"All the more reason to buy one!" said Mike. "I'll teach you to drive!"

Sharkey and Stott stowed their stuff, got leave papers, packed their meager civilian duds, and caught the 1310, 1:10 p.m., bus into Fayetteville. They got off the bus at a strip of highway where there were about a half dozen used car lots. The second lot they came to had a number of late model cars that were pretty expensive, but way back in the last space in the lot was a 1950 two-door Pontiac.

The used-car hustler Mike and JJ talked with was pushing them to buy one of his later models. As he was showing JJ a decent '58 Chevy, Mike walked back and opened the door of the Pontiac. It was a black "torpedo-back" model with grey cloth seats. He noticed it was a straight-six and had a manual transmission. The tires looked good and then Stott saw there were only 29,400 miles showing on the speedometer.

"How much for the Pontiac?" Mike asked.

"Christ, Stott! That's the ugliest car I ever saw! I'm not riding in that thing!" JJ scoffed.

"You boys need something fancier than that if you're gonna pick up any chicks!" the hustler chided.

"How much?" Mike asked again.

"We're asking $495. It's clean, a real one-owner and it runs good. Clear North Carolina title. But you need something better!" the car salesman whined.

"Tell you what. We're going to take it for a test ride. If we like it, and if you'll change the oil for us right now and fill the gas tank, we'll give you $250 cash money! Now, don't you deal me! Take the $250, or we're going back across the street and buy that '50 Ford coupe over there for $245! Yes or no?" Stott was holding twelve twenties and a ten out where he could see the cash.

"Three hundred!" he said.

"Goodbye," Mike said and motioned to JJ to follow him.

"Hold on! I'll get the keys. Let's take a ride."

It was slow as heck, but it was a solid old car that had been taken care of. Stott knew they couldn't get into any trouble with a 1950 Pontiac!

"Two hundred fifty cash and we drive it away as soon as you service it," Stott said.

"All right, damn it! Gimmie the cash! Johnny, change the oil and gas the Pontiac! Right now! You boys come on in here, and I'll sign the title over to you!"

Sharkey and Stott got the title put in both their names and pulled out onto North Carolina Route 24 headed east, just before 1600 hours. They stopped at a pharmacy on the edge of Fayetteville and bought hamburgers and Cokes from the lunch counter, two pairs of sunglasses and a North Carolina map.

Sharkey said, "Man, this is great! We're gonna make it in the Special Forces! I own half of a car with my best friend, and we're headed for a beach with seven days leave! And we're going to Panama when we get back! Our first foreign country! Show me how to drive!"

"Tell you what, JJ. How about you just enjoy the ride right now. Tomorrow when we're out in the country with no traf-

fic, I'll teach you. You be the navigator for a while. Find us a
route to the Outer Banks, and we'll drive all night 'til we get
there!" said Stott.

JJ busied himself with the map and then said, "Mike, I
never thought I could be this lucky or this happy. Thank you.
Looks like we take Route 24 almost all the way, right past
Camp LeJeune! Maybe we should stop and kick some Marine Corps ass just for the hell of it! Look what I brought!"

JJ produced a quart bottle of Jim Beam whiskey that he
had stashed in his travel bag. "I'll drink, you drive! To the
beach, sonny, and step on it!"

They gassed up the old Pontiac just outside Jacksonville,
North Carolina, around 8:00 p.m. and stayed on Route 24
toward Morehead City. There, Sharkey directed Mike to turn
onto Route 70, and just before ten o'clock they came to a
wide spot in the road called Williston. A sign read "Ferry to
Cape Lookout National Seashore—6 Miles," in front of an
old-fashioned motel with metal lawn chairs out in front of
the rooms and a "Vacancy" sign in the window. JJ had been
taking pulls at the Jim Beam bottle and was pretty tipsy.

"Let's hole up here for the night and take that ferry ride
in the morning, JJ. I'll go in to get a room! You smell like an
old bar," Mike said.

"I love my car; let's just sleep in it!" Sharkey said. He
was slurring his words and Stott wondered if the Jim Beam
had hit him harder than he realized. Mike rung the night
bell, and, eventually, an old man came and looked out at him
through the screen door.

"Help you, sonny?" he asked.

"Yeah, me and my buddy are on a seven-day leave from
Fort Bragg, and we want to go to a beach for a while. How
far are the beaches from here?" Stott asked.

"Prettiest beaches in the world just over the ferry about
five miles up the road. Two beds for one night?"

"How much?"

"You got any army ID?" he inquired.

"Sure. Here. And our leave slip."

"Sixth Rangers? You look pretty young to be a Ranger, son," the old man said. "Since you're in the army I'll let you have a room for fifteen dollars a night. If you were a Marine, I'd charge you twenty-five. Gotta pay up front, though."

Mike gave him fifteen dollars and got a key. Stott got back in the car to pull it up in front of their room, but Sharkey was out like a light! Mike opened the room, carried JJ in over his shoulder, and put him on the inside bed. Mike took a shower and walked down to the ice and Pepsi machines in his Levi's. He bought a 7 Up and sat out on a metal lawn chair in front of the motel drinking Jim Beam and 7 Up over ice listening to JJ snoring like a beached whale! It was after 2300 hours, 11:00 p.m., but it was still eighty-five degrees. Mike could hear John's snoring over the window air conditioner that he had put on "max-cool." Every five minutes or so a car would pass by, usually with the radio blaring a country-western song.

Stott realized it was the first time in fourteen months that he could sit by himself and just relax and reflect. He thought about his parents and turning nineteen in a couple of months. Mostly, Mike thought about the army and his friend JJ. Until tonight, when JJ sipped his Jim Beam and floated into the sound slumber he was now enjoying, Stott had never seen him let down. Mike remembered JJ thanking him earlier in the evening as they rode down highway 24 in their old car. Their car!

Stott recounted the incredible experiences of the past fourteen months. From his encounter with John Sharkey and Syl Mobliano on that first day of basic training right through finding JJ in the orderly room earlier that morning. Mike thought of Labor Day weekend 1963 when he had entered into the pact with JJ and Big Howie. How different his path with Sharkey into the Special Forces selection process had been from Howard's to the military police. Mike believed that Howie was still in Germany, but they hadn't heard from him for several months.

Struggling with the reality of being where he was, Stott felt that his fate was somehow tied to John Sharkey in ways yet to be revealed. The damn pact and Sharkey's inspiration had gotten him through the training to date. For Mike, Ranger school had been far more difficult than the Special Forces training. He remembered JJ's challenge to Captain Gonzalez at their Ranger graduation ceremony. One more phase to get through and he and his best friend would be Special Forces troopers! It seemed surreal.

Then Mike thought about the last nine hours. He and JJ had bought a car, driven to the beach, and were about to chase girls for a week before returning to group and unit training in Panama. Mike realized how much their friendship meant to John Sharkey and how lucky he was to have JJ as a friend. He downed the last of his mixed drink and went back inside where it was at least a few degrees cooler. Despite the thunderous racket of JJ's liquor-inspired snoring, Mike Stott fell asleep dreaming of earning a green beret.

When he awoke at 9:00 a.m. the next morning, Sharkey's bunk was empty. On the nightstand between the beds was a big glass of orange juice. A note from JJ said, "Running. To stay ahead of you. Back later."

At 1000 hours, JJ came double-timing down the road carrying a sack with coffee and doughnuts.

"Finally up, huh, sonny! Here's your breakfast! We got pussy to go find! Move your ass!" JJ was back in form.

"You're not my fucking sergeant, so sit down and shut up! Drink your coffee, before you make me kick your ass on general principles!" said Stott.

"Who do you fucking think you are? First Sergeant Turner?" was JJ's quick reply. But then their day got better real fast!

From a room two doors down, a very pretty but slightly overweight lady appeared and said, "Could you guys hold it down! We're trying to get some sleep in here!"

Fast as lighting Sharkey said, "Who's we?"

The door slammed as she went back inside. "Did you see the size of those tits? Had to be 40D's!" JJ said.

"Yeah, but the rest of her was a little oversized, too," Mike responded. "And she was a lot older than us!"

"Never stopped you before, Corporal! Besides, I like older women! Let's clean up and go get 'em some coffee and doughnuts! I got a good feeling about this!" JJ was on the hunt.

The boys performed the Three S's, fired up the Pontiac and retraced JJ's steps to the general store, where he'd gotten the coffee. It was way down the road, next to the entrance to the ferry.

"You ran all the way down here and back?" Stott asked.

"Yep! Only about six miles! It's Sunday, dickhead! Only thing open was this place, because of the ferry. Get a dozen glazed and four big cups of coffee. We'll ambush 'em as they come out!" said JJ, referring, Mike presumed, to the heavy-boobed lady back at the motel.

"And what if she's with a guy or her parents?" Mike asked.

"Won't be her parents! I'll guarantee you that! Don't you know by now to always trust my instincts? Move your ass! I don't want to miss them!"

Mike and JJ sat outside their room hoping Miss Big Tits would emerge with a girlfriend in the near future. Again, JJ's instincts proved correct. At about 1050 hours, Miss Big Tits emerged with another slightly heavy lady with flaming-red hair. Fortunately, her boobs also were oversized.

"Good morning, ladies! And a beautiful morning it is! We brought you coffee and doughnuts! I'm bettin' glazed are your favorite! Cream and sugar?" Silver-tongued Sharkey was off and running.

"Well, I just never encountered anyone as brash as you, young man! What makes you think we'd even talk to you, much less accept coffee and glazed doughnuts?" said the redheaded one.

When she referred to the "glazed" doughnuts as opposed to just plain "doughnuts," Mike and JJ knew they were in business! "Miss, you can trust army Rangers anytime, any-place! I'm John Sharkey and my young friend, here, is Mike Stott. Let's move to that picnic table over there and get acquainted. You are?" JJ was fast!

The woman that had shushed them earlier responded, "Well, okay, but we're headed for the beach! You guys look like you should be headed for the playground!"

The women had arrived at the motel about 0200 hours the night before from Washington, D.C., for a week at the beach. They both worked for the government. The redhead was celebrating her recent divorce.

For the next six days, they fucked Mike and JJ's brains out!

JJ moved in with the redhead and Mike shacked up with the first queen they had met, Cindy. They did it at the beach, in the cars, in the parking lots of barbeque restaurants, and once, when it wasn't crowded, in the car on the ferry in route to the outer islands! This late in the season there was hardly anyone else around and they had the outer islands to themselves. Over the next week, the partiers consumed six bottles of Jim Beam purchased from the local "bootlegger," and drank more Budweiser than Stott thought existed. The girls were great! Actually, they weren't girls; they were women. Mike and JJ figured they both had to be well into their thirties. They could out drink the boys, and all they wanted to do was party!

Very early Saturday morning, September 19, 1964, Cindy and "Red" headed back to D.C., and Mike and JJ took off for Fort Bragg. The last thing Cindy said to Mike was, "I'm gonna give you a blow job that'll make you come to find me in Washington! Here's my phone number! Now, come over here!"

Stott decided to keep her address.

They had been so busy with the girls that Mike hadn't taught JJ to drive, and there wasn't time on the way back to Bragg. Besides, Sharkey was worn out! As they pulled away from the motel and "their girls," JJ said, "Buying this car was the best decision I ever made! Now shut up and drive me back to the post, sonny! I need some rest!"

It took Stott six hours to get back to Fort Bragg. Sharkey woke up only once to pee when they stopped for gas and mumbled something like, "Why should I learn to drive? I've got you as a chauffeur!" JJ was snoring again in about three minutes. Mike had to shake him awake when they got to Bragg to change into fatigues and report. There was a storage lot where army personnel could stow their vehicles, and they left their Pontiac there at 1400 hours, September 19, 1964. At 1500 hours on that memorable day, Sharkey and Stott were abruptly reimmersed into army life.

Chapter Thirty-One

"Well, well! You boys look like shit! Where you been, troopers?" asked Sergeant Major Snook.

"Sergeant Major, if we told you we'd have to kill you! But a good time was had by all, Sergeant Major!" JJ barked out.

Sharkey's response caught Sergeant Major Snook off guard. "Is that so, son? Did it involve alcohol and pussy, Corporal Sharkey?"

"Yes, Sergeant Major, it did! Now we're relaxed and ready to give 'em hell in Panama, Sergeant Major!" JJ was on a roll. Stott wanted to strangle him because he knew they were on shaky ground, talking like that to a sergeant major.

"Uh-huh. How about you, Corporal Stott? Did you guys really get laid, or was it Sharkey's imagination?"

"Sergeant Major, Corporal Sharkey's telling it straight, Sergeant Major!" Mike said.

"Big tits involved?" Sergeant Major Snook inquired.

"Sir, yes sir!" JJ mistakenly yelled.

"Don't call me sir, I work for a living you miserable little dickhead! Drop and give me 200! You too, Stott! For being goofy enough to hang out with Rat II here!" Snook commanded.

Sharkey and Stott did the 200 push-ups and returned to attention. "Now, since you're back relaxed and ready to give us 'hell,' go out there and start double-timing on the cinder track until I come get you! Now! Dismissed!"

As they got into double-time discipline, Mike said to Sharkey, "Why'd you have to open your mouth, goddamn it? Now look what you got us into!"

"Doesn't bother me! I slept all the way home! Shut up and keep up," JJ screamed.

At 1800 hours Sergeant Major Snook came and got them. Stott had puked three times and JJ had puked at least once, but they were still double-timing! Had been for about two and a half hours.

"Well, looks like you boys got your color back! Report to the flight line at Pope at 2100 hours! Combat-packed and good to go! We're leaving a little early! Jungle warfare starts now! Move!"

Double holy shit!

It probably wouldn't have made any difference, but Mike blamed JJ for getting them off to such a tough start after their leave. Every time Stott reminded JJ of it he would say, "Remember the size of Cindy's tits? Remember that last blow job? Shut up and go! You're back in the army now!"

Six "A" trainer teams with support cadre loaded up that night and headed for Panama. The air force refueled the four C-130s at least once in route to the jungle paradise known as Fort Sherman, Panama. At 0430 hours on September 20, 1964, the green jump light came on in the airplane. The troopers jumped into the darkness of the jungle below from 800 feet.

Unfortunately, Stott landed in a tree. He cut himself loose, fell about ten feet to the ground without breaking anything and found the gathering point. So began the hardest thirty-two days of Mike Stott's life. The jungle terrain in and around Fort Sherman is some of the toughest turf anywhere in the world. Daytime temperatures in September and October regularly exceed one hundred degrees, but at night it cools down to ninety! All soldiers who have attended jungle warfare school in Panama will remember it as being as challenging as any noncombat experience in the army! Maybe worse than some combat duty! There are snakes, scorpions, and all kinds of other critters to make one's life miserable, not to mention a concentration of biting insects like no place else in the world. And ticks! The variation of attacking ticks and leeches was simply amazing.

Sharkey and Stott got assigned to different A training teams. In his first team exercise, Mike functioned as the assistant weapons sergeant, but in the next maneuver he cross-trained as an assistant communications sergeant. The teams set night ambushes and ran night recovery operations. They

ate "off the land" with occasional ration supplements. Water
came from muddy streams via purification tablets. All the
while the trainees were getting the shit kicked out of them by
their training cadre. Once, around day twenty, Mike's team
rendezvoused with a jeep that brought them more insect
repellant and water purification tablets, both badly needed.
Stott caught a glimpse of himself in one of the jeep's side
mirrors and realized that his face was un-recognizable from
a combination of bruises and swelling from insect bites.

Men had to field-shave every day, of course, and the ra-
zor caused a lot of bleeding as they cut off the scabs created from scratching the insect bites. The bleeding caused
the ticks and leeches to intensify their attacks. It truly was a
kind of hell on earth.

One night as Stott lay on a hillside, camouflaged to spring
an ambush and in absolute silence discipline, he felt something drop on his shoulder. Stott managed to maintain silence only because he was more afraid of the consequences
of making a sound than of being bitten by whatever had
landed on his shoulder. Mike could feel the weight of the
critter and something was tickling his neck. Fearing a taran-
tula or some other menacing insect, he slowly raised his left
hand to flick it off, all the while concerned with giving away
his position through movement. The creature on his shoulder stepped softly into the palm of his hand. It was a tiny,
two-toed sloth less than ten inches high. It put its little paws
around his left index finger and began gently sucking it as
though it were trying to nurse. As Stott got it down in front
of him he could see its little yellow eyes staring up. Those
eyes reminded him of Captain Gonzalez Gonzalez's yellow
eyes. Mike wondered if they were related.

Slowly, gently, Mike stroked the top of the baby sloth's
head, and it went to sleep, right in his hand! He tucked it
into the left front pocket of his fatigue pants and focused
on the ambush setup. After the exercise was complete, Stott
remembered his new pet. As he lifted it out of his pocket the
damn thing peed on him! The smell of its urine was reminis-

cent of a skunk! Mike had to live in those fatigue pants for several more days! No good deed ever goes unpunished.

Fort Sherman sits on the eastern side of Panama very close to a miserable little city called Colon. Colon, a violent, lawless town filled with sleazy bars and whorehouses, services sailors from around the world on shore liberty as their ships wait access to the eastern entrance of the Panama Canal. Toward the end of Special Forces jungle warfare training, an exercise brought Stott and his team to the eastern edge of Fort Sherman, relatively close to Colon. As they trekked to yet another of the endless night exercises, a very senior master sergeant named Hawkins, who was one of the team's observers, gave them the "stop-in-place/silence" signal. As he did so, Mike became aware of an unusual and really foul odor in the air. Master Sergeant Hawkins and two of the observer officers began searching the jungle near them and discovered two human bodies in an advanced state of decay.

One cadaver was female; the other wore the remains of a British naval officer's uniform. As darkness set in, an officer used his radio to call a team of U.S. Army Military Police, Panamanian army officers and Panamanian civilian police to deal with the obvious crime scene. The Panamanian police insisted that Mike's team hold in place until another group of civilian cops arrived to deal with what appeared to be a double homicide. As they waited for the Panamanian authorities to finally place the remains in body bags and carry them down the mountainside, Stott and his mates got their best six hours of rest during the entire thirty-two days in the jungle. It was also the first time most of the trainees had smelled decaying human flesh and seen cadavers bagged and hauled away like so much trash. It was a smell they would never forget.

At the end of day thirty-two, Stott and all the members of his training squad were informed that they had successfully completed the Special Forces version of the army's jungle warfare school. The men were trucked to Fort Clayton on the western side of the Canal Zone and given three "down days" to recover from the training. When Stott caught up with Sharkey at Fort Clayton, JJ looked as bad as Mike felt, but his spirits were soaring.

Despite being amidst all the remaining Special Forces trainees, JJ hugged Stott. "Mikey, we made it! We really did! We're gonna be two of the youngest Special Forces soldiers ever! God, you look like hell! Do I look that bad?"

"Worse, dickhead! I bet you lost ten pounds! I did! You okay?" Mike responded.

"Hell yes! We fuckin' made it!" Sharkey screamed.

In fact, they had. After three fun days drinking and celebrating in Panama City with the other fifty-one Special Forces candidates, they all flew back to Fort Bragg on Sunday, October 25, 1964. Nearly all of the other candidates that been in Panama with them had to complete a languages course as a final qualification to earn their berets. But JJ and Stott had already done that!

On Friday, October 30, 1964, John J. Sharkey and Mike Stott, along with nineteen other candidates, were awarded their green berets and inducted into an elite brotherhood. Both men cried tears of joy and relief at having made it. Truth be told, other guys cried too. Stott was still eighteen years old and was, at that moment, the youngest member of the army Special Forces. JJ turned nineteen the next day, Halloween, October 31, 1964. They both made E-5, buck sergeant, at the same ceremony, but because "Sharkey" came before "Stott" alphabetically, the "little dickhead" made sergeant ahead of Mike!

First words out of Sharkey's mouth when the ceremony concluded were, "I did it! I got my stripes before you! You owe me the best steak dinner in Fayetteville, plus a month's pay! At E-5 rates!"

Stott didn't mind. In his heart, Mike knew he never would have made it if it weren't for their pact and his determination not to let Sharkey beat him.

The partying was about to start at the end of the ceremony when Colonel James Hyatt spoke. "Listen up! I know you boys deserve to go party, and we want you to! But I've got a little more business! I'm the executive officer of Five Group. The following troopers are hereby assigned to The Fifth, effective immediately: Sergeant Mike Aswann; Sergeant Mike Ceiake; First Sergeant Howard Jones; Staff Sergeant Michael Maloney; Sergeant Bill Murphy; Sergeant Pete Netting; Staff Sergeant Barry Norris; Sergeant Kyle Ryan; Sergeant John Sharkey; Staff Sergeant Jim Stein; Sergeant Mike Stott. Need to huddle up with you troopers right now. Just take a few minutes, and then I'll buy!"

Colonel James Hyatt sounded like a right guy! And Sharkey and Stott were both assigned to Five Group! Next stop, Vietnam!

The soldiers met in a classroom in a building in back of the parade grounds. Master Sergeant Dennis Dokes introduced himself. "Morning, boys! I'm Master Sergeant Dennis Dokes. Been with the Fifth since I was a pup, like some of you! You're lucky bastards! You've made it to the finest team in the army! Ten-hut! Colonel James Hyatt and Major Bill Harper!"

Men snapped to attention as their officers entered the room. "Stand easy, sergeants! In fact, take a chair. Welcome to the tip of the spear! Some of you are veterans. Some of you are 'Boy Scouts,' but you are all now part of the army's elite! Look around the room, look at us. We are your brothers, now. Fight for 'em, die for 'em, if necessary. We're still working out the individual team assignments, so we'll give you that info later. But know this: each of you will be assigned directly to a southeast Asia combat force immediately, most likely out of Nha Trang, Vietnam. I know some of you just completed jungle warfare school in Panama. You look it! The rest of you look a little frazzled, too, so here's the deal. You're all gonna be out of country for quite a while, so take some leave. How much, you decide, but you all must report back here to Bragg by 16 November, 0700 hours. Here's something for each of you from the officers of Five Group!"

Master Sergeant Dennis Dokes then called names and had each man come to the front of the room to receive his green beret with the Five Group's insignia, and experience the "grasped" handshake that they came to know so well. Colonel James Hyatt and Major Bill Harper also shook their hands.

Stott was energized beyond description! He felt as though he could fly!

"That's it, boys! Welcome! See me for leave papers, the fun starts 16 November! Dismissed!" said Master Sergeant Dokes. JJ and Mike shook hands with their new comrades, some they had met before and some they hadn't. As the meeting broke up, Mike and JJ went to see Dokes.

"Master Sergeant Dokes, is there anything we can do, Master Sergeant?" JJ asked their new Top.

"Yes, sergeants, there is! Get the fuck out of my military sight until 16 November! See your family, get laid, whatever, but get ready! I'm cutting leaves for you through 15 November. Pick 'em up in an hour! Move, before I change my mind and put you on KP!"

JJ and Mike walked out into a crisp, sunny autumn day in the Carolina hill country of Fort Bragg. "This is our home," JJ said. "Now, this is the best day of my life! That beret looks pretty good on you despite your basic ugliness! We got sixteen days leave, money in our pockets and a car to drive! Where we going, sonny?"

Chapter Thirty-Two

Mike and JJ packed dress greens along with their civvies. They had sewn on sergeant's stripes and Special Forces patches in anticipation of their promotions; their new jump boots were mirror-shined. "Let's travel in civvies, but take our uniforms," Stott suggested. "First, if it's okay with you, I want to see my folks in Cincinnati for a few days! I say we call Cindy and Red in Washington, D.C., and go do some sightseeing!"

"Sonny, you read my mind!" exclaimed JJ. "But first, teach me to drive so we don't waste time or money sleeping! We got some livin' to do! Let's hit the road!"

They gathered their gear and Mike double-timed down to where they'd left the Pontiac. He was worried it wouldn't start after sitting for six weeks, but it fired right up! Stott got back to JJ at about 1500 hours, 3:00 p.m. They loaded up and went back to the parking area to put Sharkey behind the wheel for the first time in his life. To Mike's surprise and relief, he got the hang of it right away, even shifting the gears without grinding. Then it hit him! "JJ, you don't have a driver's license! What if we get stopped?"

"For Christ's sake, Stott! If we can't talk our way out of the problem, I'll just kill the cop!" Sharkey said, matter-of-factly.

Just for a second, Sharkey's statement really spooked Mike, but then he could see the little bastard grinning. "What dumb-ass cop is gonna fuck with a couple of Green Berets, dickhead?" JJ asked. "I'll drive 'til it gets dark! Relax!"

They drove straight through to Ohio, stopping only to gas up, eat and pee. Mike drove through the mountains of Tennessee on Friday and then Kentucky. When JJ awoke, he was all fired up to drive! Stott tried to get some sleep, but JJ decided it was a good time to review and practice their Hmong and Mandarin! He made Stott repeat words and answer questions for about two hours. Finally, Mike said, "Look, goddamn it, you slept for the last eight hours! Now shut up and let me rest!" He finally dozed off as JJ was drilling him on some Hmong sound he couldn't remember.

On Sunday, November 1, JJ and Mike were waiting outside his parents' house in their old Pontiac when his folks returned from church. They stayed with Stott's parents for two nights and spent time with all the extended family. Raymond still threatened to kick their asses for "going Green," but thought better of it after he saw them. JJ and Mike showed him how they could do 200 perfect push-ups, nonstop, and Ray decided to give them a pass on the ass-kicking. He made a good decision.

By Wednesday, anxious to go have some fun, JJ and Mike said good-bye to his mom and dad and headed for D.C. Stott had checked in with Cindy, who said she and Red were anxious to see them. "I guess that blowjob did the trick, huh?" she teased. "Did you get your berets?"

"Yes and yes!" Mike said. "We're driving straight through, so we'll see you in ten or twelve hours."

Sharkey and Stott started driving east on Ohio-U.S. Route 52, winding their way along the Ohio River. They crossed into West Virginia and picked up Route 50 in Parkersburg and drove through the Maryland mountains all the way into Washington. The Pontiac held up fine, it didn't burn any oil, and it got good gas mileage. When they arrived at Cindy's place in Georgetown after twenty-two hours on the road, she wasn't home, but had left a key. The boys let themselves into a beautifully decorated and classy town house. A note read:

Mikey and Dickhead:

I work until 5 PM. Make yourselves at home, but don't pee in my sinks, I know about Special Forces Troopers! Help yourselves to a shower. Use the guest bathroom on the third floor. There's Bud in the frig, and Jim Beam in the side cabinet. Meet

*Red and me at Flaherty's Bar on K Street around
5:30 PM or 1730 for you military types! Red says
she wants to fix us dinner at her place after we
have a few drinks. Mikey, get some rest! You are
going to need it!*

Love-Cindy

Love! Holy shit!

JJ was reading the note over Mike's shoulder. "Whoa, Sergeant Stott! You better watch your ass, boy! This broad's after you! Let's get some rest and get ready to party!"

They looked around Cindy's townhouse, and JJ observed, "Mikey, this is a classy place! I bet it costs some serious cash! Did she ever tell you what she does for a living? How old is Cindy, anyway?"

Sharkey was right again, Cindy's pad was high-class. "She just told me that she works for the government, JJ. She didn't say, but my guess is she's at least thirty."

JJ went to shower as Mike continued to look around. He happened to glance out the window and saw a cop about to write them a parking ticket. Stott hustled to try to talk him out of a fine.

"Excuse me, officer, but we just left our car here a minute ago to make sure we were in the right place. I'm on leave from the army, visiting a friend here. Could you please maybe give me a break? I don't have a lot of cash," Stott was putting on his best face.

"Gotta have a sticker to park on this street, mister. Let's see your registration and license."

Fortunately, it was Mike and not Sharkey talking to the cop. Stott had a license! JJ still didn't.

After reviewing the requested documents, the policeman asked, "Who you visiting, son? We don't see many cars like this in Georgetown."

"Cindy, um, uh, I don't remember her last name, officer," Mike admitted.

"Really. And where does this Cindy live?" the cop challenged.

"Right there, officer. That's her front door that's open," said Stott.

"You by yourself?" the cop asked.

"No, sir. A buddy of mine from the army is in taking a shower."

Another squad car pulled up, and a police sergeant got out from the passenger's seat. "Trouble, Smitty?" he asked the first cop.

"Don't know, Sarge. This kid claims he's on leave from the army, visiting a woman who lives right there, but he doesn't know her last name. I saw the North Carolina plate and knew the car was wrong. He's got ID, but it just doesn't feel right," Smitty said.

"How'd you get in?" asked the sergeant.

"She left us a key. I've got her work phone number, maybe we could call her," Stott suggested.

"What unit are you with, son?" the sergeant asked.

"Fifth Special Forces Group, sergeant. We—" But the sergeant cut Mike off.

"Bullshit! You're nowhere near old enough to be a green hat. Gimmie your military ID! Now! Turn around and put your hands on the squad car. Frisk him, Smitty."

Holy shit!

The sergeant got back in his car and got on the radio.

"He's clean, Sarge," Smitty said.

Mike stood there for maybe fifteen minutes trying to figure out how things had gotten so bad, so fast. Finally, the sergeant got out of his car again and walked back toward Stott and Smitty. About this time, JJ came strutting out of Cindy's place, all dressed up in his greens, wearing his beret. He walked right up to the police sergeant, and said, "I'm Sergeant John J. Sharkey, Fifth Special Forces Group. We are in town for meetings at the Pentagon, and you are about to make us late. Explain yourself, officer!"

Both cops stood there for a minute, trying to figure out who the hell this brash young sergeant was and what was going on. But JJ was way ahead of them.

"Here is a restricted number at the Pentagon. Call Specialist Edward Hale. He'll vouch for us. Now, please. We need to make that meeting. Sergeant Stott, get in there and get in uniform! Now, sergeant!"

Mike followed JJ's command. The cops just stood there. Stott could hear Sharkey as he entered Cindy's townhouse. "Sergeant, make that call! I'm not fooling around here much longer! We don't need this shit! Now call!"

The police sergeant got on his radio and had someone back at his headquarters make the call "to the Pentagon." JJ had looked out the window, saw the cop hassling his friend and called Fast Eddy Hale, their man in the Pentagon! The police sergeant was told to release Sergeant Stott immediately and to give him a special sticker allowing him to park on any street in Georgetown, as Stott was on "army business."

JJ came back in the house, poured a drink, and said, "Stott, I can't even let you park my car without supervision! Clean up and get dressed! We're meeting Fast Eddy for lunch! At the Pentagon, of course!"

It was true! Sort of, anyway. Mike and JJ picked Fast Eddy Hale up at a bus stop just across from the Pentagon. They barely recognized Hale when they spotted him. Eddy had gained about thirty-five pounds and had relatively long hair, certainly longer than real soldiers could have gotten away with! He was wearing E-4, specialist rank, and he was smoking a fucking pipe! Standing there waiting for his friends, he looked about thirty years old instead of twenty. Mike was driving, and as they pulled up in front of Eddy, JJ jumped out, flung his arms around Hale and literally threw him into the back seat.

"Take it easy, goddamn it, Sharkey! Hi, Mikey! Look at the two of you! Holy shit! Sharkey wasn't lying! You're both wearing green berets!" exclaimed Hale.

"Sergeant Sharkey to you, dickhead!" JJ barked. "What'd you do? Go on a milk shake diet? You must weigh 200 pounds! And what's with the fucking pipe? Don't even think of lighting that in my car!" JJ's animosity toward Eddy held over from basic training.

"That's how you thank me for saving you from the D.C. cops? Fucking with me? Come on, guys!" Eddy lapsed right back into his whining mode that had so irritated JJ and all his buddies, in basic.

"Hey, Ed! Good to see you! Where can we get a good breakfast? We're starving, and you remember how Sharkey gets when he's hungry!" Mike tried to lighten the air.

"Breakfast, huh? Corned beef hash and eggs sound good? Turn right at the next street!" said Hale.

"I've got about two hours, and then I have to report back. You guys look fantastic! How the hell did you get into the Special Forces?" Eddy's compliment seemed genuine, and it cooled JJ down a bit. Over a great corned beef skillet in an Irish bar where everyone seemed to know Hale, JJ and Mike told him their story. Sharkey, of course, took all the credit for getting them into and through Special Forces School.

"So you're both posted to the Fifth? Guess that means you'll be going to Nam, soon," Eddy calculated.

Sharkey and Stott had been ordered not to disclose their next posting, so they changed the subject by asking Eddy what was up with him.

"Well, not much compared to you guys! I went to a six-teen-week MOS school for intelligence clerks and then came right here to the Pentagon. All I do is type letters and answer the phone for my captain. Boring as hell! I got housing 'cause no enlisted guy can afford to live off base around here. But the food is damn good! Now I'm in for a 'top-secret' clearance. If it comes through, the captain says I got a shot at Spec Five in another six months or maybe a more interesting duty assignment. I take the train back home to Brooklyn every other month or so, and I stopped to see the Mobliano girls, but they're stuck-up college broads now.

Syl has his own apartment in Manhattan. He's getting married next summer. Oh, by the way, Syl's mom talks to Barry Smeall's folks all the time. Barry already got married to some farm girl from Indiana! How about that! And Allsmeir is in an artillery unit with the Big Red One as a gunner! He's threatening to sue the army!" Eddy was full of news.

"Smeall got married? Damn! And Syl bites the dust this summer? When you gettin' married, Hale?" JJ asked.

"Soon as Briggetta asks me!" Fast Eddy fired back.

"You know, Hale, I still owe you an ass-kicking!" said JJ, not liking the reference to Briggetta.

"What are you guys really doing in Washington?" asked Hale, attempting to change the subject.

"We got leave before we report to our team back at Bragg and came to see a couple of ladies we know in D.C." Stott said.

"Yeah? Man, I haven't met any chicks here! Are they lookers? Where did you meet them?" Eddy wanted to know.

Sharkey recounted the story of their trip to the outer banks and hooking up with Cindy and Red. JJ finished with, "Stott's lady is a little older, but we're staying at her place, and she must be loaded! It's some joint! How'd you get the cops to give us the parking sticker?"

"Told them I represented General Wheeler, you know, army chief of staff, and they were pretty impressed! Remember, my dad and brothers are cops! I know how to bullshit the fuzz!" said Hale. "You guys hear from Big Howie?"

"Mr. Howard to you, as I recall!" JJ reminded Hale. "No, we haven't heard from him in several months. Last we heard he was doing a stint in Germany with the 101st MP's. You knew he got through jump school, right? We figure the army had to come up with a special chute to hold his big, sorry ass!"

All three soldiers smiled at the mental image of the 250-pound-plus Big Howie falling from the sky.

"So you two and Howard, maybe Allsmeir, are real soldiers while me, Mobliano, and Smeall are just fuckin' paper pushers, right? I still don't know why the army didn't make me a sniper!" Fast Eddy lamented.

"Maybe it's because you're a pussy and barely qualified on the M-14 range," Sharkey theorized, his dislike for Hale obvious.

Seeing that JJ's words had hurt Hale's feelings, Mike said, "Lay off, Sharkey! You need to get laid!"

Fast Eddy had to get back to his desk job at the Pentagon, and he surprised Mike and JJ by picking up the tab. "Thought you were hurting for money, Hale," JJ said.

"I didn't say that! I said housing is too expensive here! Actually, I've got a full-time night job," Eddy told them as Mike drove him back to his duty station.

"What?" JJ and Mike said at the same time. The concept of an active-duty soldier having time to work any job was beyond their comprehension based on what they had been through over the past sixteen months.

"Yeah. I tend bar six nights a week from 7:00 p.m. to 1:00 p.m. at the bar at the Hay-Adams Hotel! Swankiest joint in town! Sometimes I make fifty dollars a night in tips! Plus, I've got no watchers! Come on over! You can drink anything you want for free! As long as you tip me, of course!" Hale seemed sincere.

"Are you serious, Hale?" JJ asked. "You make that kind of money tending bar?"

"Come on over and see, dickheads!" Hale screamed as he ran from our Pontiac back to the Pentagon, giving us the finger over his shoulder!

"I'm gonna kill that asshole!" said Sharkey.

"Wait 'til after we drink free for the next ten days!" Mike replied. "We can impress the girls by taking them to a fancy hotel bar, and it won't break us! And ease up on Hale! He's not so bad, JJ."

"I don't trust him, and neither should you," Sharkey emphatically stated. "Come on! Let's find that bar and get a head start on the girls!"

Mike and JJ located the bar and a spot to park before 1700 hours. It took them that long because of the traffic! As they walked around the corner to Flaherty's, two white-helmeted MP's stopped them.

"Papers, troopers!" the sergeant demanded.

Stott thought they were going to have trouble with them because they just wouldn't believe their rank and unit. "How the fuck did two punks like you make it to the Special Forces?" the older-appearing MP asked.

"If we told you, we'd have to kill you," said JJ. "And frankly, I'd enjoy that!"

"I'm gonna be on the lookout for you two dickheads!" promised the ranking MP.

When he got to a barstool, Mike said, "JJ, stop messing with MP's! That's just asking for trouble!"

"Bullshit! I wouldn't mind kicking their ass on general principles! Come on, get out your money! You're buying 'cause I saved your ass from the D.C. cops! Bartender! Couple of double Jim Beams with Bud chasers!"

It wasn't even 1700 hours yet! Holy shit! The boys had another round while they were waiting for the girls, and the bar was filling up. At about 1750 hours, Red walked through the door dressed up in a blue wool suit and looking fantastic! All the guys in the bar gave her the eye as she came over and kissed both JJ and Mike.

"Wow! You look great," Sharkey said. "You never dressed up like that at the beach!" She looked absolutely stunning, but also much older. Red leaned into JJ and rubbed her boobs up against him.

"We'll go to my place for dinner later, but right now I'd like a double Beefeater's martini on the rocks with olives. You guys look fantastic! Look at those berets! I'm proud of you both!" Red kissed them both again.

"Where's Cindy? Not here, yet? She rarely leaves Langley before 7:00 p.m. and will probably be late," Red commented.

"Langley?" Mike asked. "As in CIA headquarters Langley? By the way Red, what's your real name?"

"Well, Sergeant Stott, you're just full of questions! Next thing you'll want to know is how old I am, which I'd rather kill you than disclose! But, yes, that Langley. My name is Virginia, but I prefer 'Red.'"

Virginia, "Red," had two quick drinks to catch up, but by 1845 hours, they still hadn't seen Cindy. Mike was more than a little anxious. Right at 1900 hours, 7:00 p.m., the bartender asked him, "You wouldn't be Sergeant Stott, would you?"

Since his name was prominently displayed above his right breast pocket, Mike felt like smacking the guy. "It's what it says right here, pal! What's up?"

"Phone call for you. Take it at the end of the bar."

It was Cindy. "I'm so sorry, honey! I should've known I'd never get out of here on time! Tell you what! I'll go straight to Virginia's house! You guys go ahead. I'll be there when I can. Sorry. Love you! Bye!"

Double holy shit! There was that four letter word again. Mike went back to the lovebirds and told them what Cindy had said. They left immediately. Mike paid the tab. Nine drinks, thirty-five dollars! Plus tip!

JJ rode with Red and Stott followed. They drove for quite a ways, at least ten miles. The farther they drove, the nicer the neighborhoods got, until they arrived at a beautiful brick home that Stott's mother would have described as "Georgian." It had a circular driveway lined with coach lights! Red rolled down her window and said, "Leave your car there, Mikey! I'm gonna pull around back to the garage. Go to the front door."

The old Pontiac seemed out of place in that driveway, but so was Stott! In about two minutes, Red and JJ opened the door already ripping their clothes off! "Make yourself at home, honey! The bar's over there! JJ and I have some business upstairs!"

They disappeared up a beautiful mahogany staircase as Mike stood there thinking he should have picked Red back at the beach that day! If this was her house, she was rich! Her bar had more liquor than most taverns. Lots of brands Mike had never heard of. There was a refrigerator right next to the bar and he selected a Bud. Stott could hear the "fun" upstairs, so he settled into a big maroon leather chair in what appeared to be the library, hoping Cindy would show up sometime soon.

Stott fell into a deep sleep, but awoke to find Cindy leaning over him. She took his privates in her right hand and pulled him to her by his tie with her left. "It's after 10:00 p.m. Sorry. Too late to eat. Ginny has lots of bedrooms! Get up!"

It was a good thing Mike had taken a nap. He needed all his strength. They finally dozed for a bit around 4:00 a.m., but at 0500 hours Cindy handed Stott a big glass of orange juice and snuggled back in beside him. "I've got another hour before I have to go. You can sleep later. Perform!" she commanded.

Mike was in a semi-coma a little after 6:00 a.m. when Cindy once again shook him and said, "Go back to my place when you want. Ginny says JJ has to stay here. She's taking the day off. See you tonight. Call me if you want to. Love you. Bye."

At 1000 hours, JJ shook Mike again and told him, "Hey, Ginny's making breakfast. Get up and shower. Eat fast and leave. I'll see you in a few days. You know where to find me."

By the time Mike got downstairs, JJ and Ginny were back at it upstairs. There was a big plate of scrambled eggs and bacon with another plate of toast on the side. A pot of the best coffee Stott had ever tasted got his strength back to a level that allowed him to find his way back to Cindy's. He left the Pontiac—sticker on the inside lower left part of the windshield—around the corner from her house where the sign said you could park all day if you had that precious sticker.

Just as Mike was falling asleep in what he presumed was a guest bedroom, Cindy called to see if he was okay. "Get some rest, Honey. I'll be home by 1900. Love ya!"

Cindy arrived at a little after 1900 hours, and she brought Chinese! "Mikey, it's Friday night, and I took Monday off. I hope you got plenty of rest today!"

By 5:00 p.m. Saturday afternoon, Mike was raw and exhausted. "Cindy, I never thought I'd have to say this, but I need a break! Let me take you out for dinner, please!"

"Well, okay. But we're coming home early! What do you feel like?"

Stott told her about their connection at the Hay-Adams. "That sounds like fun, but we don't want to have dinner there. It's one of the most expensive restaurants in town. How did your friend land that gig? I would have thought they'd be standing in line to work the Hay-Adams Bar!"

"Don't know. Should we call JJ and Red?" Mike asked.

"Let's go alone. Do you have a fresh army shirt? You'll need to wear your dress greens at that hotel," Cindy said.

"Can I ask you something, Cindy?"

"Depends. You can ask, but let's not screw up a good thing here by asking awkward questions, okay?" Cindy advised.

"Cindy, I'm an eighteen-year-old soldier, and you're an attractive and successful woman. Okay, we met at a beach and had fun, but I had no idea you lived like this. I'm from a different world. Why am I so lucky?" Mike asked.

"You're on the border of too serious, Mikey! The fact is, I don't know. The last thing Red and I expected on our beach getaway was to meet a couple of guys like you and JJ. Fact is now, though, I'm getting attached. Scared, sergeant?"

"Maybe," Mike said.

"Let's just enjoy, okay, Mikey?" She kissed him.

"Okay. I'm done after this question. Don't you have lots of guys chasing you? Don't you have a boyfriend?"

"Chasing, yes, boyfriend, no. Just you. Still want to go out?"

Stott was a little spooked. He knew he was in way over his head, but then Cindy stretched and yawned, showing off those fantastic boobs! Holy shit!

Mike got ready in about twenty minutes, but it took Cindy an hour and a half. Stott was touching up the shine on his jump boots when she finally came downstairs. Cindy had piled her dark hair up on her head, and she was wearing a dress off her shoulders revealing ample cleavage. Cindy normally wore little makeup, but tonight she had gone all-out. Mike was mesmerized.

"Holy shit! You are beyond gorgeous!" he said, and he meant it. Mike had no idea makeup could be so flattering.

Cindy actually blushed. Then she did the unexpected! She started to cry. Mike held her for maybe five minutes. "Don't say a word," she whispered. "Just hold me awhile."

Mike stood there, holding Cindy in his arms, now convinced he was not only in over his head, but about to drown. After at least ten minutes Cindy recovered. "I'll just fix my face," she said. "Then we'll go."

They drove Cindy's Chrysler in silence to the Hay-Adams.

"There's a valet. Just pull up front, there. Mike. Before we get out I've got to say something. I know we're from different worlds, but I am really getting attached to you. When we get home, I've some things to tell you. But let's just have fun in here, okay? We may see people I know in here. I hope that's all right."

It was 1900 hours, and the hotel bar was filling up. Most of the men were in formal evening dress, and the women were really decked out. None of them looked as good as Cindy. To Mike's great relief, sure enough, there was Fast Eddy Hale in a dinner jacket behind the bar! Stott noticed there was a second, older bartender on the far end of the bar so he headed for where Eddy was very busy mixing drinks. Mike folded his beret under his left shoulder band as he had been instructed to do when indoors, and steered Cindy in Eddy's direction. Eddy noticed Cindy first.

"Good evening, ma'am. What can I . . . holy shit, Mikey! Hi! Is this, I mean, are you with her?" Eddy's face turned bright red as he realized how he was staring.

"Hi, Ed. This is Cindy Strand. Cindy, this is our friend from basic, Fast Eddy Hale."

"It's a pleasure to meet you, Miss Strand. You are even prettier than Mike said. What may I get you to drink?" Eddy recovered quickly.

"I bet I can guess why they call you 'Fast,' Eddy," Cindy teased. "Beefeater martini, up with olives, please." She turned and whispered to Mike, "So you really do think I'm pretty?"

Before Stott could respond they heard, "Cindy? Cindy Strand, is that you?"

A very distinguished looking older man with snow-white hair combed back in matinee idol style was just behind them at the bar with an equally distinguished looking lady and two other couples.

"It is you! Good evening, Cindy! You remember my wife, Madeline, and this is Bob and Helen Josephson and James and Barbara McNeil," said the new arrival.

"Good evening, Senator. Hello, Madeline. How are you? I know James and Barbara, of course, and it's nice to meet you, Mr. and Mrs. Josephson. Please meet my friend, Sergeant Michael Stott." Cindy's cool was incredible. "Mike, this is Senator Warren Oakes and his wife, Madeline."

As Mike shook hands with the senator and his entourage, the senator focused on him. "Sergeant, I believe that is a Green Beret folded under your epaulet. It is a great honor to shake the hand of a Special Forces soldier. May I ask how long you've been in the Special Forces?"

Stott was trying desperately to keep his cool, for Cindy's sake if nothing else, but that he could be standing at a bar in Washington, D.C., with a lady who could introduce him to a U.S. senator was incomprehensible. Mike was impressed beyond belief but managed to respond, "It's my honor to meet you, sir. I just earned my beret on October 30. It will always be the proudest day of my life, Senator."

All this happened as Senator Oakes continued to shake Mike's hand. His grip was amazingly strong for a man his age, and he kept his eyes focused on Stott's. It was easy for Mike to see why this man was a U.S. senator.

"Congratulations, Sergeant. Thank God our country has young men like you," Senator Oakes said.

The senator turned his attention to Cindy, and they chatted as Mike stood there biting the inside of his jaw to make sure he wasn't dreaming. He looked at Hale and got an interesting nod. It made Mike flash back to the nod Hale had given him that night early in basic training after he had told him about his brother, James—the night they had met Captain Albert with the missing arm and leg.

Stott tuned back in to his current surroundings and heard Senator Oakes say to Cindy, "Well, congratulations again. It was the best analysis I've seen in three senate terms! Refreshing and downright encouraging when a staffer has the courage to offer an intelligent opinion that goes against the politics of the day. Don't give in! Stick by your guns! How are you doing personally, dear?"

"Better, sir. And thank you for the kind words. They meant a lot to me," Cindy said.

Senator Oakes called to Mike as he and his party worked their way down the bar, shaking hands, "Good luck, Sergeant! Give 'em hell!"

"Holy shit, Cindy! What's going on? How in hell do you know a U.S. senator?" Mike asked.

"When we get home," was all she said.

Eddy Hale was working his tail off behind the bar, his customer's three deep. Cindy and Mike sipped their drinks, but she had become pensive. Just as Stott was about to call for another round, Eddy delivered two more drinks and said, "Best of all worlds, Sergeant. You and the lady are on the senator's tab, right through dinner. Martini the way you like it, ma'am?" he asked Cindy.

"You call me 'ma'am' one more time and I'm gonna come right over this bar and kick your ass!" Cindy said to Eddy.

Mike was more surprised than Eddy! Where did that come from? Up to that point Cindy had exhibited an even temperament despite her passion in the bedroom. When she threatened Eddy, she sounded like she had every confidence that she could kick his ass. Not that kicking Hale's ass was all that hard! Eddy was staring at Cindy.

To lighten things up, Mike said, "Well, Cindy, you are full of surprises! But you'll have to stand in line behind JJ to kick Eddy's ass! That's Sharkey's specialty!" Over Hale's protest, Stott told Cindy the story of the Sharkey-Hale fight in the reception center. He finished the story by observing, "It's almost impossible for me to believe that was sixteen months ago. Hey, Eddy! What do you mean about being on the 'senator's tab' for dinner?"

Cindy showed the faintest of smiles, and Mike hoped he was getting her back in good spirits, but then she said, "I'll accept a drink from that asshole, but not dinner! Drink up! Let's get out of here!"

Stott was totally confused. It seemed to him that Cindy and the senator and his wife were on good terms, maybe even friends. Now she was referring to him as "asshole" and wanted to leave.

Mike started to leave Hale a tip, but Eddy said, "For Christ's sake, Mike! I was kidding you guys about tipping me! Come back anytime."

"Let's leave the car here. I know a good little steakhouse within walking distance." Cindy had only the jacket to her dress as a coat and the night was turning quite cool.

"I'm sorry I can't give you my waistcoat, but I don't want to be out of uniform with all these MP's around," Mike said.

"I'm not cold, but put your arm around me anyway," Cindy said.

They walked the two blocks to the restaurant in silence. The maitre'd greeted Cindy as they walked through the bar, "Good to see you Mrs. Strand. We're booked tonight, but I'll always give you that corner booth. Good evening, Sergeant. Please enjoy your evening."

The waiter had followed them to the booth. "May I get you a cocktail?"

"Two double Beefeaters martinis straight up with olives, please," Stott ordered.

As the waiter left to get their drinks, Cindy said, "That's right, Mike. You heard the maitre'd right. He called me Mrs. Strand. I was going to tell you later tonight, but I need to talk now. Please just listen. My husband died on the USS Thresher on April 10, 1963. He was an Annapolis graduate, a career naval officer. The fact is, we were separated when the Thresher was lost. I wanted a divorce. He did not. I'm not able to have children. That was the beginning of our troubles. I've been living with his loss, and my guilt, these nineteen months, and, frankly, not doing all that well. After Virginia's divorce, she talked me into taking that trip with her to the Outer Banks. I guess you could say our timing was right that Sunday morning when we met."

Mike didn't know what to say. For some reason, he wasn't that surprised at Cindy's story.

"There's more, Mike. Let me just get it all out, okay? I work at the Central Intelligence Agency. That's how I met my husband. I have a relatively responsible position there. More than that, I can't say. I'm thirty-five years old, Mike, old enough to be your mother. I don't feel that old, at least not physically. I won't pretend that my marriage was a good one. We never were that happy. I am very attached to you for some reason that I don't really understand. I'd like us to continue until it doesn't feel right anymore, if that makes any sense."

Mike sat there in silence trying to comprehend all that Cindy had just revealed and what if any difference it made to him.

The martinis arrived, and Cindy ordered a second round even before they tasted the first ones. They sat there, silently sipping their drinks.

"It would help me if you would say something, Mike," said Cindy.

"Okay, here goes. For as long as I can remember, I've always felt older than I am. Maybe that doesn't make any sense either, but it's true. Until I joined the army, I was a kid who had experienced almost nothing. I was thirsting to escape from an ordinary life like my parents live. But then the army consumed me in ways I still don't pretend to understand, but the army feels like home to me now. You are the real first woman I've been with. I wasn't a virgin when I met you, but I wasn't exactly experienced, as you know. I'm sorry about your situation, but it doesn't figure into the equation from my perspective. You're every man's dream, and I'm totally thrilled to be here with you. It's that simple to me. Thank you for allowing me to share a part of your life. I hope my inexperience, particularly in this environment, doesn't get in our way."

Cindy sat and stared at Mike for a very long time. He didn't know if he had hurt her, made her angry or what. Finally, she spoke. "That was quite a speech, Mike. I believe you spoke from your heart without any agendas. I hope you keep that honesty. I'll be here for you until you tell me not to be. That's my definition of love, and I love you. But don't let this conversation change the sex! I'm serious! Don't let my affection for you drive you away, please."

"What man could hope for more?" Stott said to her.

Their second martini arrived, and Cindy told Stott about Senator Oakes. But just as she started her story she leaned across the table and kissed Mike like he'd never been kissed before. He was so aroused he thought he might lose it, right there in the restaurant. She held his hand as she continued her tale.

"Senator Oakes sits on a certain unpublished committee that my section gives briefings to on a regular basis. Usually my section chief handles the oratory, but, of course, several of us are always there to back him up with detail should the need arise. Oakes is the second ranking senator on this committee and, as such, often challenges our findings and recommendations. Just before I met you, the Friday after Labor Day, one of these briefings turned pretty ugly as Oakes and a senator from the other party nearly got into a fistfight over one of our recommendations. Oakes holds himself out to be a moderate conservative, but a flaming, left-wing pinko lurks under all that silver hair!

"Then, the next day, Saturday, Oakes held a press conference and came close to violating the National Secrets Act by talking all around a certain issue that was absolutely off limits to open discussion. At that committee's briefing last Friday, my section chief was summonsed to a more critical briefing at the White House. I was called on to fill in for him. I read his briefing notes to the committee, and they contained a strong warning about confidentiality. Senator Oakes cursed at me for 'daring to impune his discretion,' so his public, sweet-talking to me this evening made me want to kick him in the balls! Enough of this! Tell me about Special Forces school."

Over a great steak dinner, Mike recounted first his 18-B training and then tried to describe Ranger school. Cindy was surprised about the physical beatings. Stott's story about JJ and Captain Gonzalez brought tears of anger to her eyes.

"It's really like that? Ranger training is harder than Special Forces school?" she asked.

"Well, it was for me. Ask JJ when you see him; I'm sure he'll agree. I wonder what he and Red are doing right now."

"Probably what I wish we were doing! Finish up! Let's go home!"

"You don't have to say that twice," Mike said.

The next sixty hours with Cindy Strand changed Mike's life. Not that the rest of the week at Cindy's house wasn't fantastic, but the memory of her tenderness and passion on that Sunday and Monday would sustain him through difficult times for many, many years.

Sharkey finally called his buddy from Red's home on Tuesday, November 10. "You finally come up for air, JJ?" Mike asked.

"Yeah, Ginny had to go to work today. How are you doing?" JJ inquired.

"I'm thinking about deserting and staying right here with Cindy until she screws me to death!" Stott said.

"Don't say things like that, even to me Mike! Can you come get me? Let's do some sight-seeing!"

"Do you have the strength?" Stott teased JJ.

"Barely, but yes. How long 'til you get here?" Sharkey asked.

"About an hour. And JJ, wear your dress greens, I want to go to Arlington," Mike said.

After a moment, JJ responded, "Yes, let's go there this morning. See you soon."

After only one wrong turn, Mike found his way back to Red's mansion. He had gotten up early to have coffee with Cindy, and after she left he washed and waxed the Pontiac. As Stott pulled into Red's big circular driveway, there was JJ, standing at parade rest, absolutely resplendent in his uniform. He had "styled" his beret to peak on the left front, showcasing the Group Five Patch. His jump boots gleamed with an incredible sheen. JJ looked like a career soldier.

"Looking pretty sharp, trooper," Mike said as John got in the car.

"Sergeant Sharkey to you soldier. Remember, I'm the senior NCO here! I got my promotion one minute ahead of you! Which reminds me, you never made good on our bet! By the way, my car looks pretty good! About time you cleaned it up," JJ was in rare form.

"Sharkey, if I wasn't all dressed up right now I'd kick your ass on general principles!"

That made JJ smile. "Yeah, yeah! Looks like you lost weight! You holding up okay?" Sharkey asked.

"Better than you! How many push-ups can you do now? Or has she been on top all the time?" Mike asked as they headed down Wisconsin Avenue.

"Very funny, Sergeant Stott. Let's stop for coffee before we get to Arlington. You know how to get there?" JJ asked.

"18-B's never get lost! What do think, I'm some communications sergeant or something?" Mike wasn't cutting JJ any slack.

Sharkey started speaking in Hmong and made Mike practice with him through their coffee stop and all the way to Arlington. When they arrived, JJ said, "Mike, thanks for asking me to come here with you. It means a lot to me."

The soldiers stopped and got a directory and Sharkey guided them to Mike's brother's grave. They had to park some distance from the actual site. As Mike and JJ got out of the Pontiac, a spit-and-polish army corporal greeted them. "Good morning, sergeants! Are you here for the funeral?"

"What?" JJ and Mike asked.

"We are expecting some Green Berets to serve as honor guards at this morning's funeral ceremony. I expected you to be them. You're not here for that?" the corporal was puzzled.

"No, we're not. We came to visit a grave," JJ said.

"Perhaps I can help you, then. Do you know where it is? What's the name, please?" asked Corporal Brown.

"Captain Stott, James William," Mike said. "We have this directory. I think we're pretty close."

Corporal Brown consulted first their directory and then a larger one that he had with him. He glanced at Mike's name tag and said, "Your father, Sergeant Stott?"

"Uh, no. My oldest brother."

"You must be extremely proud to have a Congressional Medal of Honor winner for a brother. His grave is just up on that ridge line there. Are those Five Group patches?" the corporal asked.

"They are."

"Good luck over there. A number of Special Forces troopers are coming for this funeral. Just over the hill there, for your information. There are several dozen people there already."

He saluted Mike and JJ and took up his watch again.

It was a perfectly clear, cool autumn morning. An intense early sun shone in their faces as John and Mike walked about a hundred paces up an incline and then in from the aisle several headstones. There it was: Stott's brother's final resting place. Overcome with emotion, Mike simply could not hold back the tears. JJ put his hand on Mike's shoulder and also had tears in his eyes.

Mike barely remembered James, but he'd grown up listening to the family's memories of him. James was a big man, six feet, four inches, and 220 pounds. In pictures of him, James had his mother's good looks, but their father's intensity in his face. In his room at home, Mike still had a little windup toy car that James had sent him from Germany before he shipped to Korea. As Stott stood there, he could imagine how incredibly difficult it must have been for his mom and dad to visit this spot. Seeing the endless rows of heroes' graves was moving beyond description.

As Mike and JJ stood before James' grave, Corporal Brown led a group of Green Beret officers up the hill toward the funeral. When they saw the two young green hats standing at a grave, the ranking officer, a major named Taylor, stopped the group and walked over to them. Mike and JJ snapped to attention and saluted.

"At ease, Sergeants Sharkey and Stott," Major Taylor said as he read their name tags. "I see you're with Five Group. Congratulations! We're here to honor one of your guys, Major Michael Kohn."

At this point, Major Taylor looked directly at James' marker. He looked again at Mike's name badge. "Your father, son?" he softly asked.

"Sir, no sir. My oldest brother, sir," Mike said.

"My condolences. You must be very proud. Come stand with us, if you will. Major Kohn was my good friend." Sharkey and Stott saluted Major Taylor again as he departed.

"Do you suppose he could see that I had been crying?" Mike asked JJ.

"No matter, Mike," Sharkey said. "Are you okay to walk over to the burial? It would probably be the right thing to do. We could come back here later, if you would like."

JJ and Mike walked over the hill and saw that the honor guard was already carrying the casket from the caisson to the gravesite. There were perhaps a hundred people attending the service. About half were in uniform. Mike counted nine Green Berets and about two dozen airborne berets. The ceremony, of course, concluded with the playing of taps and a three-gun salute. Major Taylor presented the flag to a pretty blond-haired woman and a small boy. It was all Mike and JJ could do to hold back their tears.

As the attendees began to make their way back toward their vehicles, JJ whispered, "I hope to be buried here someday, but not too soon."

They stopped again at James' grave on their way out and placed a small flag they had received at the funeral in the slot at the bottom of his marker. JJ and Mike came to attention and saluted, then walked to the car in silence. They rode most of the way back toward the Washington Monument before Sharkey finally broke the silence.

"That was even more emotional than I imagined. God, how hard it must have been on your folks. Thank you for taking me with you this morning. Let's find a bar!"

The boys found a tavern just around the corner from the Hay-Adams Hotel and had a couple of beers and a hamburger. Mike told JJ about his experience at 'Hale's' bar the past Saturday night. Stott told his friend everything, including his conversation with Cindy about their relationship. They left the tavern and past the White House over to the National Mall. Sharkey wanted to walk more, and they went first to the Lincoln Memorial and then on the Washington Monument. The conversation was constant, but light. Mostly JJ recounted their training experiences and laughed about the good memories, ignoring others that weren't so good. They walked back to the car and drove to the Capitol, marveling at the building's beauty and design.

"Before I joined the army, I wanted to be an architect," Mike told JJ. "Wouldn't it be something to learn how to construct buildings like the ones we've seen here in Washington?"

"Maybe. But you were born to be a soldier, just like me," JJ responded.

"Why in hell do you say that, John?" Mike asked.

"Look what we've accomplished! We've been in the army only sixteen months, and we're sergeants in one of the most prestigious units in all the armed services! And now that I understand a little about the army, I know exactly what I want to do for the next forty years!" Sharkey's enthusiasm made Mike grin.

"And what, exactly, would that be, JJ?" Stott asked.

"I want to become the ranking command sergeant major in all the Special Forces!" John exclaimed.

Mike knew he meant it. Sharkey loved the army.

"Well, I bet you'll make it, JJ! But I'll still kick your ass when you need it! Let's call the girls and see if they can meet us at the Hay-Adams and drink on Hale!" Stott said.

"Ginny said she for sure will have to work late tonight and not to expect her until 2200 hours at the earliest, so she won't make it. But call Cindy if you want," JJ said.

Mike called Cindy, but she said she had to catch up too, and she'd see him at her house "whenever."

"Do you know how weird this feels to me, Mike?" JJ asked.

"What feels weird?" Stott responded.

"You know, us staying with these older women. Them being interested in us. I don't really understand it; do you?" JJ seemed confused.

"JJ, one thing my dad has told me a thousand times: 'Never, ever presume to understand women because you never will.' I'm pretty sure he's right, so I'm gonna take his advice and just enjoy this thing with Cindy for as long as it lasts. When we head back to Bragg this weekend, we may never see them again or, who knows, you may wind up marrying Red!"

"That's it, goddamn it. Pull over! I'm gonna kick your ass right now!" JJ shouted.

Of course, he didn't mean it. Mike stashed the car in a lot about two blocks from the Hay-Adams and waited for Hale to show up for work. They weren't about to pay hotel bar prices for booze, especially when Fast Eddy could soon

take care of them. Mike and JJ sat on a park bench right outside the hotel from which they could watch the bus stop for
Eddy's arrival. Hale got off the bus at 1835 hours, and they
were drinking Jim Beam with Bud chasers by 1845!

The bar was quiet on Tuesday night, so Eddy had time to
shoot the shit with his friends.

"I still can't believe you guys are Green Berets!" Hale
said. "Tell me about all the training and stuff you've been
through. I want to hear it all!"

For the next two hours, Mike and JJ relived their first sixteen months in the army as they explained it all to Fast Eddy.
Stott told the story of Sharkey challenging Captain Gonzalez
at the conclusion of Ranger training, and Eddy asked him to
repeat it three times.

"That's like the best army story I've heard yet!" Hale exclaimed. "What's next for you guys? Do you know if you're
going to Vietnam?"

"Eddy, we can't say, but we can say it will probably be
many months, if not years, before we see you again after this
week," JJ told him.

"Well, I've got a little news for you guys, but it seems
pretty tame compared to your stories. My top-secret clearance came through, and I'm getting transferred to a section
that handles intelligence for southeast Asia! Maybe I can
help you guys from here!" Eddy said.

"Congratulations. Eddy! That's great! We're going to
bring our lady friends here Friday night if that's okay, sort of
a going away party. We've got to start driving back to Bragg
Saturday. We're not sure how long it will take in the Pontiac," Mike said.

"Sure, bring 'em! What are you gonna do with your car?
Sounds like maybe you guys won't be needing it for a while."

Frankly, Mike hadn't thought about what to do with the
car. He could see by the look on JJ's face that he hadn't either, but Sharkey was always thinking! "Tell you what, Hale!
We'll sell it to you for $500! It's got new tires and brakes,
and it runs great! What do you say?"

"I'll give you $400 cash!" Hale came back quickly.

"We'll split the difference with you and let you have it for $450, but you gotta pay us cash, Friday night! You can take possession right then and drive it back to your quarters that night," JJ had turned into a deal maker.

"Deal!" said Hale.

"Uh, JJ, how we going to get back to Fort Bragg? What if we can't get a flight? It's only four days away," Mike said.

"I'll handle that!" said Sharkey. "We better get outta here while we can still find our way home. See you Friday night, Hale, and bring our cash!"

Stott was too drunk to drive legally, but managed to deliver Sharkey back to Red's house at 2215 hours. She was just arriving home.

"Come in for a nightcap, Mikey! Cindy's still at work, I talked to her fifteen minutes ago. She said she'd see you by midnight."

"In that case, okay, but I'd better have a Coke. I'm already buzzed," Mike said.

"Hey Ginny, I've got an idea! Hale wants to buy our old Pontiac, but if we sell it to him we need a ride to Bragg. Can you get us a flight Saturday or Sunday?" JJ asked.

"Sure, I'll do it the morning! That means you can stay a day longer and leave Sunday, right?" Ginny said.

"Right, so we'll have one more night together," JJ said.

"Oh, Johnny, that's great!"

As Red went to get comfortable, JJ whispered to Mike, "You may not understand women, but I do! Drink up and get out of here, I've got work to do upstairs!"

Stott went back to wait for Cindy and do a little work of his own.

As it turned out Ginny, "Red," worked for the FBI and had all kinds of connections. She got Mike and JJ a military fare on Piedmont Airlines Sunday, November 15, 1964, leaving Washington National at 1000 hours through Charlotte, North Carolina, connecting to a puddle jumper that got them into Fayetteville at 1740 hours for fifty-eight dollars each. Perfect!

JJ made a reservation in the main dining room at the Hay-Adams Hotel for Friday night. They spent the proceeds from the sale of the Pontiac to Hale plus some on a blowout dinner for Cindy and Ginny to thank them for all their hospitality. Mike spent all day and night that Saturday in bed with Cindy as JJ did with Red. On Sunday morning, the women took the soldiers to Washington National Airport in Cindy's Chrysler.

Mike and JJ had to travel in dress greens to get the military fare. At the curb at Washington National, Cindy produced a fancy camera and had a skycap take their pictures, all dressed up in their uniforms. She had him take couples' pictures as well as individual pictures of JJ and Mike and, of course, several pictures of the four of them.

"Until next time. I'll come anywhere in the world to see you, Mikey. Just give me as much notice as you can. I mean it. Just tell me where and when. Stay safe, honey, I love you," Cindy said.

Sharkey and Stott watched them drive away and then flew back to their world in the Special Forces.

Chapter Thirty-Three

On November 16, 1964, at 0700 hours, Sharkey and Stott reported to Five Group headquarters at Fort Bragg. The next four weeks and five days went by in a blur of vaccinations, processing, and reorientation that made those thirty-three days seem like three. The men were required to make out a will. Sharkey named Stott and St Agnes Orphanage as his beneficiaries.

JJ and Mike were part of a Five Group contingent that reached Nha Trang, Vietnam, by way of Phuket, Thailand, on December 18, 1964, two days before Mike's nineteenth birthday. Nha Trang was in the process of becoming the Fifth Special Forces Group headquarters, controlling the group's operations not only "in country," but also directing its "non-existent" operations in surrounding nations. Nha Trang had an aura of excitement, anticipation, and fear about it that made the atmosphere electric with energy.

On December 19, Sharkey and Stott received their first A Team assignments. It happened in a way that seemed a bit odd, but just about everything that happened to them from that point forward was unconventional.

There were several hundred Special Forces soldiers at Nha Trang in December of 1964 and hundreds of indigenous tribesmen that had been recruited to support special operations. Many of the tribesmen's families were with them, helping to build and expand the camp. The contingent of new troops that had just arrived numbered about a hundred, but the majority of these were veteran SF men, many returning to Vietnam for the second or third time. Sharkey and Stott were the most junior members of the new contingent.

For security reasons, the new arrivals attended briefings in groups that were multiples of the basic A Team configuration of twelve men. Their briefing group consisted of thirty-six "newbies" addressed by their commanding officer, Colonel Robert Besuden and Sergeant Major Mike Franke. Colonel

Besuden's executive officer, Major Lawrence Royalty, was also in attendance with three captains. The briefing was conducted in a bunker and, to Mike and JJ's surprise, was completely informal.

Colonel Besuden began, "Welcome to Nha Trang. I see many familiar faces that I've served with before; it's damn good to see you again. I see some new, young faces. I'm proud to welcome you to the army's finest group. We tell it straight here at Nha Trang and share all that is prudent to share, all the way down the line. Put as straight as I can put it, the shit's about to hit the fan in several ways.

"More supplies than ever are finding their way down the Ho Chi Minh Trail. Our recon teams are seeing beaucoup North Vietnamese regulars infiltrating to help train the Vietcong. The ARVN's [Army of Republic of Vietnam] are trying to gear up for the challenge, but they got a long way to go. Corruption abounds within the army of the South, at all levels. My best guess is that the communists control half of the South, either through out right land domination or through the influence of their sympathizers.

"Our mission here has been expanded in both official and unofficial ways; more on that in a sec. You've seen the tribesmen and their families here. They may be the South's best hope in the short run if we, the men in this bunker and your brothers 'on the ground' out in the countryside, can keep the Montagnards and Hmongs motivated and on our side! And if we can keep them from going to war with each other again! And if we can keep the opium use down to a manageable level.

"We have been given increased intelligence gathering missions including arms-for-opium monitoring, all the way up to the Golden Triangle. Most, but not all, of you men speak at least some Hmong. I can't exaggerate how important it is for you all to be proficient in this language. Most Montagnards and Shan speak it too, so it's critical! We can't win their hearts and minds if we can't communicate with them!

"Today you will receive your A Team assignments. Most of you are going to join existing teams as replacements. A few of you will be assigned to newly formed teams. We have preliminarily assigned personnel based on the interviews and skills assessments that were done back at Bragg. In rare cases, your team commanders may request reassignments based on their own gut feel about how you fit in with their particular team. Should any of you get reassigned, do not personalize it or feel disgrace! Your team leaders must be 100 percent comfortable with their team members! If they're not, the team's effectiveness is diminished! We cannot afford teams that aren't in harmony! It's dangerous for all involved.

"We've made every effort to maximize experience in the new teams. Still, we must get new teams in the field. Some will have half their members who will be in their first combat assignments.

"Men, make no mistake, this is a combat assignment! All team members qualify for the Combat Infantry badge on recommendation of their team commander after an appropriate interval.

"I wish we could give you longer to acclimate here at Nha Trang. The fact is, though, many of your teams will be 'heading out' as soon as your proficiencies with weapons and communications have been demonstrated and proven to your team leaders.

"Men, hear this! Five Group tolerates no drug use nor alcohol abuse, period. Not to say we don't celebrate our successes with the occasional booze party, but only in the right environment! Never in the field. In this there are no second chances!

"I see men in this room that have served in southeast Asia as far back as the mid-fifties. I know that there are men in Five Group with children in some of these mountain villages. So be it, but Five Group and your team comes first! Understood?"

"Yes, Colonel!" said the newbies. Besuden's statement about children surprised Stott. He hadn't even considered that possibility.

Colonel Besuden continued, "You've all worked or practiced in the twelve-man A Team configuration, and that's normally the way we'll operate. However, you may hear about
some half A's or C Team experimentation that we're looking
at. I'm not convinced this is the way to go, but for certain
black operations, it may make sense.

"For you new guys about to experience your first incoming, be it small arms fire, mortars, rockets, or whatever, hear
this! You will feel fear! If you don't it's because you're already dead! It's how you handle that fear that counts! Measure up! Conquer your fear. Make me proud!

"Sergeant Major Mike Franke will call your name, followed by the names of your detachment commander, executive officer and operations sergeant. One or more of these
men will be in the designated place in camp waiting to meet
with you. They may choose to meet with you individually or
together with other new members of the team, depending on
the situation. We depend on your team commanders to complete your orientation to Nha Trang and Vietnam and explain
your part in our mission here.

"One more thing, I need an aid/interpreter to assist my
headquarters team here in Nha Trang. Ideally, a senior
trooper with lots of 'in country' experience, but, candidly,
we're looking for the soldier with the best languages skills,
period. If you believe you speak good Hmong, I want to hear
from you. This isn't the other army, so any questions?"

"Sir, First Sergeant Morgan, just back. Proud to rejoin the
group, sir! Last night I actually got a good night's sleep; is
Chuck on vacation?"

A ripple of laughter swept through the bunker. Even Colonel Besuden grinned. "Good to have you back, Morgan!
Heard you did some good hunting in Latin land. We're all
proud of you. No, Chuck's not taking the week off just cause
you're back!"

More laughter. "Fact is, last night was the first quiet night
in a long time, so I'm glad you got some sleep. Chuck still
tests our perimeter most nights. We get hit with rockets and

mortars several times a week. You could probably see that we've got decent fields of fire out 200 to 300 meters in most directions now, and our patrols have kept the mortars relatively quiet, but Charlie's still working twenty-four seven. Other questions?"

"Sir, First Sergeant Jans, just back from Panama. Good to see you, sir. Is it true you now have an ice cream machine in HQ, sir?"

Now the group roared with laughter. "Are you sayin' I've put on weight, First Sergeant?" Besuden said through a grin.

"Sir, no sir! A Ranger colonel named Downs put me up to the question, sir! Said you'd understand, sir!"

"Uh-huh. Don't you know better than to listen to a Ranger colonel, Sergeant Jans?"

More polite laughter.

"Well, okay. Welcome, men. Good fortune with your team assignments. God bless you all. Sergeant Major Franke, they're all yours! Stay seated men! Save your energy, especially you old farts!" Colonel Besuden and all of the officers left the bunker.

"Listen up, men of the Fifth! I'm gonna read your name and then your report contact, along with location. If you don't know the location, ask. Here goes: Staff Sergeant Roy Adams; Captain Jim Haas and Warrant Officer Ken Jones-C Hooch . . . " Sergeant Major Franke started reading through the list.

As Sharkey and Stott waited for the S's, Mike looked around at his fellow sergeants. How proud he was to be in that room! Finally, JJ got his team assignment, then came Mike's turn. "Sergeant Mike Stott: Captain Bill Freeze, detachment commander; W-3 Rick Myers, executive officer; Master Sergeant Jim Harper, ops sergeant. Blue Hooch."

Sergeant Major Franke read three more trooper's assignments and then said, "Remember, you brand new guys, we do have some practical jokers in our group! You'll just have to survive their shit! Dismissed!"

Practical jokers in a combat environment? Holy shit!

Mike got directions to the Blue Hooch, which turned out to be a six-man bunker with a blue shooting star painted on the upper support beam. A diminutive native woman was exiting the bunker carrying what looked a bundle of dirty fatigues as he arrived. From the bunker opening Mike called, "Sergeant Stott, reporting, sir!"

"Don't call me sir, goddamn it! I work my balls off for this lousy $500 a month!" a voice from the bunker replied. "Did you bring my Hershey bar, goddamn it?"

"Master Sergeant Harper, is that you?" Stott asked.

"Well, it's not your goddamn girlfriend now, is it? You got my Hershey bar?"

"Master Sergeant, where would I find a Hershey bar?" Mike inquired.

"Up your ass, I guess sergeant! Step in here! No fuckin' HB, huh? You're pissing me off already! Can you shoot straight? Cause if you can't shoot straight we can't use you! Come on down here and let me look at you!" Harper demanded.

As Mike's eyes adjusted to the dim light in the bunker, he could see that Master Sergeant Harper appeared to be alone. He was sitting on an empty .50 caliber ammo box and had on no shirt and no headgear. Just fatigue pants and jump boots. Stott guessed his age to be at least fifty, and he was smoking a really foul cigar. Mike could smell alcohol. Not the rubbing kind.

"What makes you think you're worthy to be on my team, Sergeant?" Harper asked.

Instinct drove Stott to answer him in Hmong. "I am young, strong, and tough. I am worthy to serve with honorable men."

Master Sergeant Harper gave Mike that deer-in-the-headlights look, revealing that he didn't speak Hmong. "You dumb enough to fuck with me, shithead?" Harper was incredulous.

"That's enough, sergeants!" came a voice from behind them. "Step on in there, Sergeant! You're off to one hell of a bad start!"

Stott turned to see two men, both wearing captain's bars, make their way into the bunker. Mike came to attention and held a salute as they looked him up and down. Finally, they both returned the salute, and then one of them said, "Your Hmong sounded pretty good; how're your reflexes?" He lashed out at Stott with a left hook!

Reflex took over, captain or not! Mike ducked the hook as he had hundreds of others during his boxing days, and closed in tight to his assailer. Stott crossed a leg to avoid his possible knee. Stott's hands were shoulder high in front of him with his thumbs about four inches from the captain's eyes. Mike didn't hit him, but the captain knew he could have.

Mike's movement brought Master Sergeant Harper up off his seat. That old fart was not an officer. When he felt Harper's hand on his shoulder, Mike dropped straight down and brought his right hand firmly into Harper's crotch so that he pitched forward into the captain.

"You asshole!" Harper hissed as Stott upended him to his right side, leaving him staring up at Mike and the two captains from the floor of the bunker, holding his balls in agony.

The other captain said, "Bill, if you don't want him, I'll take on my team anytime!"

Captain Bill Freeze stuck out his hand and said, "Two nice moves, Sergeant! Welcome! Get up, Sergeant Harper! Looks like you tested one who won't back down to your bullshit. How'd you pick up such good Hmong, Sergeant Stott?"

"Sir, I went to languages school with my buddy who's got a real gift for all languages! I've spent a lot of time with him, and he makes me practice constantly, sir!" Mike said.

"That so? What's your buddy's name? Did he come in with your same contingent? And drop all those sirs, just call me 'Captain' here, but 'Cap' or Bill works in the field. And no saluting outside, ever."

Immediately, Stott regretted speaking about JJ's language skills. Now he had no choice but to answer his detachment commander. "Sergeant John Sharkey, captain."

"Okay. Your records indicate you're good with weapons. Come show me. Stay here, Sergeant Harper. I know you're on stand down."

As they exited the bunker, Mike met Warrant Officer Rick Myers.

"Myers, this might be our new 18-B, Mike Stott. We're going to see how he shoots. Got time to come along?" Captain Freeze's informality surprised Mike.

Stott remembered the captain's orders about saluting and said, "Nice to meet you, Mr. Myers."

"Troops call me WO M, Sergeant. How old are you?" Myers asked Mike as looked him up and down.

"I'll be nineteen tomorrow, sir—er—Mister Myers."

Captain Freeze and Warrant Officer Myers both stopped dead in their tracks. "Repeat that, Sergeant!" Freeze demanded.

"I'll be nineteen tomorrow, sir," Stott repeated.

"Well, I'll be goddamn! How long you been in the army?"

"A little over seventeen months, Captain," Mike responded.

"Well, I'll be goddamn!" Captain Freeze said again. "How in hell did you get here?" Freeze seemed genuinely amazed.

As they walked down to a makeshift range on the south side of the base, Stott recounted his time in the army to date as concisely as he could. Both Captain Freeze and WO Myers shook their heads. Myers yelled for the armory sergeant to bring up an AK-47.

"Silhouette target between the fifty-five-gallon drums, 200 meters," the armory sergeant said as he literally tossed the AK to Mike.

"Dead sited? Full mag?" Stott asked the sergeant.

"Gun's right," he responded.

Stott checked the safety and then fired all thirty rounds into the target, one shot every two to three seconds. Captain

Freeze was watching the target through binoculars given to him by the armor.

"Well, I'll be goddamn! Bring Stott out a new M-14E2. See if he's as good with our rifle as he is with Chuck's!" Captain Freeze directed.

"That far fifty-five can is 350 yards if you want a little more challenge, Sarge," the armorer said.

"First ten 200, second ten 350," Mike said. He made all twenty hits.

"Ever fire the sniper version of the 14, Sergeant Stott?" Captain Freeze asked.

"Yes, captain! I loved the ones we had in 18-B school!"

"Can you shoot a pistol as well?"

"Yes, captain, I can!"

"Here. Try mine at that close-in can," Freeze said.

Again, Stott did not miss.

"Well, it looks like you can shoot," WO Myers observed.

"Tell me again why you wanted to earn a beret, Sergeant," Captain Freeze said.

"Captain, when I joined the army I'd never even heard of the Special Forces. But during Ranger training we began to hear about the 'green-hat guys' and my buddy Sharkey was determined to make it to the Special Forces. Once I made it through Ranger training, I was hooked. And I didn't want to let Sharkey down."

"Was your dad in the service, Sergeant?" Freeze asked.

"No, captain, he wasn't. He had six kids and was in his late thirties when World War II began, so he was never called. My brothers were, though," Mike said. As soon as Mike spoke about his brothers he knew he was talking too much.

"Yeah? How many brothers you have? What branch?" asked Freeze.

"Uh, three brothers, Captain. All in the army, sir."

"Any of them lifers?" Captain Freeze seemed extraordinarily interested in Mike's family background.

"Uh, no sir."

"Why'd you hesitate on your last two responses, Sergeant?" asked WO Myers. "Hiding something?"

"No, Mr. Myers, I'm not," but Mike spoke too quickly and too passionately.

"Tell me about your brothers, Sergeant Stott. Everything." It was a direct command from Stott's potential commanding officer.

"Okay. I have two brothers back in Ohio that were in the paratroopers. I grew up listening to them talk about jumping and the esprit de corps in the 101st. That probably influenced me to go airborne. My oldest brother, James, was killed in Korea. He was a captain in the Tenth Rangers. He won the Congressional Medal of Honor. I also have two sisters," Stott added.

"Why in God's name were you reluctant to tell us that, Sergeant?" Captain Freeze wanted to know.

"Well, I don't want special treatment, and I don't want to be compared to James. I just want to be a good soldier," Mike said.

Captain Freeze got a nod from WO Myers, shook Mike's hand, and said, "Come meet your team, Sergeant Stott."

They walked across the base from the range to a large bunker that was actually under a twenty-man tent. There were seven men in the bunker, cleaning weapons and talking shop. Stott noticed that none of them got up when their commanding officer entered.

"Men, heads up! This is Sergeant Mike Stott, our new assistant weapons NCO. He just arrived with that last contingent. His Hmong sounds as good as anybody's here. We just saw that he can shoot, at least at targets! Stott will be nineteen tomorrow, so wish the kid happy birthday! Sergeant Stott, meet our ops and intel man, First Sergeant Jake Dunigan. Staff Sergeants Jim Barnett and Dave Beamer, our engineers. Sergeant First Class Bill Adams and Staff Sergeant Dan Meeks, the communications guys. Our medic, who's way better than most MD's, First Sergeant Bo Brackett. First Sergeant Gary Helms, our weapons sergeant and you're go-to guy. We call him 'Mr. Sixty!' He's pretty good with his namesake!"

As Captain Freeze introduced the team they each got up and shook Mike's hand. None of them said anything. They just looked him in the eye and nodded.

"We're light an assistant medic and, frankly, probably will be for quite a while. You met Master Sergeant Harper already. Sergeant Stott, I wish we had time to get to know you better while we're here in Nha Trang, but the fact is we're going 'up country' day after tomorrow. Team, while the ten of us are here together, I've got some poop."

Mike was new, but could feel a certain tension in that bunker as Captain Freeze introduced him. But he didn't feel it was because of his arrival. Something else was bothering this group.

Captain Freeze continued, "Mr. Myers and I have made another personnel decision this afternoon besides bringing in Stott, here. Master Sergeant Harper has been reassigned to HQ staff. He's staying here in Nha Trang. It means we'll be two short in Lac Do, with a new kid, here, to bring along. Congratulations Master Sergeant Dunigan, you're our ops sergeant, effective right now.

"Let's clear the air men. This was not Master Sergeant Harper's desire. It was my decision. Some of you may not agree, but get over it! I know Harper has served his country long and well and for that he'll always have my respect. I believe you all understand this decision, even if you don't agree with it. It's done! We're a ten man 'A' until such time as we can fill in with an assistant medic and a qualified replacement for Jake's old slot. Questions?"

The bunker atmosphere seemed somehow lighter.

First Sergeant Helms spoke. "I've a question for Sergeant Stott, Captain. Did you join the army right out of grade school? I mean, how fucking long you been in the army, for Christ's sake, kid?"

No laughter, but grins all around. Stott knew it was one of many tests this group would put him through, so he decided to come back at his new boss. "Seventeen months, First Sergeant Helms! I was so smart I skipped high school after learning all I needed to know through four years in the eighth grade, Dad!"

Everybody laughed except Helms. "Uh-huh. Just what I need, a fucking comedian for an assistant! Do you shave yet, kid?"

"Everything but my balls, First Sergeant!" Mike said.

"All right, now that all this love is in the air, let's talk," said WO Myers. "Here's the scoop. Of the three Yard villages you all know well, we've decided to make Lac Do home, at least for a while. It's the farthest from Nha Trang, so hopefully we won't get too much direction from staff. It's as close as we can get to the triangle and still be in Vietnam. It's also probably the hottest spot for Chuck! We know it won't be easy to stay in Chief Won's good graces!

I can see by the looks of delight on your faces that you all agree that Lac Do is a good choice! Captain?"

"Lac Do has the best natural defenses based on its elevation and natural topography, but there's a lot of work to do on its perimeter. We've been authorized to offer Won several solid incentives, including weapons and a school, to stay friendly. We know a lot of opium passes around Lac Do. Disrupting that flow and the cash it provides Charlie is a very important part of our mission. But charting the Trail up in the border region is of prime importance. If our little war goes upscale as it almost surely will in the coming year, knowing where to hit 'em to choke off their supply lines will be of paramount importance. We will be the most northerly deployed A team in Vietnam. You know what that means from a support standpoint. We will be dependent on air support and the Yards, period. Questions?"

No one raised a question. Stott had about a hundred, but decided not to ask any.

"Okay. Tomorrow, I want you guys to tutor Stott on our team's operational variations. Helms, take him back to the armory now and get him some weapons. Fire a sixty with him! He's good to go on our other stuff! Watch him sight 'em if you have time. Stott, hang with Helms, let him show you around a bit. I wish we had more time to work with you, but we're goin' north at first light 21 December. Transport via Huey's. Birds will be standing by to shuttle more supplies, assuming things go okay on the ground up there. Oh, I almost forgot. Found new flak jackets for all! Try not to lose these, they're getting hard to come by! I've got to go to a team commanders' meeting for chow, but I'll be back after that. Maybe tonight will be as quiet as last night! Oh, yeah. Congratulations, Dunigan! Later!" Captain Freeze and Warrant Officer Myers departed.

The team members all congratulated Master Sergeant Dunigan.

"Thank fucking Christ the old man is out of our hair," said First Sergeant Brackett. "I don't think Harper could have handled more time up North."

"You heard the captain, let's go get you some weapons, kid," said First Sergeant Helms.

"I'm gonna tag along and watch the kid sight his toys," said the new operations sergeant.

It occurred to Mike that he would probably be "the kid" to these guys for a very long time.

Chapter Thirty-Four

Master Sergeant Dunigan introduced Stott to the armory sergeant when they went to get his weapons. "First Sergeant McCoy, meet my team's new 18-B, Mike Stott. Stott, meet First Sergeant McCoy."

"We already met, sorta!" McCoy said as he shook Mike's hand. "I'll tell you this, Dunigan! The kid can shoot! At least at targets! Are you gonna have him carry a sixty?"

"Maybe. But I hear you got in some new 7.62 snipes! Is that true, Sarge?" Dunigan asked.

"How the hell did you hear that? They just came in with the new troops! Are there no fucking secrets around here?" McCoy seemed truly upset.

"They got the new design silencer-suppressers? Get one out here, goddamn it! I know you've already squirreled one away for yourself, and you never leave the fucking armory!" Master Sergeant Dunigan commanded.

McCoy brought out a brand new M-14E-2 LB sniper's rifle with a sight like Stott had not seen before. "Got new scopes, too. Don't know how well they're set up, but I guess we could play with one before it gets too dark."

Dunigan, Helms, McCoy, and Stott stepped down to the range just as the sun was starting to drop behind the hills. McCoy tightened the scope set-screws and sighted the hundred-meter target. "Got some hot rounds loaded, let's see how they kick!"

First Sergeant McCoy was a skilled craftsman. It was a pleasure to watch him handle the rifle. "Hundred meter, mark!" he said.

But instead of the expected "BLAM!" all the soldiers heard was what could best be described as a light handclap! Maybe a lady's gloved handclap! McCoy's round hit one ring from dead center on the hundred meter target.

"How sweet is that?" Master Dunigan said. "No visible flash and the quietest 7.62 round I ever heard!"

Sergeant McCoy made a slight adjustment to the scope and reset the weapon on the sight stand. Again, he said, "Hundred meter, mark!"

Dead bull's-eye! McCoy then ranged the rifle all the way out to 400 meters. "Fuckin' perfect!" he said.

"Can I try, Sarge?" Mike asked.

"Wait your turn, kid!" Master Sergeant Dunigan exclaimed. "I gotta try it!"

Dunigan and Helms both fired a dozen rounds through the weapon. They didn't miss, up to 300 meters. Finally, it was Stott's turn. When Helms handed him the rifle, Mike was surprised at how light it felt.

"Okay, kid! If you're such a hotshot, start at 300 meters," Dunigan ordered.

Mike ran his left hand down the stock and felt the heat of the barrel. As he shouldered the rifle, it felt absolutely perfect! "Can I use the armor's stand just for the first round, Sarge? And I want to sight the 200-meter target 'cause you old guys tore up the 300!"

"Thought you were a hotshot! Yeah, go ahead!"

The trigger pull was much lighter than the sniper rifles he'd worked with in 18-B school, and the view through the scope was amazingly clear! Mike felt that he could see the projectile as it tore through the 200 meter bull's-eye. "Four hundred meter, top-ring, mark!" Stott said as Dunigan and Helms adjusted their binoculars to check his worthiness.

"Four hundred meter, bottom ring, mark!"

"Four hundred meter, third ring, three o'clock, mark!"

"Four hundred meter, second ring, nine o'clock, mark!" Mike's fifth shot completed the cross on the 400-meter target.

"Where the fuck did you learn to shoot like that?" Master Sergeant Dunigan asked.

"Dunigan, the kid didn't learn that! That's a fucking gift!" McCoy stated.

"I want this one! I love this rifle!" Mike pleaded.

"Fucking rookies! You gotta hump a sixty, too, and a forty-five. Let him have it, McCoy. We're gonna see if real targets spook the kid soon enough," Dunigan said. "Got another one of those, McCoy! We're gonna need it up north!"

As they walked back to the team bunker, Helms said, "Kid, that was impressive, but I'm gonna assume you haven't shot a human yet, is that right?"

"Yes, Sergeant, that's right," Stott said.

"Just think of Chuck as that paper target! Except the paper target's worth more!" First Sergeant Helms advised.

When they got back to the bunker, there was John J. Sharkey drinking a Budweiser and telling his new team what a complete dickhead Mike was! As Stott entered, the first thing Sharkey said was, "You're on my shit list, goddamn it! You ratted me out! I'm gonna kick your ass!"

Mike's new team members seemed pretty amused at JJ's tirade. "Good to see you, too, dickhead! What the hell are you so fired up about?" Stott asked.

"You know goddamn well what I'm mad about! You told your CO about my languages and now I'm a goddamn staffy! You get to go to the field, and I'm stuck here at fucking base camp! I am abso-fucking-lutey going to kick your ass!"

"Well, I guess you all have met my good buddy, John J. Sharkey," Mike said to his team. "Isn't he a swell guy?"

"Don't try to fucking appease me, goddamn it! Did you or did you not rat me out?" JJ just would not back down.

"JJ, it's your fault! You made me practice Hmong so much that I sounded like I knew what I was doing! So I had to give you credit for tutoring me, and I couldn't withhold information from my CO! Besides, you'll be in the know on everything!" Mike knew how much JJ liked to be on top of everything.

Before JJ could respond, Master Sergeant Dunigan said to Sharkey, "Hey, kid! How old are you? You look younger than Stott!"

"I'm two full months older than this dickhead, Master Sergeant! And I've never ratted him out, goddamn it!"

"Cool down, son," Dunigan said. "Captain Freeze asked Stott direct questions. The kid had no choice but to answer him candidly. He gave you credit for his Hmong being so good! So, do you know other languages, Sergeant Sharkey?"

"Uh, yes Master Sergeant, I do," JJ responded.

"Tell us what else you speak, son," Dunigan directed. "Sit down and have another beer; we got chow being delivered any minute so you might as well eat with us."

Mike's entire team was now focused on the discussion and awaited Sharkey's response.

First Sergeant Brackett handed JJ and Mike a Bud and said, "Let's see if you kids can handle a couple of brews instead of warm milk! Start talking, Sharkey!"

"Well, I had a chance to learn a couple of languages where I grew up," JJ began, but Dunigan interrupted him.

"And which orphanage was that, son?" Dunigan asked.

Stott almost dropped his beer! How in the hell did Dunigan know that JJ was raised in an orphanage? Had he somehow checked Sharkey's records? That didn't seem likely in that he had just met JJ.

"St. Agnes in Bedford, New York, Master Sergeant," Sharkey coolly replied. "And what orphanage did you come from?"

"St. Mary's in Columbus, Ohio. Barnett, Adams, and Meeks are orphanage products too, as you probably guessed, Sharkey. Continue," Dunigan directed.

Mike was dumbfounded! Again, just like back after Ranger school, he was surrounded by guys who had grown up in orphanages and recognized it in each other!

"How about Warrant Officer Myers?" JJ asked.

"Oh, yeah. I forgot; him too. St. Rita's in St Louis," Dunigan confirmed. "Now tell us about your language skills."

Sharkey related the story of whaling magnate Captain Sharkey's sponsorship of St. Agnes and how Sister K had tutored him in three Chinese dialects. He continued talking about how he and Stott had met in the reception center, and he outlined their time in the army right up to arrival in Nha Trang. JJ spoke for more than thirty minutes. Not one of Mike's team members said a word. They listened intently to everything Sharkey said, particularly when he talked about Stott personally. Just as Sharkey was finishing his narrative, the native woman Mike had seen earlier and two other equally tiny females brought in dinner. They had prepared an absolutely delicious meal using components from C rations, locally grown vegetables, herbs, and rice. They served the men on metal army trays just like in the mess halls back in the states. The team all got another beer and settled in to eat.

Sergeant Beamer asked JJ a follow-up question about something, but Mike had to respond because JJ's mouth was full.

"Guys, when Sharkey gets a shot at food you might as well wait until he's full, and that takes a while. This chow tastes great! I've got a question, Master Dunigan. How did you know JJ grew up in an orphanage?" Mike just couldn't understand how he knew.

"Most orphans know when they meet other orphans. I can't explain it beyond that," was all Dunigan said.

"Why are there so many orphans in Ranger and Special Forces units?" Mike asked the group.

Staff Sergeant Dan Meeks, silent until then, said, "For me, and I expect for most of us, the army is the family I never had. You'll come to understand how tight the Special Forces are, especially at the team level. Let me ask you what your team is wondering; why did you make the sacrifices to earn a beret, Sergeant Stott?"

Unfortunately, Meeks' question caught Sharkey between bites, so JJ answered for his buddy. "He comes from a military family. Had a brother in the Tenth Rangers that earned a CMH in Korea. Two other brothers that were paratroopers. Plus, I brought the kid along!"

That last line made all Mike's team members laugh out loud. "Who you callin' a 'kid,' dickhead? I ought to kick your ass right now!" Stott said to Sharkey.

But Stott's team was enjoying Sharkey's harassment of Mike. "Have another Bud, Sergeant Sharkey! Tell us more about the kid, here!" Master Sergeant Dunigan commanded.

So Sharkey told them about their New York adventures and, worse, he told them all about Cindy! Sharkey finished by saying, "Yeah, the first chance he gets Mikey will probably marry Cindy so he can share her social security checks!"

Every one of Stott's team members howled with laughter! Mike went for the little bastard, but Brackett and Adams restrained him! "Sit down, kid-sergeant," Master Sergeant Dunigan directed him. "We're having too much fun getting the poop on you from your buddy, here!"

"Kid-sergeant! Sergeant Kid! That's fucking perfect!" said the medic, "Doc" Brackett. "What else can you tell us, Sergeant Sharkey?"

"Well, as you can see, the kid has quite a temper! And a real weakness for the ladies! Especially the older ones! You guys are going to have to watch him every minute, especially around any toothless mama-sans!" JJ was on a roll and he once again had all the guys laughing, at Stott's expense, of course.

"Goddamn it, Sharkey! You'd better stay in your fucking headquarters hooch all day tomorrow 'cause if I catch you outside, I'm gonna kill you!" Mike was steamed!

That made his teamies laugh even harder! "Threatening a fellow trooper can get you court-martialed," said Staff Sergeant Beamer. "But I guess you're too young to stand trial!"

The fucking laughter continued! "Don't you have to report back to your office job?" Mike asked JJ. "I mean, shouldn't you staffies be in before dark?"

"What a lame retort!" JJ exclaimed. "I'm telling you guys, you're gonna have to look after this kid every minute!"

Mike realized that Captain Freeze had returned to the hooch sometime during Sharkey's oratory. Freeze was standing in a corner enjoying his harassment too.

"Do you have this Cindy's address?" Freeze asked JJ. "Sounds like she's perfect for some of our older guys!"

Again, everyone howled with laughter. That's when Mike heard the whistling sound.

"Incoming!" team members yelled concurrently.

The whistling sound rapidly increased followed by an explosion close by. "Defensive assignments!" screamed Captain Freeze. "Stott, Sharkey! Take that sixty and all the belts you can carry and follow me! Move!"

The evening sky was totally dark now. Leaving the dimly lit bunker made the men strain to gain their night vision. Sharkey and JJ hadn't gone more than twenty steps from the bunker following Freeze when a perimeter trip-flare illuminated the night sky. They heard a M-60 open up off to their left and Captain Freeze led them in the direction of the small-arms fire. They could also hear the pop-pop-pop of AK-47s signaling that an aggressor force was on their wires.

"Stott, Sharkey! Set up on that second ridge! There's a bunker there, but watch the far wire! Careful not to fire into any of our Yards, they're on that third, lower ridge two clicks ahead of you! Fuck! Hit the deck! Incoming!" screamed Freeze.

Again that unmistakable, descending whistling sound signaled rockets on the way! A far-off thump-thump-thump told them mortars had also opened up. Stott and Sharkey dove into the closest bunker and heard ordinance explode very close to where they were. JJ and Mike scrambled back out of the first bunker and crouched-ran to where Freeze had pointed, diving into the second bunker as more incoming arrived. Stott landed literally on top of Captain Freeze.

"For young guys, you're not that fast!" the captain exclaimed. "Set up your sixty on that right corner and wait! Make sure who you're shooting at! There're two lines of Yards in front of you! Christ, Charlie's early tonight! How many belts did you grab?"

"Ten 200s, Captain! Plus a box of 7.62 clips!" Mike shouted.

Thump-thump-thump! More incoming mortars! Captain Freeze was peering over the lip of the bunker, as were Sharkey and Stott. As they watched, a VC stepped on a perimeter mine. His body was blown ten feet in the air and landed on another trip wire. They could see twenty to thirty black-pajama-clad bad guys trying to follow the path cleared when their dead comrade tripped the mine. For some unknown reason, the two Yard lines in front were not firing. Freeze said, "Fuck! Where's our defensive line! Stott! Lay some fire high in that direction! Now!"

Stott cradled the machine gun to his shoulder and checked the elevation setting. He lined-up the sights, preparing for his first real test as a soldier.

JJ shouted in Mike's ear, "Hooah! Hooah! Get 'em Mikey!"

More flares were tripped just as Stott was preparing to fire. They hung in the air, slowly descending over the VC, 200 meters out. Right where the captain had said their outer perimeter should be.

At about 2100 hours, on the day before his nineteenth birthday, Stott fired the first of what would be thousands of bursts from an M-60 at the enemy over the coming months. To Mike's surprise, there were tracer rounds loaded in that first belt just like in training exercises! The VC hit the ground, but Stott had an excellent down-elevation field of fire. With every sixth round a tracer shell, Mike "walked" his line of fire right down their line. Many of the insurgents screamed in agony as the 7.62 millimeter rounds tore into them.

As Charlie realized where the tracer bullets were coming from, Stott's position began to take fire from their AK-47s. Mike emptied the first ammo belt, and JJ did a masterfully quick reload. Stott was firing from the second 200-shot belt even before the first flare hit the ground. About twenty VC started up and at them even as the screams of their wounded and dying comrades filled the air.

Stott continued to hear enemy screams as he emptied a second, then third belt as JJ reloaded him a fourth time. To their utter disbelief, Captain Freeze said, "Hold your fire, Sergeant!"

An even brighter, closer illumination flare lit the sky, revealing the remainder of the initial line of VC, perhaps four or five of them, still coming at them 150 meters distant. A second line of thirty-fifty bad guys about one hundred meters behind the first emerged from the outer darkness charging at their position.

"Watch closely," Captain Freeze said.

An incredible line of fire then opened up from the previously silent defensive line one hundred meters to their front, cutting down the remainder of the first wave of VC and most of the second. Vietcong screams echoed through the night air.

"Lift your sights a click and empty another belt about 300 meters out," Freeze directed Stott.

This time Mike was firing blindly into darkened landscape beyond his original field of fire. Oddly, another crescendo of screams reverberated over them. JJ had reloaded the M-60 yet again.

Freeze, Sharkey and Stott could hear small arms fire coming from other parts of the camp's perimeter, but it seemed that the main thrust of the attack, so far, had come directly at them. Mike felt JJ's hand on his shoulder. Sharkey gave his friend a pat and whispered, "Un-fucking-believable!"

They stayed in the bunker, waiting on another wave of VC for quite a while. A flare revealed no further movement, but lots of bodies on the far wires.

Captain Freeze was still peering out into the darkness when Master Sergeant Dunigan rolled into the bunker with them. "You okay, Cap?" he asked.

"We're good! Casualties?"

"So far, so good! Two Yards wounded by shrapnel, but none killed, as far as we know," said Dunigan. "You on that first sixty, Stott?"

"He was," Captain Freeze confirmed. "With Sharkey reloading! Why did the second line hold off so long?" Freeze questioned.

"So the first line could grab a few VC for interrogation as they retreated! I think we got three prisoners! Looks like maybe as many as fifty dead VC. Helms was on the other sixty! He fired several thousand rounds. And at least six mines got tripped! Good job, kids!" Sergeant Dunigan said. "Specially for a staff guy!" he said to JJ through a grin.

"I'm no goddamn staff sergeant!" Sharkey yelled, but Dunigan was already moving to check other positions.

Captain Freeze turned and stared at Sharkey and Stott. "You did real good, kids! I am truly impressed. Let's sit tight for a while and see if it's over. By the way, looks like you both pissed your pants."

Mike looked down at his crotch and realized the captain was right. He was soaked. So was JJ. "Happened to me the first time, too, sergeants! And it'll happen again! You both did fine. I'm proud of you both."

Only then did Mike start to shake. He realized that a significant portion of the dead VC had been killed by rounds he had fired. Again, JJ put his hand on Mike's shoulder and gave him that thumbs-up air check.

"How lucky was this?" JJ said. "Our first combat experience, and we were together by dumb luck! But you're still on my shit list for ratting me out, goddamn it!"

Mike and JJ didn't think Freeze had heard them, but the captain said over his shoulder, "Drop it, Sergeant Sharkey! Be thankful you were here with us. Being the colonel's interpreter is maybe the best job in the Fifth. You ought to pay Stott for his recommendation! They may be looking for you at HQ, especially if we got prisoners. Can you find your way back?"

"Yes, Captain," JJ said. "I'm on my way. Take care of the kid, sir."

As Sharkey left the bunker, First Sergeant Adams came by with more ammo. "You okay with the kid, Cap?" he asked.

"We're good," Freeze said.

Stott spent the remainder of that night right in the bunker with Captain Freeze, taking turns on watch. The rest of the team stayed on the line too. No further attacks occurred. The official body count in Mike's sector after first light revealed sixty-seven dead VC. Master Sergeant Dunigan said he reckoned the VC had recovered at least that many more of their bodies during the night.

Stott's team regrouped in the bunker where they'd had dinner the night before. Dunigan brought Mike some clean fatigues. Dry pants! First Sergeant Helms claimed he got most of the kills because he fired more rounds.

Captain Freeze said, "I'm not so sure of that, Sergeant Helms."

The same native woman from the night before brought hot coffee from somewhere and Captain Freeze told Mike they called her Mia. Mia placed another drinking vessel by Stott's coffee. Mike looked around and noticed none of the other guys had one. It was an earthen pitcher shaped like a jug with a lid on it.

In Hmong, Mike asked Mia, "What is this?" But she only bowed and smiled and left the bunker.

WO Myers spoke, "Heads up, team! Lift your mugs to the kid. He wet himself, but Cap says half the kills last night come from his sixty! He and his buddy JJ followed Cap's directives exactly. Kid, that's hot sake in the pitcher. It's a tradition! Drink it down and thank God or whatever you believe in for the courage you showed last night. Happy birthday, Sergeant Stott!"

Each of his team members came and clicked their tin coffee cup against Mike's sake pitcher and shook his hand. Not many words were spoken, but Stott sensed that he had made it through his first, all-important test in an acceptable way.

"Okay, guys, try and get a few hours rest. At 1200, we'll start packin' up. First light tomorrow we head to Lac Do. Not sure when we'll get back to base, so do what you need to. Probably be good if you could all say something to Harper. He's hurtin'. Cap and me are off to a briefing. Helms, make sure the kid gets properly rigged." WO Myers and Captain Freeze exited the bunker, leaving the rest of the team contemplating Lac Do. Stott should have been exhausted, but wasn't. He felt strangely invigorated, and older.

As the team settled in to sleep, Doc Brackett came and sat across from Mike. "You okay, kid?" he asked.

"Sure, Doc, I guess. I'm not sure it has hit me yet. I mean, did last night really happen like I remember?" Mike asked him.

"It did. Fate put you in an unusual situation your second day in country. You did fine. Talk to any of us if you need to, but last night's action gave you about a six-month jump-start with your team. Lac Do is very different from Nha Trang. Stay close to one of us all the time when we get there. It's a very dangerous place. Get some rest," Doc advised.

Like Nha Trang wasn't dangerous! JJ and Mike had been in country less than forty-eight hours and had been shot at, mortared, and rocketed!

Some of the guys were already snoring. The light in the bunker was very dim as Doc stretched out on his cot. Mike lay down, too, but couldn't close his eyes. As he relived last night in his mind, the scenes played in slow motion. JJ's words, "Un-fucking-believable," kept coming back to him. Stott had not been allowed to go view the VC bodies, a special team cleared the kill zone, checking for booby traps that might have been rigged on the bodies during the night.

Mike Stott realized that he had shot and killed many men, perhaps twenty or thirty, on only his second day in the country of Vietnam. That first flare illumination that enabled him to sight on the charging VC was indelibly etched in his brain. VC screams remained a vivid memory as well. It seemed like an eight-millimeter movie projector like the one he had operated as a member of his high school projection club kept replaying the scenes from the night before on a screen just behind his eyes.

Mike wondered if he would ever be able to turn that projector off.

Chapter Thirty-Five

At 1200 hours on December 20, 1964, Stott awoke to Sergeant Helms shaking him. He had finally dozed off sometime during the morning and gotten a couple of hours sleep. "Up and at 'em, Sergeant Stott! Freshen up! We got work to do!" Helms stated.

Again, Mia was there with hot coffee and ham and eggs! Mike ate, cleaned up and put on fresh fatigues. For the next six hours, he shadowed First Sergeant Helms, assisting him with cleaning and checking out all the team's weapons and packing ammo, grenades, and other ordinance for their deployment to Lac Do. They drew extra boots and fatigues, even soap and towels from the supply bunkers and packed them in duffel bags to load on the Hueys. All of the team members were doing the same thing, focusing on the supplies to support their individual specialties.

Captain Freeze wasn't visible during the day, but WO Myers seemed to be everywhere, making sure the preparations were coming together. He came and spoke to Stott several times. Mike had the feeling he was checking on his state of mind more than anything else. Just before 1800 hours, Top Dunigan announced the team would take mess together in the bunker just like the night before, but that only team members could participate. "If you want to talk to Sergeant Sharkey before we leave you better go look him up now. No telling when you'll see him again," Top said.

Mike went to the HQ Bunker as dusk was settling in, but two heavily armed sergeants he'd never met before told him Sergeant Sharkey was unavailable. Just as he was turning to go back to his team bunker, Colonel Besuden and several detachment commanders came out. Mike's first impulse was to salute, but, fortunately, he caught himself. Captain Freeze was in the group.

"Hey, Sergeant Kid, get back here," Freeze commanded.

Again, he had to overcome the impulse to salute. "Yes, Captain Freeze!" Mike said.

"Colonel, gentlemen, this is the young sergeant I spoke to you about earlier, Mike Stott. The team has dubbed him Sergeant Kid, and I'm afraid they have me calling him that too. Sergeant Stott, shake hands with our CO," directed Freeze.

"It's an honor to meet you, sir," Mike said.

Besuden's handshake was incredibly powerful. "The honor is mine, son," Colonel Besuden said. "Good work last night! Baptism by fire, you might say. I understand you are a friend of my new aide, John Sharkey."

"Yes, sir."

"My guess is you came up to speak to him before you deploy in the a.m. Am I right?"

"Yes, sir."

"Go on in. Make it quick. Sergeant Sharkey is a busy man today. Good hunting up north! Keep doin' what you did last night!" Besuden and his entourage of officers departed.

One of the "guard" sergeants walked Mike in to where JJ was sitting, bent over what appeared to be a sort of diary. The handwritten characters were in Chinese. Sharkey the interpreter had become Sharkey the translator. He was so intent on his work he didn't notice Mike. The rest of the men in JJ's vicinity were officers, so Stott was reluctant to butt in.

Finally, Mike said, "Hey, dickhead! See you in a while!"

JJ looked up at the sound of Stott's voice and said, "See, I told you gentlemen he had no class, and he just proved it! Sirs, meet Sergeant Kid, otherwise known as Sergeant Mike Stott."

To Mike's surprise, two captains and two lieutenants got up and shook his hand. A captain named Mooney said, "Class or not, good work last night! Captain Freeze debriefed us this morning on what happened on the north wire last evening. And, of course, we've had to listen to Sergeant Sharkey retell it about a hundred times today! Nevertheless, well done, Sergeant."

Stott was embarrassed. JJ said, "Sirs, I told you he was really too young to be in the army, but I've been able to bring him along very well!"

The officers actually laughed! JJ had already established himself with these men.

"Sirs, please don't let my association with this dickhead prejudice you against me! I'm not as bad as he says!" Mike offered.

"Why don't you guys go for a smoke," Captain Mooney said. "Not too long Sergeant Sharkey! We've got to verify by midnight."

Regardless of the fact that neither of them smoked, Stott and Sharkey went outside the HQ bunker and stood there looking up at the night sky. After several minutes, JJ said, "Hard to believe what happened last night, huh?"

"I'm still playing it back in slow motion in a camera just behind my eyes."

"You know, Captain Freeze put us in for a commendation, right?" asked JJ.

"What?" Stott was dumbfounded.

"Yeah, he told the CO he'd never seen a trooper, young or old, handle a sixty better than you did. I'll never forget it! On our second day in country!" JJ commented.

The two friends stood there for several more minutes. "Look, Mike, I know where you're headed tomorrow. Sitting here with all the officers, I pretty much hear everything. They say Loc Do is the most dangerous place in Vietnam. That team you got assigned to is one of Besuden's best and toughest. Keep your head down, for Christ sake!"

After more staring at the stars, JJ said, "I've gotta get back. Turns out I'm now the only trooper in Nha Trang that can actually read Chinese. Mikey, there's all kinds of bad guys up there, and not just North Vietnamese. Watch your ass!"

"Okay. See you whenever, JJ."

"See ya, Mikey."

Charlie took the night off. Mike lay on his cot in the team bunker and tried to rest, but excitement and anticipation made sleep impossible. At 0500 hours, they were all "saddling up" as Master Dunigan phrased it.

Mia served them coffee and something that tasted like a rice casserole. A look that passed between her and Doc Brackett made Mike think they knew each other pretty well. As they left the bunker, Stott could hear the Hueys warming up. Captain Freeze and WO Myers were already on the flight line when the rest of the team got there. As the first light appeared over the far eastern hills, Stott's A Team loaded up and lifted off from base camp into the darkness on a north by northwest heading. Civilization as Mike knew it stayed in Nha Trang.

As the morning sun came up over the fog-laden valleys and green-forested hills of Vietnam, Stott was struck with the country's beauty. The Hueys were flying just above the treetops, occasionally climbing dramatically to skirt a fogged-in area. They seemed to be zigzagging a lot as they followed the valley cuts. No one said a word.

Mike was in a chopper with WO Myers, Staff Sergeant Jim Barnett, First Sergeant Bill Adams, and Doc Brackett. Stott met the door gunner, Staff Sergeant Peter Pound, who told Mike to set on his flak jacket. "Always protect your balls first," he advised.

After they had been in the air about thirty-five minutes, Doc Brackett asked, "You okay, kid?"

"Yeah, Doc, a little nervous I guess. It hit me that it's just us, a long way from base camp."

"That's the idea," yelled First Sergeant Adams. "In Lac Do, it's all ours!"

Mike wanted to ask him what he meant by "all ours," but the door gunner yelled, "Heads up! Signs of life!"

The Huey seemed to speed up and hug the trees even closer. Stott thought he felt the chopper scrape tree branches; they were that low. Or so it seemed.

Doc said, "We must be less than ten clicks out! I see Paint Creek!" Adams, Myers, and Barnett turned to look where Doc was pointing.

"You know, I'm gonna miss Mia's coffee," Barnett said. "Belt your sixty, kid, but don't chamber a round. Point it out the other side."

The left side doors opened; it seemed they were surfing over the treetops on a green sea.

"Five out!" yelled the copilot.

"Chamber a round! Keep it on safety. When we set down, crouch with your sixty about fifty feet out from the bird. Keep scanning your outward 180. We're hoping for a reasonable welcome, but you never know. Say nothing. Cap will speak directly to Chief Won," Myers shouted over the noise of the helicopter.

Although Stott's Huey had lifted off after Captain Freeze's bird back at Nha Trang, they were the first on the ground in a clearing that appeared to be about three clicks—300 meters—from the edge of a village that Mike assumed was Lac Do. The landing zone was slightly lower than Lac Do, providing a defensive field of fire from the perimeter bunker line that surrounded the village. Lac Do seemed to occupy the highest piece of ground for miles around. The way the Huey was positioned caused Mike to set up his sixty directly at Lac Do. He could see armed men peering over the lips of their bunkers watching his chopper and then Freeze's land. Mike saw Helms jump out with his sixty as he had done and scan Lac Do's defensive line. The door gunners from both choppers had their 50-caliber machine guns trained on the forest line beyond the LZ, covering the opposite 180 degree arch. The pilots kept the rotors turning, causing even the low grasses in the LZ to ripple in the wake. A dozen Montagnard tribesmen came out to meet the choppers. They were heavily armed with a combination of weaponry including M-14s, shotguns, and AK-47s. Captain Freeze and WO Myers engaged in a conversation that lasted for several minutes. WO Myers signaled the team excepting Helms and Stott to offload their supplies. First Sergeant Helms and Stott remained on their M-60 scans.

Two large piles of supplies were quickly dropped to the ground. The Hueys lifted off, cleared the first ridgeline and were gone within ten minutes of touchdown. As the roar of their engines faded, a discernable stillness settled over Lac Do. Stott was still crouching with his sixty, waiting further orders. He could see smoke from cooking fires in the village and smelled pungent aromas.

"Reverse your scans, sergeants! We're home!" Master Sergeant Dunigan instructed them. Helms and Stott turned their machine guns toward the wood line past the LZ. Several dozen Montagnard women came out and carried the supplies from the choppers back to the village. When this was completed, Helms and Stott backed their way inside Lac Do's defensive perimeter, machine guns still trained on the distant forest.

The Hmong militiamen closed a large concertina wire gate behind them, and both male and female villagers began restacking sandbags against the closed gate. For the first time, behind Lac Do's security perimeter, Stott looked around at his new home.

Despite his combat exposure during that second night at Nha Trang, backing into Lac Do was Mike's first real in-country experience. Nha Trang seemed almost an extension of Fort Bragg or Camp Darby, so strong was the Americanization of the base. There at Lac Do, however, nothing was familiar. Most foreign were the smells. They were unlike any aromas from Stott's past.

Holy shit!

Lac Do had dozens of native hooches. These were huts, really, made of mud bricks, wood, straw, and other materials Mike didn't recognize. Some had corrugated metal roofs; other roofs were woven straw. The center of the village was an open area that appeared to be a commons where women were cooking and performing other domestic functions. Stott saw a woman breast-feeding her baby while another woman combed her hair. The residents of Lac Do were very small. The tallest man in sight couldn't have been more than five-foot two. Mike thought, *JJ would love this! He'd feel like a giant!*

First Sergeant Helms said, "Well, what do you think? Is it what you expected?"

"No, Sergeant. I mean, I didn't know what to expect, but this is different! Everyone is so small! I feel like Gulliver!" Stott told him.

"Who the fuck is Gulliver?" Helms asked.

Before Stott could respond, Master Sergeant Dunigan called to them. "Helms, Stott! Split up with the engineers and check out the perimeter defenses! Cap says Won has accepted our terms of deployment here, so we'll be settling in. He says Charlie hasn't been here for days, but my guess is he's out there observing us right now. And when the birds return with all the supplies, Chuck will know what's up! Get ready!"

Mike went with Beamer, and Helms took Barnett to walk the defensive lines. Stott was encouraged by the good fields of fire in nearly every direction. "Looks like the villagers cleared out the fire zones pretty well," he said to Staff Sergeant Beamer.

"Bullshit! We did all that when we were here before! They've let some of them grow back too much," Beamer replied.

"When was the team here last?" Mike asked.

"'Bout three weeks ago when it was still monsoon. At least the rain seems to have stopped early this season," Beamer said.

"How many people live in Lac Do?" Stott asked Beamer.

"Depending on how you count 'em, around 600 as near as we can tell. There are some farmers that come and go, though. Could be as high as 750."

"What kind of farmers?" Mike asked.

"Sergeant Stott, let me start your education of Gookland right now. There are two kinds of farmers here, rich and poor. The poor guys grow rice to feed their families. The rich ones grow opium. The rice growers are on our side, sort of. The opium growers are on their own side, or whichever side protects them.

"The war you're in is a drug war, pure and simple. It's not about politics or stopping communism! It's about drugs. Specifically, opium. Lac Do is to opium what Abilene, Kansas, was to cattle back in the frontier days. There's a little spot across the border up there in Burma that's the Dodge City of the opium business, Won Da, or 'One Day' to us. It's the town that's gonna make this team very, very rich," Sergeant Beamer told Stott.

Mike was stunned. "What the fuck are you talking about, Beamer?"

"You'll see, soon enough. All that counts for you now is your A Team. By dumb luck or whatever, you're in the right place at the right time with the right team! We need warriors and you just might be what we're looking for! Capice?" Staff Sergeant Beamer looked Mike straight in the eye. "Your Boy-Scout days are over, Sergeant! The 'One Day' A Team is gonna perform its mission and get rich! Now go unpack your sniper rifle and let's get down to business."

Stott heard Beamer's words, but could in no way comprehend their true meaning. His first instinct was that this was yet another team test. How would he react to Beamer's advice?

"Are you for real, Beamer?" Mike asked.

"You have no fucking idea, son," Beamer said. "Get your rifle."

Captain Freeze, WO Myers and Master Sergeant Dunigan were in a powwow with a group of village men who appeared to be some sort of council or governing body. Stott collected his sniper rifle from First Sergeant Helms, his "boss," as he was inventorying the weaponry. Mike was about to ask Helms if he could speak to him privately when Helms said, "Beamer talk to you? What do you think?" First Sergeant Helms, like Staff Sergeant Beamer, stared straight into his eyes, waiting for an answer.

As Mike looked back at Helms, chopper blades cut the air. "We'll continue this right after we unload," Helms said. "Come on! You need to learn what I'm about to do!"

Instead of the Hueys that had brought them to Lac Do, a giant Chinook helicopter dropped over the southern hills and came straight for Lac Do. The pilot hesitated about 500 meters outside of the LZ, hovering in the morning air. Stott could see that WO Myers was on his radio, presumably talking to the big chopper's pilot.

The Chinook then proceeded to fly directly over the commons area of Lac Do and hover just above the hooch roof tops. Both side doors opened and several troopers began dropping out all kinds of supplies. The troopers appeared to be wearing Navy "greens"!

Two piles quickly built up under each helicopter side door. As quickly as it had appeared, the Chinook was gone. The dust storm created by the Chinook's huge blades had obscured visibility to some degree during the supply dump, but when the dust settled Mike was amazed at how much had been off-loaded from the big bird.

"Load one," Helms said as he and Mike made their way toward the drop area. "So, you cool with what Beamer talked to you about?"

"First Sergeant Helms, I don't have a clue as to what Beamer was talking about! This is my fourth day in country and my third day with you guys! What's all this shit about opium?" Mike asked.

Master Sergeant Jake Dunigan walked up in time to hear Stott's question to Helms. "I'll handle this, Helms," he said. "Look, kid, let's take five in that bunker over there. Never just stand upright in the open at one spot for long. Charlie's got snipers too, you know! Be a hell of a shot from a thousand meters out, but you know it is possible, so don't give them an opportunity! As you learned on your second night back at Nha Trang, things happen pretty quick here in Vietnam. Frankly, if you weren't so handy with weaponry we would have reassigned you to HQ or another team. Fact is, you impressed Freeze in the bunker at Nha Trang, and he calls the shots.

Son, I've been in the army since 1941. Three years combat experience in World War II and three more in Korea. I've

just described. You are our seventeenth partner. You became our partner when the Huey lifted off from Nha Trang this morning."

"Seventeenth? I thought you said it was our team? Who else is in on this? What would I have to do?" It seemed unbelievable.

"You don't need to know who else just now. Basically, your role will be identical to what every assistant weapons sergeant on any A Team does. You'll be paid much better. Now you know. You're here. You're on the team. A couple of days after Christmas, your work starts. Tonight, we'll conduct a little membership ceremony.

"Now, go with Helms and Beamer and sight in your sniper rifle. Got to be sure the scope's right after the ride. See that farthest tree line? With binoculars you can locate fifty-gallon drums camouflaged there. You can use the dark brown ones as 500-meter targets. Don't hit the dark green ones; they're rigged. I want a twenty-five-meter-deep minefield completely surrounding Lac Do by New Year's. You'll need to be covering the Yards as they set the charges. If everything stays on schedule, we're gonna receive another six to eight birds full of supplies by nightfall, so get to work and start earning your money!" Jake Dunigan shook Mike's hand and departed, saying, "You'll be amazed at what you see and learn here in Lac Do starting right now!"

That night, Mike Stott swore an oath to support the Day One A Team—DOAT—in all its endeavors. It was 2230 hours, December 21, 1964. Mike's life was changed forever.

Chapter Thirty-Six

Larry Allsmeir was sitting in the airport in Kansas City on December 22, 1964, trying to get on a flight back to Boston for the holidays. As he sipped a Budweiser, Allsmeir reflected on the past few days back at Fort Sill. He couldn't decide if his army luck was improving or getting worse. The good news was he had finally escaped from the middle of nowhere. Following his twenty-one day holiday leave, he was to report to Fort Ord, California. He had just received a promotion to specialist fourth class. Larry was taking his first real leave since joining the army. He hoped by saving leave time he could get out early enough to start graduate school at Harvard during the summer term of 1966. Allsmeir mentally calculated again, as he did almost constantly, that, if all went according to his plan, he would "cross over" the halfway mark in his army enlistment sometime during this leave. If he could stand to keep banking his leave time, Allsmeir hoped to get discharged from active duty in May 1966. Maybe even April with a little luck!

As he waited for his military standby seat to clear, two very young-looking army sergeants strode by the gate area sporting Ranger patches and wearing the deep-maroon berets signifying they were assigned to an airborne unit. They had that cocky walk that Allsmeir had come to associate with gung-ho army types. They made him think of John J. Sharkey and Mike B. Stott, the two crazy kids from his basic training company. He had heard from Barry Smeall that they were both headed for a tour of duty in Vietnam. What dumb bastards they were to volunteer for everything! Smeall's mother had heard from Maria Mobliano that both Sharkey and Stott had actually been accepted into the Special Forces! Fucking nuts!

"Specialist Larry Allsmeir, please report to the ticket counter," a voice pleasantly announced over the airport public address system.

Please God, get me a seat! I've got to get out of here,
Allsmeir prayed.

As Allsmeir stood in line at the Kansas City airport, Specialist Five Fast Eddy Hale was at his bar tending job at the Hay-
Adams. Since his top-secret clearance had come through in November, his day job had definitely gotten more interesting, and
his new boss got him a Spec Five slot immediately. Hale was
beginning to understand that the army could do things completely around the system when necessary. Just today, his new
commanding officer, Major Olivia Stroth, had asked him if he
had a girlfriend who caused him to start watching the clock
around 1730 hours every day. On an impulse, Eddy had explained to her that he had a night job at a Washington hotel bar.
He half expected her to demand that he quit it. To his surprise,
the major had said she understood, but that she might need him
seven days a week for a while right after the holidays.

"Yes, ma'am! Happy to serve every day, Major," Eddy had
enthusiastically responded through a snappy salute.

"You never know, specialist, I just might have to stop in
the Hay-Adams for a drink sometime. Do you mix a good
martini?"

"Ma'am, yes ma'am! Best in town! Please do stop in,
ma'am!" said Hale, ever the optimist. Perhaps the major
needed male company. He began to fanaticize about becoming her sex slave.

Hale had worked a deal with the valet at the hotel to park
his Pontiac in the hotel garage free in exchange for a "coffee
cup" of Crown Royal whiskey each evening. As he got out
of his car, he thought as he often did about the car's previous
owners, Mike and JJ. He had seen Mike's friend, Cindy, enter
the hotel dining room twice since Mike had introduced them,
but she never came to the bar. *What a dish!*, he thought. But
just as quickly he put that out of his mind. She was Stott's
girl, and Mike Stott was not a guy to mess with!

Eddy changed into his bartender's jacket and took up his
station behind the bar at 1759 hours. *Made it by one minute,*
he thought.

"Hale, what the hell are you doing in a dinner jacket?" Syl Mobliano barked out. "I thought you'd be in stripes at Leavenworth by now!"

"Hey! Syl, how you doing, man? What are you doing here in D.C.? Thought you were a big time New York City lawyer!" Eddy was glad to see the brother of the goddesses.

"Client meeting, Ed. Meet one of the firm's senior partners, Mr. Jack Wasserman. Mr. Wasserman, this is Fast Eddy Hale. He went to school with my little brother, Paulie, and then we were in the same basic training company at Fort Dix, summer before last. Christ, Ed, can you believe that was a year and a half ago? You still got that great duty gig at the Pentagon?"

"Sure do, Syl! And I just made Spec Five! And I got my top secret clearance! What'll you have to drink, gentlemen?"

"Bombay Gin martini, straight up with olives, please," said Jack Wasserman.

"Do you have a decent red wine by the glass, Ed?" Syl asked.

"How about a Montrachet burgundy '58?" Ed asked.

"That works! So Ed, heard from any of the guys from basic?" Syl asked, still checking on everyone.

"Have I! Sharkey and Stott were in here at those two very bar stools where you guys are sitting 'bout six weeks ago! You should have seen them! They both made it through Special Forces school and look about ten years older than when you saw them last. And you should have seen the women they were with! I mean, seriously classy stuff! I bought their car!" Eddy went on to detail all he knew about their basic training buddies.

"Were they headed for Vietnam?" Syl inquired.

"They didn't say, but I know for a fact they are 'in country' right now," Eddy said with a wink. "I've got access to stuff you wouldn't believe!"

"Better be careful with that, Ed. Even to friends like me. You could get in real trouble." Syl's tone turned extremely stern.

Eddy Hale was chagrined. "Come on, Syl. I would only say it to you!"

"So they were with some real cuties, huh, Ed?"

"Not cute, Syl! Gorgeous, older women! I bet they were in their thirties!" said Hale.

"Watch it, son! I just had my sixtieth birthday!" said Mr. Wasserman.

"Uh, sorry, sir. But, I mean, Mikey and JJ aren't even twenty yet!"

"Never met kids as gung-ho as those two!" said Syl. He went on to explain to Jack Wasserman about how the seven basic trainees had formed an unusual friendship.

"But it was clear that Sharkey and Stott really bonded," Syl stated. "I'd be surprised if they don't remain best friends for life."

"Another round, gentlemen?" Hale inquired. He still wished he had gone on to be a real soldier like Mike and JJ. "I wish I could have stayed with them, Syl."

"Um-hum," Syl said. But Syl Mobliano had to suppress a chuckle. That Eddy Hale thought he belonged with John Sharkey and Mike Stott amazed Mobliano. *Some people just don't get it*, thought Syl.

"Are you coming home to Brooklyn for Christmas, Ed?" Syl asked.

"Still waiting to hear if I get leave. But I don't mind staying here! The tips are great at this time of year!"

As Eddy Hale and Syl Mobliano were reminiscing in the comfort of the Hay-Adams bar, Mr. and Mrs. Barry Smeall were even more comfortable in the guest wing of the Smealls' family home in Pittsburg. "You're beautiful pregnant!" Barry said to his wife. "Are you feeling okay? Can I get you anything? I love you, Bevey," Barry said.

"And I love you, honey! Your parents have been so wonderful to me! I was, you know, afraid they'd be mad about us getting pregnant. But they seem genuinely pleased! Are they, honey?" the new Mrs. Smeall needed some reassurance.

"Yes, they truly are! We've only got six months and four days left in the army! Can you believe it? Only a half year and this shit's over! We can come back to Pittsburg. I'll go to work in one of Dad's companies; life will be great!" Barry was counting the days.

"Can we get a house? Should I look for a job after the baby comes? Do you want more children?"

"Bevey, how long can we, you know, continue to do it? Do we have to stop at some point?" Barry asked.

"Well, yes, at some point, but not now!" Bev pulled her husband to her and stuck her hand down his pajama pants. "Turn out the light, honey. See if this works."

Two floors below Barry and Bev, Milt and Bessy Smeall were sitting at their bar between the kitchen and dining room. "Better go easy, Bess! That's your fourth martini, and you've had no food! Calm down! Life's not so bad," Milt said to his wife.

"Don't fucking tell me to calm down, goddamn it! I have one son, and now he's married to a farm girl from nowhere! He could have had any socialite on the East Coast! It's the army's fault for drafting him and sending him out west!" Bessy Smeall was distraught.

"Bess, he loves her! She's good-looking and no dummy! The kids will be fine! Stop worrying!" Milt said.

"Easy for you to say! I'm going to be a grandmother, for shit's sake! How could this have happened? I talked to Maria Mobliano this week, and she's all excited planning a huge wedding for Syl and Maria. I'm sure we'll be invited. That wedding will make the New York Times social pages! And Barry got married at a justice of the peace! Goddamn!"

"Bess, did Mrs. Mobliano mention if her daughters still hear from John Sharkey or Mike Stott?"

"What do you care? But yes, those two young men are in some special army unit headed for Vietnam," Bessy told her husband.

"See there! Barry could be headed for a combat zone instead of married to a pretty little farm girl! Now, that would be something to worry about, Bess! Barry will be out of the army and back in Pittsburg in six months. I'll find him a business to run. And you'll have a grandchild! Cheer up!"

"What if they get killed?" Bess asked.

"Who?"

"JJ and Mike Stott, you idiot! What if something happens to them? They're just kids!" Bessy began to cry.

"Now you're worried about those two? Bess, get a grip! What's wrong with you?"

"I'm starting the change, goddamn it! That's what wrong! How would you feel if it was happening to you?" screamed Bess.

With that new information, Milt Smeall mixed himself another double martini. *Oh brother!* he thought. *I'm gonna be sleeping with a change-of-life grandmother!*

Across the Atlantic, Specialist Fourth Class George Washington Howard was having another sleepless night in the barrack. Two days before Christmas, he was stuck in a country where nobody liked him, and his duty NCO was a Georgia cracker! He hadn't been home to Mississippi since joining the army! But what was keeping him awake that night was something else entirely. After being posted to Germany, Howard had little to do in his spare time but read. Thankfully, the base at Ramstadt had an excellent library that was almost never used. The library became George's sanctuary.

Over the past ten months, Howard had become friendly with, of all things, an officer! Major James Waterman had noticed Howard's appetite for books and became a sort of mentor, encouraging the young specialist's quest for knowledge. The more Major Waterman talked with Howard, the more he appreciated George's intelligence. Then, one week ago, the major had shocked Big Howie.

"Son, I'm beginning to understand you a bit. Let me give you something to think about. Take advantage of your situation. The army is desperate for black officers. Put your name in! Get a slot in OCS! You could do it! Go for it!" Major Waterman encouraged him.

At first Howard thought Major Waterman was crazy to suggest such a thing. After considerable reflection, he decided that OCS might be a way to realize his longer-term ambition to make something of himself. George knew he had the brains to be an officer, but did he have the drive? Howard thought about the only two real friends he had made in the army, John Sharkey and Mike Stott. He had made a pact with those guys that he thought about often. The last letter he got from JJ confirmed that both he and Mike had actually made it through Special Forces training and were now Green Berets. George assumed from the tone of Sharkey's letter that his two pals were probably already in Vietnam. *Goddamn it!* he thought. If Mike and JJ could put up with all the shit to become airborne Ranger Special Forces troopers, he could make through OCS! He'd gotten through jump school! But what to do next? Howard decided to confide in Major Waterman. Wouldn't Mike and JJ be impressed if he became an officer? The thought of his two buddies having to salute him made George laugh out loud.

"Are you fucking losing it, Howard? Shut up the laughing and get some sleep, goddamn it!" a fellow MP in the bunk across from him yelled.

Officers live better than regular troopers, Howard thought. *And they make a lot more money!* He promised himself to seek out Major Waterman the next morning.

Chapter Thirty-Seven

On December 23 and 24, 1964, the Day One A Team, DOAT, received more than a dozen Chinook helicopter supply drops. Mike was amazed at how much the big choppers could carry and then off-load with incredible efficiency. DOAT got enough building supplies to construct not only the school promised to Chief Won, but several other structures as well. The Yards had dug a deep munitions bunker within the village security perimeter, and it was filled with all types of ordinance by Christmas Day.

On Christmas Eve morning, Stott helped First Sergeant Helms account for and store their recently arrived ammo and grenades in the munitions bunker. As they worked, Stott asked him the questions that had been on his mind for two days. "Sarge, did all the stuff on those Chinooks come from Nha Trang? It seems we've received more supplies than I saw at base camp! And should the Yards have constructed this munitions bunker right in the middle of the village? What if it takes a direct rocket hit? Can you tell me more about our 'other' mission?"

"I need a coffee, let's take a break. Fire up the sterno burner, and boil some water," Helms directed Stott. "No, this stuff is not all from Nha Trang. We cut a deal with the Seabees that are doing some work at Da Nang. Most of the building supplies are from there. And most of the ammo came from the South Korean marines. The ROK's get their ordinance through some special deal they cut with the CIA. Seems to be no limit to what they can get! The Christmas dinner you're going to enjoy tonight and tomorrow, as long as Charlie stays quiet, is from a deal Colonel Besuden made with some admiral. As far as the location of this bunker is concerned, you are right! It's not ideal! But we couldn't have them locate it outside the perimeter, now could we? You notice our team hooches are as far from it as possible, right?

Hopefully, all those support beams and sandbags will prevent a rocket from blowing all this to kingdom come!

"As far as our other mission—getting rich—is concerned, you'll learn more about it as we work it. Actually, you will play one of the key roles starting next week. I hope you like the bush! We're gonna be humpin' on over to Burma real soon! Stay sharp with your shooter, you're gonna be needing it! Oh, I almost forgot! We have guests for dinner! Be a bit of a surprise for you!"

The last Chinook made its drop about 1200 hours, noon, on Christmas Eve day. By 1400 hours, they had stowed the last of the 7.62 ammo. Helms and Stott went to Captain Freeze's HQ bunker for chow. Freeze, WO Myers, Adams, and Beamer were there, the rest of DOAT were on watch. Everyone seemed to be in a holiday mood.

DOAT had a Lac Do equivalent of Mia, the house maid and cook in Nha Trang, already on the job in the HQ bunker. Her name was Coni. Coni had prepared a K ration meal that tasted pretty good.

"So what do you think so far, Sergeant Stott? This beats the shit out of Ranger school doesn't it?" Captain Freeze asked Mike.

"Yes, Captain, but then just about anything would be better than Ranger training, especially 'Run!'" Stott said.

"I heard you saw Gonzalez eat a snake! Isn't he a piece of work?" Freeze stated.

Mike was tired from having unloaded supplies for thirty-six of the last forty-eight hours, but he was sharp enough to catch Freeze's implication about Captain Gonzalez.

"How'd you know I saw him eat a snake, sir? I heard he pulled that stunt with various creatures," Mike said.

"Sergeant Stott! Sergeant Stott! You continue to underestimate us! We know virtually everything about you from your AIT forward! Surely you don't still think you got here by chance, do you? You have specific talents that DOAT demands! We've been watching you and Sharkey ever since jump school. You're two lucky bastards! You sight in your

EB yet?" Freeze's comments shocked Stott. None of the other men in the bunker reacted at all.

"Captain Freeze, I'm confused," was all Mike could say.

Stott's team members laughed out loud. "Stott, you're on the team now. Listen up. From the time John Sharkey told Sergeant Patterson that he could speak and write Chinese back at St Agnes, we've had our eye on him. When the two of you hit it off in AIT, we added you to our watch list. Then we learned that you were Captain Stott's little brother! A natural for us, we figured.

Don't misunderstand! You had to get through all the training on your own! But you must have wondered about going directly from one training school to the next while other troopers waited months, if not years, for those slots! Frankly, we were all surprised at how well you did in languages school. We knew Sharkey would excel! Christ! He's got a 200 IQ! But you surprised us!

And Sharkey's stunt at the Ranger awards ceremony! What a classic! So Sharkey was made on languages capability, and, of course, being an orphan. But your M-60 shooting on that second night in Nha Trang sealed the deal for you. Near as we can tell, you killed at least twenty VC and slept the next morning! Very cool! So here you are, about to get very rich as you serve your country! Might make even you get religious!"

Stott looked at each of the men in the bunker. They were staring back at him, waiting on a response. Mike returned his focus to Captain Freeze. "Are you saying my being assigned to this team was planned long ago? And that JJ's languages skills were known to the army even before he enlisted? And that 'someone' has been watching us for the last year?" Stott could barely comprehend all the implications of what had just been revealed to him by Captain Freeze.

"Bravo! The young sergeant is beginning to catch on! Yes, Sergeant Stott, that's exactly what I'm saying. But, seriously, I wasn't convinced about you until that night in the bunker at Nha Trang. So now, what do you think?" Freeze asked.

"How much money are we talking about?" Stott asked. "When do we get it?"

His team members actually cheered! "That's what we were hoping to hear, Sergeant!" WO Myers said. "That's the spirit!"

Captain Freeze continued, "We don't actually know, Mike. Lots! Mostly U.S. dollars, but some gold. Go clean up. We're gonna have some fun tonight!"

DOAT had rigged up a decent shower in Lac Do utilizing two big water bags. The water was cold, of course, but at least a man could get clean. Stott showered, shaved and put on fresh fatigues. Mike checked his weapons and started back to HQ. He thought he heard distant chopper blades, but Mike knew they weren't expecting any more supplies drops on Christmas Eve.

As Stott got closer to HQ, the sound of a chopper was unmistakable. Mike peered out over HQ's big upper support beams and saw a blacked-out Huey appear on the horizon. It came in fast and settled in the LZ close to where he had first landed at Lac Do. To his surprise, he saw Captain Freeze and Master Sergeant Dunigan along with Sergeants Beamer and Barnett hustle out to meet the chopper.

The first person out the right side door was Sergeant John J. Sharkey. Next was the group's executive officer, Major Lawrence Royalty and then came Colonel Besuden himself!

What the fuck?

The seven soldiers hustled back inside the gate at Lac Do and headed in Mike's direction. As always, a collection of Montagnard men and women restacked sandbags against the closed gate and Sergeant Adams began rewiring the explosive charges he had placed there. The black Huey lifted off. Apparently, the guests were staying for a while.

Sergeants Beamer and Barnett separated from the others, presumably back to their duty stations. Besuden, Royalty, Freeze, and Dunigan came straight toward where Mike was standing outside the group bunker. Sharkey was with them carrying a puppy in his arms! Stott still had to resist the temptation to salute his CO and executive officer. He did manage to get out, "Good afternoon, sirs! Welcome to Lac Do."

"Afternoon, Sergeant Stott," Colonel Besuden responded. "We brought along the man responsible for getting you through Ranger school, languages school and Special Forces training, at least according to him! You remember your mentor, John Sharkey, right sergeant?" Everyone laughed except Mike.

"Right. Hey, JJ. What's with the puppy?" Stott asked.

"Your Christmas present, dickhead! Half shepherd and half collie. At least that's what the Seabees told us! Actually, Colonel Besuden thought you guys needed a camp pet, so here he is!" JJ handed the mutt to Stott. The dog immediately licked Mike's face and peed on him at the same time.

Again, everyone roared with laughter, except Stott.

"How'd you teach him to do that?" Master Sergeant Dunigan said through his laughter. "Now, that's worth something!"

More laughter.

"Did you already name him, or do we do that?" Stott asked.

"I started calling him 'Dickhead' in honor of you, Mikey! What do you think?" JJ's humor appealed to the officers. Mike didn't think it was that funny.

Stott sat Dickhead down as they entered the bunker, but the dog wouldn't leave his side. "I've gotta go change my fatigue jacket where this mongrel peed on me," Mike said to Dunigan. More laughter.

"Hold a minute, Sergeant Stott," Colonel Besuden commanded. "Before you change, let's have a toast!" Major Royalty produced a quart bottle of Crown Royal whiskey from his rucksack and WO Myers rounded up seven steel canteen cups. Colonel Besuden took the bottle from Royalty and poured out seven equal portions of the liquor, emptying the bottle completely. Major Royalty, Captain Freeze, WO Myers, Master Sergeant Dunigan, Sergeant Sharkey, and Mike each took a cup.

"Here's to getting rich as we serve our country," Colonel Besuden said. "Merry Christmas!" The soldiers all took a good, long pull of the excellent whiskey.

Stott was staring at Sharkey for a sign, but he just winked and gave Mike that air-check sign of his. So he already knew!

Colonel Besuden observed the look between JJ and Stott and said, "Sergeant Sharkey was partner sixteen. You are partner seventeen, Sergeant Stott. We won't need many more, just a few. What we're going to do over the coming years will be legend! We'll use a large part of our take to do good back home. That's part of the deal! Congratulations, sergeants! You two take a walk! We've got some details to go over concerning our day job. But tonight you'll hear more about the good stuff!"

Sharkey, Dickhead, and Mike left the HQ bunker and walked out under a rapidly darkening sky. Dickhead stopped to pee about every ten paces. "We'll go to the hooch I share with Adams and Beamer. We can have some privacy there," Mike said. He and JJ still had their cups of Crown Royal. Several villagers stopped Dickhead to pet him, but the mutt stayed close to Stott.

Mike changed fatigue jackets and said, "Holy shit, JJ! Is this for real?"

"Yeah, Mikey, it's for real! I'll try to tell you all that's happened to me since I got to Nha Trang, but you just won't be able to believe it! First off, the Special Forces planners had been watching us from the beginning! It turns out that recruiter that came to St. Agnes, Sergeant Bill Patterson, reported my Chinese language skills to Special Forces command right after I first met him! You know how we wondered why we got immediately sent to our next training assignments while other guys waited? Turns out that was all coordinated somehow! And when we became friends the army decided to pair us up! It wasn't the luck of the draw at all! Colonel Besuden himself told me this the morning after you came off strong with your M-60! We've got a chance to do it all! Serve our country and get rich! And together!"

Mike listened to JJ's enthusiasm and wondered what he was missing. It all seemed too improbable to Stott. "JJ, does it make sense to you that we're getting this so-called opportunity?" he asked.

"Don't you go negative on me, goddamn it! We wanted to be soldiers, and now we're going to get rich too! What could be better?" Sharkey was euphoric. "Look, Mikey, it's our big break! Do you know what percentage of army personnel speak both Hmong and Chinese? It's incalculable, it's so small! Colonel Besuden, Major Royalty and Captain Myers have been working on this for three years! Get that skeptical look off your face or I'll have to kick your ass!"

Mike sipped on his Crown Royal and thought about what JJ had just said. Clearly Sharkey had bought in hook, line, and sinker. In the back of his mind Mike thought, *How perfect! He's an orphan. He has nothing to lose.*

"And why is Chinese so important, JJ? Why not just Hmong?" Mike asked.

"Sometimes you really are slow, Stott! Chinese is the language of the opium trade! You're gonna hear more about that over the next twenty-four hours! That's why we're here! To bring it all together and get operational and celebrate Christmas, of course!" Sharkey was on a roll.

Dickhead had curled up and gone to sleep on Mike's boots as he and JJ talked. When Sharkey tried to pick him up and move him away from Stott, Dickhead actually growled at JJ.

"At least the mutt's got good instincts," Mike said.

"Ungrateful little bastard!" JJ said. "No wonder you two immediately bonded! He's an ingrate, just like you! Cheer up, Mikey! We're gonna be heroes and rich!"

It occurred to Mike that JJ was going to be doing a lot of translating and talking; he was likely to be doing a lot of shooting.

"I guess this trumps our pact with Big Howie," Stott said.

"That's been bothering me more than anything," JJ confessed. "Colonel Besuden told me right away that you were 'in,' so I only had Howard to worry about. We'll have to figure out a way to take care of him without divulging too much. Are you going to be all right with this?"

"JJ, neither you nor me really had a choice, did we? Yeah, I'm gonna be fine, but you know there's big risk with all this, right?" Mike said.

"No more risk than serving in combat with the Special Forces! We're not going to shirk our mission! We're gonna do it all! They've even figured out how we can launder our take. Did you take an oath before you knew I was in?" JJ didn't miss a trick.

"Yes, JJ, what choice did I have? I figured I could find a way to take care of you just like you were worrying about how to take care of Howie. By the way, Captain Freeze also told me they've been watching you and me since AIT!"

"Besuden told me the same thing. He also explained to me that the army focuses on orphans because, on average, they are more likely to be both lifers and totally devoted to their units. I never dreamed I would come to think of being an orphan as a positive, but I'm starting to think it is!" exclaimed JJ.

"I'm on line tonight, so I'm gonna check back in to HQ. Probably need to get some sleep. I've been unloading and storing ordinance for two days," Mike said.

"We're here 'til 0800 hours. Then we're visiting a couple of other remote A Teams, spreading Christmas cheer! I want to do your rounds with you tonight!" JJ was as gung-ho as ever, maybe more.

Dickhead was still sleeping, so JJ carried him back to HQ. The officers were done with their meeting and were all smoking big cigars and working on more Crown Royal. They offered JJ more booze, but not Stott. Mike was on the night shift.

"No thank you, sir," JJ said to Major Royalty. "I want to stay on line with young Stott, here. This is my first real night in country!"

"We thought you'd say that! Sit down and have dinner with us! Sergeant Stott doesn't go on line until 2200 hours," Captain Freeze said.

Coni and another village woman served a turkey dinner with all the trimmings! The men even had pumpkin pie for dessert! Turns out the meal had arrived on the CO's Huey. Doc Brackett helped them warm it up.

"Got plenty for tomorrow too!" Doc said. "The guys on line are getting served as we speak! Just like home!"

"Doc, this is home," said Master Sergeant Dunigan.

"I'll drink to that!" said Colonel Besuden. He and the officers and Dunigan tossed down another round. Mike could see JJ was licking his lips.

"You're in the field now, Sergeant Staffie," Stott said to Sharkey. "You can't just party like back at Nha Trang!" Mike spoke softly enough that he thought the officers wouldn't hear.

"I'm not a staffie, goddamn it! I ought to kick your ass!" JJ didn't try to keep it down.

"Give it a rest, you two. You got plenty enough fighting to do real soon," Major Royalty said.

How right he was!

That evening the officers, led by Colonel Besuden, explained how DOAT was going to accomplish the dual missions of serving the army and getting rich. Actually, they made it sound completely logical.

"Conquering armies have enjoyed the spoils of war for centuries. The spoils available to us are more grand than most," Besuden began. "Your command structure is the same for both missions, sergeants. I give you my word that the army's mission will always take precedence over our secondary goal. But the facts are that the two objectives overlap in numerous ways, not the least of which is to disrupt the opium trade and the funding it provides to Charlie. In case you are wondering, should any partner be killed in action his share will reach whomever he named in his will. We will have no more than twenty-five partners. Each partner will receive an equal share. My take will be exactly the same as yours, boys.

"The code name we will use for getting rich is SPEND. SPEND launches in two days. How long we can work it depends on conditions beyond our control, so we're going to maximize the take as soon as possible. Word is the army will begin a major buildup in Vietnam starting in March 1965. The Third Marines are already here, so there's no time to waste. And, of course, we'll have to contend with CIA spooks here and there, but they don't usually get involved in the heavy lifting! They leave that to us!"

Besuden's comments about the CIA brought a chuckle from the officers. The colonel continued. "Actually, we have two CIA types in SPEND. One is a former green hat that worked for me. The other is in Langley. You may or may not ever learn the names of all the team. We expect total and equal loyalty from all partners, period. A formula has been developed for when the proceeds from SPEND will be distributed. You probably won't like it, so just accept it as necessary. The first distribution, other than to cover expenses, will occur ten years after we shut SPEND down. This accomplishes several necessary objectives not the least of which is to keep the heat off all of us who might be tempted to 'live beyond our means.' Secondarily, we expect every SPEND partner to continue their Special Forces or other military careers!

DOAT is the heart of SPEND. Lac Do is perfectly located to be the tactical center of SPEND. DOAT team members can slip in and out of Laos and Burma undetected. Sergeant Stott, JJ tells me you know enough Chinese to get by. Are you comfortable with that?"

Mike was amazed to hear Colonel Besuden refer to John Sharkey as JJ. "Sir, I'm nowhere near as good as John, but I understand probably 80 to 90 percent of what I hear in Chinese. I'm much better in the Hmong dialect."

"Good enough. Twenty-eight December, you, Beamer, Adams, and Meeks leave for recon across the border. Laos is friendly, so a bird will sit you guys down right on the border with Burma. Sergeant Adams is senior NCO and will be in charge. Mike, they all shoot just as good as you do, but you'll be the designated 'first shooter' on this mission. We're all proud of how you handled the M-60 in Nha Trang. This will be a different kind of shooting. You four men will be DOAT's 'C' Team. That blacked-out Huey you saw earlier and a couple more just like it will be on standby for extraction should that become necessary. We hope it won't. We'll send birds across the Burmese border only as a last resort. Mike, JJ will be the main link of communication between your 'C' Team and the rest of us. Speak in Hmong or Chinese. English, never."

Besuden and the officers then spent another hour defining SPEND's initial objectives. Their plans were amazing. Beautiful in strategic simplicity, yet very challenging from a tactical implementation standpoint.

At the end of the officers' discussion, Colonel Besuden said, "Sergeant Stott, do you have any questions?"

All Mike could say was, "Wow!"

"Yeah, it's a big 'WOW' Mike," Captain Freeze confirmed.

It was 2120 hours on Christmas Eve 1964. Despite having been tired earlier, Stott was hyped up. "You still going to stand watch with me JJ?" Mike asked.

"Let's go!" Sharkey said.

"You have ammo in your weapons, Sergeant?" Mike asked.

"Goddamn it! Yes! Let's go!"

It was only Stott's second night at Lac Do, but the routine was straight forward. The Montagnard militiamen manned their perimeter defenses, relieving on a four-hour rotation. DOAT team members checked the positions on a constantly rotating walk around. Little was spoken between DOAT and the Yards. They had as much vested in their security as the soldiers did. Maybe more! Most Yards had wives and children in Lac Do.

JJ and Mike moved down the north side perimeter and then crossed back through the village and started down the west line. They carried no gear, though both were heavily armed and carrying fragmentation grenades and several hundred rounds of ammo, just in case. Although there was plenty of ammo stored at all the lookout points, Captain Freeze rightfully insisted that each trooper carry his own extra rounds just to be sure.

The night was clear and fairly cool. JJ and Mike both had field jackets under their flak jackets. "Always wear that flak jacket, Mike," JJ said. "Even when it gets hot."

"Okay, dad," Stott said.

"I'm serious, goddamn it! Remember where we were last Christmas Eve?" Sharkey asked.

"I'm not senile, yet, dickhead! We were with our family in Cincinnati."

Sharkey was quiet for longer than usual. "I'll never forget Raymond calling me 'little brother.' I think about your family often. Christ! Here we are one year later about to get rich in the Special Forces! Quite a plan the officers have put together, huh?"

"Yeah, JJ, it is. I'll tell you more after my trip. You know, the next youngest guy in DOAT is Staff Sergeant Beamer, and he's thirty-four! And he's got fifteen years in the army! It feels a little strange being about half as old as the other guys!" Mike told his friend.

"Actually, Captain Freeze is only twenty-nine. He's a Pointer, like Besuden and Royalty. He'll be a major in about sixty days. I saw the paperwork!" JJ said.

"Is there anything you don't see?" Mike asked.

"Sure, but nobody seems to hide anything, at least about the regular missions."

"Do you know who else at Nha Trang is in SPEND?" Stott asked.

"I don't think anyone else there is a part of it. Colonel Besuden said I was to speak about SPEND only to him and of course, Major Royalty. I guess this whole thing was Royalty's idea going back three years ago when he was a captain running a recon team up this way. They were looking for the right sergeant who had both Hmong and Chinese. We get radio transmissions relayed to us that are all in Chinese. Now SPEND knows what's happening, thanks to me!" JJ was pretty proud.

"Okay, but watch your ass, John. The rest of the staff is bound to resent your relationship with the CO and XO. Maybe you can get away with it because you're so young," Stott speculated. "But watch your ass!"

JJ and Mike spent the rest of Christmas Eve walking the line and talking. Charlie took the night off, and at 0400 hours Stott rotated off duty. He and JJ went back to his hooch and lay down on the cots, but they were still too excited to sleep. Dickhead crawled out from under Beamer's cot and started to pee, but Mike grabbed him and sat him outside. "Now I've gotta housebreak this mongrel!" he told John.

JJ didn't respond. John was already asleep. Mike fired up a sterno burner and boiled water for coffee. He sat there listening to Sharkey's snoring, reflecting on the last few weeks. Less than six weeks ago, he and JJ had been on leave in Washington, D.C. with Cindy and Ginny. Mike thought of Cindy's last words to him at National Airport, *Until next time. I'll come anywhere in the world to see you, Mikey. Just give me as much notice as you can. I mean it. Just tell me where and when. Stay safe, honey, I love you.*

Stott wondered if he'd ever see Cindy again. He wondered if he'd ever see the states again. Could SPEND really work? Would they all get rich? Would any of them be alive to enjoy the money? The only thing Mike knew for sure was that he was humping into Burma in three days. Burma! Officially, the U.S. Army could not enter Burma's sovereign space. But Stott wasn't in the regular army. He was in Colonel Besuden's SPEND group! As a shooter!

Mike looked at his watch and saw that it was 0630 hours on Christmas Day. "Hey JJ! Wake up! Here's a coffee. You better do the Three S's and get moving! You're traveling with the man!"

"What time is it?" JJ yawned. "This isn't as good as the latte at The Plaza, dickhead!"

"Move your ass before I kick it!" Stott said. "Merry Christmas!"

At exactly 0800 hours, the black Huey dropped into Lac Do's LZ. Besuden, Royalty and Sharkey jumped on board, and the chopper roared away over the southern hills. Mike went back to his bunker and crashed. He dreamt of Cindy and big stacks of hundred dollar bills. Mike Stott was hooked.

Chapter Thirty-Eight

There are many definitions of what makes up the Golden Triangle, but, in 1964, it was a no-man's land of some 350,000 square kilometers of rugged, mountainous terrain covering portions of Burma, Laos, Thailand, and Vietnam. The Shan and Hmong peoples who make up most of the population considered themselves part of no country. Political borders simply had no meaning for them.

Shan and Hmong civilizations were thousands of years old. Their traditions and values were never understood by outsiders and certainly not by the members of western armies. The inhabitants of the Golden Triangle grew various strains of the poppy plant from which they refined opium. They also made various by-products or variations of opium-based drugs including diacetylmorphine—heroin.

In 1964, much of the world's heroin came from the poppy crop of the Golden Triangle. The wealth generated by the heroin production and distribution pipeline was simply indescribable. The governments of communist China, Laos, Burma, Thailand, and both Vietnams vied for some portion of the profits generated from those poppy harvests off the mountainsides of the Golden Triangle. There were no rules or laws or even working agreements. He who had the power ruled. As Mike Stott soon learned firsthand, the Russians were also cultivating their own interests in this part of southeast Asia. This put them in direct competition with the other rival nations, particularly the Chinese.

One of Besuden's black Hueys picked up DOAT's 'C' Team at dusk on December 28, 1964 and flew them at treetop level over Laos and the northeastern-most tip of Thailand to a drop zone just outside the border with Burma. Before the men lifted off from Lac Do, Captain Freeze collected their dog tags. Adams, Beamer, Meeks, and Stott were about to enter forbidden territory with absolutely no personal identification of any kind. First Sergeant Adams had several thousand dollars in hundred dollar bills. He said that was the only identification they needed.

The flight lasted far longer than Stott had anticipated. They crossed the Truong Son Mountains and flew at maximum sustainable speed for more than two hours. "This bird got the range to get home?" Mike had asked First Sergeant Adams.

"She's not going home," was all Adams said. The Huey's pilot and copilot wore no name tags, and there was no door gunner on board. Mike realized how cut off they were from the rest of the Fifth Special Forces Group and the world. How the pilots were able to set them down was a mystery since the night was pitch black and there were few clearings.

First Sergeant Bill Adams, Staff Sergeants Dave Beamer and Dan Meeks, and Sergeant Mike Stott dropped from their Huey with more than a hundred pounds of gear each, about two-thirds of which was ammunition, grenades and C-4 explosive. The Huey also left them an inflatable rubber boat. As the bird roared off into the night the men secured the boat in the wood line and waited. After three hours of watching and listening in absolute silence, they determined that the only sounds were the natural sounds of the night. Their insertion had gone undetected.

First Sergeant Adams guided them some 1,000 meters to the northwest, where they encountered a wide and rapidly flowing river. Silently, they crossed that body of water, drifting about a half mile downstream in the process. It was 0200 hours on December 29, 1964 when DOAT-C deflated the boat and cut it up into very small pieces to disperse downstream.

Adams consulted his compass and they set off in a north-by-northwest direction, making their way through dense forest and carefully crossing the occasional highland trail. As dawn broke, the four troopers settled into a deep thicket and concealed themselves in the classic four-man defensive quadrangle. Stott drew first watch and was told to be sure no one snored.

As Mike watched the first morning light descend through the highland forest, he thought about Ranger training. Then he thought about the jungle in Panama and how miserable that heat had been. Stott looked at the three hardened combat veterans that he was with and wondered what the hell he was doing there in Burma. A movement caught his eye some distance away, and Mike strained to make out an image. Slowly, carefully he lined up his sniper rifle in the direction of the movement and waited for what came next. Stott thought they were well enough concealed that a man would literally have to walk on them to see them, but he had been told that the mountain people could usually smell Caucasians several hundred yards away. Carefully, Mike placed his hand over Adams's mouth to wake him as they had practiced doing.

Adams was instantly alert. Mike cautiously pointed in the direction of his concern. Adams motioned for Stott to focus on the movement while he woke Beamer and Meeks. Mike again saw movement and this time Adams saw it too. Through his sniper's scope, Stott saw one, then two, then several men. They appeared to be on some kind of trail that angled toward DOAT-C's position. Stott had the lead man squarely in his crosshairs perhaps a hundred meters distant. There were six of them, still coming directly toward him. The second man from the rear was Caucasian. The men were carrying very little other than their individual weapons. Beamer and Meeks also had targets in their crosshairs.

At a point no more than fifty meters away, the trail must have taken a ninety-degree right turn. The party angled away from Mike's position. The team waited a full fifteen minutes before moving or speaking.

"Close," Adams whispered. "Let's back off a click and watch that trail."

They repositioned themselves a hundred meters back and dug in again. Over the next four hours, three more groups of armed men came up that path, all moving in the same direction. Adams had selected the concealment well. The prevail-

346 **Philip B. Storm**

ing winds came from the direction of the trail so the men burrowed in and watched.

For two more days and nights, DOAT-C stayed where they could monitor the movement on what they dubbed the A Trail. The four men wished each other a happy 1965 from deep concealment camouflage one hundred meters from the A Trail deep inside Burma, a country the U.S.A. never acknowledged putting troops in!

Both Adams and Beamer had been in the area previously. The team was very near an objective that was revealed to Mike on the third day of their insertion. On that third night, the soldiers moved up a mountainside they'd been watching for the past two daylight periods and set up near the pinnacle. A sweet and pungent aroma drifted up the hillside, and Stott saw the occasional wisp of smoke. On the morning of the fourth day, Mike crawled up to the mountaintop with Adams to see firsthand an expanse of poppy fields spread farther than the eye could see.

"Harvest is nearly over; what you see is the last of this season's crop. They've been cooking it for days," Adams whispered. "On the far side of that ridge line is Pong Dai, one of the banking centers for the Golden Triangle. Ping the radio to see if we get a signal."

With the incoming volume turned all the way up and the radio snuggled against his ear, Stott had no faith that he could possibly have contact. But he did. Mike nodded to Adams that he had a signal, and Adams gave him the "cut it off" sign.

Stott gave Adams a shoulder shrug and whispered, "Where could that be coming from?"

"Friends in Thailand," was his answer.

From their elevated position, Adams and Stott could look down on the area where Beamer and Meeks were concealed. Though they knew exactly where to look, Beamer and Meeks weren't at all visible.

Suddenly, a Mil-8T Russian helicopter appeared on the far ridge line. Adams and Stott saw it at about the same time they heard it, the chopper's roar masked by the rugged hills.

Sergeant Adams softly said, "There's our guy, right on schedule."

The helicopter bore no markings. It was painted in green-brown camouflage and was flying directly at Mike's position. He wasn't concerned about being spotted, but it was unnerving to have the bird swoop right over their location.

"Let's see how long it takes 'til she returns," Adams said.

As they waited, Stott thought he could hear very distant gun fire. He pointed to his rifle and gave Adams the shoulder shrug to see if he heard it too.

"Very distant, I hope," Adams whispered.

After more than two hours, the Russian helicopter flew back at them, though not directly over their position as it had before. Beamer and Meeks had worked their way up to the mountaintop by then, and all four troopers watched the chopper cross the far mountain top and start its descent.

"Know it?" Adams asked Meeks.

"Can do," Meeks answered.

"Same one as last month?" Adams asked.

Both Beamer and Meeks nodded "yes."

"Okay. Tomorrow then," Sergeant Adams told them. "Get some shut-eye, I'll watch. We go to work tonight."

Despite the conditions, Stott fell sound asleep. Beamer woke him just as darkness was setting in. "Okay, kid. Let's travel."

During that fifth night, the team made their way down through the valley and up and over the mountain behind which they'd seen the Russian-made chopper descend. From the top of "Big Hill," Stott could see lights spread out for some distance. At the bottom of Big Hill, Adams spoke for the first time since they had started their night's journey. "There she is," he whispered.

Through the darkness, Mike struggled to see what Adams was pointing at. Then he saw the silhouette of the Russian helicopter.

"Kid, at first light you get to kill some bad guys," First Sergeant Adams stated. "Don't miss."

Just before first light, Staff Sergeant Dan Meeks, U.S. Army Special Forces engineering sergeant, crawled on his belly some 200 meters from their position in the wood line to within twenty meters of the Russian helicopter. Stott's team had identified four men guarding the chopper, each about fifty meters out from the aircraft in a basic defensive square. Meeks was well inside their perimeter. It appeared all four guards were asleep. On Meeks's signal, Adams, Beamer, and Stott each shot a designated target with their silenced sniper rifles as Meeks buried his K-Bar knife into the fourth guard's heart.

Nothing stirred in the vicinity of the helicopter, so Sergeant Meeks pulled himself up and into the pilothouse of the chopper. Three minutes later, just as light was coming up, the helicopter's crew appeared at the opposite wood line and headed for their aircraft. As one of the pilots called out to the guards, Mike shot him through the head. He then killed the crew member to his immediate right. Beamer and Adams shot and killed the other three crewmen. Still no reaction of any kind; the new-design silencers on the M-14EB's emitted essentially no sound.

Beamer and Stott crouch-ran to the far wood line and set up watch on the trail from which the crew had emerged. They confirmed that all of the targets were dead. First Sergeant Adams climbed in the Mil-8T as Meeks fired up the engine. The helicopter needed three minutes of warm-up before she could lift off. Those three minutes were critical to DOAT-C's plan.

Two minutes and thirty seconds into the chopper's warm-up, four more men entered the far end of the trail that Beamer and Stott were guarding. They, of course, expected the chopper to be in warm-up mode and were taking their time walking toward the chopper—and the soldiers. When they were within twenty meters of their position, Beamer and Stott killed all four of them with two shots each. Still no repercussions.

Staff Sergeant Beamer and Mike covered each other back to the Russian chopper and hopped in the right side door as Staff Sergeant Meeks lifted her off into the morning air.

"She's real heavy," was all Meeks said.

By prearrangement, Stott took the helicopter's right side gun, and Beamer took the gun on the left side, leaving First Sergeant Adams to the all important task of inventorying the aircraft's payload.

"Looks like we might have hit it just right," Adams said. He then took the second seat next to Meeks in the pilothouse and handed a headset back to Mike. "Watch and listen, kid, watch and listen."

Meeks flew the bird right over Pong Dai. The village was still asleep. It was 0550 hours on January 2, 1965; no one still alive had seen Stott and his team. First Sergeant Bill Adams, Staff Sergeants Dave Beamer and Dan Meeks, and Sergeant Mike Stott were clearing the Burmese village of Pong Dai in a stolen Russian Mil-8T Helicopter.

"In Chinese, radio Sergeant Sharkey that we scored and are headed for rendezvous one," First Sergeant Adams directed Mike. "As briefly as possible."

Staff Sergeant Meeks had set the helicopter's radio to their designated frequency, and Stott got through to JJ on the first try. Hearing Sharkey's voice responding in Mandarin was the sweetest sound Mike had ever heard.

In Mandarin, Stott said, "Scored. Rendezvous one."

"See you in an hour," JJ responded in perfect Mandarin.

The entire radio transmission took less than twenty seconds.

"You know the coordinates. Fly this mother to Thailand!" Adams told Meeks.

The Russian helicopter had a nearly full fuel tank, and she roared along over the treetops at maximum speed as Meeks showed a masterful grasp of the chopper's avionics.

"Where did Meeks learn to fly a Russian helicopter?" Stott asked Sergeant Beamer.

"Meeks was a flight instructor at Fort Rucker before he joined the Fifth. He can fly every type of helicopter used by any army in the world! Meeks practiced on captured birds for years! Relax and enjoy the flight," Staff Sergeant Beamer said. "You cool with that Russian side-loader?"

"Yep! We fired them a lot in 18-B School! Never thought I'd be a door-gunner on a Russian chopper, though!" Stott said.

Adams left the right seat and came to talk with Beamer and Mike. "Okay, boys! So far, so good! Way more loot than we had estimated! Start chain-rigging C-4 in half-kilo packs. When we rally with Blackbird One we need to be ready to turn this bird into scrap metal!"

Somewhere over northern Thailand, one hour and nine minutes after they stole the Russian helicopter, Staff Sergeant Meeks announced, "Got a visual on Blackbird One! We're right where we want to be! Get ready!"

Meeks lifted the chopper several hundred feet higher than they had been flying and then dropped her down into an isolated clearing in a tight valley between two mountains. Blackbird One landed next to them, just far enough away to ensure rotor clearance. Sergeant John J. Sharkey was out of the black Huey even before she hit the ground.

"Hey, dickhead! Hi, guys! Let's transfer!" JJ was actually giving orders!

As Meeks and the Blackbird's pilot conferred, Beamer, Sharkey, and Stott transferred the dollars and gold from the Russian helicopter to the Huey. First Sergeant Adams packed C-4 explosive literally all through the Russian helicopter's superstructure and then along its rotors and tail section.

"What's the weight on the gold?" asked the Huey pilot. "We may have to leave it!"

"No fucking way! What's on board that we don't need?" Adams screamed.

"Nothing! This bird's rigged with the long-range tanks, so I'm fuel-heavy!" said the nameless pilot. "Unless you guys want to leave your weapons and other gear!"

"How will you know if the weight's too much?" demanded Adams.

"When she won't lift off, Sarge," Meeks told Adams. "How you feel about humping back to Nha Trang?"

"We can't leave any U.S. gear at this sight, goddamn it!" Adams responded.

"We've been here too long already, Top," the Huey pilot said. "We're outta here in two minutes. Make a decision!"

"Load up and try it!" First Sergeant Adams commanded.

JJ and Mike looked at each other and nodded. "If she's too heavy, we'll stay and wait on another bird," Sharkey told Adams.

"Are you out of your fuckin' mind, Sharkey? Mount up! Worse comes to worse we'll ditch the gold!" Adams said.

Adams, Beamer, Meeks, and Stott plus Sharkey and the pilot, loaded up in the black Huey with their stolen cargo. Sergeant Meeks was in the copilot seat. The chopper strained against the weight, but she lifted up and away toward the eastern horizon with little problem. As they cleared the tree-tops, First Sergeant Adams said, "In about thirty seconds there's gonna be one hell of an explosion!"

Mike was on the right-side 50-caliber machine gun, and Beamer had an M-60 scanning the left side. They were no more than 500 meters distant from the Mil-8T when an explosion of amazing intensity rocked the morning calm. Stott thought he could feel the concussion as he watched the 8T fragment into a million pieces. It disintegrated as the remaining fuel created a fireball several hundred feet high.

"Holy shit!" Sharkey exclaimed. "How much C-4 did you use, Top?"

"All we had! Musta been close to eighty pounds! Plus a lot of ammo that the Mil had on board," Adams confirmed.

"Plus half a tank of fuel!" Meeks yelled from the second seat. "Makes you want to avoid any hard landings with full fuel tanks, huh?"

As the black Huey screamed along over the treetops, Adams spoke to Beamer, JJ, and Mike. "We've been planning this first action for three years. We were 90 percent certain that Russian chopper would be loaded with cash, but we weren't absolutely sure. We left no trace of U.S. soldiers anywhere in Burma unless the gooks find our buried shit and analyze it! Now that we've confirmed what goes down in Pong Dai around harvest, we've got a plan for next year that will make this take seem like chicken feed. Hopefully, the Shan will blame the Russians or Chi-Coms or rival drug traders for today's raid. They have absolutely no reason to suspect U.S. involvement! Relax and enjoy the ride to Nha Trang! But keep a scan going with the guns. Let's not celebrate just yet!"

They arrived in Nha Trang two hours later without incident. First Sergeant Adams kept counting and recounting the contents of the Chinese duffel bags, right up until they touched down in Five Group headquarters. From time to time, he muttered, "Un-fucking believable!"

Colonel Besuden himself came out to the Huey to greet them along with Major Royalty. "Welcome home, men! How'd we do? Everybody okay?" Besuden asked.

"Colonel, you're not going to fucking believe it! Near as I can tell there's about six million dollars U.S. and maybe two million dollars in gold bars! No one saw us! No one fired a shot at us! It went just like we planned it!" Adams said.

"Kills?"

"Thirteen, confirmed. Should start an internal feud of some magnitude in Pong Dai," First Sergeant Adams told Besuden and Royalty through a grin.

As their commanding officer debriefed them, a crew refueled and serviced the Huey that had brought them back to Nha Trang. Major Royalty had actually brought out a duffel bag for JJ as well as about a dozen empty duffels. The empty bags were stenciled with white letters that read "U.S. Army—Official Records—To Be Opened By Authorized Personnel ONLY." Each duffel had a locking mechanism that secured the zippered top openings.

"Ready for a little R & R, Sergeant Sharkey?" Royalty asked him.

"Yes, sir! Let's roll!" JJ's enthusiasm made them all laugh. On the flight back to Nha Trang, Sharkey had explained to them that he was to accompany Major Royalty on "R & R" to safely deposit the proceeds of the raid in an affiliate of The Bank of Switzerland located in Hong Kong. The gold would be traded for U.S. dollars and 80 percent of the total, some $6.4 million would be equally deposited into twenty-two secret, eleven-digit accounts, one for each SPEND team member. The remaining 20 percent, $1.6 million, would be set aside in SPEND's master account to cover "expenses" including bribes to the bankers to ensure that their accounts were untraceable.

"Mikey, in a few days you'll be given an eleven-digit number to memorize. After January 15, 1975, your $290,900 plus interest, will be available to you to do with what you want! And this is our first raid! Can you believe it?" JJ had told Mike over the noise of the Huey's engine.

Frankly, Stott couldn't believe it. But he had seen the cash and gold with his own eyes. Mike was relieved to hear that Sharkey was accompanying Major Royalty to make the deposits. "It seems unreal, JJ. Watch your ass. I'm still trying to comprehend what we're into," Stott said to Sharkey.

"You did the heavy lifting, Mike! You and your C Team. We all owe you guys!" JJ said. "How many?"

Mike knew what JJ meant, but he made him clarify his question. "How many what, JJ?"

"You know what I mean, goddamn it! How many kills did you score?" JJ asked.

First Sergeant Adams's hearing continued to amaze Mike. He answered Sharkey's question. "Stott had five clean kills, Sergeant Sharkey. You can be proud of your buddy. I'll take him anywhere, anytime, on any black assignment we draw."

Sharkey surprised Adams and Mike by saying, "Goddamn it! Mikey's got over thirty kills, and I still haven't done anything but talk and translate!"

"Your time will come, Sergeant Sharkey! Your time will come!" Adams had gone back to his counting.

"You okay?" JJ asked Mike.

"Why wouldn't I be?" Mike responded.

Adams, Beamer, and Stott went back to Besuden's HQ bunker as the Huey carrying Major Royalty and Sergeant Sharkey roared away toward a rendezvous with a military airlift command or MACS flight to Thailand from which they would make their way to Hong Kong. The C Team sat in Besuden's bunker office and rehearsed the briefing they would give Besuden's staff. The content of the briefing reflected a successful reconnaissance mission to northern Thailand. There was even some truth in the debriefing story!

As First Sergeant Adams did the talking to Besuden's non-SPEND staff officers, Mike thought about the trip JJ was taking. If it all went according to plan, ten years from now he would have more money than his father made in ten years of hard work in a General Motors plant!

When the debriefing was complete, Adams, Beamer, Meeks, and Stott cleaned up and had their first real meal in six days. Mike had lost about ten pounds during the Burma adventure, but he felt great! And rich! When they returned from their showers to the bunker to crash for a while, another pleasant surprise awaited them. Four young and relatively attractive girls were waiting, in the nude. They were all Eurasians, most likely fathered by French soldiers, and two of the girls had green eyes! Mike's girl was named was Sosh, and she appeared to be older than the others. "JJ explained to us that you like older women, Stott! Enjoy!" Adams teased.

Mike did.

The next day, the C team returned to Lac Do where the remaining DOAT team members learned of the success of the mission. Captain Freeze summed it up best. "Absolutely un-fucking-believable, but just like we planned it! Mission one accomplished!"

The high spirits DOAT enjoyed due to the success of SPEND's first mission abruptly ended that evening. An estimated battalion-strength group of bad guys hit Lac Do at dusk and kept coming until dawn. Thirty-one Montagnard fighters were killed with another forty wounded. Ten women and seven children were killed with another dozen sustaining various levels of injures. Staff Sergeants Beamer and Barnett were wounded, though not seriously. WO Myers temporarily lost the hearing in his right ear due to concussion from a mortar shell that miraculously did not otherwise injure him.

The next morning, the confirmed body count of North Vietnamese regulars numbered more than 200. The wounded and removed dead must have been twice that many. The courage and resolve the Yards showed defending their village was simply astonishing. For some unknown reason, the enemy stopped their assault and melted back into the highland forest shortly before dawn.

Stott was on an M-60 that night, firing belt after belt of 7.62 rounds into the lines of VC that seemed to just keep coming. Enemy gunfire and mortar shells landed all around him, but he wasn't touched. A bizarre thought kept running through Mike's head all during the battle; how pissed off would JJ be when he heard Stott got more "kills"!

One month after arriving in Vietnam, Mike Stott had seen more combat than most men experienced in a twelve-month tour of duty. As DOAT braced for another night of attacks, he wondered if Sharkey had deposited their money in Hong Kong. He wondered if it mattered. It seemed highly unlikely to Stott that he would ever see JJ again, much less live to spend his money.

Stott helped Doc Brackett for a while on that awful day after the first battle that made Lac Do famous. Doc worked to exhaustion saving the lives of tribesmen and their wounded family members. Seeing and helping to treat the injured children was, for Mike, harder by far than the actual combat. The battles were surreal. The wounded, suffering children were very real and tested his mental resolve like nothing before.

Stott's team spent all day bracing for the attack that would surely continue as night fell. Captain Freeze had F-4s at the ready to help defend them on the second night of combat, but the soldiers from the north did not return.

In fact, Lac Do and the Day One A Team experienced a period of unusual calm for the next six months. DOAT helped the villagers of Lac Do construct a school, a clinic, and a meeting hooch for Chief Won's tribal council.

Word of DOAT's defense of Lac Do spread through the countryside. Several hundred additional tribesmen and their families from smaller, less defendable settlements around Lac Do sought shelter under Chief Won's protection. The expanded population of the town strained its infrastructure, especially the water supply. Doc Brackett became a full-time caregiver to Won's extended community and Staff Sergeant Meeks started teaching English to both the children and adults of Lac Do in the new school. Although Mike's main duty was to support their defensive and intelligence gathering endeavors, he found himself assisting Meeks in his so-called "off time." Stott's Hmong improved further as he conversed with the people in the village.

DOAT ran patrols around their extended perimeter constantly. Reconnaissance teams consisting of two or three DOAT team members and ten to twelve Yards fanned out in all directions on a random basis, focusing mainly to the north and northwest of Lac Do where they could monitor the activity on the many branches of the Ho Chi Minh Trail.

In a bizarre way, the men of the Day One A Team settled in to a kind of normal existence, if life in an active combat zone could ever be considered normal. Colonel Besuden organized their R & R so that they got a break every four months or so. As the junior member of DOAT, Mike's first leave came in July 1965.

Captain Freeze called him to HQ one Tuesday morning and said, "Stott, you need a break! Colonel Besuden is sending Sergeant Sharkey on a combination of business and R & R to Bangkok and we think you probably ought to go with him. Pack your stuff! A bird will pick you up at 1500 hours today and take you and Doc to Nha Trang.

Doc's on official business, and he can't go with you and JJ, so you'll have to take care of Sergeant Staffie yourself. By the way, you'll get a nice surprise from Major Royalty to liven up your trip. Take your .45 and ammo. You won't have any trouble keeping it with you because you're on MACS flights right into Bangkok. Watch your ass there. Try not to kill anybody, but if you have to, cover it up well. Just kidding! Have fun! See you in a week!"

Holy shit! R & R with JJ in Bangkok! No time to call Cindy!

Chapter Thirty-Nine

When Doc Brackett and Mike arrived at Nha Trang they received a stand-up salute from the headquarters staffies. "Best intel we get is from Freeze's guys at Lac Do," a young captain named Lykins told them. "Now that the regular army is here fucking up everything, nothing seems to be going right!"

Mike was surprised to see Sergeant Sharkey all packed and ready to go. "Come on, dickhead! We're on a flight to Da Nang in thirty minutes! Got you some new duds!"

JJ took Stott back to his hooch where he had three new sets of tailored khakis for him. They were made of officer-grade material and fit him perfectly! There were also two new pairs of the shiniest jump boots Mike had ever seen and two new green berets.

"How'd you get these to fit me so well?" Mike asked Sharkey.

"Sosh took your measurements during your last visit! Be careful who you sleep with! Shower and let's go!"

Stott managed to shave and shower in ten minutes. JJ and Mike were humping out to the flight line when Major Royalty double-timed up beside them. "Here you go boys! Have a good time! Remember what I told you, JJ! No more than a thousand home!" Royalty handed them each an envelope. "Get a blow job for me and bring it home!"

Sharkey and Stott sat away from the four other troopers that were also going on R & R from Nha Trang. Careful not to be observed, they opened their envelopes. Each contained fifty hundred-dollar bills.

"Holy shit!" Mike said to JJ.

"Colonel Besuden told me to tell you not to send more than $1,000 home, Mike. We could put another $1,000 to $1,500 in a regular banking account, but we need to spend the rest! Think we can do that, dickhead?" Sharkey said.

"Holy shit! Yes!"

Sharkey then produced a fifth of Crown Royal whiskey from his traveling bag and two crystal tumblers! "Where the hell did you get the glasses, JJ?" Mike asked.

"Same place we get the booze! Trading with the ROKS! Here's to R & R! Before I get too drunk, let me fill you in on those dickheads we were in basic with!"

JJ talked nonstop through the two MACS flights that took them to Bangkok. He began, "Here's the big news! George Washington Dickhead Howard just graduated from Officer's Candidate School at Benning! He's a fucking second lieutenant! He wrote me a letter and said he expects the snappiest of salutes from both of us next time he sees us! We're gonna have to fucking salute that dickhead!

"Big Howie just got assigned to a first cavalry unit as an airborne infantry platoon leader! He'll be in Nam by the end of the year! Maybe as early as October!" JJ said.

"Howard's a fucking officer! I can't believe it! Seriously, JJ, that shows me Howie is a right guy. You know how hard they must have been on him at OCS!" Stott said.

"Yeah, you're right about that! He was the only black guy in his class. He also said that he thinks about our 'pact' all the time. Not letting us down got him through to his gold bar! Imagine that big dickhead as a grunt platoon leader! He's gonna make one hell of a big target!" JJ said. "Mikey, we heard you did us proud again at Lac Do during the big assault. All the troopers know your name. I am so proud of you."

Stott didn't know what to say, so he changed the subject. "Heard from anybody else?"

"Sure, everybody except Smeall, and Fast Eddy tells me about him! Hale must have a lot of time on his hands in his cushy job at the Pentagon; he writes often. Says he's banging that broad we went to languages school with, Major Stroth! His commanding officer! You know Hale! Always full of shit! But he's got a top security clearance and he has access to all kinds of stuff. Hale says Barry Smeall got discharged from active duty in June. He's back in Pittsburgh with a wife and a kid on the way! That intel he got from Mobliano's sister, whose mom, Maria, talks with Bessie Smeall."

"Which sister?" Mike asked.

"Oh, still thinking about Briggetta, huh? Hale says he talks to both of them and that they ask about us. Can you believe Smeall is a civilian with a wife and a kid coming?"

"So you must have word on Mobliano, too," Stott said.

"Yep! He's now married and living the good life in Manhattan! Hale said he stopped in the Hay-Adams bar a while back and asked about us. His wife's dad is some big-shot politician. Mobs is getting involved in New York City politics with him, just like he said he wanted to do. He'll probably be a senator someday, but we're gonna make more money!" JJ said.

"Hope we live to enjoy it," Stott said.

"Come on, asshole! Of course we will! We're in the sweetest spot in the world!"

Mike stared at JJ in amazement. "You really believe that? You think we're in a sweet spot? Man, JJ! You need to come do a little time in Lac Do! I think that might change your mind!"

"I want to! But Colonel Besuden says I'm too valuable as an interpreter! I get to go to most of the other A Team sites, though! I tell you, Mikey, Lac Do is where it's at!"

"That leaves Allsmeir. Any word on him?" Mike asked.

JJ nearly choked on his Royal Crown as he laughed out loud. "Remember how Allsmeir was so negative on the army and how he hated being posted to Fort Sill? Guess what! He got re-assigned to the Big Red One, and he's 'in country' right now! He's a Spec Four on a 155 squad at a new firebase under construction up in R Sector! He arrived about ten days ago! The regular army guys are on one year tours, so, unless Allsmeir gets an 'early,' he'll have his active duty extended by a few months! Can you imagine that sissy in a combat zone?"

"Allsmeir wasn't so bad, JJ. But you're right! I bet he's one miserable son-of-a-bitch right about now! So, you, me, and

Allsmeir are in Vietnam, and Howie's on the way! Smeall's
a civilian and Mobs is weekend warrior! Think Hale will be
permanently posted to the Pentagon? He was in for six years,
right?" Stott asked Sharkey.

"Who cares?" JJ said. "I never liked that smart-ass son
of a bitch! I think I'll kick his ass next time I see him just
on general principles! Mikey, do you know how rich we're
gonna get?"

"JJ, I feel rich already, but I'm worried about living to
spend what we've already got! Ten years is a long time!"
Stott said.

"We play our cards right and stay here in Nam, we'll be E-
7s by then, maybe even E-8s! We ought to get our rockers by
year's end! The colonel is gonna take care of us!" Sharkey
told his friend.

"You have no fear about doing what we're doing, JJ?"
Mike asked.

"Mikey! What have we got to lose?" JJ said it with absolute sincerity. "We're about to party in Bangkok with unlimited funds! We're in the best damn unit in all the U.S.
military! You want to be back in the states writing English
compositions for some sorry-ass faggot professor to yell at
you about? Come on, man! Let's live!"

As he listened, Mike realized he was still trapped in thinking about a return to normalcy at some point in the future.
Part of him knew that would never be possible.

"So what's next for SPEND, JJ? Heard anything?" Stott
asked.

"As a matter of fact, I have! That Burmese town you guys
scored in, Pong Dai, is just one of several banking centers
where big bucks change hands at harvest time. There's a
North Vietnamese town called Dong San just north of the
DMZ right on their border with Laos. Actually, it's right on
the border with the South, too. Major Royalty says Dong
San is becoming the biggest of the dollars-for-dope banking centers around the Triangle because Ho Chi Minh gives
his personal protection guarantee to all sides for a piece of

the action. Plus, it's real close to the South China Sea. San pans can ferry the heroin down a river and out to third world freighters in open water. No port involved!"

"JJ, stop! Whoa! Hold on! Beamer, Adams, and I just got back from a recon right in that area! Hell! I could've picked off targets on the outskirts of town! Took us a week to hump back to a pickup zone on this side of the border," Stott told his buddy.

"Hello, Earth to Mikey! I know that! That piece of the trail you guys filed the intel on when you returned is about five clicks south of where we're going to score big time this harvest season!" Sharkey said. "What was up there?"

"Not much, just a lot of bad guys. Very tough terrain along the three borders there. We got in and out with no problem. Beaucoup arms for Charlie coming right through those mountain passes!" Stott said.

"Well, Mikey me boy, remember that area well! This January DOAT will be there, setting up a really big takedown! Colonel says I may get to go along because the language intel is so important. Not that your Mandarin isn't improving! You got a slant broad up there in Lac Do teaching you the lingo?" JJ asked.

"Maybe! But how come you know all this and we don't?" Stott asked.

"Major Freeze and WO Myers know! And now, so do you! Mikey, now that the 3rd/3rd Marines and the regular army units are arriving in force, we've got access to air support like you wouldn't believe! B-52s out of Guam, F-4s out of Phuket, and even jarhead pilots off carriers in the gulf are gonna be there to support us! We're gonna kick some serious ass! And get rich! Have another tumbler of Crown!" JJ said.

"I would, JJ, but you drank it all! Are you carrying?" Mike asked.

"Of course, dickhead! Forgot to show you!" JJ went back into his traveling bag and pulled out a Smith & Wesson .357 Magnum revolver with a four-inch barrel and black rubber grips.

"What do you think of this?" JJ asked Mike.

"Good belly gun. Can you hit anything with it?"

"Fuckin' A! Wait a minute, though." Sharkey reached into his bag again and pulled out another, identical .357.

"Here, this one's for you! Think you can hit anything with it?" JJ retorted.

"This one's mine?" Stott asked.

"Don't I always take care of you, Mikey? Yeah, that one's yours. Cost me a case of Cutty Sark each, so be grateful!" John said.

"Cool! Thanks! But now I've got two pistols 'cause Freeze told me to bring my .45!"

"Don't try to one-up me, goddamn it!" JJ said. Again, he reached in his bag and produced two fragmentation grenades.

"Just in case we need some excitement!" JJ said.

Mike just shook his head. At least Sharkey had the pull-pins taped down for the flight.

"Any other surprises, JJ?" he asked.

"Yeah, one more. But you'll have to wait 'til Bangkok for that one! I'm gonna take a quick nap. Wake me up just before we land!" Sharkey was instantly snoring.

Mike looked out the window of the C-130 into total darkness. The MACS flight they had connected to in Da Nang was starting its decent into what he presumed was Bangkok. There were no lights visible on the ground. Looking out the eastern side of the plane, Stott could see a glimmer of first light and looked at his watch. It was July 14, 1965, 0530 hours. Sharkey and Stott had been in the army for two years and three days.

Mike's family wrote him lots of letters to keep him posted about life back in the world, as soldiers referred to the states. He even got letters from Kathy Giuseppe and, of course, Cindy. For some reason, answering those letters was very difficult for him. He realized that he no longer felt much of a connection to the civilian world. To Mike's surprise, he had never really felt homesick since joining the army. Not even in the beginning back at Fort Dix. In basic training, some of the young soldiers had actually cried for home.

Stott thought over what JJ had told him about their five buddies from basic training. The thought of Barry Smeall about to become a father was far more frightening to Mike than being in Five Group. And Sharkey was right about college too. What John and Mike had experienced over the past two years made any other experience boring and mundane. And now he and JJ were about to land in exotic Thailand!

But it wasn't their first time in that country! They had landed in Phuket, Thailand, on their way to Vietnam. And Stott had been in Laos! And Burma! Mike had $5,000 in his kakis and nearly $300,000 in his Swiss account. Mike thought about the number of men he had killed in the past seven months. All bad guys, enemies of his country.

The only negative thing Mike could think of on that Wednesday morning as he and Sharkey approached Bang-kok was having to salute Big Howie when they saw him!

Now that was aggravating!

Chapter Forty

JJ and Mike spent five fantastic days in Bangkok partying as only young soldiers going back to a combat zone could. They rented a suite of rooms in an old, traditional Thai hotel not far from the royal palace. The boys also rented four of the most gorgeous young Thai girls one could imagine. Five dollars a day got them the pick of the working ladies. Mike and JJ had no trouble spending more than a thousand dollars each on their R & R. For five days, they drank, ate, and screwed, literally around the clock.

When they first got to the hotel, JJ gave the hotel manager a hundred dollar bill and said, "Four of your best and no pimps, get it? My friend here has no problem killing pimps, so don't fuck with us! We'll pay the girls directly, and we want rooms with dead bolts! Got it?"

Alone in their suite waiting for the girls and sipping on two fresh bottles of Crown Royal, Mike asked Sharkey, "So how'd you know about this place? And what was that spiel about no pimps?"

"This is Colonel Besuden's favorite Bangkok whorehouse. He said we'd have to pay double for the girls unless we played tough, which we have no trouble doing!"

When the girls arrived, the prettiest of the lot, who called herself Patti, said in Chinese to her three partners, "These two are young! Maybe we can get them to take us out where we can take all their money!" Never suspecting that Stott and Sharkey understood her every word, she gave them the most radiant of smiles as she plotted against the boys with her friends.

Sharkey spun her around, looked her in the eye and put his .357 pistol against her temple. In his perfect Cantonese, JJ said, "Bad start. Don't make me kill you. Want to stay or go back downstairs?"

It was the first time Mike had seen John act that way. He absolutely terrified the girls.

"He speaks Cantonese!" the one called Rita said. "We thought you were just dumb Americans!"

"One more crack about Americans and I will kill you all on general principles. What'll it be ladies? Stay or go?" Sharkey asked.

They stayed four days. JJ and Mike never slept at the same time. Mike thought Sharkey actually hoped Patti would try something. JJ never got over her original scheme.

On their last day of leave, JJ and Mike wired money back to his brother in Ohio with instructions to deposit their "army pay" in savings accounts in the 5/3 Bank in Cincinnati. Each opened two accounts and put $1,000 in both of them. Later, they received letters from Mike's parents congratulating them for being so frugal with their army pay. Those letters made the soldiers laugh out loud.

Sharkey and Stott caught a MACS flight out of Bangkok's main airport on July 20, 1965, and arrived in Da Nang in time to shuttle back to Nha Trang the same day. Both slept all the way back.

Mike overnighted at base camp and arrived back in Lac Do the following morning. Major Freeze told him he looked like he'd lost ten pounds. "Son, you better come back on duty and rest up! You okay on line tonight, or are you all worn out?"

"I'm fine Maj! Good to go! Charlie still quiet?" Stott asked.

"Has been. In ten days we need you back on recon up towards Dong San again. Looks like that will be SPEND's next target. WO Myers is going with you, Adams, and Meeks. What's your eleven digit account again?" Freeze teased.

Mike just smiled. Stott knew his Swiss account number and Sharkey's. John J. Sharkey, however, had memorized nineteen SPEND members' account numbers. Only Besuden and Royalty knew them all.

"Range open?" Mike asked. "I need to sharpen up, sir."

"Hey! I'll go with you!" said Freeze.

Major Freeze and Stott spent several hours firing and cleaning weapons. "So, did you miss us back here in Lac Do while you were on R & R?" Freeze asked. He was staring intently at Mike as he asked the question.

"Actually, Major, I did. I found myself thinking more about Lac Do than that world! Does that happen to you too?" asked Mike.

"Happens to all of us who were meant to be soldiers, Sergeant. Welcome back home!"

Mike settled back into the routine of walking the security lines at night and working around Lac Do during the day. All the soldiers slept erratic patterns, catching two hours here and three hours there between their other duties. Once, and sometimes twice, a month, Mike went on extended recon missions of varying distances and duration. These were based on the assignments DOAT got from Nha Trang and their need to monitor the perimeter.

Between August and mid-December 1965, all of the men of the Day One A Team pulled several recons in the Dong San area, mostly on the north side of the DMZ that in theory separated North and South Vietnam. Every one of them became familiar with the roads and paths in and out of Dong San. The soldiers from North Vietnam seemed totally focused on the DMZ geography. They didn't suspect that American soldiers would be on their side of the border. Skirting around their lines and patrols became a familiar maneuver. DOAT's mission was not to engage the enemy, but rather to monitor his movements and the southward flow of supplies on the Ho Chi Minh Trail.

DOAT team members were all amazed and concerned with the ever-increasing volume of those supplies. From rice to mortar shells, supplies from the north seemed to constantly ooze across the border.

The rainy season in 1965 was rated normal by the army's weathermen. It seemed pretty extreme to those men who were living in it. For months, they never really got dry or clean.

DOAT members all shaved their heads and bodies as they fought the leeches and other parasites that were ever present. Returning from five to fifteen day recon patrols, the men routinely cut off soiled fatigues and deloused. Touching the parasites with heat from a cigarette lighter or match usually caused the ticks and leeches to extract their claws and teeth cleanly. If the soldiers pulled them off, the teeth and claws left behind were sure to cause infection.

DOAT endured the difficult conditions and performed its missions with dedication and, most of the time, enthusiasm. In December 1965, Mike celebrated his first year as a Five Group shooter. When he turned twenty on December 20, Stott felt as seasoned as the rest the team.

Mike had gone on another five day R & R with Doc Brackett in mid November. He had a good time, but it was not like the experience with JJ in July. Stott and Doc had become really good friends; all of DOAT had closely bonded during Mike's year with the team. Occasionally, one of the guys still referred to Stott as "kid," but he had done at least his share of the heavy lifting—and more than his share of the killing.

On December 22, 1965, Mike Stott was promoted to E-6, staff sergeant, after only thirty months in the army. Regular army guys usually waited at least twice that long before getting an E-6 slot. Unfortunately, Staff Sergeant John J. Sharkey sent Mike a message via a supply chopper that read: *Congratulations! I got my rocker last week! Actually, ours came through on the same day, but I had one of the officers hold yours back a week! I'm still the senior Staff Sergeant in our pact and don't you forget it! Happy birthday! Hope to see you over Xmas.*

Mike received a long letter from Cindy just before his birthday that asked among other things when she could meet him for R & R. He wrote her back that maybe they could meet in Hawaii in the spring. Stott's parents and family sent packages with homemade chocolate-chip cookies and other goodies to both Mike and JJ for Christmas. The cookies were pretty broken up, but all his DOAT teamies enjoyed them anyway.

As during the previous Christmas in Nam, Colonel Besuden made the rounds to many of his A Team locations,
spreading holiday cheer. Besuden, Major Royalty, Staff Sergeant John J. Sharkey, and a fourth man Stott had never seen
before arrived on the colonel's Huey early on Christmas Eve
1965 and stayed until 1200 hours the next day.

The fourth visitor was a CIA operative named, of course,
Jim Smith. In his time with DOAT, Smith said almost nothing but listened carefully to DOAT's recounting of their many
recons to Dong San. Smith appeared to be old for a spook
fieldman. Mike guessed him to be pushing fifty.

When they were introduced, he looked Stott in the eye and
said, "Knew your brother. One of the best. Do him proud."

Charlie stayed quiet over the holiday. On Christmas morning, eight DOAT men sat down with their visitors to discuss
an upcoming deployment. Beamer and Adams walked the
line during the meeting; DOAT never left security totally to
the Yards.

Colonel Besuden briefed them. "You've now all met
Smith. He wore a green hat until a year ago. Now he's a government guy. I vouch for him. Jim's been in SPEND since
the beginning. We were set to go to Burma again this harvest, but something else has come up. You all know we had a
long, wet monsoon. Last summer was the one of the hottest
and sunniest summers ever in the Triangle. This year's poppy
crop is the best in twenty years. They started harvesting and
processing early. Intel has it that Dong San is where it's at
this year for deal making. Seems there was a little trouble in
Pong Dai last year!"

That brought a cheer from the assembled group.

"Jim," Colonel Besuden gave the floor to the CIA man.

Mr. Smith spoke. "A feud of some magnitude broke out
over a certain lost Russian helicopter last year. Security from
all sides in and around Pong Dai is quadrupled this year. Just
too hot to go back. That feud has pushed a lot of the cash
exchange to Dong San. Security there is also extremely tight

now, as you men know firsthand. So we've put together what I would characterize as an extreme plan. Reasonable odds of success, but we can only do something like this once."

For the next two hours, Besuden, Royalty, and Smith explained the opportunity. It made last year's raid on Pong Dai seem like a Boy Scout outing. The scope of the operation that Besuden and Smith described was mind-numbing.

"All right men. I know it's off the charts, but it will work! I'm asking all of you to commit right now. Language interception and interpretation is absolutely critical. Sergeant Sharkey has volunteered to join DOAT to facilitate information interception effective immediately. He's staying here now. Everybody in?" Besuden demanded.

Mike looked at JJ, who was grinning ear to ear.

"Staff Sergeant Stott?"

"In, Colonel," Mike said.

Besuden went around the room. Only Doc Brackett hesitated. "Doc, yes or no? No hard feelings, but if you aren't certain you reassign to Nha Trang immediately. Your team needs a medic."

"I'm in, sir. But holy shit!" Doc had the balls to say what they were all thinking. It was the opportunity of a lifetime. So was the risk.

"Okay. Done. Smith stays here too. It will go down sometime during January, most likely toward the end of the month. Try to get rested. Let's hope Chuck stays quiet. Any questions?" asked the colonel.

"Colonel Besuden, why did Sharkey get his rocker before me? I'll never hear the end of it!" Mike's question lightened the air. Everyone laughed.

"Submitted at the same time, Stott. Guess the alphabet got you!" said Besuden.

Besuden and Royalty left on the Huey just before 1200 hours Christmas Day. Smith bunked in with Major Freeze, and JJ set up in Stott's hooch with Beamer and Meeks. Freeze and Smith brought Beamer and Adams up to speed on the new SPEND mission.

When First Sergeant Adams returned to their hooch from his briefing, he said, "HOLY SHIT!" as he entered the bunker.

Christmas night, Charlie sent a small squad of sappers against DOAT's western berm and dropped several rockets in the vicinity of where Besuden's Huey had landed and departed earlier. Lac Do suffered no casualties but did kill five gooks. One of the VC they shot that night was a girl no more than twenty years old. Mike was pretty sure he'd seen her in Lac Do, but that surprised no one. Chief Won had her head placed on a pole in the center of the village. Three of the girl's family members disappeared from Lac Do that night. DOAT took it to mean that Chief Won was still on their side.

Chapter Forty-One

It was good to have JJ in Lac Do, but Mike had a lot to teach him in terms of how DOAT worked together in the field. Helms, Major Freeze, and Stott went to the range with Sharkey the day after Christmas. John was steady and good as ever.

"Staff Sergeant Sharkey, you're good on the targets, but have you shot anyone yet?" Helms asked.

"No, First Sergeant, I have not. Don't worry about me. I'll have no problem killing bad guys!" JJ said.

"Okay, Sarge. If you're half as steady as your buddy here, you'll do fine. Shadow Stott on tonight's perimeter patrol. Watch his movements." Freeze directed.

Mike could see that Major Freeze's direction to "shadow" him irked JJ. Back in their hooch, Sharkey said, "Mike, I've been in country the same time as you and I haven't really been in the shit yet except that first night in Nha Trang, and you did all the shooting. How many?"

JJ was still obsessed with the number of enemy his friend had killed.

"I'm not positive, JJ. More than a hundred. But the individual, targeted kills are the ones that count. Eleven of those. I guess maybe another fifty or sixty kills defending our perimeter." Stott said.

"Eleven! No shit! I know about the five in Burma, but where did you get the others?" John asked.

"JJ, you know we go on recon all the time. When conditions are right, we kill VC. It's no big deal," Mike told him.

JJ and Mike sat and stared at each other for several minutes. "No problems with it?" Sharkey asked.

The cold fact was that killing enemy soldiers, male or female, did not bother Stott at all.

"No, JJ. None," Mike confirmed.

"Are we, you know, winning the hearts and minds of the Hmong villagers here in Lac Do?" Sharkey asked his buddy.

That was an oft discussed subject among the men of DOAT. "I don't know, JJ. My guess is that, right now, we're simply the lesser of two evils. Compared to the Vietcong, we try hard to do good for the people of Lac Do. But, between you and me, I think they will be thrilled when we're gone. What's the intel you hear from the marines and regular army units? Are the ARVN's measuring up?" Mike asked.

"Hell no! It's up to the U.S. to win this war! The army of the South is corrupt and inept! The ARVN officer core is more concerned with profiting from the war than winning it! Half of them stay hopped up on heroin or smoking dope. Looks like Westmoreland will be asking for beaucoup more American GI's to make this thing work," JJ said.

"Well, get some sleep. We're on line tonight, and there's some things I need to show you." Stott said.

"Hey, where's Dickhead?" JJ asked.

"He disappeared while I was on an extended recon. Hmongs probably ate him. He was the fattest dog in the village," Mike said.

"No shit? You think they ate him?" JJ was dumbfounded.

"Yeah, JJ, I do. We're not in Manhattan, you know! I couldn't leave him with a doorman for safe keeping!"

"Man! Remember our Labor Day in New York? What a time! You fell in love with the Mobliano girls!" JJ said.

"Yeah, and you lusted after Smeall's mom! I'll never forget when you started speaking Chinese at the New Peking! And the look on Allsmeir's face!" Stott said.

"And how about Ranger school? Was that fun or what?" JJ said.

"Only good day I recall from Ranger training was at graduation when you challenged Captain Gonzalez! Now that, I'll never forget!" Mike said.

"That motherfucker! I'd like to run into him again here!" JJ said.

"And what would you do, JJ? He is an American officer!"

Staff Sergeant John J. Sharkey, Mike's best friend, looked him in the eye and said, "Kill him, of course."

Stott knew he meant it. "Just don't get caught, JJ," was all Mike said.

During the first two weeks of January 1966, the men of DOAT, including Staff Sergeant Sharkey and their spook, Jim Smith, readied for the mission to Dong San. They went over the details of the plan again and again. Every team member knew his individual assignment as well as every other team member's job. DOAT memorized the maps of the area. They practiced their Hmong. DOAT would communicate only in Hmong from the time they deployed until they returned.

As the middle of the month approached, Stott and his teammates were on edge, anticipating the mission. Colonel Besuden was bringing in a backup A Team, non-SPEND of course, to remain in Lac Do while DOAT went north. On January 19, 1966, Major Freeze talked to his men in groups of two or three where he found them at their duty stations. "We go tomorrow, men. Colonel Besuden and the backup A will be here in three hours. Saddle up."

"At last!" JJ exclaimed. "I couldn't have waited much longer! Hooah!"

"Stay cool, Sergeant Sharkey. This may not be as much fun as you think!" Freeze said.

Besuden's Huey and a Sikorsky brought the backup troopers from base camp at 1530 hours. Major Freeze, WO Myers, and Master Sergeant Dunigan began briefing the replacements about their responsibilities at Lac Do. Interestingly, the backup team was comprised of more officers than enlisted men. Sharkey knew most of them from Nha Trang. The backups knew only that DOAT was going on an extended reconnaissance mission.

A baby-faced lieutenant named Pike brought the mail around to DOAT.

"Hey, Sergeant Sharkey! How you doing! We miss you at the poker table. Other guys are actually winning! Looks like you got more mail than the rest of the guys up here combined!" First Lieutenant Pike handed JJ a stack of mail.

"Good to see you, sir! You're not moving in on any of my girlfriends while I'm gone, are you?" JJ asked.

Pike laughed. "Sergeant, who'd want your girlfriends? Have a good field trip! Have you put on weight out here in the boonies?"

"Sir, no sir! Just added muscle, working! This isn't a plushy base camp, sir!" JJ said.

"Good luck, Sharkey! You, too, Sergeant Stott! Watch out for your buddy!" Pike said.

After Pike left their bunker, JJ said, "Fuckin' Pointers! You know they earn their berets at a shorter school, right?"

"No, how would I know that? You're the guy who sees all the group stuff, staffie!" Mike said.

"I'm NOT a goddamn staffie! Don't make me kick your ass before this mission!" JJ said.

Sharkey was opening his mail as they talked. Mike was cleaning his sniper rifle for the umpteenth time when JJ said, "Damn."

Sharkey handed Stott a letter from Fast Eddy Hale.

John,

I don't know if you heard, but Larry Allsmeir was killed in action on November 20, 1965. His firebase came under heavy attack that night, and Allsmeir's bunker apparently took a direct rocket hit. His body arrived back in the states just before the holidays. Major Stroth let me off to attend the funeral in Boston. Saddest thing I've ever seen. His folks were absolutely devastated. I'd never been to a Jewish funeral before and I didn't know what to do. I guess there's really no difference in funerals. Just sadness and grief. Syl Mobliano showed up at the funeral too. When we introduced ourselves to his folks, they knew our names and asked about all of us that were buddies in basic. I was really sur-

prised that they even knew about us, but they said Larry wrote to them about us all.

Mobs and I both just lost it and cried our eyes out talking to Allsmeir's parents. I rode back to New York with Mobs, and we talked all the way about how the seven of us had become friends at Fort Dix. Mobs and I agreed that he and I and Smeall had really lucked out at not having to serve in Vietnam. We pray that you and Stott make it through your tours and get home safe to the states. We also talked about Second Lieutenant George Washington Howard, who I'm sure you know is in Vietnam now with the First Cavalry. We prayed for him, too, of course. Mobs said he thought Big Howie making it through OCS was almost as hard as what you and Stott went through to earn your berets. I doubt that, but then, Mobs is an officer.

Tell you the truth, Mobs and I each feel guilty that you guys are serving in Vietnam while we didn't have to. I guess I could get assigned to an intel unit in Nam, but right now that doesn't look likely. Frankly, if the U.S. is still in Vietnam when it's time to re-up, I'm getting out.

On a brighter note, Smeall is now the proud father of a baby girl!

Mobs and I send you our best. He said he'd write you, too, but asked me to say that. Tell Stott to keep his head down. Looks like he's really in the shit up where he's at. Maybe you guys can hook up with Big Howie over there for a visit. Remember, you're going to have to salute him!

Spec Five Ed Hale

PS: I still have the Pontiac. I think of you guys every time I get in it.

Mike read Hale's letter a second time, and then read it again. He handed the letter back to JJ. The two friends sat there, absorbing the news about Allsmeir, trying to keep their composure.

Finally, JJ said, "Allsmeir's the first guy I really know who got killed over here. We lost two men from another A Team down south, but I had only just met them."

"I mentioned him before you handed me Hale's letter. I was still thinking about that night at the New Peking as you were opening your mail. What lousy luck! Here we are in the shit by choice and all Larry wanted to do was get back to graduate school. Have you heard that the new firebases are getting hit a lot?" Mike asked Sharkey.

"Yeah. Constructing those outlying firebases is like saying to Charlie, 'Here we are! Come attack us!' The ones I've seen are really vulnerable to rockets and even mortars 'cause they don't keep wide fields of fire and run constant patrols like we do," Sharkey said.

"Think Hale will get a tour over here, JJ?" Mike asked.

"Probably not! Long as he keeps his CO girlfriend happy! How old was Allsmeir, Mikey?"

"I think twenty-five, maybe twenty-six. Wonder if Big Howie knows about Allsmeir?"

"Probably not, until someone writes to tell him. Damn! We need to shake this off! We're going north!" JJ said.

"I'm going to write to his folks when we get back, JJ. You should, too," Mike said.

"Deal. Now, let's go kick some gook ass and get richer!" Sharkey said.

It occurred to Mike that this was JJ's first real mission "in the shit." Stott wondered how it would affect him.

"JJ, don't be a hero. We've got a good plan; just do your job. We want to get back for another Bangkok R & R, right?" Mike advised.

"Goddamn it, Mikey! You've made your mark! I still got to prove myself!" John said.

"JJ, you don't have to prove shit! You're here in a combat zone with the Special Forces! Stay cool, or I'll kick your ass!"

Mike and JJ's intellectual discussion was interrupted by Master Dunigan. "Good to go, boys? You didn't pack a pillow, did you Sergeant Sharkey? I know you Nha Trang troopers are used to the good life!"

Not even Staff Sergeant John J. Sharkey would smart-mouth back to a master sergeant. "No, Master Dunigan, no pillow! And remember, I'm a DOAT trooper now! Not a staffie!"

Dunigan just smiled. "Hump it, boys! Choppers are waiting!"

As darkness descended on Lac Do, Vietnam on January 19, 1966 all eleven DOAT team members, including Sergeant John J. Sharkey and CIA spook Jim Smith, loaded up in three blacked-out Hueys and headed north.

The mission was code named "Out of Bounds." DOAT had organized into three four-man "C" Teams. Alpha Team was led by Major Freeze, supported by First Sergeants Helms and Brackett with Staff Sergeant John Sharkey functioning as communications NCO. Warrant Officer Myers headed up Bravo Team with First Sergeant Adams, Staff Sergeant Barnett, and the CIA man Jim Smith. Delta Team consisted of Master Sergeant Dunigan and Staff Sergeants Beamer, Meeks, and Stott.

The Hueys flew to a rallying point on a high clearing just south of the border between North and South Vietnam. DOAT and the Huey pilots secured the LZ and waited for the radio signal that would confirm that two divisions of ARVN soldiers had started their pre-Lunar New Year's thrust toward the border with the North. The ARVN troops moved northwest from their staging area outside Dong Ho just after midnight on January 19. It was DOAT's hope that the ARVN offensive would divert most, if not all, of the North Vietnamese Regular Army units strung out along the border toward the southeast away from Dong San, and operation "Out of Bounds."

At 0300 hours on January 20, 1966, the Hueys dropped the C Teams into three preselected areas inside Laos just across the border from North Vietnam. Alpha landed closest to the Bon Hai River with teams Bravo and Delta getting out two and four miles farther north. All three teams were within five miles of their objective, Dong San.

Like their insertion on the Burmese border a year earlier, troopers got out quickly and watched the choppers streak back into Laos to hug the border and then cross into South Vietnam on their way home to Nha Trang. DOAT dug in, hoping that their arrival had gone undetected.

By 0500 hours, all three teams were moving steadily, cautiously toward Dong San. Major Freeze estimated that they crossed into North Vietnam right at first light around 0600 hours. Alpha Team was the closest to Dong San.

In perfect Hmong, Stott heard Sharkey confirm Alpha's position on his radio, "In sight." By 0700 hours, Bravo and Delta were positioned and camouflaged, waiting. So far, so good. Now DOAT needed a little luck.

At 0900 hours on January 20, 1966, Colonel Besuden, commanding officer of the Fifth Special Forces Group in Nha Trang, Vietnam, hooked up to General Westmoreland's command center in Da Nang. Besuden reported that Five Group had a stranded A Team returning from reconnaissance in Laos that needed help. Besuden reported that his A Team was cut off from returning through Laos by a division of North Vietnamese Regular Army that had crossed into Laos to intercept them. Colonel Besuden further stated that he believed the best option to rescue his A Team was to saturate bomb the North Vietnamese border village of Dong San, creating a "wiped-out" corridor of retreat that would allow his troopers to cross back into South Vietnam by skirting just west of the target area.

Westmoreland's staff was, of course, focused on the ARVN exploratory thrust north of Dong Ho. The plan was that the offensive would catch the NVA (North Vietnamese Army) off guard and allow the ARVN's a much needed battlefield victory. Colonel Besuden explained that the stranded A Team were the same troopers who had successfully defended Lac Do in mid-1965.

Besuden requested the support of B-52s to attack Dong San with 1000-pound bombs. He further requested that F-4s out of Phuket "get in the air" after the B-52s had done their job to help clear the path back across the border. Besuden reminded Westmoreland's staff that such a strike would undoubtedly cause the NVA to redeploy at least some of their troops away from the ARVN offensive, increasing the odds of success for that endeavor.

The colonel ended his request with the following, "We owe it to my boys to help them get home. Let's show Uncle Ho just what the B-52s can do and make an example of Dong San! Let's make those bastards look up as well as sideways to see what's coming next! We need to do this NOW!"

The success of SPEND's mission, "Out of Bounds," depended on the decision from Westmoreland. If they got no saturation bombing of Dong San, DOAT would cross back into Laos and work its way back to one of several possible pickup LZ's over the next few days. If the ploy worked, and Westmoreland gave the go-ahead for the first really big B-52 deployment on the northern side of the border, DOAT would go into bombed-out Dong San and raid four pre-selected dollars-for-drugs "banks" identified by CIA intelligence.

During DOAT's previous reconnaissance missions to Dong San, they had identified these locations and mapped the entire area. If the B-52s were deployed and hit the pre-selected targets with sufficient bomb tonnage, "Out of Bounds" could work. The three DOAT teams waited outside Dong San, North Vietnam, to see if the bombers would be deployed.

As Mike lay in the lowland jungle grass just outside Dong San with Dunigan, Beamer, and Meeks, he pondered their fate. His stomach churned in anticipation of the action about to commence. Even if the bombers did not deploy, and they retreated through Laos, DOAT was in for several tough days.

If the B-52s bombed Dong San, they would need a lot of things to go their way if they were to be successful.

Stott wondered how Sharkey was feeling. Was he still excited? Or was he scared and excited, like himself? Or was JJ scared shitless now that he was really "in the shit"? Mike looked down at his black-taped dog tags. If he had been killed last year in Burma, no one would ever have known what happened to him. Adams, Beamer, Meeks, and Stott would have been just four more MIA's. This time they were "official." Their dog tags were black-taped to keep them from reflecting light and to keep them silent.

Superstition prevented Mike from thinking too much about what DOAT might find in Dong San. The fantastic sum recovered from the Russian helicopter had been far more than Stott could have imagined, but he now understood that Colonel Besuden had CIA assets working for them. The Golden Triangle growers had had the best poppy harvest in twenty years. According to Jim Smith's CIA information, this was the highest volume sales week of the season for the opium growers, just before the Lunar New Year on January 21. Allegedly, Dong San was filled with drug buyers from all over the world, basking in Ho Chi Minh's protection.

Mike thought of their operational agreement for "Out of Bounds." "If we get in, kill it if it moves. Do not hesitate. We must get in and get out and leave no trail behind us! Agreed?" Colonel Besuden had said.

"Agreed," they had all confirmed.

However, Besuden was back in the relative safety of Nha Trang. He was probably drinking coffee and waiting for the decision that would dictate DOAT's next move. Invade a bombed-out Dong San, or hightail it back across the border into Laos and wait for another opportunity.

Stott began to think about the concept of borders as he lay there in the bush in North Vietnam. During the briefing, when Besuden, Royalty, and Smith had described "Out of Bounds," Smith had referred to the point where Laos, North Vietnam, and South Vietnam came together as the "tri-country" area.

Mike reflected back to the "tri-state" area of Ohio, Indiana, and Kentucky where he had grown up. Lawrenceburg, Indiana, was where Mike had seen his first dirt-track stockcar race. Stott remembered the excitement as he watched the stockers sling mud from the track against the chain-link fencing that protected the spectators from the race cars. He imagined the roar the small-block Chevy engines made running through unmuffled headers. Mike Stott hoped to survive Vietnam and go back to the Lawrenceburg Speedway someday.

Mike looked at Dunigan and Beamer, Meeks was just out of his line of sight. Who would ever believe what DOAT was doing? Master Sergeant Dunigan seemed to read Mike's thoughts. He looked Stott in the eye and rolled his eyes back as if to say, "Can you believe this?" Staff Sergeant Beamer kept that level "I can do anything" expression on his face that Mike had come to know so well.

At 1542 hours on January 20, 1966, the ground shook beneath Stott as the Arc Light Operation commenced. DOAT heard and felt the first of what proved to be twenty-five minutes of continuous B-52 bombardment. Mike had never seen or heard 1,000-pound bombs explode before; he was mesmerized by the sound and concussion.

All three C Teams were within a mile of the bomb drop zone called Dong San, risking their lives that the B-52s would be on target.

At 1615 hours, Stott's C Team got the radio ping from Major Freeze that meant move in. With blackened faces and hands, wearing matte-black head scarves to be as native as possible, the most dangerous part of "Out of Bounds" began. The three teams double-timed down their designated corridors toward Dong San, leaving only a few yards between each trooper as they rushed towards their objectives.

As the men neared the town center, they began to see a few signs of life, but not many.

The B-52s had been amazingly accurate and thorough. Through the smoke and fire, Stott saw that very little was left of Dong San. The town had been essentially destroyed.

Three shell-shocked males emerged from a bombed-out hooch and looked toward Mike's advancing team. Stott shot two and Beamer shot the third, using silenced sniper rifles so as not to alert other survivors.

What little remained of Dong San seemed devoid of life. The only sounds were follow-up explosions as fires continued to collapse the remaining buildings. DOAT was counting on that post-bombing chaos and the shock factor to minimize initial resistance.

Delta team's number one objective was an old French-era hotel that CIA intelligence had identified as sitting on top of Dong San's largest heroin exchange. It was identifiable only because Delta knew where it had been. The remains of one of the hotel's verandah columns marked its front entrance. The upper floors of the hotel had been blasted away. The hotel must have taken at least one direct hit because there was literally nothing left to burn.

As Stott entered what had been the hotel lobby, he saw bodies strewn everywhere. Most of those corpses wore North Vietnamese uniforms. Pieces of AK-47s and other weapons were scattered among the ruins. The few survivors were silenced.

The center lobby entrance to the cellar/vault was obstructed by the debris from the second story staircase remains. Sergeant Meeks expertly rigged two C-4 packs that blew open good access to the lower level. Master Dunigan and Stott kept watch as Beamer and Meeks made their way down to their lower-level objective. Stott recognized the whoosh-whoosh-whoosh of Beamer and Meeks's silencers, followed by the unmistakable blast of more C-4 explosive.

In Hmong, Master Sergeant Dunigan whispered, "I'll go down; stand here." Mike continued his 360-degree scan of the area. Three minutes later, Dunigan and Meeks climbed back up through the wreckage to where Mike stood guard. They were both smiling.

Again in Hmong, Dunigan asked, "Concerns?"

"None, yet," said Stott.

Meeks had humped an M-60 to set up as a cover gun. Mike went back in with his team leader. When they were safely below ground, Dunigan said in English, "No gook words for this! You ain't gonna fucking believe it! Beamer and Meeks iced a few still-breathing guards and then blew the door."

Stott peered into a steel-reinforced room sixty feet long and thirty feet wide. The concrete ceiling was low, just high enough for Mike to stand up. On one side of this vault were plastic bags filled with processed heroin. On the other side of the vault was a combination of stacks of gold bars and Chinese duffel bags full of U.S. one hundred dollar bills. The dollars and gold appeared to be divided into sections that were labeled in Chinese.

"Where's Sergeant Sharkey when we need him?" Dunigan said.

"Christ, Sarge! How much is here?" Mike asked.

"More than we can move, son! More than we can move! Go up and see if you can raise Alpha and Bravo. This must be the mother lode!"

SPEND had identified four objectives within Dong San as potential storehouses for heroin and/or cash. Alpha team was to search two of the four locations and Bravo the other, larger site on the south side of the town. Depending on what the teams found, one or two of the sites would be selected for exploitation. DOAT would destroy the drugs but confiscate the cash. The C teams had devised a series of codes to help quickly identify and select the prime consolidation objectives.

Stott hustled back to the surface, leaving Dunigan and Beamer to start moving the cash closer to the exit. He clicked JJ and said in Hmong, "Number?"

Sharkey responded in Hmong, "Three."

"Alive?"

"All."

"Friends?"

"Three. All. Number?"

"Seven. Seven. One."

This coded exchange identified Delta team's site as the highest priority and verified that, so far, DOAT had taken no casualties. Mike's "seven, seven, one" to Sharkey signified that Delta's site was loaded with cash and that Alpha and Bravo teams should converge on the hotel location to assist with security and cash retrieval.

Stott checked that Meeks was okay and went back down to help Dunigan and Beamer. "Report," Dunigan said.

"All alive. Two threes. Alpha and Bravo are on the way here."

Dunigan, Beamer, and Stott began transferring the cash to the modified backpacks they had brought with them. They brought additional cash close to the exit to fill their teammates' packs when they arrived.

"My God! What we're going to have to leave behind!" Sergeant Beamer voiced what Stott was thinking.

Master Sergeant Dunigan said, "Keep bringing the cash up here."

Beamer and Stott exchanged glances, but obeyed Dunigan's command. As they made their fourth or fifth shuttle from the vault to the exit, Major Freeze and his team arrived.

"Bravo and the rest of Alpha are setting up the perimeter. What have we got?" Freeze asked Dunigan. Jim Smith joined them as Master Sergeant Dunigan answered, "It's beyond estimation. Smith was right. This was their main hold."

Freeze and Smith followed Mike and Dunigan back to the vault to get their first look at the treasure. It was an awe-inspiring sight.

After an initial walk-around evaluation, Major Freeze said to Smith, "Well?"

"At least a half a billion in cash. Half that in gold and maybe $2 billion in H, if it's pure. And it probably is," said Smith.

"So, 'Up one,' right?" Freeze said to Smith.

"Get's my vote," Smith grinned.

"Okay. Smith, tell Sharkey. 'Up one,'" DOAT's CO said.

Smith departed, leaving Dunigan, Beamer, and Stott staring bewilderedly at Major Freeze.

"Modification to plan, men, code named 'Up one.' We thought we might find something like this based on Smith's CIA info. If all goes well, in less than twenty minutes Dong San gets hit again by beaucoup F-4s. Everywhere except this grid. Immediately following the F-4 strikes, two Hueys and a Sikorsky are going to sit down right out front. We're gonna load all the cash and gold they can carry and haul ass across the border.

"Dunigan, rig that wall of H with enough C-4 to obliterate this entire grid. Beamer, Stott, go switch places with Doc and Barnett. WO Myers should have the best defensive positions identified. Kill anything that moves. Doc and Barney are gonna move the loot. You two are better on the sixties. We're outta here in one hour!"

Beamer and Stott hustled to comply with Freeze's orders even as they tried to comprehend the modification to "Out of Bounds."

"Motherfucker!" Beamer said.

Mike passed JJ using a radio unlike any he'd seen before in the army. Sharkey was speaking rapidly in Hmong. The little bastard gave his buddy that thumbs-up air check of his. Mike knew at that moment that JJ had been aware of "Up one" all along.

Stott took Doc's post and Beamer took Barnett's as those men hustled to move money. As Mike scanned their perimeter, he saw First Sergeants Helms and Adams also scanning for bad guys. WO Myers came over to him and said, "Cool?"

Mike just nodded. Sharkey stood up and signaled "ten" to everyone. Two figures staggered into the open one hundred meters out. Beamer and Helms shot them dead. DOAT settled in to wait for the F-4s.

Nine minutes later, Stott heard the scream of jet engines as a flight of F-4s with USAF markings began dropping ordinance all around DOAT's position. Another flight of F-4s followed the first and another after that. The F-4s were using a "softening" fire pattern designed to eliminate ground personnel in the target area. It was the first time Mike had seen such a maneuver.

Several North Vietnamese soldiers emerged around their position only to be taken out immediately by DOAT shooters. Even before the last F-4s departed, Mike heard the glorious sound of helicopter blades cutting the air. Two blacked-out Hueys hovered in covering positions as the first blacked-out Sikorsky Stott had ever seen sat down in what once had been the hotel courtyard.

DOAT shooters focused on their individual defensive fire corridors as Major Freeze, Master Sergeant Dunigan, Doc Brackett, and Staff Sergeant Barnett formed a human chain and loaded duffel after duffel of cash into the big chopper. Mike wondered who was loading up in the helicopter since he could not see into it from his position. Twice during the loading the 50-caliber machine guns on the hovering Hueys opened up on targets only they saw.

Forty-nine minutes after Major Freeze had said, "We'll be outta here in an hour," WO Myers began directing the members of DOAT into one of the three helicopters. Freeze, Dunigan, Brackett, and Barnett piled into the Sikorsky with the last hand-up of cash. Sharkey, Meeks, Helms, and Beamer loaded into one Huey. WO Myers, First Sergeant Adams, and the spook, Jim Smith, pulled Mike up into the second Huey and roared away at 1805 hours on January 20, 1966.

"Happy New Year, motherfuckers!" Jim Smith said as he spat out the side door of the Huey on what little remained of Dong San, North Vietnam.

Chapter Forty-Two

Stott and his DOAT buddies had been expecting at least a week or maybe even longer "in the shit," on mission "Out of Bounds." They were in a state of near shock at what had just transpired under "Up one" as the choppers lifted up and away from Dong San. Mike's Huey was last off the ground. WO Myers spoke, "Any second now it's gonna—"

Myers was interrupted by the sequenced rumble of C-4 as the charges set to destroy the heroin went off. It wasn't a fireball like when the Russian helicopter exploded, but DOAT knew the drugs were history. Stott kept looking back at what had been a town of maybe 3,000 people about two and a-half hours earlier. He saw no movement whatsoever.

Jim Smith pulled a handful of Cuban cigars from his tunic pocket. "Every once in a while those dickheads in Langley get something right! Here's to you, boys! We're rich beyond our dreams!"

Sergeant Adams said, "Smith, you really think there's a half billion dollars in Besuden's Sikorsky?"

"Besuden's Sikorsky?" Stott and Beamer asked together.

"Maybe more, Sarge, maybe more! But in any case, enough to make every SPEND team member off-the-charts rich! We even got a few gold bars loaded before weight became a problem!" Smith said.

"Besuden's Sikorsky?" Stott repeated.

WO Myers, Jim Smith, and First Sergeant Adams laughed together. "Who do you think was stacking the cash in the Sikorsky?" Myers answered. "The old man wasn't going to stay home on this caper!"

"Here's to the colonel with the biggest balls in the army! Not only a patriot, but a soldier's soldier! In the shit with his troops!" Smith said.

"So 'Up one' was the plan all along?" Mike asked.

"Hell yes! When we learned the ARVN's were going to launch an offensive up on the border around their New Year, we knew we had a shot at taking down Dong San! Perfect post-harvest timing! Westmoreland has been itching for an excuse to get the B-52s more involved in ground support. What better reason than to rescue an A Team! We put the odds at eighty-twenty he'd say yes to the air strike. We got lucky that the bombers were so perfectly on target! But then, you guys had it gridded from your recons! How many 1,000 pounders do you think they dropped?" Smith asked.

"More than I thought they had!" First Sergeant Adams said. "Holy shit, they leveled the joint!"

"Must have been a couple hundred! So much concussion destruction there wasn't much left to burn!" WO Myers said.

"So now what? DOAT wasn't expected back to Lac Do for at least a week. Won't the backup A Team get suspicious?" Stott asked.

"DOAT's not going back just yet, Sergeant Stott. Remember that abandoned mountain-top fortress we checked out just across the border in Laos? You guys are gonna hole up there awhile and hump back to Lac Do in about a week. Tomorrow, we'll get a good count. Then the colonel and I will take the Sikorsky with the loot to meet up with a C-130, whose captain is one of us." Smith explained.

"So are the pilots of these three choppers all in SPEND?" Adams asked.

"You don't want to ask too many questions, Sarge, but yes, all six of them. Stott, you probably recognized our left-seater from last year, right?" Smith said.

"Yes, I did. So there's the twelve of us, six chopper pilots, Colonel Besuden, Major Royalty, and the C-130 jockey. That's twenty-one men. We heard SPEND has twenty-two members. Do we get to know who the other one is?" Mike asked Smith.

"No, you don't," Smith answered.

First Sergeant Adams changed the subject. "So the deal's the same? If there's really $500 million in the Sik, it gets split twenty-two ways after the 20 percent for expenses, right? Could be about $18 million each. Is that possible?" The amount was simply beyond comprehension.

"That's right, Sarge. Probably enough to get by on for a while, right? But the ten-year waiting period holds. It's more important than ever. We've got to be real careful about how we get that much cash into our Swiss accounts, but the colonel has it all figured out. It's worth paying out 20 percent to keep $18 million each, isn't it?" Smith teased.

Myers, Adams, and Stott continued to look from one to another in amazement. It just didn't seem possible that they could be that rich.

"So how long have you known the colonel?" Myers asked Smith.

"Since before Stott was born! Long enough to know I can trust him! Now that's enough probing, guys! Thank God you're part of SPEND, and try to stay alive to enjoy your money." Smith ended the conversation.

Mike sat there listening to the Huey's roar, pinching himself on the thigh several times. His mother had always told him, "Pinch yourself to make sure you're awake."

The lead Huey somehow found the clearing in Laos that provided access to the abandoned mountain fortress where DOAT would hole up. That pilot talked the other birds down. By 2300 hours, the men had a perimeter set up and a watch schedule worked out.

"So, what do you think now, dickhead?" Sharkey said to Stott as he knelt down where Mike was organizing his gear. "Could it get any better than this?"

"You knew it might go down like this, and you didn't tell me? I promise you an ass-kicking just as soon as we get home, asshole!" Stott told him.

It was too dark to see JJ's face, but Mike could feel Sharkey grinning at him. "And what qualifies as home now that you're a multi-millionaire, dickhead?" Sharkey asked.

Mike had no answer for JJ, so he said, "If we're all really on this mountaintop in Laos when first light comes, I'll give you my answer!"

DOAT awoke to an unusually bright and crisp day on January 21, 1966. They were in the middle of a no-man's-land on a rocky and inhospitable mountain top in Laos, about thirty clicks, twenty or so miles, from the border with South Vietnam. Six men stood watch while the rest counted money and gold and listened to Colonel Besuden discuss the future of SPEND. By 1000 hours on Lunar New Year's Day, the men determined that the take was, in fact, just under $475 million, all in U.S. hundred dollar bills, plus twelve mini gold bars.

Besuden began, "One hell of a day, yesterday. The stars lined up just right to help a good plan become a great score. Before we talk about our money, remember that we destroyed probably $2 billion of the killer drug, heroin. We called in an air strike that took out one of Charlie's key supply points. Most importantly, we did not lose a man! For those of you that worry, we stretched the truth about an "out of bounds" A Team. Get over it!"

The colonel's pun got a good laugh.

Besuden continued. "DOAT members have now met our pilot partners. Everyone knows Major Royalty, who's holding down the fort in Nha Trang. Some of you have met our C-130 partner. I hear some of you have asked about out twenty-second partner. That's info you don't need. But if I could tell you, it would make you all feel good! I've made a command decision to disband SPEND. Frankly, we've scored beyond our wildest dreams and expectations. Take the secret of SPEND to your graves. Starting in 1975, we can all enjoy our money. Everybody square?"

Each team member reaffirmed his commitment to keep their pact secret and to abide by Besuden's rules.

"There are numerous safeguards to ensure future access to your funds. You all know your specific eleven digit account numbers and personal security codes. Major Royalty and I know all twenty-two base account numbers, but by now you should all have established your new, personal security codes. There is a system to back you up if you need it, but only Royalty and I could access the backup system until thirty days ago. We made the decision to add Staff Sergeant John J. Sharkey to our security backup team. JJ now knows how to work the system if you should need it. All of you except Sergeant Stott are senior to Sharkey, so let me explain why we chose him. First and most importantly, JJ understands loyalty and trust. Second, he's an orphan whose closest friend is our partner, Mike Stott. Third, he's young enough to be around to help all of us past our normal life expectancies. And fourth, John's IQ is forty-four points higher than mine. It's always good to use the smartest man you know if you can trust him. I trust Sharkey. Questions?"

There were none.

"It will take us some time to get all of your cash into your individual accounts. That shouldn't matter because you can't touch it for ten years anyway. Should any of you develop a desperate, and I mean desperate, need for cash between now and then, you may approach me, Royalty or Sharkey. I expect such requests only for life-or-death situations. Questions?"

Again, no questions.

"Remember our pact. Stay with your military careers. A couple of you old farts are eligible to retire. I hope you'll reconsider and stay in Five Group. This war is just getting started. Your country still needs you. Happy Lunar New Year, men. See you in Nha Trang or maybe Lac Do."

Colonel Besuden, Jim Smith, and Staff Sergeant John J. Sharkey loaded into the Sikorsky headed back for Nha Trang, leaving the men of DOAT to plan their return to Lac Do. Beamer and Meeks were on lookout so the rest of the team huddled up to discuss their incredible adventure.

Major Freeze said, "Men, you know we share all the poop we can, but "Up one" we kept close because we didn't want to raise false hopes if we couldn't find the mother lode. But we found it! Our friends at Langley believe that drug profits help fund the war for the North, so taking out Dong San was the right thing to do. From the destruction you all witnessed, a lot of people died in Dong San yesterday. Civilians were among the casualties, but so were drug traffickers from all over the world. And hundreds of NVA. You're not likely to hear about the bombing of Dong San! Neither side has a vested interest in publicizing what happened!

"A secret shared by twenty-two men is by definition not a secret! But we're brothers in the Fifth! Everybody cool with what went down?"

"Can we do it again next year?" Master Sergeant Dunigan asked.

Chuckles and grins, but no outright laughter. "Boys, never tempt fate! We couldn't hope to be so lucky again!" Freeze said. "Staff Sergeant Stott, you're about half as old as the rest of these guys! What do you have to say?"

"Thank you! That's all I have to say. Thank you for taking me into DOAT! I am proud to be a part of all this. Sir, I believe you're the next youngest guy here after me. You went to West Point. You're an officer. Can I ask you how you feel right now?" Mike knew he was on thin ice, asking his CO such a question, but felt pretty sure of himself at that point. The boldness of his question caused some of Mike's teammates to raise their eyebrows.

"That's a fair question, Sergeant. There's not a man in DOAT that hasn't put his life on the line for his country numerous times. What we did up north yesterday was the right thing to do strategically and tactically from a military perspective. Keeping the money doesn't bother me at all. And remember, what's left of the 20 percent held out for expenses we'll use to help other soldiers who aren't so fortunate. I plan to spend the next twenty years in the Special Forces. I hope you will too, Sergeant. Anybody else?"

"Major, we're a good four, maybe six days hump from Lac Do. When do we start?" First Sergeant Helms asked.

"Couple of days, Helms. I'd like to get back by 29 or 30 January. Once we cross back into Nam we're likely to run into some obstacles! So let's rest up and watch our twenty. You afraid your woman's cheating on you, Helms?" Freeze asked.

That brought a good laugh from the men of DOAT. Helms shacked up every chance he got with the only woman in Lac Do who had big tits.

"No, sir! I just got a feeling we need to get back," Helms said.

Helms's intuition about the need to get back to Lac Do proved to be correct.

Chapter Forty-Three

When Major James Waterman returned from his Christmas leave in January 1965, he had a message from Specialist George Washington Howard. It read:

Dear Major Waterman,

I've thought about your offer to help me apply for Officer's Candidate School. Sir, if you're still willing to help me I'd be eternally grateful. I don't have any college, but I did graduate with honors from my high school in Ashland, Mississippi. I promise you that if you will help me get into officer's training I'll do my very best to make you proud. I've always planned to make the army a career. Now that I understand a little bit how the army works I believe I could learn to be a good officer. My two best friends are guys I met in basic training at Fort Dix. I know they'll be real proud of me if I can become an officer.

I hope it was OK to write you this letter. I'll be going to the base library every chance I get, so maybe I can see you there when you get back from your leave. Thank you for encouraging me.

Thank you again, Sir.

Respectfully,

Specialist George Washington Howard
101st MP Company

Major Jim Waterman sat and pondered Howard's letter. Waterman was a West Point graduate with all the army connections that pointers enjoyed. He knew that supporting a young, nondegreed black man for OCS would be unpopular with many of his fellow officers. *What the hell*, he thought. *Let's see if I can make this happen.*

To Waterman's surprise, Specialist Howard received good support from his commanding officer, Major Ben Humphrys. The two majors worked together helping Howard do the preliminaries to apply for OCS. On May 17, 1965, George Washington Howard, son of a Mississippi share-cropper, began Officer's Candidate School at Fort Benning, Georgia.

Howard graduated first in his class. He received his commission as a "Butter Bar," second lieutenant on August 20, 1965.

Big Howie had learned to drive while serving as an MP in Germany. He obtained a Georgia driver's license while in OCS at Fort Benning. George had sent home or saved most of his pay since joining the army, but now he had the opportunity to do something he'd dreamed about doing all his life. Immediately after being commissioned, he went to a used car lot in Columbus, Georgia, and bought a clean, 1960 F-Series Ford pickup truck. Howard had new tires and brakes put on his vehicle and headed home to Ashland, Mississippi.

Howard drove straight through from Columbus, Georgia, to Jackson, Mississippi, where he got a cheap motel for the night. On the drive, Howie wore the Levi's, T-shirt, NYPD jacket, and Converse All Star gym shoes that Sharkey had bought for him in New York City on that memorable Labor Day weekend trip from Fort Dix nearly two years earlier.

Big Howie thought about his buddies, Sharkey and Stott, all the way to Jackson. What he thought about most was Sharkey's words to him the night they had made their pact at the Plaza Hotel: "Howard, don't ever underestimate yourself again! I can see that you're smart and, more important, loyal. If you join our pact, I know you'll keep up your side of the deal. In or out? You get only one chance with us. In or not?"

How often Howard had thought about that pact with his buddies! He wondered if it would be possible to see them in Vietnam. After his twenty-one day leave, Second Lieutenant George Washington Howard was to report to a six-week air mobile assault school for officers back at Benning. He expected to be in Vietnam by Thanksgiving.

On August 22, 1965 George awoke early in his motel room to prepare for his homecoming. He shaved extra close as he inspected himself in the mirror. He was down to 235 pounds, the slimmest he'd been since eighth grade. And it was all muscle. He now had a thirty-four inch waist, but required a forty-eight inch officers' dress jacket. People asked him if he played in the NFL. The timidity with which he'd entered the army was gone. *I'm an airborne army officer*, Howard thought to himself. Folks better remember that when he got to Ashland.

It was already at least eighty degrees, even at 0630 hours and, of course, his seven dollar a night room had no air conditioning. George laid out his tailored dress kakis and once again inspected his perfectly shined jump boots. He decided to wait until just outside Ashland to don his uniform. He didn't want to arrive home all wrinkled. The last nine miles of road to his family's home was all dirt. He hoped he'd be able to stand to keep the windows shut on the truck. George did not want to arrive home all dusty.

Howard had gassed up his truck the night before. He found a restaurant on the "black" side of Jackson and got coffee and a sack of homemade biscuits. Second Lieutenant George Howard began the last one hundred miles of his first journey home since leaving for Fort Dix twenty-six months earlier.

Although it was considerably out of the way, George drove his Ford right into Ashland and around courthouse square. Ashland's courthouse had been one of the few spared the torch by Sherman's army after the Civil War. The impressive structure with its two-foot thick walls had changed very little since that war. So neither had Ashland, Mississippi. The sight of a black man driving a relatively new pickup truck around the square brought stares from all the white folks in town. Howard stared back. Something he wouldn't have dared to do two years ago.

George stopped at the Piggly Wiggly and bought four cases of ice cold RC Cola. He also bought an assortment of cookies, candy, and potato chips, all he could pack into the passenger compartment of his truck. George recognized several people, white folks as well as black. No one recognized him.

Howard drove extra slowly down the dirt track toward his home. His truck was still relatively clean and he wanted it to be as new-looking as possible when he arrived. In a cottonwood patch about a mile from the house, George parked his truck in the shade. He carefully dressed in his uniform, making sure his medals and ribbons were straight. He put his jump boots on only after getting back in the cab. He had selected a garrison cap for his gold "Butter Bar," signifying his second lieutenant rank. George slowly drove the last few hundred yards to his family home.

His timing was just right. All his brothers and sisters and his ma and pa had come in from the fields to lunch together in the shade of the willow trees on the east side of the house. Everyone stopped at the sound and sight of the truck. Even in 1965, nearly new pickups just weren't that common out here in cotton country, especially if it was being driven by a black man. George let the dust settle a bit before he stepped out of the truck.

No one said a word. His family did not recognize him. Only when George started walking toward his mother did she scream out, "LORD, LORD, my GOD! Praise the LORD! It's my Georgie!" His entire family then descended on him with hugs and kisses like he had never experienced from them before. George's father stood back and looked his son up and down.

"Son, son! How the army has changed you! You musta growed another foot!" his pa said.

"No, Pa! Just ain't as fat as I was!" George said.

His oldest brother Thomas reached out and touched the gold bar on George's collar. "What you doin' with that?" he asked. "You ain't no officer! They'll hang you for that, boy!"

In addition to his brothers and sisters and mom and dad, there was a sizable collection of extended family surrounding George. Two of his sisters had new babies strapped to their chests. Thomas's words caused them all to be silent.

"Son, what's he mean?" George's mother asked.

"Thomas is wrong, Mama. I am a second lieutenant in the United States Army! I got my commission last Friday at Fort Benning Georgia! I got cold RC's in the car! And my commission papers! Your son is an army officer!"

George's statement caused all his family to once again be silent. Finally, his mother said, "George, can it be? You really are a regular army officer? Like Robert E. Lee?"

"I am, Mama! I did it! I graduated first in my OCS class! Ain't nobody can take it away from me now! You all be happy! Be proud! I did it for all of you, and for my buddies!"

The kids had made a beeline for the truck when George mentioned cold RC's. Now everyone had one in their hand. In his family's faces, George saw a combination of pride, disbelief, and fear.

"Is it really true, Son?" his father asked again.

"Pa, it is. And that's your truck I just drove up in," George said.

Stunned silence from his family. Now, they really did not believe him! "Look! Here's the title, free and clear! It's a Georgia title, but we'll get it switched to a Mississippi title for you tomorrow! And here's the rest of my pay I've been savin' to give to you, Ma!" George handed his mother nine fifty-dollar bills. "And I'll be able to send more with my combat pay!"

"WHAT? What's combat pay? What do you mean, Son?" his mama cried.

"I get to go to Vietnam! I'll be a platoon leader!"

"What's Bietnam?" Thomas asked.

George looked around at all his family. No one had a clue what he was talking about.

Second Lieutenant George Howard arrived at the processing center in Da Nang, Vietnam, on November 24, 1965. The next day George got a pretty decent Thanksgiving dinner of turkey with all the trimmings. Monday, November 29, 1965, Second Lieutenant Howard was assigned as rifle platoon leader in A Company, Second Battalion of the First Cavalry Division. Three days later, he was directing return fire in the Ia Drang Valley.

As Staff Sergeant Mike B. Stott sat on a mountaintop in Laos on January 21 1966, and Staff Sergeant John J. Sharkey was arriving back to Nha Trang in a Sikorsky full of cash, Second Lieutenant Howard was in a world of shit. The Vietcong celebrated the New Year by throwing everything they had at A Company, Second Battalion, First Cavalry, in Ton Dai, or what the army called the Spear of II Corp.

Chapter Forty-Four

On January 24, the men of DOAT were itching to get off their mountaintop resting place in Laos. They estimated that they were twenty-four to twenty-six miles from Lac Do, but a good four to six day hump due to the rugged terrain and the need to travel under darkness. DOAT left under a half moon that evening and started making their way back home, all somewhat preoccupied with what they had accomplished in Dong San, maybe even more preoccupied thinking about their future lifestyles, assuming they could survive to spend their money.

Master Sergeant Dunigan had an uncanny ability to find the best route over the rough terrain and led most of the way back. DOAT did encounter one group of seven or eight VC about five miles out of Lac Do but got the jump on them and killed seven. Stott thought an eighth enemy might have gotten away, although Major Freeze was convinced there were only seven.

That firefight was intense, however, and put Mike and his mates on edge. A lot of rounds were exchanged so they all had "battle ear" as they made their way closer to Lac Do. Perhaps that's why they got so close before they heard the artillery.

DOAT knew the terrain within a five mile radius of Lac Do extremely well from the many recons they'd pulled around its extended perimeter. Approaching that familiar ground at 0600 hours on January 29, 1966, they thought they could hear distant artillery. The closer DOAT got, the more certain they became that something was seriously wrong at their home base. The radios they were carrying were nowhere near as good as the base radios in Lac Do. DOAT had received no warning that something was amiss.

Approaching from the northwest, DOAT had one good-sized hill to top before they got a visual on Lac Do. It was an overcast day with low-hanging clouds and generally poor visibility. When they topped "Hill K," however, the men could see more than they wanted to. Lac Do was under full-scale assault by a sizable force of NVA supported by beaucoup VC.

The NVA had somehow gotten artillery up to the top of "D Hill," where they could fire directly at the village. Lac Do's far perimeters were strewn with bodies they hoped and assumed were at least mostly NVA and VC, but they could also see that the village had been hit hard. Many hooches were destroyed, and several were on fire.

There was no indication that Charlie intended to take the daytime off and start again at dusk, as he so often did. DOAT immediately tried calling for air support, but had no luck getting through.

"Christ, they've got no air support!" Freeze said. "How in the hell did they get surrounded like this without calling in the F-4s?"

As the major spoke, his men spread themselves out along the ridgeline. Beamer and Meeks were watching the flank, Adams had his sixty covering their back. As Stott and the team took up positions, the NVA started another artillery barrage to support a company-strength assault on Lac Do's northern perimeter. Another aggressor force was flanking south, preparing to charge across the area used as a landing zone. Sergeant Meeks tried again and again to radio the troopers inside Lac Do, but got no response.

DOAT knew Lac Do was in serious trouble, possibly about to be overrun by the enemy. Major Freeze made a quick and gutsy decision.

"Listen up! We can all see that Lac Do is in deep shit! Maybe they got air support coming, but my guess is they don't! Looks like this attack started during last night. I estimate at least a thousand gooks in the aggressor force. If they penetrate, Lac Do is history! Let's hit Charlie's flank from two directions, there and there. Maybe we can make them think there's enough of us to withdraw!"

The eight sergeants knew that was a long shot.

"WO, take Helms, Doc, and Barney around to their left rear, just behind the artillery. Set up your sixty on that high spot just behind them. Dunigan, you, me, Adams, and Meeks will hit 'em from the right flank. Sergeant Beamer, Stott, work your way to that high ground three clicks ahead. Stay separate, but in sight of each other. At 0700 hours, I want you two to start picking off the crews around their guns! When you get their attention, we'll move! Men, conserve ammo! We've got what we've got! Maybe we can grab some of Chuck's AK's! Let's try to divert their attention before the charge starts across the LZ. Rally back here at 0900. Backup rally point is that ammo dump we buried five clicks out on the south side! Meeks, keep working the radio! Inside and for air support! Everybody got it?"

"Yes, sir!" from all.

"Shoot straight! See you in two!" Freeze was already moving toward the NVA artillery.

WO Myers's team moved out right behind the major. Beamer and Stott looked at each other.

"Motherfucker!" they said at the same time.

Mike had been toting one of the two M-60 machine guns, but Helms took it for their flanking move. Stott had 300 rounds of ammo for his sniper rifle, six clips for his .45 and fifty .357 bullets for the revolver JJ had given him. He and Beamer each had six fragmentation grenades.

As Beamer and Stott moved toward their sniper's perches they heard fire from the direction their buddies had gone, way sooner than they should have heard fire from that direction.

"Maybe Chuck IS watching their flank," Beamer said.

Even as he spoke, Mike saw seven VC cross a path just ahead of them. The VC were heading toward Lac Do and did not see the Americans. Beamer and Stott followed them until they crossed open ground behind the perches where Major Freeze wanted them to set up. The VC were walking upright, not even moving quickly. Stott gave Beamer the selection signal and opened fire, killing the back four before the others knew they were being fired on, so efficient were their silencers. Stott knew they hit the fifth and sixth targets, but the lead gook dove forward into the bush and out of sight.

"Shit! We gotta get him!" Beamer said.

Stott flanked right and Beamer went left. As Mike crawled along, he noted it was 0649 hours. Major Freeze expected them to start shooting at the artillery batteries in eleven minutes. When Mike looked up from his watch, the VC they had missed was backing directly toward him, looking in Beamer's direction. Stott remembered Freeze's directive to conserve ammo. He choke-gripped the VC and buried his K-Bar knife in the gook's heart. No sound, but the VC's blood spewed forward like a geyser. Mike had blood covering both hands as he lowered Chuck to the ground and cut out the back of his black silk shirt. It wasn't very absorbent, but Stott managed at least to get most of the blood off his trigger hand.

Beamer had seen Stott stab the VC and raised just enough to give him a thumbs-up. They cautiously took up two well-concealed firing positions behind rock outcroppings no more than a hundred meters behind the NVA artillery, at 0658 hours on January 29, 1966.

Then Beamer and Stott got a little lucky again.

As they were selecting their initial targets, an NVA trooper ran out of the wood line and approached a dugout position just behind their guns. Three men got up out of the bunker and looked back in the direction the first NVA was gesturing. Then a fourth, obviously senior officer got up to take a look. Beamer gave Stott the "you, right" signal. Beamer shot the two NVA on the left and Mike got three on the right. All fell to the ground, causing one of the artillery commanders to spin around and peer in the snipers' direction. Beamer took his head off with a perfect neck shot.

Beamer and Stott continued picking off NVA artillery tenders before they realized they were being fired at. Then they all hit the deck. Supporting infantry on both sides of the artillery battery began firing in Stott's general direction, but not right at him. A platoon-sized group of VC moved off to their right, apparently to start a flanking move at the snipers' position. Stott heard an M-60 open up, cutting down several of the NVA before they got twenty meters from their holes.

There was a scurry of movement all around the NVA guns as the enemy stopped focusing on Lac Do and started worrying about their flank. Stott heard a firefight break out in the direction of where WO Myers' team should be. Beamer and Mike both sensed that their initial five hits had taken out at least a part of the NVA senior command.

Suddenly, everything got quiet. For several minutes, no shots were fired. The artillery was temporarily silenced as the gun crews hunkered down to avoid fire.

Mike saw that only fourteen minutes had elapsed since their initial volley at the NVA gunners. It was 0714 hours.

From their high vantage points, Beamer and Stott could still see virtually all of Lac Do, even the LZ on the south side of the camp. Unaware that their artillery support was being attacked, several hundred NVA and VC rose up from the far wood line beyond the LZ and charged Lac Do's southern berms. They charged in two long, loose lines screaming and firing their weapons.

Stott knew where Lac Do's far southern defense line should have been. When the advancing enemy cleared that line without really taking much defensive fire from inside, Mike was stunned. Then when Charlie's line got to within a hundred meters of Lac Do's inner berm, all hell broke loose. The replacement team inside the village and the Yard tribesmen showed incredible discipline waiting almost too long to begin firing. But fire they did. At least fifty, maybe even a hundred, VC went down from that first barrage. It made Stott want to cheer.

A second wave of gooks ran from the wood line, backing up the first charge. These NVA were on a slightly different angle toward Lac Do and begin tripping the Claymore mines planted there. Many VC catapulted into the air as they tripped the mines. Realizing their mistake, that second wave began backing away, circling toward the left flank.

Suddenly, firefights broke out very close to the hilltop Beamer and Stott were on. No fire was coming their way, but hundreds of rounds were coming mostly from AK-47s close to where they were concealed. The NVA artillery gunners resumed their bombardment of Lac Do. As the first gun crew resumed its place, Mike shot two VC and Beamer got three more. Their kills caused the other gunners to once again hit the ground. Unfortunately, a NVA spotter must have seen their muzzle flash because the infantry on both sides began firing in Beamer and Stott's direction again. This time, the bullets were getting close.

Mike glanced at Beamer who pointed to his ear and then at the sky. As Stott looked back to the south side of Lac Do, he thought he could make out several black specs in the sky, but still far out from the village. He again looked at Sergeant Beamer who gave him the "F-4" hand signal!

Could it be? Had the troopers in Lac Do gotten through to Nha Trang? Several rounds landed very close to Mike and he refocused on their immediate predicament. Then he saw Beamer roll to his right and begin firing almost directly at him! But not right at him. Beamer shot two VC who were no more than thirty meters behind Mike. Stott and Beamer repositioned to protect each other's backs. Charlie was all around them.

The unmistakable sound of F-4s filled the air. Two of those beautiful birds began firing at the NVA assault on Lac Do's southern perimeter. Two more came right at Beamer and Stott. The closest F-4s had spotted the NVA artillery and dove at the guns. As the F-4s fired their rockets, several VC stood up and fired into the sky at the planes. That enabled Beamer and Mike to shoot five more bad guys, all within fifty meters of their position.

The F-4 pilots were spot on! Their rockets hit four of the six NVA howitzer placements and the explosions killed many of the gunners. The jets swooped right back at the artillery positions and began strafing the entire area. The pilots, of course, had no idea an A Team was just behind the bad guys.

Mike knew DOAT wasn't throwing friendly smoke for the F-4s to see. That would have marked their position for the NVA. He hoped his buddies weren't caught in the F-4s' cannon fire.

Stott heard an M-60 open up very close to him. He turned to see if Beamer had a visual on it. But Staff Sergeant Dave Beamer wasn't seeing anything. He was on his back, not moving. Mike knew immediately that Beamer was dead.

Stott did a 360-degree scan and could see no one. He belly-crawled to Beamer and touched his throat, hoping for a pulse. There was none. Mike could see two penetrations on Dave's chest. There was a rapidly spreading pool of blood beneath him.

Mike's head was no more than two feet off the ground as he examined his friend, but a VC had seen him. Rounds rained down all around Stott, but, miraculously, he wasn't hit. Two VC came charging at him standing nearly upright. Stott shot them both. One of the wounded VC landed so close that Mike could touch him. As the enemy turned his head toward him, Stott put a .45 round through his ear.

Stott was aware of the F-4s making another sweep back toward him. He wondered how they could have any munitions left.

A line of six or seven NVA troopers rose from the bush not forty meters distant. As they charged toward Mike he was aware of an M-60 somewhere behind him opening up. Mike fired the remaining rounds in his Colt at the NVA, but they were firing AK-47s directly at him, and throwing grenades.

The muzzle flash of the VC weapons was the last thing Stott remembered.

Chapter Forty-Five

When Lac Do's replacement A Team missed their morning report to Nha Trang, Staff Sergeant John Sharkey was in the orderly room drinking coffee. He was already concerned that DOAT had not made it back to Lac Do. Nha Trang command expected them to be back on January 28.

Colonel Besuden was on a long overdue R & R, this time in Hong Kong. Sharkey knew the colonel's trip was a combination of rest and business. He had taken $100 million to deposit in SPEND members' accounts. A recently arrived green hat colonel named Spitz was temporarily in command until Besuden's return. Major Royalty entered the orderly room at 0550 hours.

"Hey, JJ. Heard from DOAT?" was Royalty's first question.

"No, sir, we haven't. Worse, we haven't heard from the troops in Lac Do since 1800 hours yesterday. No pings; nothing!" Sharkey told his major.

"Damn! They've been good about the check-ins up 'til now, right? Try raising them again," Royalty commanded.

"Nothing, Major. Their radios are dead. Have been all night," Sharkey said.

"Did we hear from DOAT yesterday?" Royalty directed his question to Sharkey.

"No, sir. Major, can we walk outside a sec?" Sharkey asked.

Outside the command bunker and out of earshot of other troopers Sharkey said, "Sir, I know something's wrong up there! Let me call in some air support! We got F-4s in the air out of Tan Son Nhat could be there in minutes, sir! Please, sir!"

"Sergeant we've got to go to Colonel Spitz with this. DOAT's still coming in, right? Let's use that!" Royalty said.

Colonel Barry Spitz was just getting his first coffee of the day when Major Royalty requested a meet. "Come on in, Major! I see you have our 'ear' right behind you!"

One of the Nha Trang troopers had hung the nickname "Ears" or "The Ear" on Sergeant Sharkey because of his mastery of languages. Sharkey didn't appreciate the handle, but he knew if he protested it would only enforce the nickname.

"Morning, sir!" JJ said.

"What's up, men? It's mighty early, and I'm still on Bragg time, so go slow!" said Spitz.

"Sir, we've got our Lac Do A Team coming home from an extended recon over in Laos. I hope Colonel Besuden briefed you about them, sir. Kind of an off-the-charts deal for our friends in Langley," Royalty said.

"Yep, he did. So?"

"Sir, we can't raise them and now the backup team in Lac Do has gone silent. We're worried. There's a squadron of F-4s just got up out of Phuket. We'd like them to take a look, sir," Royalty said.

"Why is Sergeant Sharkey with you, Major?" Spitz asked.

"His best bud, Staff Sergeant Mike Stott is a DOAT shooter. They're bonded at the hip. JJ, er, Sergeant Sharkey is worried about his pal," said Royalty.

"You psychic or something, Sergeant Sharkey?" Spitz asked.

"Yes, sir, I am. I just got a bad feeling, sir. Can we send a Huey too?" Sharkey asked.

"You're ballsy, Sergeant! What do you think, Major? Send the jets, huh?"

"Yes, sir. Lac Do is way up there, sir! You know about Dong San. Maybe Charlie's hitting back," Major Royalty said.

"Okay, get the Fours to take a look. Warm up a Huey! I've been wanting to see some of the outlying locations anyway. This is a good excuse," Colonel Spitz said.

"Sir, can I go too? I'm on stand-down, but I need to go! Please, sir!" Sharkey begged.

"That's enough, Sergeant Sharkey! You may be needed here," Royalty said.

"You know what? I want to talk to this kid anyway, Major. Get me a couple of shooters! Let's take a ride depending on what the F-4s report," Colonel Spitz said.

"Can I go too?" Royalty asked.

"What's with you guys? You got women in Lac Do? Damn! No, you hold down the fort here, Major! I'll take Captain Drew and his shooters. Get ready, Sergeant Sharkey! I want to hear how it is you speak so many languages on the ride up!"

"Sir, thank you sir!" JJ literally ran out of Spitz's office.

Sharkey's gut was in a knot.

After what seemed like a long time, Colonel Spitz arrived at the flight line with Captain Drew and two of Five Group's best snipers. At 0730 hours, January 29, Spitz's bird lifted out of Nha Trang for the hour and a half flight to Lac Do. Sharkey once again had to tell the story of his life in St. Agnes. He did it from rote. All JJ could think about was the bad feeling he had in his gut about DOAT and Lac Do.

Chapter Forty-Six

As Colonel Spitz's Huey winged its way north toward Lac Do, Lieutenant Colonel Michael Collins rolled his F-4 over hard and took another look at the battlefield below him. "What do you make of it, Pete? We got that artillery battery, but looks to me like Lac Do's in deep shit! Gooks all the fuck over the place!"

"You bet, Colle! I'm out of ordinance! Can we call in Birddog's wing?" Major Peter Hill said to his CO.

"I'll raise 'em through OPS, but I think they're out of range to help soon. Radio base. Get word back to the green hats that they've got serious shit in Lac Do!" The F-4s pulled up hard and headed for home, after dropping all ordinance in support of Lac Do.

The relay of Colonel Collins' report on Lac Do got held up a bit as the air force coordinated with the army. Then the army had to talk to Five Group in Nha Trang. Nha Trang reported to Colonel Spitz's pilot when the helicopter was no more than fifteen minutes out from Lac Do.

"Colonel Spitz, hold up! First F-4s report a full-scale assault on Lac Do by beaucoup NVA! Two more flights of Fours are about to hit Charlie again all around the encampment. Repeat, DO NOT go in! Lac Do is crawling with VC!" the duty officer from Nha Trang said.

Staff Sergeant John Sharkey heard the report on Lac Do, so loudly was the duty officer screaming his warning over the radio. "Ask him if they've heard from DOAT!" Sharkey pleaded.

"Any word from DOAT?" Spitz asked.

"No, sir."

From the front of the chopper the copilot called out, "Here come the Fours!"

JJ could hear and then see two wings of F-4s streak by on the left side of the Huey.

"Follow them in, Captain. I want a look at the ground around Lac Do," said Colonel Spitz. "Get Nha Trang for me!"

As Spitz knelt between the pilots, waiting to be connected to HQ, Captain Derrick Drew said to Sharkey, "You okay with a sixty, Sergeant? I'm thinking you're about to get some real 'in the shit' experience!"

"Captain, my best friend is down there! You just watch me!" Sharkey said.

Colonel Spitz to Nha Trang: "Major Royalty, gimme all you can spare in three bailout teams, NOW! I want you in the air headed for Lac Do ASAP! Come back at me when you're airborne!"

As Spitz's helicopter got in visual range of Lac Do, the eight F-4s were making their third run at the area surrounding the village. Major Thomas "Pole Cat" Polinski dropped his bird right at Lac Do's northern berm, firing his 20-mm canons. "SHIT! Friendly marker smoke at twelve o'clock five clicks due north!" he screamed to his wingman.

"GOT IT! SHIT! We hit that grid first, Major!"

Polinski saw yet another "friendly" smoke canister pop as he pulled up and rolled for a better look. "What the fuck!"

On the ground, five clicks north of Lac Do, Major Freeze took stock of DOAT's situation. First Sergeant Bill Adams had been instantly killed by a barrage of AK-47 rounds as the first firefight had begun. Master Sergeant Dunigan had been wounded in the left arm and left thigh but was still mobile and still fighting. Freeze and Staff Sergeant Meeks had dragged Adam's body back to the first rally point just in time to see Staff Sergeant Dave Beamer go down. Then Staff Sergeant Mike Stott got hit, even as Meeks had been covering Stott with M-60 fire while Stott checked on Beamer.

It appeared that the remaining NVA infantry that had been supporting their artillery and preparing to charge Lac Do had been redirected to counterattack DOAT. Although that had temporarily relieved the pressure on Lac Do's northern perimeter, Freeze now realized that there were far more enemy troops than he originally estimated.

First Sergeant Helms and Doc Brackett arrived at the rallying point. Helms had been shot through his right side, but it was a glancing wound and the bullet had passed through cleanly. Freeze could see the wrap-around bandage that Doc had put on Helms.

"Myers and Barnett?" Freeze asked Brackett.

"Dead, sir. F-4 bomb landed right on them. I've got their dog tags. Wasn't much else," Brackett said.

"SHIT! Here come the Fours again!" Freeze decided to put out smoke, marking the remainder of his team's position. Two F-4s pulled up and began rolling back toward the enemy artillery as the NVA resumed firing in DOAT's direction. The F-4s then came back in very low, strafing the VC positions in front of where Freeze was dug in. This distraction enabled Doc Brackett to display incredible bravery. He sprinted the thirty yards to where Stott and Beamer were down. Brackett verified that Beamer was dead and retrieved his dog tags. The medic then threw Staff Sergeant Stott over his shoulder and ran back to his team. Amazingly, Brackett got Stott back without being hit himself.

"Christ, Doc! Stott?" Freeze asked.

"Stott's alive, sir! Right arm's hit bad, and he's got some fragmentation wounds," Doc told Freeze. "Got to get the bleeding stopped!"

"Your courage saved Stott's life!" Major Freeze said.

Yet another pair of F-4s strafed the NVA positions in front of DOAT. Freeze made another courageous decision. "Helms, Meeks! Cover us with the sixties! Doc and I are gonna move Top and Stott into those rocks just up there. Then I'm gonna ask for a blast!"

Somehow Freeze and Doc got Dunigan and Stott to the relative safety of the rock ledge as Helms and Meeks laid down covering fire. Helms and Meeks then crawled up to the rocks and set up their sixty to cover their CO. Major Freeze ran directly toward the enemy and heaved a green smoke canister as far as he could toward the NVA position.

Major Pole Cat Polinski spotted the "hit here" smoke immediately. Polinski directed the remaining two flights to saturate bomb and strafe the area no more than one hundred meters in front of the rocks where the surviving DOAT men were holed up.

Colonel Spitz's Huey crew saw both colors of smoke set off by Major Freeze. "Gotta be DOAT! They called it in on themselves! SHIT! Where can you set us down, Captain?" Spitz asked his chopper pilot.

"No fuckin' way, sir! That's suicide! Ground's crawling with VC!" the pilot retorted.

"Can you get on that high ground behind the smoke?" Spitz asked.

"But, sir! There are hundreds of gooks down there!"

"Do it, son! NOW! And get me more air support!" ordered Spitz.

As Spitz, Captain Drew, Staff Sergeant John Sharkey, and the two snipers threw out their gear and extra ammo from the hovering chopper, a ground-shaking explosion rocked the mountainside. An errant last bomb from a departing F-4 had "skipped" into Lac Do. The bomb landed squarely on top of the munitions dump air vent in the middle of the village. That initial blast was followed by several minutes of continuous explosions as mortar shells, grenades, C-4 explosive and thousands of rounds of ammunition devastated the center of Lac Do.

"What the fuck!" Colonel Spitz exclaimed.

"Has to be the ammo bunker, sir! Nothing else would have lasted so long!" Sharkey said.

The hit on the munitions bunker, as devastating as it was for Lac Do, undoubtedly saved the lives of the remaining DOAT team members. The bulk of the NVA force was once again redirected to the assault on Lac Do's northern perimeter. Charlie left a company of NVA troopers to defend his

northern flank and try to kill Spitz's men, who were positioned on the mountainside behind DOAT.

The NVA had underestimated the resolve of the Special Forces troopers on that mountainside, especially Five
Group's best linguist.

Chapter Forty-Seven

The Huey that dropped Spitz and his men took serious fire as it sped away from Lac Do's northern-most gridded area. "Motherfucker! Spitz is nuts! You got it marked, right? You know we're gonna have to go back!" the chopper's copilot said.

"Yeah. I know," said the pilot.

As always, Nha Trang was thin on manpower. Major Royalty got twenty-two troopers on a Sikorsky and Huey and headed for Lac Do. The Huey was much faster than the loaded Sikorsky and reached its objective twenty minutes sooner. The pilots had coordinated with Spitz's pilots and knew to skirt five to six clicks north of the main battle zone. As the Huey approached a potential LZ not far from Spitz's position, it was hit with small arms fire from the NVA surrounding the mountainside.

"Radio the Sik pilots to set down farther north, maybe two clicks," Royalty commanded.

"That you Major Royalty?" came Sergeant Sharkey's familiar voice. "Hold for the colonel!"

"Royalty, how many troops you bring?" Spitz asked.

"There are six of us in the Huey and another sixteen in the big bird about fifteen minutes behind us. Situation?"

"We estimate minimum two battalion-strength NVA assault on Lac Do from all directions. Right now a company of regulars is pinning us and the remaining DOAT guys down about 300 meters apart on this hillside. Lac Do's ammo dump blew a bit ago. That seemed to reenergize Charlie's attack. Any minute now we got more F-4s weighing in. Mark smoke when they get here, the Fours are gonna be hittin' real close to us! Let's form around this ridge and get the men in the Sikorsky to go at Charlie from a western flanking position. Then we'll try to relieve Lac Do. DOAT got hit bad. Four dead and two, maybe three wounded need to get to hospital. I want them on that Huey that's dropping you, so tell the pilots to go out a few clicks and wait for our signal to come get our guys!"

As Major Royalty's team got on the ground, the Sikorsky came into view. Spitz got through to the troopers in the bird commanded by Captain Bill Rushing. "Your LZ is two clicks behind Charlie's western flank. Move on 'em as quick as you get organized! I want all Charlie's attention on your team so we can get wounded out on Royalty's Huey!"

"Yes, sir!" Captain Rushing said. Colonel Spitz had been an unknown quantity to the seasoned men of Five Group, but was rapidly earning total respect. Rushing's men were in the battle even before hitting the ground. NVA bullets ricocheted through the Sikorsky's troop cabin. As the big chopper lifted off, Rushing's team came under heavy fire from two directions.

"Colonel, Major, we landed 'in the shit' here! Gonna start working around, but it may take us a while!" Rushing radioed.

"Colonel, the Huey pilots are sayin' they've got fuel range issues! We got to get our guys loaded soon!" Sergeant Sharkey relayed the chopper captain's message to Spitz.

"Roger that, Sergeant! But we've got to get the DOAT guys consolidated back to this position somehow! Two wounded or three?" Spitz asked Sharkey.

"Doc bracket says all three MUST get on that chopper, sir!" JJ said.

"Your buddy is one of the wounded?"

"Yes, sir!"

"Freeze's radio still working?"

"Got him, sir!"

"Freeze, in two minutes we're gonna lay down all the cover we can on your front door! Get your wounded back to us if you can! Royalty's Huey is their ride home, and she's fuel short! So haul ass when we let loose! Got it?" Spitz said.

"Got it! We move on the covering fire!" Freeze confirmed. "Doc, you heard that! How we lookin'?"

"Stott just came to, sir, but I'm not sure he's mobile. You take Dunigan, Helms. I'll move with Stott. Meeks will bring up the rear with sixty cover!"

Spitz's team began their covering fire right on the mark. The remaining DOAT men made their dash toward Spitz's defensive line. When DOAT got to within a hundred meters of Spitz's position, four platoons of NVA emerged from DO-AT's flank and charged the retreating soldiers.

Staff Sergeant John Sharkey saw Mike Stott moving his legs with support from Brackett and Helms. JJ saw Major Freeze carrying Master Sergeant Dunigan over his shoulder. He also could see that he was closest to the line of NVA that rose up to cut off DOAT's retreat. Sharkey had clipped together two two-hundred shot belts in his M-60. The NVA troops rose up directly in front of JJ's position, strung out in a perpendicular line with the closest enemy soldier not twenty feet in front of him.

Staff Sergeant Sharkey counter-charged the line of NVA troops with his M-60 blazing. Sharkey's angle was good. The bullets from JJ's M-60 tore through the charging NVA from their left flank at point-blank range, some of his rounds passing through one enemy and striking another.

Sharkey's bold move so startled the NVA that they hesitated briefly. Sharkey emptied the 400 rounds from his M-60 into the NVA troopers' line, killing eleven and downing six more. His counter charge brought Sharkey to within twenty meters of the remaining NVA. With his M-60 empty, Sharkey hit the deck and lobbed four fragmentation grenades at NVA positions. When the last grenade exploded, Sharkey was on his feet again with a fresh double belt in his gun. JJ fired another 400 rounds into the remaining NVA as he effectively positioned himself in the middle of the surviving enemy soldiers.

Colonel Barry Spitz and Major Royalty watched Sharkey's feat in utter amazement. Sergeant Sharkey's heroic individual counter charge had not only stopped an entire NVA rifle company, it had driven the remaining enemy force into retreat. As Charlie withdrew back in the direction of Lac Do,

Captain Drew and his sharpshooters picked off many more of the enemy from their elevated position as they covered Staff Sergeant Sharkey.

When the NVA resumed their retreat, Sergeant Sharkey literally chased them, firing his machine gun and lobbing two more fragmentation grenades. Sharkey's last grenade exploded on top of an NVA captain, his radioman, and two other bad guys, killing them instantly. JJ then drew his Colt .45 and continued his attack.

Screaming at the top of his lungs, Major Royalty yelled, "STOP! JJ! HOLD UP! WE'RE COMIN' FOR YA!" Royalty was some 200 meters above Sharkey on the hillside where DOAT had hooked up with Colonel Spitz's remaining team members. "GO get him back, Drew! Move! NOW!"

Captain Drew and his two sergeants advanced to where Staff Sergeant John J. Sharkey was holding his ground. Captain Drew confirmed that Sharkey had personally, single-handedly killed at least thirty-seven NVA soldiers including a captain and two lieutenants. When Drew reached Sharkey, JJ had recovered two AK-47s and was firing them in the direction the NVA had retreated.

"SERGEANT SHARKEY! STOP! COME ON! GET BACK! LET'S GO!" Captain Drew screamed.

"Is Stott in the chopper?" Sharkey asked Captain Drew.

"YEAH! LET'S GO!"

Staff Sergeant Sharkey followed Captain Drew and his shooters back toward where Colonel Spitz and the troopers were dug in.

"CHRIST, Major! There must be fifty dead gooks down there and Sharkey killed most of 'em! UN-FUCKING-BE-LIEVABLE!" Colonel Spitz exclaimed.

"Never saw anything like it, sir! How JJ didn't get hit I'll never know!" said Major Royalty.

When Staff Sergeant John J. Sharkey got back to Colonel Spitz's position, the entire group was moving to get the wounded men to an LZ on the other side of the hill. No one said a word.

Sharkey got to Mike Stott just as the Huey was about to lift off.

"Hey, dickhead! You all right?" JJ asked his friend.

"Don't call me dickhead, goddamn it! I'll kick your fuckin' ass!" Stott responded.

Staff Sergeant John Sharkey smiled. He knew his buddy was going to make it. "R & R in Bangkok in sixty days! Get ready, asshole!" JJ said. The chopper lifted up and away.

F-4s arrived just as the Huey converted to a medivac got airborne. Colonel Spitz ordered Doc Brackett to go with his wounded team members to take care of them on the flight back to Nha Trang. As the Fours began their attack on the NVA troops all around Lac Do, Colonel Spitz and Major Royalty hooked up with Captain Rushing's team and began to plan how to relieve Lac Do. Including Freeze and Sergeant Meeks, Spitz had twenty-nine Special Forces men in the detachment.

Colonel Spitz, Majors Royalty and Freeze, and Captains Drew and Rushing huddled to formalize their next move.

"F-4s are tearing 'em up good, sir! Maybe we can reach Lac Do after nightfall," Captain Drew began.

"Hold a second, Captain. I want all of you officers to hear this and remember what I say! Major Royalty will back me up on this because he saw it all too from our perch on that hillside. So did most of the troopers! In my twenty-two years in the army I've never witnessed anything like what I saw Sergeant John Sharkey do today! I will recommend him for the Congressional Medal of Honor. If I get hit today, I command you officers to make that happen! His heroism was beyond description. I'm gonna tell you that he personally saved all our bacon today with his one man countercharge," Spitz said.

Major Royalty actually butted in. "One hundred percent with you, sir! And the kid's only twenty years old! Unbelievable courage!"

"I saw it, too, sir!" Captain Drew said. "Bravest thing I ever saw! I'll certify his kills! Hell, he was still firing an AK at Charlie when we pulled him back!"

"Agreed, then?" said Spitz. "Staff Sergeant Sharkey deserves and will receive a CMH! Now, let's get a plan together! Hold Sharkey back! He's done enough for one day!"

Two more flights of F-4s hit the NVA and VC positions surrounding Lac Do that afternoon. From their position on "K" hill, Spitz's men watched the air strikes and Charlie's continued assault on Lac Do. It appeared that the NVA had decided to set up a containment zone on their northern flank to isolate Spitz's soldiers.

"Still no radio contact with our guys inside, Sergeant Sharkey?" Major Royalty asked JJ.

"No, sir! I keep trying, but just nothing!" JJ said. "When we going in, sir?"

"We're watching the strikes and Charlie's moves, Sergeant. JJ, listen up! Every man on that hillside saw what you did this morning. It's an honor and a privilege to serve with you, son," Colonel Spitz said to Sharkey. "We get through this shit today, we'll talk!"

"What made you do it, Sergeant?" Major Royalty asked.

"Do what, sir?" Sharkey seemed genuinely confused.

"SERGEANT! None of us have witnessed greater bravery than what you showed today! This morning! When you countercharged Charlie's line!" Colonel Spitz said.

"Oh! That! Needed to get Mikey on that chopper, sir! Fuckin' gooks were in the way! He'd have done it for me, sir!" JJ said.

Colonel Spitz and Major Royalty were speechless. Spitz clapped Sharkey on the shoulder. "We could not be prouder of you, son," he said.

That night, January 29, 1966, as Spitz's men prepared to try to reach Lac Do in a flanking move from the southwest, the NVA withdrew. They simply vanished. An advance C Team of Spitz's best shooters began working their way toward Lac Do's southwest berm around 1900 hours. The whole area was strangely quiet. The night became clear and stars filled the sky.

Assigned to Colonel Spitz's radio, Staff Sergeant John J. Sharkey knew that Chuck had left.

"What do you make of this quiet, Sergeant?" Spitz asked JJ.

"I think Chuck's gone, sir. I'm just feelin' this one's all over," Sharkey said.

Staff Sergeant Sharkey was right. The NVA and VC forces were gone. They took many of their dead with them, but the enemy body count was still more than six hundred killed. All of the Five Group soldiers in the replacement A Team that had been sent to Lac Do to fill in for DOAT were killed in the battle that became known as Lac Do Two. Of the nine hundred or so Montagnard tribesmen and family members in Lac Do when the battle began, only two hundred and eleven survived uninjured. Over six hundred tribes people were killed and more than a hundred were severely wounded. Spitz's rescue team discovered that the VC had infiltrated Lac Do's communications bunker and sabotaged the radios just as the battle began, eliminating the air support that might have prevented such disastrous results.

On January 30, Colonel Spitz and his men entered what was left of Lac Do. The explosion in the ammo bunker had left a crater in the ground twenty feet deep and more than one hundred feet across. Chief Won and all of the village elders were dead. Of the two hundred eleven survivors, there were only ten men between the ages of sixteen and thirty.

Many of the Montagnard survivors wanted only to be left alone to return to other central highlands settlements. Others were so traumatized from the horrendous battle they wanted to go with the Americans. After careful consideration Spitz made the decision to abandon Lac Do. The village was essentially destroyed and totally vulnerable to another attack from Charlie. There simply wasn't enough left to defend or rebuild.

In later years, Colonel Spitz's decision to abandon Lac Do was highly criticized because the village had stood at the northernmost end of what became known as the A Shau Valley. NVA and VC exploited the demise of Lac Do and its defensive position to increase the quantity of supplies entering South Vietnam via the portion of the Ho Chi Minh Trail that came through the high mountain pass formerly known as Lac Do, South Vietnam.

On February 2, 1966, all twenty-nine surviving Group Five personnel from the second battle of Lac Do were back in Nha Trang, recovering. Colonel Besuden returned from his R & R in Hong Kong and learned of the loss of Lac Do and sixteen of his men. Colonel Spitz, aided by Majors Royalty and Freeze, debriefed Besuden on Five Group's worst defeat in Vietnam.

"Christ, what a cluster fuck! How the hell did our guys let their radios get gooked? Goddamn it!" Besuden exclaimed.

"Sir, there is one positive from Lac Do. We wanted to get all the bad news out of the way first, but now we need to explain what Staff Sergeant John J. Sharkey did in support of the relief effort," Spitz said to Besuden.

"Well?"

Spitz, Royalty, and Freeze all recounted their own versions of Sharkey's bravery for Besuden. "And, sir, truth be told, it was Sergeant Sharkey who first argued to get the F-4 jockeys up to take a look at Lac Do on the morning of 29 January," Major Royalty concluded.

"How's his buddy, Sergeant Stott, doing? Going to be okay?" Besuden asked.

"Stott's arm is bad, sir. He still may lose it above the elbow. Sergeant Sharkey's waiting to see you. He wants to go visit his buddy in Da Nang before Stott gets shipped off to Walter Reed," Royalty said.

"Well, okay. Let's get Sharkey that CMH. Colonel Spitz, sounds like you did all you could. Thanks for all your efforts. I'd like to speak with Freeze and Royalty on a personal matter. Be back with you in just a minute," Besuden said.

When Spitz was gone, Besuden said to Royalty and Freeze, "Give it to me straight! You think Lac Do was retaliation for Dong San?"

Major Royalty spoke first, "No, sir. I don't. I think Charlie had been planning the Lac Do attack for a long time. There were probably two if not three NVA battalions committed to the assault. Chuck's been setting that one up for a while."

"Major Freeze?"

"I don't know, sir. If DOAT had gotten back sooner, the radio room would not have been fragged. I just don't think we would have been blindsided so badly."

"Major Freeze, you saw Sergeant Sharkey's heroism. You convinced he deserves a Congressional Medal of Honor too, right?"

"Absolutely! You would have been proud to see it, sir," Freeze said.

"Okay. We lost four SPEND members at Lac Do. Only two of them had wills, so we need to think about what to do with the extra cash. I was able to open the deposit boxes in Zurich. The guys are all set if they decide to put some of their cash into boxes. No interest, but no sweat taking untraceable cash as needed," Besuden said. "After 1975, of course."

"No problem getting in and out of Switzerland with your backup docs?" Royalty asked. "The C-130 made it to Ramstadt okay?"

"None at all. Let's get docs for all the SPEND guys now that we know how well they work. But a lot of cash has to get moved! Any new ideas?" Besuden asked.

Neither major responded.

"Okay. We'll keep working on that one. Get Sergeant Sharkey in here. I want to shake his hand and tell him what we're putting him in for. He doesn't know yet, right?"

"No, sir. We wanted to clear it with you first, sir," Royalty said.

Staff Sergeant John Sharkey reported to Colonel Besuden and was surprised to see Majors Royalty and Freeze in Besuden's office. In the privacy of the colonel's bunker, JJ came to attention and saluted.

"Staff Sergeant Sharkey reporting, sir."

"At ease Sergeant Sharkey! Major Freeze, ask Colonel Spitz to step back in here."

When Spitz rejoined the group Sharkey, saluted him. "You do something you want to tell me about, Sergeant Sharkey?" Besuden asked.

For a moment, JJ wondered if Besuden had heard about last night's poker game. Sharkey had cleaned out all the lieutenants and captains in a poker game that lasted far into the night. "Ah, no, sir. Well, maybe, sir. I put in a request for R & R so I can go see Mikey, er, Sergeant Stott, before they ship him back to the states to heal up, sir!"

"Anything else, Sergeant?" Besuden asked.

Sharkey was getting nervous. He didn't think he'd screwed up, but you never knew! "No, sir!"

"I hear you broke a line up in Lac Do. That right?"

"Sir?" Now Sharkey was worried.

"Did you or did you not leave your position on Colonel Spitz's right flank while manning an M-60 at Lac Do Two? Yes or no? Don't even think of fucking with me, Sergeant!" Besuden had shifted into that authority-of-command tone he was famous for.

For once, Staff Sergeant Sharkey was speechless. JJ thought he'd done okay at Lac Do. Now Besuden seemed displeased.

"Sir?" Sharkey repeated.

"I REPEAT! DID YOU OR DID YOU NOT BREAK OUT OF YOUR ASSIGNED POSITION AT LAC DO?"

"Ah, yes, sir. I did," JJ said.

"And killed about fifty gooks, right? Basically saving your buddy's bacon by securing an LZ for Stott's ride home, right?" Besuden formed it as a question.

"Yes, sir!" JJ said.

Colonel Besuden got up from his seat and stood directly in front of JJ. "Son, you're going to get the Congressional Medal of Honor for your heroism. Colonel Spitz will be the sponsoring officer, and Majors Freeze and Royalty will substantiate as eye witnesses. God bless you, John Sharkey." Besuden shook JJ's hand. Then he hugged him.

426   **Philip B. Storm**

Sharkey felt his knees buckle. Could it be? He felt he'd
done what any trooper in that situation would have. Sharkey
accepted congratulations and thanks from Spitz, Royalty,
and Freeze.

"What do you say, Sergeant? Where's that quick wit of
yours?" Besuden asked.

"Well, I thank you all for what you're doing if you think I
deserve a medal. But, sir, I'd trade that medal for leave to go
check on Sergeant Stott, sir," Sharkey said.

"Son, you earned that CMH! And you got five days to go
see your buddy. Catch the noon shuttle. And try not to get
in any trouble down there, Sergeant! Son, I hope you know
how a Congressional Medal of Honor will change your life!
You are a true hero!" Besuden said.

"Thanks, sir, but can I go? I don't want to miss that shuttle!" JJ asked. Sharkey saluted and made a beeline for his
hooch to pack.

"I don't think he understands, gentlemen! Get the paperwork together. I want to get him that medal ASAP! I've got a
hunch the army public relations guys may want to use Staff
Sergeant Sharkey! Plus, it may take some heat off what happened at Lac Do. Major Freeze, are Dunigan and Helms going to recover 100 percent?" Besuden asked.

"Helms, yes. Master Sergeant Dunigan's got a nasty infection in his thigh wound. I'm worried about him. What's up
for my team, sir? We'll be ready to redeploy soon!" Freeze
said.

"Take a few days, Major. I'm working on something for
you," Besuden concluded the meeting.

Staff Sergeant Sharkey arrived at the hospital in Da Nang
at 1640 hours. Activity throughout the compound was at a
crescendo. Wounded were arriving faster than the staff could
handle.

"What's up?" JJ asked a duty sergeant.

"Bad shit in the Ia Drang Valley! First Cav's knee-deep in
VC! Wounded been arriving around the clock since yesterday morning, Sergeant."

"Too bad. I'm looking for a green hat, Staff Sergeant Stott. Where can I find him?" Sharkey asked.

The duty sergeant consulted his log. "D Ward, but I don't think you can get in there. It's restricted right now."

"Yeah? Why?" Sharkey asked.

"It just is, Sergeant!"

"Point me in the direction, Sergeant! I will get in!"

"Move it, trooper! Comin' through!" As Sharkey made his way back toward D Ward he had to dodge the stretchers and push-beds full of wounded soldiers.

"Where'd you put that nigger lieutenant?" a very young looking doctor wearing captain's bars asked a nurse.

"Uh, right there, sir!" she responded. Sharkey naturally followed her gesture and looked straight at Big Howie. Howard's eyes were closed, and he still had blood all over him. Howie had an IV in each arm and bandages binding them. His head and left ear were wrapped. Blood oozed through the bandage under his ear.

After a momentary hesitation, Staff Sergeant John J. Sharkey recovered from the shock of seeing his friend in such serious condition. JJ grabbed the young doctor's arm and spun him around in front of the nurse and two orderlies. "You ever call this officer a nigger again I will kill you! That's a promise! Now, HELP HIM!"

Dr. Peter Allen was shocked! "Who the fuck are you?" he responded.

Sharkey didn't flinch. "The guy who will kill you if you call Lieutenant Howard a nigger again, dickhead! NOW MOVE!"

"JJ! Is that you? Where are you?" George Howard recognized Sharkey's voice.

"SIR, YES SIR! IT IS! AND YOU BETTER BELIEVE I'M SALUTING!" JJ barked out.

Big Howie couldn't see Sharkey, but he smiled and reached his hand out in the direction he'd heard the voice. JJ took his hand. "You're gonna be fine now, sir! I'm here, and Stott is here somewhere too!" Sharkey said.

428 **Philip B. Storm**

"Mike's with you?" Lieutenant Howard asked.

"Ah, no, Howie, er, sir. Mike got wounded at Lac Do Two. I came here to see him before they ship him back to Walter Reed," JJ said.

"Is he okay? Can I see him? Where is he?" Howard asked.

"If this mouthy sergeant will get the fuck out of my way we're gonna start working on you, Lieutenant," Dr. Allen said. "You can see your buddies later!"

"Is he gonna be okay, Captain?" Sharkey asked Allen.

"Yeah, his wounds aren't life threatening. But he's lost a lot of blood, so move out of the way!"

"Remember, Doc! LIEUTENANT HOWARD IS A FRIEND OF MINE!" JJ said. "RESPECT HIM!"

Dr. Allen started to respond to Sharkey, but thought better of it. Some of these green hat guys were truly nuts! Captain Allen realized Staff Sergeant Sharkey was someone not to fuck with. It was one of Dr. Allen's better decisions.

Sharkey found D Ward with a female captain sitting at a desk blocking the entrance. Sharkey saluted and said, "Staff Sergeant John J. Sharkey representing Colonel Robert Besuden, commanding officer of Five Group up at Nha Trang. I'm here to debrief Sergeant Mike Stott, ma'am!"

Captain Alice Higgins looked JJ up and down and said, "I think you're full of shit, Sergeant! But Sergeant Stott told me if his little brother, Sergeant Sharkey, showed up, I had to let him in! So go on in, but don't try to bullshit me, Sergeant!"

"LITTLE brother? Why, I'll kick his ass on general principles! Where is he, er, ma'am?"

Captain Higgins smiled in spite of herself. "That's exactly what Sergeant Stott said you'd say! Third bed on the left and keep it down! Most guys in there are in worse shape than Mike, er, Sergeant Stott."

When Sharkey first saw his friend, his heart sank. Mike's arm was in an elevated sling and his head was shaved. A bandage covered Mike's right ear. Stott appeared to be dozing. Quietly, JJ walked to Mike's bedside. As Sharkey bent closer to see if Mike was asleep, Stott grabbed JJ by his collar and jerked him forward.

"Never try to sneak up on a Green Beret, dickhead! I will kick your scrawny ass!" Mike said.

Sharkey wrapped his arms around his friend. "Goddamn you! If you weren't hurt I'd kick your ass for that!" JJ said. Sharkey drew back and looked at Mike.

"Well? You never seen a guy with his head shaved before?" Stott asked.

Sharkey turned serious. "I knew about your arm, but what's with the ear bandage and those stitches on your scalp?"

"The ear is infected from shrapnel, but it'll be fine! The scalp wounds are from Captain Higgins' fingernails!" Stott said.

Sharkey smiled. "Uh huh. Next you'll be telling you got laid in here! Mike! Big Howie is here! Right out there in the hall! He got fucked up in the Ia Drang, but he's gonna be fine! First thing he did was ask about you!"

"Howard's here? No shit! How bad is he hit?" Stott asked.

"He'll recover, quicker than you!" JJ told his friend.

"JJ, how bad did Lac Do get it? What about our replacements? Who's there now?" Stott wanted to know.

"Mikey, we had to abandon Lac Do. All our replacements were killed. Charlie fragged the radios, so there was no air support. Over 600 villagers were killed. Charlie had to have lost two to three times that many. The ammo bunker took a direct hit. Left a hell of a crater!"

"I know Beamer was killed. What about other DOAT guys?" Stott asked.

"Adams, Barnett, and Myers were also killed, Mikey. Dunigan and Helms got hit too. Helms will be fine. He was treated in Nha Trang. Dunigan is here somewhere with a bad infection from his leg wound," JJ said.

After several minutes of silence, Stott asked, "If they had no radios where did the F-4s come from?"

"Uh, we called 'em in from Nha Trang to take a look when we didn't hear from DOAT or the guys in Lac Do," JJ said.

"Christ! Somebody was thinking! Otherwise, we'd all be dead," said Sergeant Stott. "Who made that call?"

"I believe it was Major Royalty. Mike, I've gotta tell you something. I'm not supposed to, but I gotta! Colonel Spitz has put me in for a Congressional Medal of Honor, just like your brother!" Sharkey said.

Mike Stott stared at his friend for a very long time. "Tell me about it," he said.

Sharkey told Stott his story. "Officially, I'm ahead of you, now, dickhead! Fifty-seven confirmed kills! Now you gotta buy the booze!"

Staff Sergeant Mike Stott smiled at Sharkey's last statement.

"You did it to get me on that chopper, didn't you?" Mike asked.

"You still owe me a month's pay and a steak dinner, goddamn it! How else was I gonna collect, dickhead?" JJ said.

"So now, I'm gonna have to hear how you saved my ass for the rest of my life, right? I don't know if it's worth it, dickhead!" There were tears in Stott's eyes as he reached for Sharkey's hand. "But thanks, anyway."

"You'd have done it for me," JJ said. "So what's the word on your arm? They shipping you back to Walter Reed?"

"They haven't told me anything yet. What did you hear?" Stott asked.

Before JJ could answer, Captain Higgins took Sharkey by the shoulder and said, "You're way over your time limit, Sergeant! Now get outta here so we can shoot him up! You can come back tomorrow. I won't let you in here again today!"

"What's that shit?" JJ asked looking at the hypodermic needle.

"OUT! NOW! Or I'll kick your ass, Sergeant!" Higgins said.

"RIGHT! See you in the a.m., Mikey."

As Staff Sergeant Mike Stott slipped away under the morphine's effect, he thought of Sharkey with a Congressional Medal of Honor around his neck—and about $20 million in his account in Switzerland. Stott thought maybe he'd give some money to Big Howie.

Chapter Forty-Eight

As Captain Higgins exited D Ward she was surprised to see the young green hat sergeant standing next to the ward desk. "I told you, you're not getting back in tonight! Sergeant Stott will be out cold for several hours anyway. Now, scram, Sergeant!" Captain Higgins said.

"I'm waiting for you, ma'am! When do you get off?" JJ asked her.

"Are you fucking nuts, Sergeant! I'm an officer, I'm a foot taller than you and twenty years older! Get out of my military sight. NOW!" Captain Higgins said.

"I won't tell if you won't! Now, what time and where do I meet you, ma'am?" Sharkey asked again.

"Are you lookin' for a Section Eight, Sergeant? I'll be here 'til late! Now, beat it!"

"I know you don't mean it! I'm gonna hang around outside the officer's club until you let me buy you dinner! So you might as well give in! I'm gonna be here five days, and I'll bug you 'til you say yes!" JJ persisted.

At 2330 hours that evening, Staff Sergeant Sharkey found himself toes to nose with the well-endowed Captain Higgins. "DO THAT AGAIN, SERGEANT!" she commanded.

"Only if you promise to take special care of Mikey!" JJ teased.

"YES! YES! AGAIN!"

Fucking captains is even better than I imagined, Sharkey thought.

The next morning JJ got right into Stott's ward. He'd been given an "unrestricted" hospital pass and could come and go as he pleased. Sharkey was not pleased to see the pain in his buddy's face. "You don't look so good, dickhead! Bad night?"

"I'll be okay. I'm due another shoot-up, so the pain's pretty bad right now," Stott said.

Sharkey knew the pain had to be bad for Stott to admit he was hurting. "So, can I do anything?" JJ asked Stott.

"Yeah! Take me to Bangkok!" Stott said.

"That was fun! We'll get back there, I promise! Did you see the doctors, yet?" JJ asked.

"Looks like him now," Stott said.

Sharkey turned to see Dr. Peter Allen entering D Ward. "What the hell are you doing here? Where'd you get the pass? I'm still considering reporting you for threatening me yesterday!" Allen said.

"Wasn't a threat, sir. It was a promise. And I keep my promises," said Sharkey. "What happens to Sergeant Stott next?"

"Well, in about two hours we're gonna operate on his arm again. If we can, we're gonna put a steel pin in the elbow joint. If there's any sign of infection, the arm will come off," Allen's matter-of-fact tone infuriated Sharkey.

Dr. Allen was accompanied by two nurses and two orderlies. Sharkey leaned close and whispered softly in Captain Allen's ear, "Stott loses that arm, you lose your life. I promise."

Dr. Allen's team began prepping Sergeant Stott for surgery, so Sharkey went to check on Big Howie. JJ finally located his friend in a recovery ward. Lieutenant Howard was sitting up in bed eating breakfast. Sharkey gave him a hug. It made Big Howie cry.

"Goddamn it! If you start bawlin,' I'll have to kick your ass, officer or not!" JJ said.

"JJ, I woke up this morning and was afraid I'd only dreamed you were here! Thank God it's really you!" Howard said.

"You look a lot better than last night! How you doin', sir?" JJ asked.

The "sir" made Howie laugh. "The only thing that got me through OCS was the thought of you and Mikey having to salute me! How's he doing?" Howard asked.

"Sir, they're going to operate on Mike in about an hour. They decided they can't wait to ship him home. Fifty-fifty on whether they can save his arm," JJ told Howard.

JJ and Big Howie locked eyes.

"Motherfucker!" Howard said.

"Howie, I've got a feeling Mike's going to be okay. You can't believe what a good soldier he's become."

Sharkey found a chair, and he and Howard passed the morning of Stott's operation catching up. Mostly, they talked about their army experience. Howie told Sharkey about his trip home after OCS.

"JJ, no one in my family had even heard of Vietnam! Sounds crazy, but it's true! They know now, of course, but not until I told them!" Howard said.

"Uh, Howie, er, sir. One more thing. Larry Allsmeir was killed last November. We heard about it from Eddy Hale. He and Mobliano went to the funeral. Now you know," Sharkey said. "Sorry to spring it on you."

After Lieutenant Howard absorbed the news about Allsmeir, he said to Sharkey, "So now there are six of us left. Smeall's already a civilian and Mobliano was always just a weekend warrior. Hale gonna get a tour over here?"

"Hale doesn't think so, but who knows? Eddy seems to carry the luck of the Irish with him, whatever that means! He just doesn't understand what he's missing," JJ said.

"JJ, you mean that, don't you? You actually want to be in Vietnam! Man, I'd go back to Germany in a heartbeat!" said Lieutenant Howard.

"Howie, are you still thinking of staying in the army?" JJ asked.

"Sure, JJ! What else have I got? How about you?"

"Absolutely. But I'm afraid they'll make Mikey get out, you know, because of his arm," Sharkey said.

JJ leaned close to Howie and said, "I told Mike, and now I'm gonna tell you. Colonel Spitz and the other officers we were with at Lac Do are putting me in for the Congressional Medal of Honor. I still can't believe it, but they are. Mikey deserves it more than me! Hell, he's done ten times more than I have over here!"

"DAMN, JJ! That's incredible! Congratulations!" Lieutenant Howard was thrilled for Sharkey. "You're made for life in the army! Do we still, you know, have our pact?"

John Sharkey stared at Howard. "Our pact is more important to me than ten CMH's! Of course we have it! When Mike's okay, the three of us need to talk about something Mike and I got involved in that will be very good for you too. Let me go check in at the operating room. It's been four hours! I'll be back!"

It was three hours later when Sharkey returned to Howard's ward. "They put a pin in Mike's arm! They're still worried about infection, but it should be okay! HOLY SHIT! I feel better!" JJ told Big Howie.

"Great! When can I see him?" Howard asked.

"Maybe tomorrow! Hey, get some rest! I'll be back later today or early tomorrow at the latest!"

Staff Sergeant John Sharkey spent the next three days going back and forth between Howard and Stott's wards in the hospital. Stott's arm was improving daily and Lieutenant Howard was healing rapidly too.

On February 7, 1966, Sharkey got Howard and Stott into wheelchairs and rolled them out into a bright, sunny day in Da Nang. There was a smoking area with a canvas covering on the eastern side of the hospital where the three friends found some privacy.

Sharkey produced three crystal tumblers from his travel bag and a bottle of Crown Royal. JJ filled each glass and said, "To our pact! To the two people that mean more to me than anyone else in the world! GET WELL AND GET BACK ON LINE! I can't win this war all by myself! Listen up! I've got to catch the supply plane back to Nha Trang in three hours. Howie, Mikey and I have got some stuff to tell you. It sort of puts you on the spot with you being an officer, but we've agreed that our pact prevails above all else!"

For the next two hours, John Sharkey and Mike Stott explained what SPEND had accomplished.

Sharkey concluded, "So, sir! Mike and I have agreed. In the later part of 1975, when we can access our money, we're each going to give you $1 million. So don't worry about money ever again! We're going to figure out what to do with all of our combined funds later! Right now, we're gonna enjoy this war and see what other opportunities develop!"

"IS THIS REAL?" Howard asked.

"That's what you asked in our suite at the Plaza! Howie, it's real! You guys get well and stay out of trouble! I'm going home to Nha Trang! Get your ass back there, Stott! We got work to do!" Sharkey said.

But Staff Sergeant Mike Stott never returned to Nha Trang. On April 21, 1966, less than three years after enlisting in the army, Stott was honorably discharged as no longer physically fit to serve in Five Group. Although his arm was healing fairly well, Mike Stott could no longer qualify to be a Special Forces soldier. Stott wrote the following letter to Staff Sergeant John Sharkey and Lieutenant George Howard:

Dear Dickhead and Lieutenant Howard,

>*Well, guys, my army career is over. I was told this morning that I will be honorably discharged immediately and placed in a control group of disabled veterans! I still can't believe it!*
>
>*I feel completely guilty that you guys are still in Vietnam and I'm sitting on my ass getting fat here at Bragg. Truth is, I miss 5 Group. I even miss Vietnam! I will, of course, always honor our pact as the most important commitment I will ever make. So now what can I do to support you guys?*
>
>*I guess maybe I'll start college next fall and try to prepare to manage money, if you know what I mean. My arm is coming along OK, but I don't think I'll be pitching in the majors!*

JJ, I heard from Colonel Besuden that you may get your Congressional Medal of Honor as early as this summer! Guess the army can process paper when they want to! Besuden said your ceremony might be stateside because the army wants to show you off! In any case, wherever you get it, I'll be there! Unless they do it in Nam. I don't think I could get back in country.

Howie, I got your letter about being back in the field. Glad you're healed, but keep your big ugly head down! You're a big-ass target!

Soon as they process me I guess I'll head back to Cincinnati. I feel totally and completely lost. Please forgive me for not coming back, JJ. I'm going to work hard to get all three of us set up back here. With all this time laying around in army beds, I thought of the following idea. From now on we'll be the PACKMEN! JJ's Packman One, Howie's Packman Two and me, the dumb-ass civilian, will be Packman Three.

Please send me the names and addresses of any of your girlfriends you want me to take care of until you get back!

Packman Three
Staff Sergeant Mike Stott

Three weeks later, Staff Sergeant Stott processed out of the army. On his last day at Fort Bragg, Stott was ordered to report to Five Group's liaison office on post. To his surprise, Lieutenant Colonel Bill Freeze, DOAT's former CO, was there waiting for him.

"At ease, Sergeant! Mike, it's great to see you! All the troopers at Nha Trang send you their best! Even First Sergeant John Sharkey! He wanted me to give you this," said Freeze.

"First Sergeant Sharkey? HOLY SHIT! Congratulations on your promotion, sir! What are you doing here?" Stott asked.

"Coordination meeting, Sergeant. Don't open this until you are off post." Freeze handed Stott a thick 8-1/2 x 11-inch manila envelope. "I expect to see you in Washington sometime in August, Sergeant Stott! JJ will be receiving his CMH. He says he won't accept it if you're not there! I'm proud to have served with you, son. I'll never forget you! By the way, you might want to open that envelope right outside the gate before you go too far! See you in August!"

Outside the gate at Fort Bragg, North Carolina, May 9, 1966, the just-discharged Green Beret, Staff Sergeant Mike Stott, opened the envelope. In it was a letter from JJ, three hundred hundred-dollar bills, and a title to a 1966 Pontiac GTO convertible. The letter read:

> *Dear Dickhead Civilian Stott,*
>
> *Enclosed please find the clear title to a Black on Black on Black 1966 GTO Convertible. The car is waiting for you at the Pontiac dealer in Fayetteville. Try not to wreck it before I get to drive it. It's a lot of power for a fucking civilian to handle!*
>
> *Also enclosed is some college money. "We" expect you to graduate with a degree in finance from a good college. Concentrate your studies on long-term investing, if you get my drift!*
>
> *If your arm has healed up by the time I see you in Washington this summer I will kick your ass for becoming a civilian!*
>
> *You might want to look around the dealership when you pick up the GTO. Might see someone you know.*
>
> *Remember me to the family. See you in DC.*
> *Packman One*
>
> *First Sergeant John J. Sharkey*
> *5 Group*
> *Nha Trang, Vietnam*
>
> *P.S. That's right, dickhead, I'm an E-7! Goes with the medal! Go figure!*

Mike Stott caught the 1300 hours bus into Fayetteville. Sitting in front of the Pontiac dealer was a shiny GTO convertible with the top down. In the passenger's seat was Cindy Strand.

"Hey, soldier! I know a great spot on the shore! Want to get laid?" Cindy said. They stayed on the shore for three weeks.

On August 24, 1966, three years and six weeks after joining the army, First Sergeant John J. Sharkey, airborne Ranger and Green Beret communications NCO, received the Congressional Medal of Honor. President Lyndon Baines Johnson personally presented him with the medal at a ceremony on the South Lawn of the White House.

In attendance were seven sisters from St. Agnes Orphanage of Bedford, New York. Also there by special arrangement was First Lieutenant Sylvatore Mobliano and Specialist Ed Hale, in uniform. Standing in the "honor-slot" to Sergeant Sharkey's right and also in uniform was recently discharged Green Beret Staff Sergeant Mike Stott. Second Lieutenant George Howard was still "on line" in the Ia Drang Valley with the First Cavalry Division.

After the ceremony, Milt, Bessy, Barry, Beverly, and Bunnie Smeall hosted a dinner for Sergeant Sharkey and his army buddies at the Hay-Adams Hotel. The first toast was, of course, to the nation's youngest Congressional Medal of Honor winner in fifteen years, John "JJ" Sharkey. The second toast was to the memory of Larry Allsmeir, killed in action in Vietnam. The third toast was to Second Lieutenant "Big Howie" George Howard of the First Cavalry.

JJ presented the fourth toast. "To my best friend Staff Sergeant Mike Stott. This medal is more yours than mine. To our pact, to our friendship, and to what comes next!"

"Goddamn it, JJ! You always do all the talking! Tell you what, everybody. Let's agree to hold a ten-year reunion right here at the Hay-Adams Hotel! Since Labor Day weekends have a special significance for many of us, let's do our re-union over Labor Day weekend 1976! But that re-union will be on JJ and me! We'll pay for everything! The Smeall fam-

ily has done enough! Everybody agrees? Labor Day weekend 1976, right here at this hotel?" Mike Stott said.

"Sounds great, Mike! The Smealls will be there! But we'll
sponsor the party! The Hay-Adams is pricey by anybody's
standards!" Milt Smeall said. "It would probably be a year's
pay for JJ, even if he's a sergeant major by then!"

"No sir, Milt! Mikey, Big Howie, and me will sponsor that
reunion! Hell, Howie's an officer! He'll be able to afford it!"
Sharkey said.

Epilogue

John "JJ" Sharkey returned to Five Group at Nha Trang in October 1966 after a thirty-day leave in Washington, D.C. During that leave, he and Mike Stott partied with their friends, Cindy and Red, and planned what to do with their money after 1976.

Sharkey remained in the Fifth Special Forces Group in Vietnam until the group redeployed back to Fort Bragg in 1971. During 1972, First Sergeant Sharkey was reassigned to another Special Forces group and attended languages school again in Monterrey, California, to learn Farsi and Arabic.

John Sharkey served in Grenada, Panama, and the First Gulf War in addition to going "on loan" to the governments of Israel and Saudi Arabia to advise and assist the special operations sections of their militaries. In 1993, Command Sergeant Major John Sharkey retired from the army as the most decorated soldier from the Vietnam era. In addition to his Congressional Medal of Honor, John Sharkey earned four Silver Stars, three Bronze Stars and too many commendations to list. JJ was awarded four Purple Hearts for being wounded in combat; three from Vietnam and one from Grenada.

After taking a year off to travel the world with Mike Stott, John Sharkey went back to work for an unnamed department of the U.S. government until 2004. Sharkey is retired and resides in Switzerland where he helps design and construct orphanages throughout the world.

Mike Stott graduated from Georgetown University and went to work for the Mellon Bank of Pittsburgh where Barry Smeall was a senior vice president and major stockholder. By special arrangement, Mike remained in the D.C. area and lived with Cindy Strand until she died in 1980. In 1977, Stott left Mellon and started a private venture capital fund with the Smeall family and other investors. The fund is managed from Zurich, Switzerland, and invests primarily in defense industries around the world. The fund has done quite well. Mike Stott lives in Naples, Florida, when he isn't traveling the world.

George "Big Howie" Howard stayed in the army for twenty years and earned a degree in criminology followed by two masters' degrees. He retired as a lieutenant colonel in 1984 after twenty-one years of service. First Lieutenant Howard was awarded a Silver Star for Valor in the Ia Drang Valley during 1967. In 1985, George Howard joined the New York City Police Department and worked his way up to captain before retiring in 2002. George and his wife Anna and their three daughters spend their time between their condos in Manhattan and Naples, Florida.

Through the years, Mike Stott, John Sharkey, and George Howard have honored their pact. They remain the best of friends and get together as often as possible, usually in Switzerland where JJ has a mountaintop chalet.

Barry Smeall retired from banking at the age of thirty-five and lived off his family's immense wealth. He served on the board of Mike Stott's defense industry venture fund until he died of a heart attack in 1995. His wife Beverly and daughter Bunnie live in Vail, Colorado.

Sylvatore Mobliano also served twenty years in the army, but with the New York National Guard Judge Advocates Office. Mobs attained the rank of lieutenant colonel. After losing a bid to represent Brooklyn in the U.S. House of Representatives in 1984, Syl retired from law to become CEO of Mobliano Wholesale Foods, Inc. With the support and assistance of his entire family, including the goddesses, Syl took the enterprise public in 1997 just after volume reached $1 billion. He and wife Maria have three sons and two daughters and reside in Great Neck, New York.

Spec Five Eddie Hale was posted to an intelligence unit of General Westmoreland's staff at Da Nang in March 1967. Hale went missing in action during the 1968 Tet Offensive. His remains have never been recovered.

Over Labor Day weekend 1976, John Sharkey and Mike Stott organized the promised reunion marking the ten-year anniversary of JJ's Congressional Medal of Honor Ceremony. Although he had missed the first celebration in 1966, Major George Howard insisted on picking up the tab for the entire weekend celebration at the Hay-Adams Hotel. The rooms, dinners, and bar bills totaled more than $75,000. Big Howie paid with cash. He explained to the group that he had "won big" in Vegas. In fact, he still had well over $2 million in his Swiss account. Mike and JJ wanted to split the bill with him, but Howie threatened to kick their asses if they even mentioned it a second time. Sharkey told Howie that the only thing saving him from having to prove he could do it was the fact that he was an officer, and everybody knew officers couldn't work that hard.

The surviving soldiers that enjoyed Labor Day weekend 1963 together in Manhattan still get together most every Labor Day. On Monday, September 4, 2006, Mike Stott, George Howard and Syl Mobliano joined John Sharkey on his yacht, PACKMAN ONE, in Monaco. Syl could only stay for four days, but the three packmen sailed the Mediterranean for a month.

Only fourteen of the original twenty-two SPEND team members survived Vietnam to enjoy their money. During their Mediterranean cruise, Sharkey told Mike that their last surviving SPEND partner, retired Brigadier General Bill Freeze, had died in July. Sharkey said to Stott, "Guess your buddy can go ahead and write the story now, Mikey! All the officers are dead now, and everybody knows the enlisted men were only following orders!"

Printed in the United States
142013LV00003B/14/P

9 781606 938751